Vasily Mahanenko

RESTART

*Books are the lives
we don't have
time to live,

Vasily Mahanenko*

DARK PALADIN
BOOK#3

Magic Dome Books

Restart
Dark Paladin, Book # 3
Copyright © V. Mahanenko 2018
Cover Art © V. Manyukhin 2018
English Translation Copyright ©
Alexandra Tussing 2018
Published by Magic Dome Books, 2018
All Rights Reserved
ISBN: 978-80-88231-63-9

ALL BOOKS BY VASILY MAHANENKO:

The Way of the Shaman LitRPG Series
Survival Quest
The Kartoss Gambit
The Secret of the Dark Forest
The Phantom Castle
The Karmadont Chess Set
Shaman's Revenge
Clans War

The Alchemist LiTRPG series by Vasily Mahanenko:
City of the Dead
Forest of Desire
Tears of Alron

Dark Paladin LitRPG Series
The Beginning
The Quest
Restart

Galactogon LitRPG Series
Start the Game!
In Search of the Uldans
A Check for a Billion

Invasion LitRPG Series
A Second Chance
An Equation with One Unknown

World of the Changed LitRPG Series
No Mistakes
Pearl of the South

The Bard from Barliona LitRPG series
(with Eugenia Dmitrieva)
The Renegades
A Song of Shadow

You're in Game!
(LitRPG Stories from Bestselling Authors)

You're in Game-2!
(More LitRPG stories set in your favorite worlds)

TABLE OF CONTENTS :

CHAPTER ONE

THE DAY BEFORE

"PALADIN YAROPOLK!" the herald announced, and the wide double doors opened before me. Containing my worry, I stepped into the hall for official ceremonies of the Residence of the Sector 446 Coordinator, nobleman by birth, Count Bernard Kalran. My suzerain graciously put his "humble" abode at Madonna's disposal, and representatives of all the game worlds hurried to pay their respects to the Great One. No matter how great the hall was, it was unlikely that all the creatures gathered here felt comfortable – they were devoid of any personal space. In other words, the hall was full to bursting: everyone was in a great hurry to look at the reincarnated Madonna. But anyway, whom was I trying to deceive? Who would want to simply take a look at the Great one? They were all attracted by the hype that inevitably accompanied those kinds of events. Where else would one see the grand scale characteristic of the Creators, as they reward the undeserving and punish the innocent?

I was standing at the entrance to the hall, completely unwilling to move any further. Thoughts were idly circling around in my head — what would it be for me, reward or punishment? Everyone else was doing the same thing; they were not even bothering to hide sidelong glances and whispers. No one had tried to divide those who came before me into the guilty and the worthy, so for the rest of the guests our appearance and Madonna's reaction were intriguing. Since I was the last in the line of the lucky (or not) ones, I already knew that Archibald had been pronounced guilty of the problems that had occurred during Madonna's return. He was declared an outlaw, stripped of all the ranks he held and condemned to oblivion. The guests were highly entertained. After that they became somewhat bored: the moment of excitement was followed by the standard procedure of receiving rewards from the hands of the Great One. Some even dared snorting if they considered the reward useless or insignificant. The NPCs described all this in vivid detail to us as they came back to fetch the next in line. The Head of the Order of Paladins, Gerhard van Brast, was seen before me, and the crowd was astonished the second time that evening, but this time with the scale of the reward. As I was listening to my escort on the way to the Hall, I allowed myself to dream about a personal world with millions of slaves. Since I was the player who had done most of the work to make sure the Great One returned.

Casting an understanding glance over the whispering guests, I started out for the throne after all. The crowd parted, as was expected, enabling me to pass forward down the road at the end of which the powerful and eccentric Great One was waiting for me. Madonna easily occupied the throne of the host, moving Bernard aside. Meanwhile the Coordinator was nearby: he was standing to the right of the throne like a most devoted servant, and showed not the slightest displeasure about his current situation. On the contrary, he was being witty, and did everything to serve his Mistress and guest of honor. There was a reason for that. The Coordinator of a backwater sector instantly became an important figure in the Game world, and he was not about to miss his chance. I spent the entire week before the ceremony in my suzerain's residence, and had plenty of opportunity to observe Bernard basking in the attention of other Coordinators and influential players, condescendingly accepting their gifts and requests to put in a word for them to the Great One. Madonna did not like the premises provided to her by the Priests, so she stayed with the Coordinator instead, making him first among equals.

Bending her head down to Bernard, the Great One was listening to him with a fleeting smile, responding something from time to time. However, her eyes followed my approach unswervingly. Even though I had had enough time to steel myself for this meeting, I still fell out of stride. Madonna noticed that and, smirking contentedly, averted her eyes. The enemy was defeated and could now be forgotten. I did not know whether that was the deal, but at least I could continue in peace.

By the way, to the same extent that my master was demonstratively basking in the Creator's attention, he was just as demonstratively ignoring my approach. That was easy to explain. First of all, there was no way to know my future fate. Then, Bernard still retained his misconception that I was under his full mental control due to the activated Book of Lumpen. For that reason I had been for a long time assigned to one of the least valuable categories in his listing of animate and inanimate property. Even though I was considered a slave without rights, I still knew I was remembered. Before the ceremony started, Bernard's loyal guard, the vampire Malturion, handed me a looped anti-grav with Light Source so that the dear guests would not be bothered with my hundredth level of Darkness.

I almost reached my goal, when I noticed a completely impossible creature. The Necromancer Lumpen was present in the hall for official ceremonies. Not in person, of course: his status of "Enemy of all Life" did not really help him move about the Earth freely. Even the Sanctuary would not fully protect him from being attacked by other players. Lumpen came to the meeting in the form of a hologram projected by a device hovering closely above the floor. The horrid dark specter was looming over the other players, and even though the hall was chock-full, there was almost a yard of empty space around Lumpen. Only the Viceroy kept the necromancer company, and now those two were talking quietly but urgently, ignoring the ceremony. Madonna had already been presented to the world, most of the ceremony was behind us, so one could work on his own affairs without having to waste one's time dealing with the unworthy.

"Paladin Yaropolk!" I kneeled and Madonna's eyes settled on me again. The humming in the hall died down. As they say, curiosity is not a sin, but unsatisfied curiosity is a major headache. My peripheral vision seemed to indicate that even the Lumpen and the Viceroy put their conversation on hold, waiting for the outcome. "We know of all the facts as you took part in the recent events. Having measured all your deeds undertaken for the sake of Our return, and taking into consideration external evidence, We desire to fully give you your due and ..."

Madonna paused and glanced at Bernard. The Coordinator dispassionately waited for the conclusion of the statement, while those around demonstrated lamentable lack of restraint now and again. The woman did not hurry, enjoying the few tense moments as everyone felt silent; however, her sense of timing did not let her down. Turning towards me without extending the pause too much and ruin the moment, she finished:

"We pronounce you guilty!" The sentence seemed to nail me to the floor. What did that mean — "guilty"?! And of what?!

"By your stupid and presumptuous actions you jeopardized Our reincarnation. You treacherously snatched the activation process from the hands of experienced players." Apparently, that was a hint about Zangar and his teacher. Madonna was getting more and more aggravated with each new accusation. "You wasted time, which delayed Our resurrection, and spurned help. You brought Lumpen back to this world!" At this point the woman jumped up, not at all regally, and pointed accusingly in the direction of the hologram of the necromancer; that gave so much more expression to her words. Everyone hastened to turn their glances towards Lumpen, who was now serving as a visible illustration of my shame. Ignoring the necromancer's moment of fame, I stared at Madonna expectantly. Unless my eyes were failing me, a fleeting coquettish smile had just graced the face of "The Great One" and it was intended for the "Enemy of all Life"! What kind of circus was that? I was being publicly whipped for resurrecting him, while she was flirting with him? Some Creator, indeed! Or was she just trying to build a safety net for herself? Despite his Game status, Lumpen was a very interesting and, most importantly, a very, very powerful figure. In the upcoming war he would have excellent chance of winning. Apparently, I was not the only one who thought along those lines...

"The only way I was able to resurrect was by sheer luck." Madonna said, calming down and returning to the throne. "We are displeased with you, Paladin Yaropolk! We consider that you deserve a most severe punishment. However..." at that point she turned towards Bernard and smiled at him openly, patronizingly. "We value servants who are loyal to us, and accept the petition of our kind Coordinator. It does not mean that you will avoid punishment! We grant you a month to serve to everyone's benefit, and then you will suffer the just punishment at our hands! We are announcing to the entire Game community: we would be extremely displeased if due to someone's stupidity the guilty one were to not live long enough to face his sentence."

The Hall hummed with approval. Madonna waved her hand in disgust:

"Get him out of my sight!"

Immediately a couple of genies materialized next to me: they grabbed my arms and dragged me out of the Hall as if I had been a naughty kitten. They did not teleport nor escort me, but dragged me out. They deprived me of an opportunity to leave the Hall on my own, preserving my honor and dignity. The entire Game community was being shown that no one should have anything to do with me.

The genies dragged me beyond the door, and the world around me swirled in a portal. Multicolored lines started jumping in front of my eyes. Gradually the colors settled, showing me a small office. The bright setting sun flooded the room through wide French windows; for a few seconds I was blinded.

"The Paladin has been delivered!" One of my escorts boomed. I was released and lightly pushed down into a soft armchair. A friendly voice said peacefully:

"Good afternoon, monsieur Yaropolk."

Squinting from the light, I looked around the room, but could not see anyone. Feeling my confusion, Steve hurried to help me, highlighting in red a small creature next to the far wall. The stranger blended in with his environment so well that I immediately called him "Chameleon" to myself. Had it not been for Steve, I would not have been able to see through the creature's camouflage, no matter how much I turned around.

"Hm, you are quite observant: good for you, monsieur!" The creature immediately sensed that his presence and location were no longer a secret to me, and paid me the compliment in an annoyed voice. Separating from the wall, it moved towards the desk. It kept changing its shape and coloration; besides, it used light refraction masterfully. It was impossible to determine the true shape of the owner of this office; nor was it easy to look at him for a long time. I squinted, trying to single out or identify at least individual body parts, since I was unable to see the entire image. At some point it even seemed to me that the true shape of the creature was not that different from an actual chameleon that existed on Earth. Finally, I gave up on that, letting the professional do his work. Steve would process the images and show me that wonder in all its glory. The Chameleon chuckled contentedly:

"Don't burden yourself. I am used to it — members of your species have a hard time looking at us." The creature settled in an armchair in front of me and got down to business. "Monsieur Yaropolk, you are here in order to understand the role you are supposed to play in upcoming events. My name is Delcatran de Lure, and I am the personal assistant to the Great One."

The Chameleon looked at me expectantly; however, due to recent events I was unable to produce any reaction other than wariness and deep grunts. Perhaps that was the reason the creature offered:

"Would you care for some Cartanian liqueur?"

Two glasses with ominously red liquid appeared on the small table. My tired brain considered that a pretty bad sign, yet did not pass up a chance to relax. De Lure joined me. Several minutes passed in silence as we enjoyed the strong drink. I was not worried for my life. The status of the Sanctuary was reassuring; besides, if Madonna had in mind to kill me, she would not have bothered with all the trappings and bringing in personal assistants. One thing I did not doubt was that in another month I would face either a painful wiping out or tortures directed personally by the Great One. Moreover, she might stoop to not only directing, but to personally putting in a "Great hand" to it. Or foot. That would not surprise me. Such fresh thoughts popping up in my head indicated that I did in fact manage to relax. I really did need this liqueur to become myself again. The Chameleon was right.

"What a grrreat thing this is." I rolled the "r" on my tongue for a bit, cleared my throat and took control of the subject. "So what role are you talking about? The Great Madonna was very clear in her indication that I am not worthy of fulfilling her directives." It took a great effort to keep sarcasm out of my voice.

"It's not up to us to judge the words and deeds of the Great Ones," the chameleon cut me off. "The Great Mistress is displeased with your actions during preparation for Her return. For good reason, too—you nearly botched everything! And yet as the Guide you still have certain obligations to the entire Game community. And until now you have not been doing your best to fulfill them. That was what caused Her displeasure. However, She is very kind. And, as it turns out, you have worthy protectors. Rejoice! You now have a chance to right everything, prove your competence and loyalty to the great cause! You understand what I mean, monsieur Yaropolk?"

"Are we talking about finding Merlin and the Nameless One?" I ventured a guess.

"Only Merlin," Delcatran hastened to reply; apparently, he did not expect that some lowlife would know about the third participant of the Restart. The fingers on his right hand came into motion and Steve pointed that out to me. The sly chameleon was quickly typing a message on the keyboard built into the armrest of the chair. Unfortunately, neither Steve nor I were able to read the missive.

"It does not matter; I don't know anything about them anyway." I tried to look careless. Internally scolding myself. What an idiot! How could I relax! The last thing I needed was Gerhard worrying what I might know about the Nameless One. Those who know too much don't stay in the Game for long, even if they are thrice the Guides! I immediately tasked Steve with working out a plausible explanation about how Zangar had told me about the third participant in the Restart. I needed to cover all possible scenarios for future developments.

"That's what we are talking about here – that you have no information," the Chameleon nodded, pleased. "The Guide's task is to bring all the participants of the Restart together. How will you do this if you have still not identified Merlin? At this time this is the highest priority for you–the purpose of your very existence!!!"

The logic of the conversation called for me, a humble wretched creature, to become self-effacing, and I hurried to present myself as such, nodding all the way. Nobody asks much of daft people. Particularly since I already had the right kind of reputation. So off we go; follow the chosen course and make sure the interlocutor remembers the effect he wanted to see in the first place.

"You are right there–my bad. But I do have an excuse here — my training went awry, I was not trained like the others. Archibald...," I sighed for effect and made a guilty face, hoping I was not playing it too hard. But Delcatran was affected by the liqueur as well. He was inspired by my contrition and willingness to cooperate. The Chameleon even leaned back in his chair, feeling that he was in control of the situation.

"We are aware of the gaps in your education, and we are willing to help." The Chameleon was now substituting "we" and "us" for "I" and "me", copying his mistress's manner of speaking. "But only within the scope of your mission."

"Madonna's generosity knows no..." I was not even hiding my sarcasm any more, but Delcatran interrupted me so harshly that for a moment I was afraid he had figured it out:

"The Great Madonna. You must treat our Mistress with respect."

"Do I only need to find Merlin, or something else?" I was getting bored with the games. I wanted to finish it quickly and find out what it was that Madonna wanted from me.

Actually, over the past week I had been quite impressed by her "grandeur" and "saintly deeds". A hysterical woman, wallowing in her own strength and power. Given to showering rewards and punishments without any reasonable cause. Today's reception was not the only demonstration of her grace. The day before she had demoted the Heads of Clerics and Priests who somehow had not curried her favor enough, sent some players into exile as she did Archibald, stripping them of class and rank... she actively interfered with the Game on Earth without bothering to familiarize herself with current issues. There was growing discontent among the player masses, but it found no relief. Everyone kept quiet, unwilling to draw fire on themselves.

"You are instructed to find, within a month, the creature into which Merlin reincarnated." The Chameleon now assumed a businesslike manner of conversation as well. "It would be enough to simply find out who he is and report to the Mistress. Then your mission will be considered complete."

"Simply find him?" I was genuinely surprised. "I do not need to bring him to command headquarters?"

\

"Command headquarters?" The Chameleon smirked and aimed both his fantastic eyes at me. "Perhaps you happen to know where it is located?"

"What do you mean, where?" I mumbled. I simply had to confess to myself that I was not pretending to be an idiot — I actually was one. "I think it's here, on Earth. I could be wrong of course, but it seems logical to me."

"So you don't know for sure?" My interlocutor kept questioning me. In response I simply shrugged my shoulders once again and nodded. "Why do you find it logical?"

Figuring that I was not losing anything by sharing my considerations I clarified:

"Command headquarters is a standard feature in practically all Games. It would be logical to consider that it exists here as well. Would you agree? All the known key figures reincarnated on Earth: the Guide, the Keymaster, the Great Madonna. Moreover, She is certain that one should look for Merlin on our world as well. That brings about a reasonable question: why? What did Earth do to deserve such an honor? Maybe the answer is that it has the Command headquarters on it?"

"It could be, it could be..." Madonna's personal assistant said contemplatively. "But it does not matter. Monsieur Yaropolk. We are realists here and we prefer to task players with what they are capable of doing. So, find Merlin and report that to me. We do not require more from you.. My comm number has already been sent to you. If you manage to succeed, you will receive a substantial reward from the

Mistress; if not, you will lose the status of Guide–I am sure you understand the consequences."

So simply and clearly he put me in my place. I imagined the consequences quickly and vividly.

"Can I count on any help?" Since "the realists" gathered here, perhaps I could hope for some perks and additional bonuses.

"We have put in place everything that is necessary to start the search. Players have been warned that it is not a good idea to attack you. As for the eccentrics and other crazies that think they are messiahs of whatever sort, you will have to fight them off on your own. However, there are not many of those on this world." I was not particularly upset; in all fairness an extra month of life was quite a fat perk in and of itself.

"Where should I start the search?"

"There is really nothing I can do for you there. You should be in a position to know better." The Chameleon disappointed me again. "Trust your intuition. Your essential aspect will let you know where is the path that would lead you to Merlin. Let me remind you, you have one month. It's time for you to go!"

The assistant made a gesture, and the familiar genies lifted me from the armchair. Another portal trip, and I was at the Paladins' Citadel. This trip destination was unexpected to me, but everything was clarified at once:

"The Head is waiting for you, brother Yaropolk. Follow me." An orc Paladin immediately appeared next to me. Escorts and guards were replaced with more escorts and guards. That was oppressive. We moved forward and had already passed two or three halls when a belated thought struck me: we were moving away from the reception. As far as I could tell based on the 3d projection of the Citadel. I was turning my head in confusion, trying to figure out what to do. My companion noticed that:

"We can't go through the reception now. You are an outlaw now, brother. Gerhard cannot see you openly. So..."

The orc let the sentence trail off meaningfully, and sighed a few times. That made me feel wronged. At the same time, I kept walking, calmer now. We walked for another minute before I figured out what bothered me. "Gerhard!" Not a single Paladin from Earth would be so deliberately casual when speaking about the Head. Only outsiders would do that! This orc was not from our world! I rolled over, activated all my defenses and my artifact as well.

"Your debt is paid, Sharnadan." A shadow in the far corner of the room turned into an entity about which I had short-sightedly forgotten. This was really bad timing on the part of Garlion to try and satisfy his craving for revenge. In the thick of things I had already forgotten about this couple of advantage-seeking elves: Nartalim, whom I had killed, and his mean dad.

"I will take it from here." Keeping his eyes on me Garlion gestured to the orc, indicating that the latter was free to leave. At the same time, the two six-foot gremlin statues standing near the door came into motion, extracting some nets.

"Nothing personal, brother Yaropolk," the orc boomed, indifferent to my fate now, "I just needed to pay off a debt."

One of the gremlins allowed the orc to freely leave the room; then he stood motionless at the door, blocking the entrance with his massive body. A silvery net whistled through the air, trying to tie me up, but this role of prey was not to my liking. Preempting his move I dodged sideways, letting the net flash above my head, and keeping the gremlin between myself and Garlion. The elf did not follow the practice of villains from various movies wasting half an hour to tell everyone about his malevolent misdeeds. He attacked silently, but viciously. Blue lightning flashed from his hand, and I dashed away from the line of fire, jumping around like a mountain goat. The floor in the spot I just vacated exploded with shards of stone. Lightnings of this level of power from a Paladin worried me quite a bit. Steve immediately revealed to me the reason for this inconsistency: the elf was using a small staff that generated those lightning bolts.

The stone gremlin regarded his empty net sadly, then hurried, to the extent it was possible for one like him, to make another attempt. I was only happy that it took the dummy at least a couple of minutes to prepare for the next throw, or sometimes even longer; this way I did not have to be too distracted from my main opponent. I realized my mistake too late, as the silvery threads covered me head to toe. I had forgotten about the other gremlin by the door, and turned my back to him. My artifact was powerless against the net; only sparks lit the air every time I used the "Templar's Blow".

Garlion came closer, still silent, without lowering the staff that was still aimed at me. He looked me straight in the eye, and I knew full well that words would change nothing. I was counting the seconds in my mind and waiting to go for respawn without closing my eyes. Let my enemy wait in vain for fear in them. All that was there was frustration with this whole situation, and looking for it to resolve itself quickly.

Lightning flashed, but practically nothing changed. At first I did not even understand what had happened. I was steeling myself for pain, but instead I lost feeling in my legs. I stared at the elf in bewilderment, trying to understand the point of his actions. But all I received was an evil grin and another lightning bolt. That's what made his intentions clear: with each new bolt my body was becoming more and more frozen and numb. Garlion rendered me completely motionless, and I had a hard time breathing. I tried to hold my breath to try and trigger a respawn, but my reflexes worked all too well: I was gulping air raggedly, while the elf was laughing at me. Having enjoyed this view of my humiliation, Garlion, finally, started talking:

"Don't count on respawn, brother Yaropolk." His voice was dripping with hatred. "That would be too simple. I have something different in store for you. I will lock you up in a place where no one will ever find you! You will spend millennia in confinement, motionless: the only sound you will hear will be the sound of dripping water! Drip! Drip! Drip! It will drip, second after second, minute after minute, day after day, counting off your worthless existence, and driving you mad! An infinity in darkness and solitude, without any hope for welcome unconsciousness! Would that not be a worthy punishment for the death of my son?"

The elf was so carried away that he did not immediately hear a knock on the door that grew louder and louder.

"Don't let anyone in!" Garlion ordered the gremlins. The dummies obediently headed for the door and thought of nothing better than to sit down straight on the floor, creating a stone door-block. But the visitor or visitors were obviously tired of trying to gain entry peacefully, and proceeded to actively attack. Whoever was storming the door, they did not consider either the doors themselves or a couple of monumental dummies much of an obstacle. With a thunderous blow that sounded like a cannon shot, the doors splintered to pieces and the gremlins exploded into tiny stone shards. Before the dust had a chance to settle Sharda calmly stepped into the room, wearing a full battle outfit. His battle hammer shone so bright that it looked like the sun rising from the morning fog.

Garlion did not waste any time on excuses, and immediately attacked the unwelcome guest with lightning bolts. The gnome grabbed a huge shield out of the air; the lightning just licked at it and petered out harmlessly. Sharda obviously had something more to show the librarian. A few more lightning bolts flashed, with a similar result. The gnome immediately teleported himself right next to Garlion. A deceptively slight swing of the hammer, and the elf's staff, broken in half, went flying to some unknown corner. The elf's hand was now hanging lifelessly twisted while Garlion was wailing hopelessly, holding his shattered limb. The enemy was defeated. It was a pleasure to watch a real Paladin work: fast, precise and to the point. I had a lot to learn.

"I warned you, brother Garlion." Sharda said calmly, having made sure that Garlion had lost all his battle ardor. Sharda clicked his tongue, extracted an elves' potion and offered it to the elf. The gnome's care could mislead one, but his eyes did not hold anything good in store for the now quiet librarian.

"I am within my rights! He killed my son!" Garlion hissed, as if trying to justify his actions.

"You are just an old and evil elf! Had Nartalim survived the Academy, you would have had to kill him yourself!" Sharda cut him off decisively, raising his voice. "He betrayed his brethren in class! He ceased being a Paladin! Brother Yaropolk saved you from disgrace, Garlion. You are the one who brought up your son this way!"

Garlion, indignant, kept opening and closing his mouth, unable to respond anything to the gnome, and only shuffling in place clumsily. Sharda exhaled noisily, but in a few moments continued in a calm and tired voice:

"Get thee back to your library, brother. I will notify the Head of your actions."

Considering this issue settled, Sharda grabbed me by the scruff of my neck and dragged me out of the room. In the hallway there was a team of five Paladins with their weapons at the ready, waiting for the gnome's return. The support team was prepared to come to their brother's aid at any moment, but, seeing how things turned out, the Paladins sheathed their weapons. Sharda approached his team and handed me to the largest warrior. He slung my body over his shoulder like a trophy that one would grudge to discard, but that was quite heavy to carry. So that's how we started out through the corridors and halls full of echoes. The brothers joked good-naturedly about my Bucephalus. The warrior laughed at the jokes together with them, not at all offended, but did not talk back. Finally I saw a regular patterned wood floor instead of the stone slabs; then I was relieved from the need to look at the butt of my strong and patient "steed".

"Brother Shardangabat, your timing is always impeccable. I found a most curious plant..." first I heard the local doctor, and only after that was I able to see him. As a true warrior of Hippocrates, the healer immediately switched his attention to the new patient. "What happened to him?"

"Zeroed lightning, brother Dragore," Sharda explained. "He is conscious and is still breathing. How long?"

"If we are speaking about time, it would be three to four hours. We need to restore the frozen muscles. I can't send him to respawn, right?"

"Preferably not. Brother Yaropolk has changed the anchor point, and it is unclear how long it would take him to return. And we need to do it fast, the

Head is waiting for him."

"Fast?" The doctor scratched his beard in contemplation and started going through scores of little vials on his shelf, muttering under his breath. "What do we have here? No, that won't do... Or maybe... No, let's not risk too much... Oh, here it is... wait, it may have a strong adverse reaction on the digestive system... What's that...? oh, that would erase the personality... that would not do at all – no, sir! Oh! Finally! That's what we need. Fast, easy and very painful. Oh well, whatever – the result is what we need first and foremost. And the result is guaranteed in thirty minutes! But after that, no later than in four hours, make sure you let him sleep for a long time."

"Go for it. Brother Yaropolk will remember everything; he will endure now and sleep later."

Half an hour later I was sitting in Gerhard van Brast's waiting room trying to stop myself from shaking. That was not easy; sometimes my legs seemed to develop a life of their own and started to shake so hard that I had to hold them in place with my hands. The doctor had not lied. It really had been painful. Several times during the procedure I fainted as my body tried to escape the torture, but I was brought to immediately, as the method required that I stay conscious throughout.

Sharda was sitting next to me in the room, and watched my every move. The gnome did not say a word as he carried me there. Sharda generally seemed different from the gnome I used to know. He was glum and silent. He had not made any ironic comments or jests. He stared from under his eyebrows. My mood had really plummeted, and I tried to strike up a conversation, looking for topics that would interest him:

"Have you been able to find out anything about the third participant?"

Sharda's left eyelid twitched, but that was the only reaction I got.

"Did Archibald call you?"

Same twitch of the left eyelid and nothing else Maybe that was a sign for me to shut up, but I was irritated by his silence to such an extent that felt unable to stop.

"I was able to find out that they call the third participant the Nameless one. He erases all the information about himself. Who could that be, now is only known to..."

"Enough!" Sharda cut me off sharply. "Want to know nothing about the Nameless One, nor about the Restart. You have already said too much. How many times do I have to tell you, knucklehead, that even walls have ears?"

I hunched noticeably, recognizing that the reproach was justified. Yet that was his own fault; he could have said something to me – say, about the weather. I had just been frozen all the way to my brain. By the way, speaking of the freeze and its consequences:

"What will happen to Garlion? He..."

"Forget about the library." Sharda cut me off again, not hoping for my aptitude any more. "You won't be able to get in there, period. That topic is closed. Shut up and sit quietly!"

Sharda hunched up like a sparrow on a perch. Now the gnome had really destroyed all my willingness to talk, and drove away the thought that his condition had anything to do with me. Why? Simply because he cut me off on the topic of Restart, and shut me up with a reproach that I talk too much. Here he also had the last word, like the mentor of infinite numbers of dumb students. I was really not able to become the cause of Sharda's great headache. The only reasonable explanation for this behavior was Archibald being in disfavor. The gnome and the catorian had been close, and the latter's exile and the stripping of his class and rank would upset Sharda quite a bit. An indirect proof of my supposition lay in the gnome's tone of voice as he mentioned the topic of Restart. If they had not gotten themselves into this whole Restart business up to their ears, perhaps the catorian would have still been on the good side of the Head. Hm... That's it! Sharda simply feels guilty! And the things I said only exacerbated that feeling.

"If I were to see my teacher in the near future, what should I tell him?" I asked, holding the gnome's heavy stare. The silence lasted for a long time, until finally Sharda said quietly:

"Delra kan rog. Videotape it, or else you'll forget it, you knucklehead!"

"Delra kan rog." I repeated, and nodded. "I will tell him.".

Sharda puffed his cheeks, obviously about to say something else, but at that moment the doors to Gerhard's office opened and I was invited to come in. Alone. I went through the security and sanitation zone quickly, getting just three signals of the markers removed. I accepted the message telling me I was totally clean now, and finally I was standing before the Head. During the week that had passed since Madonna appeared, Gerhard had changed. And not for the better. Perhaps it was just my subjective opinion, and I simply pitied the man whose Doll was such a bitch. It seemed to me that his face was drawn, his cheeks were hollow, his eyes were red, and generally all his features looked peaked. Gerhard looked like someone who last rested a couple of Restarts ago. However, he greeted me as always, with a fatherly smile and wisdom in his tired eyes..

"You had a long and difficult week, brother Yaropolk." With this simple phrase Gerhard indicated that he was fully aware of all my troubles and the reasons why I had not been able to report to him for training earlier. Immediately after Madonna's return Bernard had taken me to his estate, and did not let me out until the ceremony. I was certain that the incident with Garlion had already been reported to the Head as well.

"Quite a few people could say the same thing." I responded. "But I do agree, calm and boredom are in fact lacking in my life."

Gerhard smiled at me supportively.

"Have you decided on the ability you would like to learn?"

"The diamond protection dome." Even though I had spent a week under home arrest, I had been able to study some of the Paladin abilities. Thanks to Alard who had not abandoned a brother in hard times. Now

I knew precisely what I wanted. The absolute protection that Gerhard had set up for me during the battle near Lecleur estate required an enormous amount of Energy. Even if my crystal had been fully charged, I would have only been able to maintain this kind of shield only for about ten minutes. With respect to my attack abilities, everything was more or less clear: several hundred bunches of scrolls with the Templar's Blow were sitting in my inventory in case times got tough. But my defense left a lot to be desired. My fight with Garlion demonstrated this one more time: the elf did not even have to work hard in order to break through. The diamond dome was not a universal method either, but it would have helped against Garlion. Probably.

"Good choice," Gerhard praised me. He spent some time looking for a clean sheet of paper on his desk, then quickly sketched a few symbols on it, and extracted a jar of golden powder from the top drawer; covering the still-wet inscription, he carefully shook off the excess. Satisfied with the result, the Head handed the paper over to me. As soon as my fingers touched the sheet, and his left the paper, the Game immediately highlighted the message on me receiving a new ability. The scroll flashed in magic fire, and disappeared without as much as a trace of ash on my fingers. My training was completed.

"You will go to Moscow." Gerhard said without wasting time. "Try to keep quiet and not be noticed by anyone undesirable. Work on explorer tasks: walk around the city, watch the ways players interact with NPCs under normal conditions. It will take time to bring everything back to normal again. Madonna's disfavor won't last forever, since women have short memories."

"I understood the subtle hint, but could not agree with the Head. Such power-seeking creatures are actually likely to bear grudges for a long time. But of course I did not say that out loud. Just shook my head and brought up another important problem:

"Moscow is full of churches." Gerhard had promised to teach me to block sources of Light. It was high time to work on that.

"Yes, clerics are fond of that city. Russia is generally an extremely strange country; under certain circumstances people are capable of latching onto an idea and start implementing it with the self-sacrifice of real fanatics. For example, there was a time when the country's rulers decided to promote atheism among the population, so immediately all the attributes and external signs of a faith were actively condemned by the authorities and mass media. All the churches and religious communities were eradicated. Then the government changed its mind, and immediately the whole county was full of repentance, preparing for the arrival of the next messiah. There are no subtle shades in that country. Even though this is the reason it wins all its wars against external aggressors. The bravest soldier is a fanatic ready to sacrifice everything for the sake of his country. Others are just not capable of that."

"I disagree." I was never an avid patriot, but this made me feel for my country. "It's not right to equate patriots with self-sacrificing fanatics! Besides:

regarding the faith..."

"I did not imply that they were equal; nor did I make any value statements as to whether that was good or bad." Gerhard grinned, making me fall silent. "It was just a statement of fact. I consider this feature of the Russian people amusing. Nothing more than that. But you are right: at this time Russia is chock-full of Sources of Light, so you need protection. Let's start with theory."

The difference between Light and Dark ones was purely in the mechanism for generating Energy. Dark ones were able to obtain it directly from their environment, while Light ones needed an intermediary that would accumulate Energy within it. The so-called "Source of Light", which destroyed all free emotion around itself. Actually, that was the main problem of the Dark ones: they continuously absorbed available free emotions from the surrounding world. If there are none available, as is very common on Earth, since all emotions are aimed at specific deities, they would have to absorb whatever is available. In this case it would be Energy infused with Light, and that is quite detrimental for Dark ones.

"What is the conclusion you make from all that?" Gerhard was not about to present it to me on a platter; rather, he wanted me to take active part in the learning process.

"In order to be able to stay near a Source of Light, one needs to conduct the absorption of emotions from the ambient space to... for example.... Now that stumped me. To oneself? But that's physically impossible. To an accumulator? That would not work either, because it did not generate emotions. Generally the only sources of emotions are living beings, but you can't continuously drag around a... I got an idea!

"A pet!" I exhaled, proud of myself, and was rewarded with an approving nod from my teacher. The gift from the Chancellor of the Academy had a twist to it!

"Specifically, the kind of pet that is capable of feeling emotions. Whether they are negative or positive, the choice is entirely yours. The important thing is that in order to overcome the effects of a Source of Light within a certain proximity to you, the pet should be nearby and feel strong emotions. The stronger the Source, the more vivid his feelings must be. Otherwise you still feel the effects of the Light. Unfortunately, pets are incapable of strong positive emotions. And no matter how noble the Dark Ones' intentions, sooner or later we take the easier path to reaching our goal. The instinct of self-preservation wins. So here is my advice to you: don't get attached to pets. Some feelings should be rejected right away, or else they make us weak. And nobody forgives that."

"Pets don't live very long, right?" The horrible realization dawned on me.

"A year, sometimes two if you work hard on avoiding Sources. At the Auction one can purchase special cages and devices that scan the ambient space, searching for Sources of Light, and initiate the torture process automatically. The Dark one will just have to remove the remains from the cage and replace them with a new pet. There is no reason to bother feeding them, either."

It probably would take time to get used to those things being common. It's easier to torture people, most of the time they are really begging for it, and, at least theoretically, they are in the same league as you. One would really have to change one's mind in order to torture a helpless creature. But Gerhard was right; guided by self-preservation I would quickly become used even to this.

The Head gave me a few minutes to think about the new information, and made sure that I fully understood everything that had to do with blocking the Sources of Light. But in any case, Darks are the way they are. One could not help but expect oceans of blood and suffering. I had known what I was getting into.

"Brother Alard requested permission to accompany you," Gerhard said, realizing I was not going to ask any questions. Orcs from Zagransh have their own notions of honor and dignity; I see no reason to deny his request. I have already approved his assignment to Moscow, all the logistical problems are being resolved now."

If a being at the level of Gerhard van Brast decided that in Moscow I would benefit from the presence of brother Alard, so be it. In this I could rely completely on the Head. The orc would be useful to me even if he had another directive, whether I knew about it or not. For a spy the Paladin would not be a suitable figure at all, so on the whole I was actually quite pleased with the news. So pleased that despite my initial intent not to be the first to bring up the issue of Madonna's task, I decided to ask for advice.

"Sir Gerhard, I need your help or advice. I think you know that Madonna told me to find Merlin within a month. If I were to fail I would no longer be the Guide. It seems unlikely that I would remain Paladin Yaropolk either, unless her anger fades. But I intend to do everything within my power. I am asking your permission to visit the classified section of the library. Archibald was certain that in there one could find references to Merlin's Diary, or, rather, indications of where one should look for it. Perhaps you know what my teacher had in mind. I don't even really need access — I just need information. Please forgive my forwardness, but one month is too short a time to rely only on one's own abilities."

Gerhard was taken aback for a moment, not expecting such direct talk from me. However, he was the Head of Class for a reason, and knew how to deal with the unexpected.

"I will think how to help you. Issuing books or copies thereof, particularly from the classified section, is strictly controlled, and even I am powerless to change it. It will take time. Now go. Brother Demitre will see you to the Auction and back.

Gerhard pressed a button on his desk, and immediately a hulking Paladin entered the room. Brother Demitre, the new Head of the Battle Wing who had replaced ousted Iven, turned out to be an interesting character. He was a typical rough warrior, one of those who intercept any attempt of speech by terrifyingly squinting their eyes and barking thunderously: "Silence! Enemies are close by!" But this particular one advanced this skill even further. At first, as he listened to his orders silently, he nodded and immediately gestured me to the door, I thought that was cool and laconic. But throughout our outing, not only did I not hear a word from him, but his face was totally expressionless. All information was conveyed to me with very spare gestures, basically reduced to orders "Stop" or "Go".

In the hallway we were joined by another six brothers, who fully surrounded me in a square formation. It was very serendipitous of Gerhard to take care of my safety. My new guards were like their commander, except they actually sported some facial expressions. At least they were capable of frowning, and, occasionally, smiling.

In the Sanctuary, one of the Paladins extracted a long feeler which he used to examine space far ahead of himself. I tried to find out the name of this strange contraption, but all six turned their heads to me and gave me such a look that it drove away any desire to communicate. So we kept moving silently all the way to our destination. The NPCs did not notice us; other players tried to clear out of the way as fast as they could, so we reached our destination without any delays. There was just one instance when the Paladin with the feeler drew back, as a portal flashed in front of him. The feeler departed in an unknown direction, and the Paladin simply frowned in displeasure and took out another. The strange portal indicated that in the foreseeable future I might be in for an unexpected trip. After I left the Sanctuary these silent Paladins would leave me, and in Moscow I would have to sort out my problems by my lonesome.

I liked the Auction. The process of purchasing items was not what attracted me the most. A host of figures and pictures, descriptions, and generally mountains of monotonous information. What I liked was a different thing: with each reviewed item my artifact experience level would grudgingly creep up by one hundredth of a percent. If I had had more time, I would have made the Auction my second home.

At the point when the hatred of my bodyguards reached a level I could physically sense, I stopped aimlessly leafing through the catalogue pages and proceeded to actual purchases: a cage, a couple of torture devices, a few other small items. It took me a record amount of time: five minutes. As I turned in my hands the steel cage with its horrible contraptions, I realized very clearly that I simply would not be able to stuff small furry Rragr in there. Having realized and accepted the thought, I started looking for a new pet for myself, preferably something disgusting both in terms of character and appearance. I did not have to search for long: there was a mean blob of fur, with fangs and claws. It emitted horrendous smells and drooled green goo. Just as I was about to confirm the purchase of the beast, I noticed a system information warning. It turned out that the rules of the Game limited the number of pets for all players, except hunters. Everyone else was only allowed one per player; the small font below indicated that if the player confirmed his purchase while already in possession of a pet, the money would not be refunded. I had to pause and verify Rragr's status.

My assistant studied the question of ownership of my furry pet and reassured me. At this time the pet was listed as the property of my Doll, and the process of transfer of ownership was successfully completed. Only in case of Helen's death would Rragr revert to becoming my pet again. With this welcome information I completed the purchase of "cannon fodder".

Having finished with the Auction, I visited the bank. A goblin with a "D" license immediately appeared from the infinite stream of employees and froze expectantly:

"Mister Yaropolk: our bank is at your service." The goblin was completely unabashed by the presence of the steely Demitre, who followed just a couple of feet behind me. By the way, it took quite an effort to get the silent Paladin to stop at the bank. It's hard to ask for something when it seems that you are being thoroughly ignored. Eventually I stooped to threatening to complain to Gerhard, and that worked.

"Only today we have special offers for deposits on extremely beneficial terms. I am sure you would be very interested to know…"

"No." I rudely cut off the clerk and his waterfall of words. I preferred to talk with their lot as little as possible. Otherwise, before you know it you would give them all your money "on very beneficial terms" and will owe them to boot. Just like peddlers from my life while I was still an NPC. "I need a normal account and exchange of one granis into gold, with subsequent conversion into Euros. That is all."

"Sure, sure, whatever you prefer." The goblin's

ears twitched, but his professional training kicked in. The goblin quickly logged in on the nearest machine, fulfilling my request, and then voiced an unexpected proposal: "I recommend that instead of Euros you take US dollars and Rubles at the rate of two to one. It would be more practical for you."

"Fine," I agreed, looking at the goblin suspiciously. He hurried to explain:

"The bank is informed about your assignment location, Mr. Yaropolk. In Moscow ordinary people tend to prefer dollars and Rubles. You would have to exchange Euros, and then you would lose money paying commission. I am sorry if I embarrassed you. Are you already familiar with the procedure for cashing granises?"

My negative movement of the head was welcomed by the goblin, who briefly outlined the method to me. As it turned out, regarding the situation with money in the Game, not everything was as transparent as I had thought at first. Just because a player converts granises into game coins, gold, securities or foreign exchange, the player's granis balance in the Game did not change. The Game would automatically calculate it regardless of the conversion. At any given time everything was calculated as granis equivalent, and the Game monitored this very carefully. As soon as it exceeded the number of basic granises, it would activate the "terror" mode. So one would not be able to get around this by converting granises into gold: it wouldn't work.

Without dragging out the formalities I signed a couple of agreements and finally received two plastic cards. The money available in those accounts would provide for decent existence, even in Moscow, which had been expensive for a couple of Game years. But one thing became obvious to me: I urgently needed to increase the number of basic granises available to me. Once I was done with the Explorer's tasks I would work on the Dungeons. Of all the ways I knew to earn some money, that one was the most effective.

Moscow greeted me with fair weather, which was suspicious in and of itself. The city I remembered as stuffy and dusty was, to my surprise, a poster-child of great infrastructure. My eyes kept stumbling on ideally clean cobblestones, while my nose wrinkled from air that smelled too fresh. The contrast with the Moscow I knew was so stark that I just kept standing in front of the stationary portal in the center of Red Square. I just stood there, astonished, getting in the way of newly arriving players.

"Paladin Yaropolk?" The player who was meeting me had to tap me on the shoulder to get my attention. I turned around, and instead of going through with meet-and-greet kept staring at a luxurious limo nearby. A limo. A government limo, no less. A well-known brand. Right in the center of Red Square. Which is closed to vehicles. The greeter cleared his throat a couple of times, making sure that I focused on him, then waved carelessly towards the limo without introducing himself:

"Get in—the meeting is in thirty minutes. I hate being late."

With the flashing beacon on, we dashed across the square and rolled up to the entrance to the

Kremlin. The gates opened as we approached and a whole dozen of guards, both NPC and players, saluted our cortege. The car rolled up to the main entrance of the Great Kremlin Palace. Several NPCs rolled out a red carpet on the stairs to the limo. Soldiers from the Kremlin Guard lined up on the sides, looking very smart at attention; an orchestra nearby played a welcome march. Everyone's eyes shone with trepidation and ingratiation. Everything was so ceremonial it made you want to take a huge spoon and scrub all that idiotic corniness to the nearest dumpster and slap everyone on the face for their slavish outlook and perpetual desire to curry favor. It is so sad that people all too frequently turn the noble concept of service into the farce of servility.

The guards opened the doors of the limo, and my companion stepped out regally. The guards stood at full attention with even more fervor. No one showed any interest in me at all. The gentleman started ascending the stairs slowly and pompously. I looked at the back of the player as he was walking between the two lines of guards, but I was in no hurry to rush after him. So who was it that had deigned to meet me?

A shortish guy rushed out from the crowd and pushed me forward a little to encourage me to follow the big boss. The latter had meanwhile reached the top of the stairs and heartily kiss the young girl holding the round bread in the welcome ceremony. Only after that did he first notice that I was not by his side. He looked back and asked in surprise:

"What's keeping you? Come on, I have to

register you still! Keep up!"

So then it was the Registrar himself who did me the honor and welcomed me personally. Not bad! Immediately following the entrance I was scanned several times for prohibited items. I was forced to leave my machine gun; that indicated that the contents of the player's personal inventory was no secret. For quite some time the guards pursed their lips at my Book of Knowledge, arguing with me about the need to surrender it as well. Only the interference of my companion protected me from being forced to feel completely naked. The registrar's vice in all of that was being patronizing and casual. As if he were a denizen of heaven deigning to descend from his official Olympus for the sale of the problems of a mere mortal.

Our journey ended in a huge office. I noticed a few players in the anteroom, waiting for their turn to register, but they were a lot less lucky than I. Once in the office, the Registrar occupied a luxurious chair at the head of the desk, and opened a shiny leather folder which had been prepared in advance. I spent several minutes in silence, waiting for the Registrar to finish his reading and speak. Notably, the room was devoid of any kinds of seats for visitors. Either because its occupant preferred communicating through his secretary, or because visitors were supposed to remember their place in that office.

"Well, well, well... So you are assigned to Moscow, then."

I nodded, confirming the obvious.

"You were allocated an initial stipend for two

months and a studio apartment in Nth street? The keys were issued to you in the Sanctuary?"

I nodded again. The Registrar looked concerned, sitting still for a while, with only his searching stare traveled over me trying to find something visible only to him. After a lengthy pause he continued harshly:

"So, then, Paladin Yaropolk, all the preliminary agreements are now void. Return the keys to the apartment to the secretary, and there is no initial stipend for you either.

"I don't get it..." I said slowly, surprised.

"What is there to get? There was an apartment allocated, but then the drift changed and no, there is no apartment. Same thing with the stipend."

The drift, eh. I would expect that this drift was not drifting from the Registrar himself. That's too petty for someone at his level; besides, he would not bother to personally welcome me if it had been so. It looked more like a woman's stupid willfulness on the part of certain pissy individuals. Bitch! Right, put some hobos under my door, too, so that I would realize more fully how powerful you are! And the local tycoon ran off to fulfill the order personally and to satisfy his curiosity about who was that guy being personally humiliated by Madonna Herself?

"Is there anything at all that is provided for me?"

"Sure there is. A room in a dorm. It's a decent room; the neighbors are good, too. Just the ticket for a beginner player." I could not understand any more whether he was mocking me or just trying to cheer me up in earnest. "My secretary will issue the keys to you."

My patience ran out. I had already opened my mouth to tell him my thoughts, but the Registrar raised his palm, stopping me:

"Before you say anything, you need to know that according to the rules of the Game you cannot say no. And for insulting an official on duty you will be designated persona non grata. I am not touchy, but the order is the same for everyone! Head hunters would be issued a permit for your respawn. You have any extra levels?"

"No." I felt deflated. My interlocutor hemmed, satisfied that he had discovered my reactions to be adequate. Relaxing, he reached for the bottom drawer of the desk, and I heard the sound of some liquid being poured. Leaning back in his chair the Registrar swished some amber drink in his glass.

"Don't fret so much. Anyone could be in your place. Never say never... to the dorm." The Registrar laughed at his own joke, superstitiously spat over his left shoulder and knocked on the desk before taking a great swig from the glass. This player, even if he were to end up in the "dorm", would only be there if he wanted it himself. People like him feel great under any kind of "drift", they always land on all fours because they are really good at adjusting to any environment. "By the way, we cannot force our guests to stay in social housing projects during their work trial period if they have their own real estate. You just have to officially notify us. You have some granises?"

The Registrar raised his eyebrow quizzically.

"I have some granises." I repeated like a parrot.

"Good deal." The Registrar beamed at me and clasped his hands exaggeratedly. "Oh, my God, why did I take my medication on an empty stomach! That's wrong, I should not do it—my doctor will yell at me! I need to correct that right away."

"I do beg your pardon, sir Registrar, but I just arrived, and have not eaten since morning. I hope it would not be too forward on my part to ask for some indication of good places for lunch?"This was a game two could and should play. What is not expressly forbidden is allowed. Can one player not provide a simple service to another player? Why not, if he is paying in granises? The Registrar jumped off of his chair immediately and pushed the speaker button on his desk:

"Sveta, I'm off to lunch. I will be back tomorrow. Today please provide the housing key to Paladin Yaropolk and tell him about the notice procedure." As he was at the door, he added quickly as he was locking the office: "It's not like it is a problem normally dealt with at my level, but why not provide some help. May everyone be rewarded according to his deeds...at some later point in time, as they say."

Followed by many displeased looks, we left the anteroom and went down to the local cafeteria, which was decorated in an old but rich design. The Registrar took a table in the corner, far from curious onlookers, and waited silently till the chef came out to greet us.

"Good afternoon! The usual?" The chef's voice was polite and his back was bowed, despite the fact that the chef was an elf.

"Yes, Master Silturine. If it is 'the usual', you know best."

Elf bowed to the Registrar again, gave me a fleeting glance, grimaced and left proudly. No one offered me a menu. Seeing that I was bewildered, the Registrar laughed:

"Master Silturine is a chef with a broad field of expertise, and is a true professional. In order to determine one's tastes in food he only needs one look. When he prepares the dishes, he takes into consideration the guests' mood or the nature of the negotiations. He likes visitors with exquisite tastes... While your attitude to food is only so-so. You are not an aficionado , to put it in one word." The Registrar laughed again.

"I see..." I replied slowly. It seemed as though I did not hear anything new, but it hurt.

"While the food is not yet here, now is time to talk business. As I mentioned, you do not have to stay in the housing that is assigned to you – just take the keys, say 'Thank you' politely, then buy yourself some property and live there. What else did you want to know?"

"Information. A detailed guide to all the interesting and useful places in Moscow. An unofficial one, of course. And some contact information for useful players. The standard set to get me out of trouble fast in case I encounter trouble."

"You are asking for a lot... two granises." The profiteer said without a pause. I nearly choked.

"This is rob ..."

"Do be careful in your choice of words." The player cut me off rudely.

"Sorry," I said calmly now, not willing to spoil relations from the outset. "I was not thinking right. I meant to say, that is expensive for a beginner player."

The Registrar hemmed contentedly and agreed:

"I know. But it was worth trying." He laughed loudly.

"One granis." I countered his proposal.

"One and a half. Or else you'll have to get by without the useful contacts." The Registrar would not give up.

I sighed sadly and crossed the useful emergency contacts off my "good to have" list.

"Fine, but please tell me, what was the precise wording of Madonna's order, and why are you still helping me? Even though this help is far from being free." I could not let this just pass by without a dig at him.

"Deal. There is nothing to hide there. 'Make his life complicated without going too far. Take away his privileges, but play within the rules.' As for the help, that really is clear. She metes out a punishment, but it is a petty one. A purely female way of doing it—just for the fun of it. This is not serious, so that means the exile will not last long. She needs you, or else we would not be talking here now. See the logic?"

"I do." I agreed. I would like to believe those convincing conclusions…

The first courses were presented and that put a stop to our conversation. It is hard to communicate when your mouth is full and all your thoughts are circling through "Divine!" Incredible!" "Delectable" "I'd kill to have him nearby!" and the whole sequence repeats with each change of course. An hour passed by before I felt any urges that did not have to do with food. I did not care anymore that at the first encounter the elf was unhappy with my tastes and attitude towards food. He was a Master, and those are allowed a lot. For him food was like a separate religion which bestowed pleasure on others, and enabled him to greet each new day with joy.

"Your granis." I offered the exchange to the Registrar and, finally, found out his name: Yurmil. In return my interlocutor passed me a substantial volume.

"This is an atlas of all the areas in Russia that are related to the Game. From nightclubs to the mysterious burial sites of giants in the Urals. I am sure that as an explorer you will be interested in this. Consider this a gift from me."

"Or an investment." I offered my own interpretation.

"We shall see, we shall see," the Registrar replied, not without irony, and we hastened to part our ways, pleased with each other.

Two hours later I was stuck in a traffic jam, "flying towards my bright future". In the past I had frequently been indignant about active road construction at the height of rush hour traffic. Some sorry bums posing as road workers would come up and dig out a hole in the freshly repaired road, then slowly proceed to take a smoke break, never bothering to as much as tape the area off. But now, as I passed by yet another construction site, I could see the complete picture, which explained a lot. There were several ugly monsters belly up in a ditch. Mages, presented as road repair engineers, were casting spells over them. That meant that every time I had seen some out-of-place road construction there had in fact been monsters breaking into the Earth, and various services worked on capturing them and eliminating the consequences. The situation was quite similar with respect to buildings: now and then I saw various airships of most improbable designs that had lost control and crashed into buildings. The aforesaid services, this time posing as renovations to historic buildings, were working on the results of those collisions. This way the Game took care of NPCs, or rather of their frail minds.

The dorm that was allocated to me was in the suburbs. There was a little local market, a couple of large malls; also within easy walking distance I saw some branches of a popular bank, a post office and a Vital Statistics registration office. It was noteworthy that right next to my building, right across the marriage registration office, there was a bus stop with a large billboard indicating "To N Cemetery". Old ladies formed a little market there. Selling plastic flowers and wreaths for the grieving relatives. But that was not the funny part. What made me laugh was that even though it was a work day, rather tipsy young men who must have been drinking to someone's health would run out of the office and buy flowers from those old hags. As I headed to my new home, I noticed one of those buyers:

"Granny, give me the nicest one! And keep the change!" He proudly handed her a hundred-ruble bill. The guy was deeply in his cups.

"Here, dearie, one moment. Here, take some lilies. They're nice flowers – for purity – and I tell you right, they'll be just the thing!" the old woman happily cajoled him. The guy grabbed a paltry bunch of flowers without looking twice and rushed right back to the marriage office.

"Good woman, why do you sell them flowers for the dead? You could make up some fit for marriage, no?" I asked the spry old lady, stopping next to her.

"Why bother, dearie? With live flowers, they're such trouble, an' they cost a bunch, too. An' them boys wouldn't even see, they won't... And that's right – sure it is – we all need to drink to the death of the girlie's freedom; there, they are dragging 'nother one, to wash an' cook an' clean them rags an' such. It's all the right way, dearie," said the old woman, her old teary eyes following yet another bride. The Judge in me did not even stir, since the truth was different for everybody.

As I was ascending the bedraggled stairs to the third floor, my heart grew heavier. Narrow dirty stairs, dank air, constant noise... That was far from an exhaustive list of features for a "normal dwelling area for a beginner player". The walls were dirty, the plaster was peeling. You could hear all the noise from every apartment, and the windows were broken, no doubt to improve natural lighting and ventilation, since there were no light bulbs at any of the landings. Dirt and dilapidation reigned everywhere. Judging by the aroma, there was only one toilet available for the entire building. Its powerful smell brought a strong note into the overall stench of food these people must have been making. Some hallways were adapted by practical gals for drying clothes, so I had every chance to enjoy ragged underwear and badly stretched flowers on someone's nightgowns and underpants.

The local denizens deserved separate mention. All along the way I felt their heavy menacing stares on my back. I was glad that was all I felt. The local thugs near the entrance way spat on the ground and turned away, moms with their offspring pretended to turn away and lose all their curiosity, and the kids ran off in the opposite direction from me, while the local hags stopped cursing at the local winos as soon as I appeared within their field of view. The Game came to my aid, creating in the head of each NPC an image necessary for their mind to activate a conflict avoidance algorithm. Had it not been for Helen, I would have never bothered showing up here. Finally, I got to the right door and opened it quietly.

"Yaropolk! You are back!" A small blond whirlwind rushed towards me and threw her arms about my neck. I never even had a chance to say anything. I was showered with kisses mixed in with little noises to show how much I was missed. That was nice. Well, not just. Actually, I was really happy that I had her and she was capable of such open and sincere joy. I was not trying to deceive myself about freedom of choice on the part of my Doll; I simply enjoyed what I had. My main mistake was that I was unable to perceive Helen as my property, despite all the laws of the Game.

The next few days flew by. I bought an apartment, a new car, and, following Gerhard's advice, did everything to simply forget that I was part of the machinery called "the Game", and that the list of my priorities starts with the item marked "urgent": finding Merlin. I dedicated all my attention to Helen. Unbeknownst to myself I was starting to fall in love with her. That comes easily when your partner is loyal to you to their last breath. I had no doubts whatsoever about it. How could it be different? The very point of existence of the Doll was to make me happy. May it be so then! We walked around for days on end, returning to our cozy nest only for the night, but not for sleeping. Sex with the Doll was outstanding, and every time I felt on cloud nine with pleasure.

The only reminders of the Game were visits from Alard and Mizardine. The hunter settled in Moscow as well. They were both making everyday arrangements, while making sure they took time to see the main points of interest in the city. Then they came back bursting with impressions from the huge megapolis with its urban ways. There was nothing of the sort in my companions' native worlds. They were particularly overwhelmed with Red Square. At the place of the historic execution platform, Lobnoye Mesto, where, as far as legends had it, many hundreds of criminals had been executed over the years. In fact, it contained a very large hole in the ground that housed quite a strange creature. It had neither eyes nor mouth — it just looked like a rounded lump of brown flesh with a few thin tentacles extending from it. The creature gorged on the emotions of the people around it. The more impressionable a person was, the more emotions he or she generated. There was a viewing bridge above the pit for all those willing to look. Mostly those who were willing were NPCs, even though they could not see the monster. They were just drawn to the bridge, and they did not resist their urges. The NPCs "felt" the atmosphere of the place, sank into thoughts about their pointless existences, and left the viewing platform deep in those thoughts. They left all the positive emotions to that bottomless pit of a creature. Players were rare guests here–understandably so. The monster affected them a lot more. So the ones that made it to the bridge were either enthusiasts who had lost a bet, or, on the contrary, wanted to win one by demonstrating their resistance to the consumer of emotional delicacies. But as far as I knew, everyone lost, ending up doubled over and nauseous on the viewing bridge. However, somehow new ones came up every time.

Carried by this wave of nostalgia, I could not resist the temptation to visit the city district where I had grown up. The things that had been my reality for the twenty-three years of my previous life demanded that of me. I wanted to see something or somebody. Not my relatives — of course there was no way to bring them back. But at least the courtyard where I used to play, or the local wino who hung out there all the time with his perpetually hungry cat. Everyone in the yard always offered Barsik some food, pitying him

---

for having a torn-up ear and only one eye. No one actually knew how or when the cat had been injured, and the guy told a different tragic story every time. We all admired the cat's courage, and pilfered fancy bologna for him from home.

However, the Game disposed of all my hopes cruelly. The building was simply not there. There was a paid parking lot in its place instead. I went into a nearby courtyard to ask when the building had been demolished, but was unanimously assured that there had never been a building there. I was unable even to find out what had been there prior to the parking lot. People were confused, and everyone came up with their own story. No one had heard about a wino with a cat, either. It could be that he still was in existence somewhere — there were all sorts of alcoholics hanging around, and some even with cats. I was even more upset when I decided to visit my first school. That was something that should have been there for sure! I would have even been happy to see our horrid home room teacher, who had scarred my young mind for life.

There was in fact a school around the corner, but it was a different type of building, and with a completely different set of teachers. Even the school name was different. I had to put up with this final hint from the Game that the past should be laid to rest, and left the area.

Helen consoled me quickly, and distracted me from all the dark thoughts. I kept immersing myself more and more into the illusionary world that we created for ourselves. There was nothing preventing me from doing so. Other players tended to avoid us remembering Madonna's instructions. I was completely satisfied with that. Alard and Mizardine worked on their own affairs and did not interfere with our lives. No one attacked me; it was as if everyone had simply forgotten about me, and that was cool! It was so cool that I would have never left that bubble on my own. But reality came to bite me precisely on the sixth day of my personal bliss:

"Paladin Yaropolk, you are instructed to immediately report to the Judge Supervisor." A low hoarse voice boomed from the speaker of my comm. The call came precisely at three o'clock in the morning. I nearly jumped out of my skin when I heard scary alarm bells instead of the usual ring tone, and did not understand why. But once I saw the comm screen light up while Helen was still sleeping, I quickly took the call.

Oh well, when I heard the orders I was very tempted to tell them all to go to hell, turn the phone off and go back to sleep, but the caller was very insistent: "I repeat! Paladin Yaropolk, you are instructed..."

The words filled my empty sleepy head, and seemed to echo on and on without the caller having to repeat them. It made you want to jump up and run headlong to pay respects to the Supervisor, whom I actually, let's be frank, had been ignoring all those days. When the voice repeated for the third time what I was supposed to do, I decided to agree with it, and thankfully the line went dead at last. Just about the last thing I needed was a reprimand from the Game for tarrying too long. As soon as I got out of bed, the portal opened next to me. The Game did not wish to waste a moment of its precious time.

A slight bout of vertigo, and then I found myself once again in the familiar place: in the middle of Red Square. A young lieutenant ran up to me right away, introduced himself and explained that he had been sent to bring me to the Supervisor. As it turned out all roads in Moscow led to the Kremlin. Particularly if you were looking for someone of higher rank.

The Supervisor of Judges, in the same way as the Registrar, and any player in general sporting any kind of high Game rank in Moscow, lived and worked directly in the Kremlin. Once Steve showed me the level of Light Energy within its territory, that explained why players were so attached to the red brick walls. The Kremlin in and of itself was a powerful Source of Light. Perhaps not as strong as the remains of saints. Yet it was plenty for the local inhabitants. That was not surprising: one hundred and fifty million NPCs living in Russia revered the Kremlin as a symbol of the unity of faith and power. The compound simply accumulated all the emanations directed at it, converting them, essentially, into free Energy. Who would ever give up such a feeding source on their own?! Nobody. They would all agree to it, and would guard it with their lives.

As I was proceeding down the hallway to the office, I noted to myself that I never felt the pressure of the Light — neither when I visited Kremlin for the first time, nor now. That meant that the new pet was coping with its task and I needed to make sure I set up the purchase of a new one in advance for that purpose. With those thoughts I entered the office of the Judge Supervisor. He was an elf. And a priest. His reddened eyes betrayed chronic fatigue and lack of sleep. His face was just physically incapable of looking friendly, and I could easily see the reasons for that: there were some jobs that simply did not include an easy life and sleeping in your own bed.

"Sit down." I received a curt nod. As he was downing the dregs from his coffee cup, the elf continued: "According to the determination of the Great Madonna, you shall receive case No. 557732. Review that."

A thin folder plopped on the desk. I was not hiding my bewilderment as I opened the document and started reading. A ritual murder. Victims: four NPCs. No witnesses. No signs of death by violence, even though the bodies had sustained odd damage. It was possible that magic was involved, but no traces of it had been discovered. No tracks or footprints were found around the crime scene. The case was being investigated by the Moscow Police Department. Priority task: find the motive for the crime. The clue: the victims' bodies had been set in a particular pattern, probably a sacrificial seal. Preliminary version: summoning a demon. There were grounds to suppose that the murderer was a player. Everything seemed to be clear and written in a way that was easy to understand. It was not clear, however, why Madonna had decided to remember me in view of these murders.

"You will report to me every day on your progress. Sign up for appointments for the entire ten days." The Supervisor finished and leaned back in his chair. From the way his eyes gleamed I guessed that whatever was in the cup, it was definitely not coffee. But I was far from blaming him: it had been a long and difficult night, and the body needed some stress relief. After that latest piece of news I would not turn down an offer of some hydration for my throat and brains.

"Why for the entire ten days?" My mind caught on the specified timeframe.

"You'll see in a moment. Take it: I have offered you an exchange. My guys took a preliminary look at the scene. In the center of the sacrifice there is an inscription. NPCs just don't have the skills for that. This was done by a player."

The Supervisor offered me a video from the crime scene. No matter how horrible it was, one could not ignore precise lines and perfect symmetry. The bodies lay on the ground like broken dolls, forming, however, an elaborate pattern. Its horrifying beauty and precision would satisfy a most demanding perfectionist. That enabled me to rule out fanatics or maniacs. The master's hand was too precise.

The pinnacle of that horror was a flaming inscription in the center of the pattern:

IN TEN DAYS CHAOS SHALL REIGN ON EARTH!

"I received instructions from my superiors to

transfer this case to you. I reviewed your file and I am wondering, what use are you?" the Supervisor added, without too much reverence to Madonna or her protégée, myself. "But an order is an order. Keep working. There are no injuries on the corpses, and no indication that they were killed by magic. If it really is a summoning, that means we have a drifter. I have no illusions that you would be able to catch him, but I have very clear orders not to interfere with your investigation, nor to start my own investigation, and generally to pretend that nothing happened. But bear in mind, Paladin, that if, through your incompetence, more NPCs die or we get into some serious kind of trouble... you'd be better off removing your sorry ass from here in whatever way you know. Got that?"

"Is this a threat?" I was surprised. From the tone and words of the Supervisor it seemed as though he genuinely cared about the Earth, which was not normal for high-ranking players, who mostly care about their own well-being rather than the motherland. And even less for NPCs.

"Just a statement of fact," the Supervisor corrected me curtly. "You have ten days. I repeat, I expect daily reports on your progress in the investigation. Unofficially, you may count on my support. It's time to remember that you are a Judge and not a piece of shit. Go on—they are expecting you at the crime scene."

CHAPTER TWO

DAY ONE

MOSCOW AT NIGHT was beautiful. Regardless of the season, after sunset it turned into a huge and tangled set of Christmas lights. Bright commercial signs blinked at each other like fireworks. Lit-up windows of tall apartment buildings posed a contrast to the mood lighting of historical buildings. In addition, few and far between and therefore fast car headlights dashed all around the city. All those who like the Christmas holiday would by default like Moscow at night. It gave you a special holiday atmosphere; all your daily troubles would seem remote and far away. Unfortunately, my troubles were not linked to a particular time of day.

The Supervisor did not bother to create a portal; instead, he was kind enough to let me use his official vehicle. It took us only about 15 minutes to reach the Tsaritsyno Park. Empty roads, flashing lights on top, a driver who did not have to obey the traffic rules for commoners... That trip was a dream for any hoi-polloi inhabitant of the great city.

We entered the park through the main Park Gate. After we passed the entry checkpoint one of the guard policemen ran up to the car and explained that we would not be able to get any further with the vehicle, and that we had to go through the night forest on foot. For about forty yards we walked along the main avenue, but then we had to leave it, straight for the thicket. There was a path there, but the ground was still uneven; periodically I stumbled on the terrain, and so did the sergeant walking ahead of me. Steve navigated by offering comments and highlighting particularly dangerous areas, but that was not enough. I was trying to look underfoot so as not to fall over, but then I missed a couple of particularly nasty trees, which then hit me across my face and hands... In this way we slowly plodded along in a south and west direction for at least ten minutes, until finally we reached a well lit clearing. It was eerily quiet: not a sound could be heard in the night forest. The trees did not rustle, birds were silent, and even moths and mosquitoes were not flying towards floodlights.

Looking at the thick brush, I thought that the case had no mention of who had discovered the bodies and when. Other than park workers I could not think of any candidates for that role. It was impossible that someone would discover this place simply by accident, was it not?

"Why are there unauthorized people at the site? Lartsov, you want to go on the beat again?" The bear-like growl floated from the darkness. Following the voice we heard the crunching of dry branches and the huffing and puffing of a body moving towards us.

"Well, it's, like... the higher-ups, they called..." The sergeant obviously had not expected this encounter, and was trying to retreat backwards from his advancing boss.

A portly figure appeared from the forest, its glasses glistening menacingly.

"Who called?! To whom?! Why did no one report anything?!" The law-enforcement officer stopped nearby, shaking his double chin in indignation, and constantly adjusting his glasses that would slide down after every question.

Expecting a logical outcome for the young sergeant, I decided to interfere, and waved my hand at Lartsov to disappear:

"Colonel Yaropolk, FSB, Department thirteen." My supervisor had provided me with a story and instructions as to what would be my position and role in the case. Naturally, I had not received any real documents confirming my employment at FSB. I simply extended my empty palm to him, letting the Game conjure up a projection of whatever paper it required with the necessary data. The local boss bent down trying to read the card, and then tried to straighten up to make his belly seem smaller.

"FSB? Fine. Hail, Sir Colonel and welcome to our humble forest." The policeman's voice was loud in itself, and here in this weird silence it was downright deafening. From behind me I heard the muffled cursing of the sergeant, who tripped over something in the dark. The kid was in no hurry to get out of the cordoned-off area.

"Good health to you, too. Show me the bodies," I ordered, following my role. There were no objections, and the policeman, waddling from side to side, turned in place. I coughed meaningfully in the direction of Lartsov, and started climbing over the warning tape. The sergeant immediately emerged from the darkness and called after us:

"Sir Colonel, asking permission to accompany you!" The youngster stared straight at me, completely ignoring his direct superior who had turned bright red from indignation. I decided to reward his courage:

"Granted. Just keep out from underfoot." I heard an indignant huff nearby, but no objections.

A minute later we were looking at four corpses. The broken bodies enthralled, urging one to admire the sight in silence. I looked over the bodies, trying to note every detail, and discussed it with Steve. Suddenly the sergeant behind my back made a hoarse sound and started slowly crumpling to the ground. Had he overestimated his endurance, or perhaps he had never seen any bodies before? The corpulent policeman, looking at him, hemmed with distaste and grumbled:

"You are no good, sergeant. You, idiot, were being sent away from here for a reason. But no, you decided to brown-nose your way into the thick of things!"

The sergeant bent over in a fit of nausea and

moved slowly, trying to get away from the corpses. The fatso continued his lecture, pointedly ignoring the sufferings of his underling:

"This will teach you for the future. What, you think I decided to engage in necrophilia and sent all the witnesses the hell out from here? Get out of here, sissy, before I slap you with an official reprimand."

I looked around. Really, why was there not a single person? What a case! What hype! After talking to my supervisor I had gotten the impression that half the city should be here. While in reality there was just one office rat, judging from his huge belly, and a young curious eager beaver. Even though the latter doesn't count. He was quickly leaving the crime scene, running away in short spurts, bending down at every bush. I turned towards the fatso, who had already forgotten about the sergeant, and who stared at me waiting for something he alone knew.

"Why is there nobody here?" I posed my question.

"What do you mean, nobody? I am here!" The strange NPC was in no hurry to explain the situation. "Don't you feel anything?"

"What is it that I am supposed to feel? Would you please explain?" This was not a good time to play guessing games.

"Major Vesnin, Senior Investigator, Tsaritsyno Police Department" The major deigned to introduce himself and extended his hand for a shake. His hand was soft to the touch, but very strong. "There is no one here because at the site of the murder my subordinates have a strange reaction. You have seen it just now. Whatever you might think, normally they don't behave like that. I have trained them well. Well, with the exception of this dolt, I guess. It's his first time at the crime scene. They are still wet behind the ears, straight from the police academy, damn it...".

I liked it that the major managed to incorporate in his explanation a way to exonerate his guys in the eyes of a "competitor". New information set in motion the gears in my brain, and I asked a logical question, looking at the investigator with interest::

"What about you?"

"For me it's the same as you," the major said, smiling bashfully and spread his hands. "You feel fine here, I can tell. Are you going to take over the case?"

Now, in the bright glare of floodlights, this not-so-young investigator did not seem dumb or funny to me. A smart and experienced NPC was looking at me through the old-fashioned horn-rimmed glasses, and it had been negligent of me to quickly dismiss him as an office rat. He quickly asked me the question that bothered him, but I could bet that his agitation was due to the fact that he did not want to give up the case in favor of "competitors". After talking to Steve I decided that it would be better to have on my team an experienced homicide investigator, so that's what I told the major:

"I am here as an observer, you should be leading the investigation."

My ideas were confirmed as I saw relief on Vesnin's face. He perked up, and shared his thoughts with me:

"That is strange. Something is going on with

my kids. Even my coroner could not deal with it. And he's seen stuff in his life that I wouldn't wish on anyone. I sent them off to take a breather, but they are not far. They'll be right here if need be. They train you tough out there in your Department thirteen. Or have you seen stuff like that before?"

I shook my head for a "no", noting that Vesnin said nothing about himself. His properties bubble indicated clearly that he was an NPC, but the aura of this crime did not affect him.

Together we again examined the bodies and the site of the crime. My certainty that a player was involved only strengthened The NPCs were unable to do things like that with the bodies of their own species.

"I need to make a call." I did not feel like diving into the darkness for the sake of calling, but I was weary of talking in front of the major. "Could you... take a walk? See how your guys are doing."

The major nodded, showing his understanding, and left the circle of light. Just to make sure, I protected myself with a "curtain of silence", and dialed my Supervisor:

"What did you find out?" He picked up immediately, as if he had been waiting for my call.

"Not much so far. I need a demonologist and a necromancer. ASAP."

"Want to talk to the bodies?" The Supervisor interpreted my request. "Good idea. They will be there in half an hour. What is your first impression?"

"It's someone from this world. Not an NPC. Those just bend over double next to this pentagram."

"Why did you call the seal a pentagram?" The Supervisor was surprised. "There are only four bodies there, not five. And there is no five-pointed star, either."

"My mistake." I had to admit my terminology error, since I knew nothing about demonology. "I thought that it's pentagrams that are used to summon demons..."

"What the hell, Paladin?! You consider yourself a Judge and meanwhile use the terms the meaning of which you don't understand precisely?!" The Supervisor blew up. "Pentagrams are only used to summon fire demons of the third circle! Any cretin is capable of finding that out! Why do you think you were sent there by car? So that you would pick your nose instead of learning your basics? Another blooper like that and I will have to bring up the issue of your competence! Keep working! I am waiting for your report at the end of the day!"

I was looking at my now silent comm, rather stunned. I did not understand what had happened just now. Not only had he yelled at me as if I were a little kid, he was now attempting to threaten me! Steve shook his head, informing me that the case materials never mentioned the seal. I did not know what the Supervisor expected, but in any case it would have been stupid to expect that a fifteen minute trip would be enough to turn me into an expert demonologist. Apparently, the elf was getting weak in the head. Too much work, too high responsibility... There was no other way for me to explain these overstated expectations. To hell with him anyway, if only he sent some help.

"Your boss rewarded you with a hearty scolding?" I did not notice the major's approach due to the "curtain of silence" that I had just removed. He was standing right next to me and smiling compassionately, extending to me a plastic cup full of aromatic liquid.

"Don't worry, I just got back and did not hear anything. It's just that you have an expression that is impossible to miss. I expect I look no better myself." I gratefully accepted the cup of coffee, and nearly burnt myself. Vesnin poured another cup for himself from his thermos. "My bosses called me as well. Wanted a result here and now. It's easy for them to make orders as they sit in clean offices, while with this one you can tell a cold case a mile away. No footprints, no witnesses, no tracks of any sort. When they were brought here is not clear. When and how they were mutilated is another hard question."

"People with special equipment will be here shortly. We'll take a look. Perhaps we'll find something. By the way, who discovered them?" I nodded towards the taped-off area. "It's a remote place, it does not seem frequented by anyone for walks."

"You shouldn't say this. I take a walk here every evening. It's pleasant and relaxing after work." Vesnin even seemed a little embarrassed. After a brief silence he continued. "So that was some walk today. I left home about ten at night, I live nearby. Discovered them about midnight. Tripped over the foot of the one we are calling Number Three here. So then I called in my guys. It's our area anyway."

The major's uncomplicated response was so unexpected that Steve had all the alarm bells going. Vesnin is not simply a pawn on this chessboard. He personally discovered the crime site. He was the only NPC not affected by the dark aura of that same site. One coincidence can be random, but two are a pattern. I made sure that the Game initiated a case concerning a ritual sacrifice and said the sentence indicating the start of an interrogation. It was time to remember that I was a Judge and not a piece of shit, according to the advice I had received the day before.

"In the name of justice I demand that you tell the truth and nothing but the truth! You are summoned as a suspect in the case 'Ritual Sacrifice'. For the duration of your testimony you are released from all physical, moral and emotional binds. Everything you say can and may be used against you in determination of the verdict."

"Whaaat?!" Vesnin was taken aback. "Colonel, did you go bonkers while your boss was yelling at you? What in hell do you mean, I am a suspect?"

Now it was my turn to be surprised, to put it mildly. What happened to the standard response "I acknowledge your right to administer justice"? I checked again. Everything was correct. Vesnin was an NPC. There could be no mistake there. Maybe I was no longer a Judge but actually a piece of shit?

According to all the rules, by now the major was supposed to play a vegetable in his patch and confess to me about all his thinkable and unthinkable crimes. Instead, Vesnin took a couple of steps backwards and was gauging his chances for victory from afar.

It was worth noting that he heard my entire statement the way it was. There was only one explanation I could think of: Vesnin was immune to magic directed at him. He read my paper as it was part of my "story"; for the same reason he saw the FSB uniform instead of my real armor. NPCs must not know anything about the Game, whoever they are! Like Monstrichello had not known, until a certain point.

It seems that here on Earth the Game had generated another immune one, even though Archibald had stated that it was an extremely rare occurrence.

Postponing this puzzle — once more — until a more opportune moment, I hurried to correct the situation:

"Sorry, major. Stress resistance check. Consider that you passed it." I reinforced my words with the most sincere smile I could produce.

"You son of a bitch..." Vesnin blurted out, but did not come closer. "That's going to scare anyone, when you hear 'you are a suspect' from an FSB guy. Don't do that any more."

"I won't." I nodded, and finally tried the coffee. It tasted really great: a little bitter, medium roast, just the way I like it. It was obviously made by a master, an expert at making coffee. As I was finishing my drink I still could not identify the unusual aftertaste. It was definitely not cinnamon, cardamom or, as an extreme, chili pepper. The secret ingredient gave it a refreshing and piquant taste.

"What is it? I can't figure it out, but it tastes great." I extended the empty cup to Vesnin, hoping for a second helping. The major must have felt generous, for he opened his thermos again. The steam immediately fogged the thick lenses of his glasses.

"Some secrets should stay secret. You agree, Colonel?" Vesnin was flattered by my reaction to the coffee. "It's an old family recipe. I felt this would be a long night. So, the coffee came in handy."

Setting all cares aside we spent a few moments enjoying our coffee. Then Vesnin asked busily:

"When are your guys coming? I need to call our meat wagons and pack those bodies up."

"Should be here in about fifteen minutes. We'll check something out. You have any ideas?"

"Nothing to write home about. Not real ideas, just guesses. Suppose the criminal is an old guy obsessed with the idea of demons. A psychopath, but not a dangerous one, or else they would have ratted him out a while ago." The major took his glasses off and started wiping the lenses methodically, squinting his already small eyes. The habitual, automatic motion indicated it was more of a habit than a necessity.

"Why would it be an old guy?" I asked evenly, so as not to derail the investigator's thoughts.

"There are four bodies; each victim is about twenty-five." Vesnin pointed at them. "Look at the mutilations. It's impossible to deform their limbs in such a way without breaking them. But there are no fresh injuries and no blood. As I was checking them for pulse I examined a couple of legs. They were mutilated a long time ago, perhaps even when they were small children. These are not simply fractures; their limbs were set like that on purpose so they would stay in zigzag shape. So then, these people lived like that for a long time, unable to move. The fractures healed, but it would be impossible to stand, walk or work with those deformities. Therefore, the criminal must have been preparing them for the ritual. That makes that butcher at least fifty, or maybe older. We would have to dig up the cases on missing children from twenty years ago or so. I expect we might be able to find some clues."

However crazy, that was a possible explanation. Without consulting with expert players it was impossible to tell whether one could use Game magic to twist the bodies of NPCs this way while still keeping them whole. Steve's answer to my question was negative: we had not encountered anything of this sort in any of the books that we had processed.

"Where are they? What, you couldn't clean it up a little here? Get rid of the damn lights!" We turned in unison in the direction of the irritated voice. The grumpy elf demonologist had been yanked out of bed, just as I had, and dumped straight into the park. The long-eared beast did not even bother to hide his annoyance with this turn of events, and shared it generously with all around. A portal blinked nearby and the necromancer joined us. Another long-eared one. As I felt prejudice against their whole race I could swear that Madonna was choosing them for me on purpose.

Vesnin did not seem to care much about the new arrivals. The Game concealed from him both the portals and the race of the newcomers.

"So?" The demonologist singled me out from the group and attacked me with complaints. "You couldn't figure it out on your own? What do you need me here for?"

Instead of explaining I pointed in the direction of the bodies, and the demonologist was enthralled. His eyes were shining, his ears trembled with anticipation, his irritation was replaced by delight.

"Amazing!" the elf said, enchanted. "What a perfect 'seal'! Were the bodies prepared in advance? Necros, what are you standing here for? Come on, get to work! We need to interrogate them!"

Vesnin beamed — some oil was thrown on the fire of his lame theory.

On the face of it, the necromancer did not share the demonologist's excitement. On the contrary, he appeared completely unperturbed and businesslike as he started working. He barely cast a sideways glance at the corpses, and extracted a cat from his inventory. Poor animal yowled and hissed loudly as if sensing its coming demise. With a quick slash of the ritual blade the sound stopped, blood flowed from the furry creature. Holding the body by its hind legs, the necromancer made a circle around the crime scene, sprinkling the bodies with the blood. That's when we heard Necros' voice for the first time. In a low monotonous chant he called on the Game, requesting for the consciousness to be returned to the dead bodies for interrogation. A minute passed, then another, but nothing happened. The bodies stayed motionless.

"Draw back ten steps." The necromancer told us. His big eyes went dull, the whites darkened, but he seemed fully sane and coherent. "Make the NPCs leave and go about a hundred and fifty yards away from the clearing. They might die. The recoil will be significant."

I did not know what major Vesnin saw instead of the cat and the ritual, but upon hearing the request of the mysterious expert, he ordered his troops to immediately retreat as far as possible. Vesnin obviously did not consider that the necromancer's request pertained to him as well. Neither the elves nor myself cared about the major. He had been warned. Now he could do whatever he felt like.

Returning to the bodies, the elf extracted a dog from his inventory now. The ritual was repeated, but the end result was the same. The dog was followed by a cow, then by an adult copy of Rragr, then by a very strange animal that was similar to a human, but without any sign of intelligence... the bodies failed to respond. Finally the necromancer addressed me:

"The bodies are dry. Their souls have been completely drained as if a demon had done it. In order to find out more I need to sacrifice an NPC. A conscious one and not subjugated. I guarantee the result. Grant permission to sacrifice an NPC, Judge, if this information is important for you. These are the rules. I have the potential victim with me."

"Two questions. Do you actually think someone summoned a demon?" This seemed to be our main theory.

"No." The elf corrected me. "I said it looks very much like the souls were drained by a demon. I will be able to tell you more after the ritual. As for the seal — ask the demonologist. What's your second question?"

"I got it. Who is the sacrifice?" I wanted to know where necromancers come up with the sacrifices for their rituals. They would not be buying them at the Auction, right? I expected that for those purposes NPC criminals were being made available. The necromancer did not disappoint me.

"A criminal from death row. Sentenced to die on the electric chair for pedophilia. Raped and murdered twenty-two minors. I have a copy of the case and sentence with me. Are you going to check it?" I had no reason to doubt Necros. Mostly just to make sure I nodded and received a copy. The first three pages were enough to make an immediate decision.

"I permit the sacrifice of this NPC for the purpose of the ritual." Good riddance. That should make the world a little better.

The necromancer decided to keep the ritual and his preparations for it secret. Both he and the maniac that he started working on were enclosed in a dark fog. I approached the demonologist:

"What do you think? Is this a summoning seal?"

"I am not certain. I am not familiar with this seal. The demon could already be here, captive to someone. It could come here because of the

---

disturbances in the Energy..."

The elf did not finish the sentence, drowned out by a horrendous scream of inhuman pain. The necromancer had started his ritual. We heard more monotonous chanting by Necros followed by a brief silence.

"A higher demon!" The necromancer fell out of his dark cloud. He looked as if he had been through a meat grinder. His arms and legs were twisted at unnatural angles, blood was dripping from his ears and nose, one eye was missing. But before he fainted he managed to nod at the "seal" that appeared from the dissipating fog. I swallowed convulsively: It's not every day that you get to see a dead body coming to life. The eyes of the nearest corpse opened, its empty gaze staring at the sky.

"The souls are not available," an unpleasant hoarse voice stated. "Drained by a higher demon. The bodies do not recall the point from which the higher demon arrived. The bodies do not recall their death or their souls."

The Energy provided by the necromancer ran out, the body shut its eyes and went silent. The necromancer, without regaining consciousness, shimmered and disappeared: the player's body could not cope with the injuries and respawned.

"Damn, a higher demon in Moscow," the demonologist grumbled despondently, impressed by the sight. "I can't help you here. We need to bring in head hunters."

"Can any of you guys determine the level of that visitor?"

"The Head might be able to." The demonologist thought for a moment. "We don't have higher ones in this world. So if anyone could say anything about the demon summoned by this seal, it would be the Head..."

The elf provided me with the coordinates of the demonologists' residence in the Sanctuary, walked around the crime scene one more time, then activated a portal and took off to do whatever he was doing.

I looked for the NPC. The major had in fact left the clearing when the fog appeared, but it turned out he hadn't gone far. As soon as I started looking around he stepped out of the shadows, completely unharmed. Another point in favor of the theory that he was an immune one.

"Major, we are finishing up. Don't mention any of the things that happened in your report. As I said, we are supposed to be observers only. Give me your phone number; if I find anything out, I will call you."

"As you say, colonel. But give me your number as well then." Vesnin gave me his official and personal phone numbers, demonstrating his readiness to cooperate, and waited for my move. I grinned inwardly: I was sure that he would immediately run looking for me in the database to find out more.

"I only have an official number. We are not allowed to have personal ones, according to our procedure. I grinned, leaving the major guessing whether I was lying or whether FSB rules were indeed so draconian. Or else Vesnin would do a search on the number and discover that today he had talked not to an FSB colonel, but to a fitness instructor,

"Evgeniy Frolov".

I left my new partner to clean up the bodies and tried to figure out a way to quickly get into the Sanctuary. I needed to talk to the Head of demonologists quickly and decisively, but how could I do it if I had no scrolls? Reluctantly I dialed the Supervisor again and listened to another bunch of insults. This time I was not so affected by it, since I felt there was a certain amount of truth to his words. After screaming to his heart's content, the elf informed me that the only player who could sell me a scroll to go to the Sanctuary was himself, and the price of this service would be at least a granis. Because, first of all, stupid idiots must be made to suffer, second, that was the night rate, third he wanted to see my ass in the Kremlin in order to give me the scroll, fourth... I stopped listening and called a taxi to leave for Zurich on a night flight like any common NPC. Since, thankfully, flights for it departed just about every hour. I wasted half a day, but saved my poor brain from all that headache, and reached the Paladins' residence. There I bought some scrolls for the future, and finally found myself in the demonologists' residence.

"What brings a Paladin to our abode?" It was weird, but the gatekeeper at the demonologists' place was an old crippled guy, same as for us. The right half of his face had been mutilated by the claws of some demon or other monster. Maybe it's some form of an ad campaign, or just a move to demonstrate the toughness of the class to visitors. Like, you come in to demonologists, say, and right from the start an old guy shows you: "Demonologists are not some silly pansies! We are tough warriors! We fight evil demons! Every time we walk the edge of the blade! And we all rush into battle! Look, even guys like me serve the common cause and die old with their boots on! Join our army!"

Maybe there was something to it, but, since I was a blatantly cynical guy, I preferred the bloom of youth, and female youth at that. Unfortunately, it's not like I had a choice.

"I need to see the Head!" I stated straight away. And it's an urgent problem."

"Just the Head? This member of the species was just about as caustic as the one we had at our Residence. "You don't want me to call the whole conclave, invite experts from other worlds? Would just the Head by himself be enough for such a high guest?"

If one were to remove the sarcasm from the old guy's voice, his reaction was not at all unexpected. Quite the opposite: it would have been extremely surprising if he had let me in right away. To save time and effort I presented my main trump card:

"The problem is a higher demon that appeared on Earth. Your demonologist already visited me at the scene. The case is managed by the Great Madonna herself, and I report daily on the progress of the investigation. And it will include a statement that the Head of demonologists denied me help. And may I explode in this very place if I am not telling the truth!"

My words were confirmed by a curtain of white light that washed over me from head to toe. The old keeper just opened and closed his toothless mouth, terrified by the possible consequences that his rudeness might cause for the Head.

"Demonologists never deny help to their brothers in the Game." Another member of the class was coming down the stairs from the second floor to aid the keeper. His cape concealed his face in deep shadows; however, four arms indicated that it was obviously not human. "First Circle Magister Erhaville. How can I help you, outcast?"

A Magister was a high rank in a class; he would be aware of various events in the Game. He called me an outcast to put me down a notch. But that did not bother me. I did not come to tell him my sob story about the unfairness of the world. Steve had prepared a video reflecting the events in Tsaritsyno Park, and I sent the file to Erhaville. I did not care if he were the Head or a Magister; I just needed some help.

"Last night a 'seal' was discovered in Moscow. The court necromancer was not able to raise the victims' bodies for interrogation. We only know that they were drained by a higher demon. The court demonologist was unable to help and referred the request to the class management. That's why I am here."

"Incompetence on the verge of idiocy." Erhaville spat out, having watched the video, and turned to the old man. "Master Glott, please revoke Master Velsar's license."

The old man started doing something hurriedly, and Erhaville switched to me:

"Come, I'll tell you what's wrong with this seal."

We went upstairs to his office. The demonologist never raised his cape, and his hands, once he slid them out of the sleeves, were sheathed in thin leather gloves. Steve was shaking his head in disappointment: We had not encountered anyone like that among the races we knew.

"It's fake," Erhaville stated unequivocally. "The seal that's made out of the bodies makes no sense and it is not possible to summon any demon using it. No demon at all."

"The necromancer..." I started, but Erhaville did not let me finish.

"He was right. The souls of those victims were, in fact, drained by a higher demon – the ritual did confirm that."

"So, then, someone made a counterfeit construct similar to a seal, brought along a higher demon which he had summoned somewhere else and got it to drain the victims' souls? That seems like total nonsense."

"Nonsense is the absence of a control line in the seal; unfortunately, Velsar did not pay attention to that. Another thing that makes no sense is the configuration of the bodies. They are set out very prettily, that's true, but they don't cover the astral loop. I understand it's hard for a Paladin to understand these fine points; so I suggest that you simply put it in your report — First Circle Magister Erhaville considers the seal is a fake."

I exhaled, upset: my only possible theory was dashed against harsh reality.

"Summoning a higher demon would inevitably

be reflected in the astral plane of the game world."
Erhaville deigned to explain things to me. "Nothing
like that has happened in our world — neither
yesterday, nor a month ago, nor over a year, nor, in
fact, for several decades. The last time a higher
demon was summoned into this world occurred in
August of 1939; that led to the Second World War.
Have I convinced you?"

"Where did the demon come from, then?" I was
bewildered.

"Someone brought one with him. Someone who
has the power to rule a higher demon. To make the
search easier for you, I will tell you right away —
there is no such player among the inhabitants of
Earth. Even the Head of our class would not be able
to stop a higher one after just four souls. It would
need at least ten to dull his eternal hunger just for a
moment. The master of the demon must have
phenomenal magic power. There is no other
explanation for what happened in Moscow yesterday."

I was despondent as I left the demonologists'
Residence. I had no idea what to do next. All I knew
about detective work I had learnt from stories about
Sherlock Holmes and Hercules Poirot. However, it
seemed impossible to transfer this "astounding"
expertise into the modern world. Should I perhaps try
the deductive method, though?

So, an extremely powerful player arrived on
Earth without announcing his arrival or his strength.
He brought a higher demon with him. What would
follow from that? That brought to mind my "beloved"
suzerain! Because everyone who arrived on Earth had

to obtain a permit to visit the world and declare especially dangerous objects and creatures. Bernard must know that player! Otherwise what kind of Coordinator is he?

I barely restrained myself from jumping up and down with excitement, and rushed to visit Bernard.

My joy was premature: there was no one at the estate. I tried calling him, but also to no avail: Malturion did not pick up and neither did the Coordinator. I did not want to hang around waiting for the host: the servants did not know how long their master was going to be away, and I would rather avoid a chance encounter with "the Great One". I passed on a request for an audience through the servants, left a voicemail for Malturion and decided to take off back to Moscow to see Helen. I needed a short break.

I felt that something was wrong when I was just approaching the building. It was the height of day, yet not a soul around. The playground, that was always bustling with noisy children, was now empty. Only a swing was creaking in the wind. No winos on the benches, no stray cats... Not even any ubiquitous pigeons! It gave me the impression that someone was lying in wait for me and wanted me to know that.

The diamond shield boosted my confidence. I decided it made no sense trying to approach the building: I was out in the open, and whoever it was, they were unlikely to let me disappear within. But outside there was not much for shelters either: the playground and a couple of cars. Not much protection however you parse it.

A light breeze touched the back of my head. I twisted around preparing to fight, but only caught the air. Again there was dead quiet, the creaking swing... and a light breeze on my neck. The bastard was trying to play on my nervousness. I had to restrain myself from fidgeting. With a curse I was about to call on my invisible opponent, but then a dark arrow appeared out of nowhere and crashed mightily into my shield, blowing it to smithereens. My inertia neutralizer did its job really well: I staggered a couple of steps backwards, but kept my footing. As it shattered, the shield completely annihilated the arrow. If the enemy planned to kill me, now was his best chance: I was stunned, disoriented and defenseless. That was the plan of my strong and experienced opponent. Her chance, actually.

Deep dark fog roiled in the path in front of me, turning into the vague, yet very familiar image of Gromana.

"Enough playing already. You will come with me. The master wants to see you!"

"Master? I don't have one, witch. You are the one who prefers a leash and collar to freedom." Another arrow shot in my direction. I rolled over and ducked out of its trajectory. The building behind me lost a chunk of wall.

"No fear at all, eh?" Gromana was obviously contradicting herself. How do you attack a player with battle lightning bolts and at the same time invite him to have a conversation? Even if you shoot without aiming, you have a high chance of sending your interlocutor for respawn anyway.

"What, truth burns if you are not the one spouting it?" As I was aggravating the witch I had a hard time avoiding more arrows. She was not aiming well, just with all her might, old bitch. Trying to scare me and show off. But she was good, damn her, she really thrived under Lumpen's wing. Seventieth level Darkness splashed around her like a pet. The Energy flows pulsed with red streaks along her entire figure, which was barely visible under her black cape. Or was it simply more fog? Gromana even freed her hair, releasing it from a tight arrangement.

It would be stupid to take this risk any further; it was time to escape. Fighting Gromana one on one I considered stupid, following her to Lumpen was not a great idea either. I made a somersault and hid behind the nearest car, hoping to gain a few seconds to activate a portal. But once I extracted the scroll from my inventory, I heard displeased, but unalarmed tsking:

"Portals won't work, Paladin. I told you, the master wants to talk to you and you will come with me. Get out of there now!"

Another arrow sank into the ground next to my foot. Instead of surrendering, I whapped Gromana with three bunches at once of the Templar's Blow scrolls, my weapon of choice. For a couple of seconds the witch was shaking her head, trying to regain her composure. The shields of the Dark witch held — I did not really count on breaching it with just three scrolls — but it gave a clear indication of what I thought about her proposition. It angered the witch, and in another few seconds I was yanked into the air.

Gromana was tired of toying with me, so a band of dark fog shot out of her hand and dashed to me, swaddling me like a baby.

"What the..." I heard her exclaim in surprise as the force that was holding me up dissipated. The fog dispersed into patches, and I, released, crashed to the ground. Not wasting any time, I quickly crawled aside and activated all my defenses.

"Fine. That's even more interesting," Gromana scowled, flying about a yard into the air. I swallowed: A three-thousand-year old witch in flight looked scary. Nothing good was in store for me; I found that out a moment later for sure. She pointed her right hand at me, and her left flew over her head, fist tight. Everything went dark as if the witch had turned the Sun off for old debts. But it was not pitch-dark: I could easily see vague shadows and hear their blood-curdling howls. The ghosts circled in an enthralling dance. I was paralyzed, unable to draw my eyes away, unable to move. The acclaimed Daro set was starting to give. A passing thought flashed through my mind that after the rust eats through the armor it will start on my body; but that was not what bothered me. I was choking on my own screams as I fell into a huge rotating funnel of my worst fears and nightmares. Gromana was not beneath combining business with pleasure and pumping Energy out of me in the process.

"Show yourself!" The witch shouted menacingly, and as if by magic, the Sun returned to the skies. Air filled my lungs with a wheeze, helping me snap back to reality, but I still was unable to move. The witch was distracted by something or someone; that gave me a respite. I felt totally drained. As if all my strength had been pumped out of me. My body was reluctant to recall who was its rightful master. I gave myself a few seconds, then forced myself to open my eyes and lifted my head. I really wanted to know where my tormentor was and who had rescued me.

"Durich? Largus? Vort?" Gromana was hanging in the air in the same place, turning her head back and forth frantically, not knowing where the next attack would come from. The visitors were in no hurry to show themselves, using the same tricks the witch had used a minute ago. Enjoying the sight, I leaned against the nearest bench and also took a look around. There was no one. The same perfect silence still hung in the air, and the damn swing was still creaking!

Grimacing with displeasure, Gromana interlinked her fingers and then pulled them apart sharply; this generated several red spheres. For a second they hung in front of the witch's face, then dashed off in different directions, looking for the enemy. Meanwhile, as my strength was returning, I attempted to get back on my feet. That attracted Gromana's attention. An arrow flashed, and I shut my eyes tiredly, cursing at the damn witch silently, bracing for a blow, but my invisible protector saved me again. The arrow exploded in a burst of festive fireworks just a couple of inches away from me, and blue Energy snakes twisted along the dome around me. Steve examined this protective sphere set by someone, and told me joyfully that it was the absolute protection dome. Gromana inhaled deeply, sniffing at the product of someone else's work.

"You are a right bitch, Gromana, but you can't smell worth shit." The space around took pity on the witch and started talking. That immediately ruined the suspense, since there was only one creature that possessed such a deep and purry voice in all epochs past and present. Being a true connoisseur of theater, Archibald was not above putting up a small but stunning performance now and then. It was that way now, too: the air around sparkled silver, and parts of the body of my teacher started appearing around Gromana, each one separately. The wide grin of the Cheshire Cat I had known since childhood appeared in front of her face. Archibald was a gentleman to the last, as his enemy was female. In his place I would have shown my ass in front of the dark bitch's face. Clicking his claws right under the witch's ear, the catorian's image became complete, and he stood between her and me. "You keep making mistakes in selecting your allies and enemies: Soluna, Bernard, Lumpen. Now you are stretching your dirty hands to my student. Are you out of your sick mind?"

"He is not your student anymore!" Gromana obviously had not expected to see my teacher here. "You have been demoted!"

"Yeah, yeah, and stripped of all privileges, rank, class, abilities, and so on and so forth," Archibald grinned. "Right, right, I remember. But I never disowned my student. And no one can take him away from me until I want it. And I don't want! He is dear to me. As a monument to boundless stupidity. Get that?"

Gromana took advantage of the long monologue to attack the catorian. A child of the previous era, she was certain of her strength, but even more so of Lumpen's strength. Together with his protection, the necromancer granted significant strength to his slaves. This played a bad joke on Gromana, as it made her overconfident to an unforgiveable extent.

She dumped a whole lot of Energy into her attack; she wiped a streak of sweat from her brow and waited for the result with a triumphant smile, particularly since Archibald was not even bothering to block her blow. The Dark force of the spells rushed towards the catorian, swirled around him a couple of times and dissipated at his feet without inflicting any harm at all. The witch realized that she had just lost that battle, while the former Paladin had not even started fighting. Losing her control, she showered him with spells even as she was retreating hastily. Archibald did not bother to respond to this outburst either. His new silvery Daro armor easily absorbed all that barrage without much ado. The amazing part was that Archibald was wearing a Paladin's armor. As if the public spanking and expulsion from the class never mattered to my teacher.

Concurrently with the attack that was supposed to distract him, first and foremost, Gromana waved her hand in the air and a portal activated next to her. However, it collapsed almost immediately. Archibald whipped his tail in glee.

"Come on, Gromana. You said yourself that

portals would not work. And now. You are so... mmm... inconsistent. Like all women... First they argue that they only want good old traditional sex, and then they throw tantrums demanding that their sex life be more varied," Archibald purred, coming practically all the way up to Gromana. "Why does Lumpen want my student? No, I am not releasing you. You will only poison yourself when I let you."

Gromana was bound tight with semitransparent silvery ropes that looked like they were live snakes. A capsule fell out of the witch's mouth, but did not hit the ground: Archibald deftly caught it in the air. Another thin silver rope easily slid into the witch's mouth and disappeared inside. Archibald pretty much completely prevented the possibility that Gromana could commit suicide.

"That will get you nowhere," the witch growled. Sooner or later the bonds will weaken. I will return to my master!"

"You will indeed. I totally share your confidence." Archibald responded gallantly while thoroughly searching Gromana for more unpleasant surprises. The witch twitched, trying to resist, but Archibald deftly took a couple of hairpins out of her hair and took a thread with a flat metal plate off her wrist. He examined the latter with distaste. Closed his fist. When he opened his fingers, the plate had crumbled to dust.

"And for little things like that I will even put a hand to your return, as a minimum, to non-existence," Archibald added, and the ability to move returned to Gromana. The bonds slackened some, but did not disappear.

"I recall you promised me something similar in the previous era as well, but my senses did not let me down in looking for my protector," Gromana croaked. The rope that had entered her mouth caused her discomfort, and made it hard for her to talk.

"I agree, you used to have a capital one. While now it's a far cry from that. I asked you why Lumpen needs Yaropolk," Archibald repeated. "This information is not critical, yet curious. Are you going to talk?"

"About that? No," the witch snorted. "But we could agree. Wiping me out won't do you any good, Archibald. We both know that. But you won't be able to guard me forever, either. The moment you become distracted I will find a way to respawn. Why all this circus? Give me this dunce of yours, hunter! Lumpen will thank you–I know your price rate. You will get a good deal."

"You might be right," the catorian nodded, his face turning sad for a moment. The game that had seemed so much fun suddenly ended. "Moreover, you are totally right. One should get rid of dunces. They are boring and predictable. Too bad there is only one dunce here, and that's you, witch. Chill out!"

Gromana wanted to shout something, but was enveloped by silver fog which turned into a huge piece of ice. Frozen into it, the witch remained alive, since she did not disappear for respawn.

"Once more that demonstrates to me that women are infinitely inconsistent twits. You are a Dark witch. You have betrayed your own many times;

you don't have even a remote idea of what is loyalty or self-sacrifice. Nastiness is your middle name. And then out of the blue! She remembered what loyalty means. And why?" Archibald, annoyed, shot that rhetorical question at the world, then turned towards me: "I am asking you — why?"

I had no ready answer and simply shrugged, puzzled.

"Because the witch met her idol. You get that, student? They do not use their mind like normal people. They follow their feelings. Everything is silent inside — damn them all to hell, I'll betray them at the first opportunity. And if he makes my soul sing — it's all completely different; I'll fight to the death for him. Stupid, in other words!"

I nodded sagely.

"Are you alive there, you small mishap of a creature? When will you grow a brain, my hapless student? I had thought you were not a woman..." Archibald started towards me.

"No, I am not a woman. I can easily show that to you, my ever doubtful teacher." I parried.

I was gradually regaining my strength. I scraped myself off the bench and took a few steps towards the catorian. He shook his head in displeasure and suddenly made a sharp move with his hand, sending a silver lightning bolt through the air. I heard a short scream from the right, and a necromancer fell out of thin air right under my bench. A silvery blade was sticking out of his throat. A few moments, and the necromancer choked on his own blood. His body shimmered and disappeared as the player respawned.

"Are you sure you are not a woman? Are you a corpse then? You are so popular with necromancers. That was number seventy seven if I am counting right." Archibald picked up the blade and examined me. His whiskers twitched in displeasure; he poured some burning hot liquid down my throat. The heat died down almost immediately, but my body felt freshly strong and energetic again. It made me want to run, jump, create. With all that Energy swirling in me I even jumped in place several times, amazed by this new ability: I pushed off lightly, but soared at least a meter in the air. Dizzy with delight, I jumped again and realized I had just broken the height of three meters or so!

"Quit playing a goat, and mucking around the fountain!" the catorian grumbled. Noting my offended look the teacher steered me back to reality:

"Why do you think Lumpen sent Gromana herself after you, and not some gopher?"

"She is familiar with this world." I was not sure I understood the question, since it seemed to have such an obvious answer.

"She'd been on Earth less than a month." Archibald responded. "If that had been the criterion, he should have sent... well, he actually did send that one as well."

"As well?" It suddenly dawned on me what the number seventy-seven meant dropped by the catorian, in the context of my quiet stay in Moscow. For almost a week I had hung around with Helen without encountering a single opponent in my way;

now as I was looking at the catorian's face I was starting to realize the extent of my debt to the teacher.

"Since the very first day?" All the euphoria induced by the infusion evaporated immediately.

"Right. There were attempts every day, and today is day six." Archibald nodded in the direction where the dead necromancer had dropped. "Of course, I could use the experience and one has to hone skills, but student of mine! How can you be so careless?!"

"I don't know, it just happened that way." Acknowledging my incompetence was painful. As I was trying to justify myself I was puzzled why the hell Archibald had spent his time and effort to protect me? No! There was something fishy about that! His mug was far too pleased as he was looking at Gromana.

"So, you were clearing out all the small fry so that Lumpen would send not some second-rate guy after me, but Gromana?" I clarified, looking at Archibald closely. He nodded condescendingly, not sensing the trap.

"Go to hell, you, 'caring teacher'! You were not protecting me, you were baiting the trap for the witch! I owe you exactly nothing!" My breath caught in indignation.

"Indeed, you are not a woman! It seems like this one has a brain and he is even trying to use it!" the catorian snorted, unimpressed. "What difference do my motives make if that's what kept you alive?"

It was useless to say anything in response. Archibald got out his comm and quickly dialed someone. A few seconds of tedious waiting, and then the patronizing and slightly arrogant voice of Bernard floated through the loudspeaker:

"I hope you are not calling me to offer your services, hunter? A connection with you may prove expensive now, even if I don't take into account your rates."

"Look who's talking, oh the nastiest of the lowly Coordinators." Archibald's every word was simply dripping with self-content.

"Has exile affected your brain, or have you caught distemper from your fleas? Get to the point, sickhead." The Coordinator ignored the catorian's insults, and his voice was full of mirth.

"As you wish, lowliest one. I decided to change my specialty the other day, so now I am into network marketing. Are you interested?" the former Paladin kept insisting.

"Another statement like that from you, Archibald, and I am dropping the line." Bernard's patience ran out.

"Being close to those in power really did ruin you, Kalran. But whatever. There is one common acquaintance of ours, visiting with me now, whom you swore by the Game to protect. But we won't state her name out loud due to recent events. I have several options for selling this rare and valuable commodity, but only for the sake of our friendship I am calling you first. Just think: a vassal who betrayed his master. It would be an ugly stain on the pristine reputation of the highly esteemed Coordinator! Do you agree?" Archibald obviously underscored "pristine" by his tone of voice.

"Really? I am indeed grateful. What are your terms?" Arrogance and condescension were replaced by metal notes. The catorian's hints had hit home.

"That's the way." Archibald's eyes sparkled as he anticipated an interesting conversation. For such ancient beings the greatest pleasure was something to dispel their no less ancient boredom. "Here are the coordinates. I am expecting just you, alone. We'll bargain. As far as I recall from the Lecleur estate, you were very effective at it."

As far as I thought, the last sentence was like a finishing shot in the head. Now I just needed to find out in whose: Archibald's or Bernard's. Kalran was not going to risk leaving alive a player who knew about the contract between himself and Lumpen. On the other hand, Archibald had never been known as an idiot. If he had decided to trot out this trump now, there must have been a reason for it. Or at least so I hoped...

Bernard showed up a minute later, surrounded by a multilayered complex protection. Meanwhile Archibald hastily created an illusion of himself and set it next to Gromana, with its back turned to us. The teacher himself meanwhile set invisibility over us and assumed the pose of an innocent girl sitting on the bench with a book in his paws.

Bernard destroyed the illusion right away with a mighty shot, using his surprise advantage. In response Archibald dispelled the invisibility and said in the smooth voice of a trained reciter:

"Gardish, a world with twenty billion inhabitants, in exchange for Earth and knowledge.

Restart is coming. You know very well that Coordinators are not included in the lists..."

"Enough." Bernard said curtly, cutting the catorian off. But my teacher continued to read with gusto the record of the conversation that had taken place between the Coordinator and the "Enemy of all life" Lumpen, demonstrating the proof that had been lacking.

"I said that's enough!" The Coordinator was losing his cool visibly, and the catorian enjoyed it just as visibly.

"Your nerves are oh so frayed... You just barely showed up and have already tried to send me to respawn. You must have a hard time sleeping, right? Your guilty conscience is bothering you. Right, Coordinator?" The book disappeared. Archibald rose from the bench, his tail whipping his boots.

"You called me for idle banter?" After a brief silence Bernard was an example of calm and self-possession. "I apologize for my flare. You are right, I have more responsibilities lately. Tired as a dog."

Since the catorian had called him rather than disclose the information to other interested parties, he would be willing to bargain.

"You want to make me an offer? I am all ears."

"For a start, you release Yaropolk from being your vassal." Archibald finally started on the goal for the sake of which the whole setup had been arranged, and now it was my turn to be surprised. "Believe me, it's nothing personal, but my student must belong to me alone. My other condition also has to do with his rather immodest person. You are now Lumpen's ally.

Use your position to make sure that he does not bother Yari again. I already have my plate full without having to constantly kill necromancer brown-nosers."

"I need guarantees." Bernard raised his eyebrows quizzically.

"Bernard, everyone needs them. What guarantees can you provide to me that Lumpen will call off his curs? None. So my guarantee is a contract sealed by the Game. While Yari plays without trouble, the record of your treason will not be made public. As a proof of my loyalty and good will you may take Gromana with you for free, as a souvenir. It's up to you what to do with her, but I would recommend you wipe her out. She's gone completely barking mad with her Lumpen."

"I don't need any recommendations from you." Bernard made a token response and fell to thinking.

"Come on, Bernard. Restart is inevitable. All you need to do is make sure that Yaropolk is safe from Lumpen, and then no one will care with whom Kalran made an alliance in whatever previous era. You don't stand to lose anything!" Archibald was persuading him calmly and smoothly. Despite obvious advantages the deal offered to the Coordinator, he was in no hurry to agree, thoroughly thinking the proposal over. Perhaps he was looking for a catch. Finding none, he said:

"Gromana and the agreement in exchange for Yaropolk. Do you confirm?" While the bosses were bargaining, I was trying to figure out why the catorian was expending so much effort to ensure my safety. It was clear why the Coordinator agreed. Indeed, he would lose nothing, as he was interested in the Restart happening as soon as possible. Why not release a vassal, particularly since in seeming fact he would still remain your mental slave? Archibald's motives were completely obscure.

"I confirm, and call the Game to witness that until and unless there are difficulties and assassination attempts initiated by Lumpen or Bernard Kalran against Yaropolk and his ability to engage in the Game, the record of the agreement made between Kalran and the necromancer Lumpen at the Lecleur estate will not be disclosed on my initiative." Archibald stated in one smooth sentence, and the Game confirmed his intent.

"I acknowledge that Paladin Yaropolk is free from the vassalage oath to me." It was now Bernard's turn to fulfill his obligations. Blue light washed over me, and Bernard's symbol disappeared from my shoulder as if simply erased. The Game acknowledged my freedom.

"I hope it will be pleasant to deal with you. Archibald grinned and his little book crumbled into dust. "Want some advice?"

"No, but when did that stop you?" Bernard countered with a chuckle.

"True. So, you made a wrong choice with Lumpen. The price of taking him to the new era is too high. You will definitely not like it."

"Let me be the judge of that." Bernard cut him off curtly. "Is that it for you?"

"It is for today." The smile never left the catorian's face, as if someone had poured him a ton of cream which he ate all by himself.

"Yaropolk, return the anti-grav to me." Bernard finally indicated that he noticed my presence and stretched out his hand demandingly. The only thing was, I was not going to part with the useful device. It was time to show my cards and notify the Coordinator that a minute ago he lost not only a vassal. I decided to do it without getting into an argument. I was simply demonstrating my disobedience. With each second Bernard grew glummer, and his eyes grew darker.

"I am waiting for my anti-grav!" The Coordinator repeated insistently.

"No." I said shortly. "It's mine now."

"I order you!" Bernard raised his voice, astonished by my refusal.

"You have no right to order me." Archibald's proximity inspired confidence in me. He did care a great deal about my safety. And I was tired of groveling. A fire jet shot at me after my second refusal and broke harmlessly against the protective dome. Archibald did not let me down.

"Bernard, settle down. I already told you that I prefer giving orders to my students myself. You released him from the oath, so now Yaropolk is free from obligations. Or did I miss something?" Archibald waited for Bernard to stop pouring fire over me and regain the ability to perceive normal speech.

"No, you did not miss anything," said the Coordinator, staring daggers at me, and unwilling to reveal to the catorian the true reason for his anger. "I detest thieves. I took care of him, and now when I request the return of my property, your student argues with me!"

Two pairs of eyes stared at me demanding an explanation:

"I just can't return the anti-grav now. It's a Light world, how am I going to play?" The simplest explanation seemed the most logical one. Archibald's whiskers twitched, and Bernard continued:

"By the way, Archibald, we missed one point. I want you to convince me that Yari will not disclose the information instead of you." After my open disobedience the Coordinator decided to ensure some extra protection for himself.

"Yari, Madonna take you, we lost such an opportunity and because of your anti-grav. The catorian grumbled in displeasure. "Deal. You let him have the anti-grav, since it is so dear to him. Don't generate assignments for hunting us, and don't pull our accreditation..."

"Of course. Don't treat me like an idiot." the Coordinator's eyebrow twitched when he heard such an obvious statement.

"Not in the least. But it would not hurt to state those things. Yari, your turn. Bernard kindly presents you anti-grav to you as a memorable gift for the days you spent under his protection. The catorian whipped me with his tail and twitched his ear impatiently. I obediently called the Game to witness, and promised to stay tight as a clam, but only if Bernard would answer a question of mine.

The Coordinator was a pleasure to behold. He was not at all deceived by my behavior, and I would be willing to bet just about anything that soon he would show up to find out one-on-one why I had not obeyed him. And both he and my teacher were even more intrigued by my added condition.

"Even so?" Archibald's eyes measured me top to bottom, yet he did not restrain me. "Surprise me, student."

Bernard said nothing, and I considered this to be a silent invitation. I needed to go forward with my case of the strange sacrifice, so I asked:

"Who among the players that arrived to the Game world Earth has a Higher Demon for a pet?"

Archibald stared at me so intently that I felt uncomfortable.

"I don't remember anyone like that offhand. I would have to look." Bernard thought for a few moments before answering. "You will have this information first-hand as soon as I find out myself."

The last sentence sounded ambiguous and only we knew what he meant. At least, Archibald pretended not to notice anything.

"So, to recap: the parties have reached an understanding, and are satisfied with the outcome of the talks."

"I consider the agreement valid. I call the Game to witness."

The light washed over the Coordinator, Archibald and me, confirming the treaty we made. Archibald exhaled loudly. He was again unhappy about something. I suspected that the 'something' was me.

"When you two decide to leave my sector, I will

personally petition the commission for a positive decision," Bernard added in a businesslike manner, hinting that we would do well to disappear from Earth. "All the best to you. I hope this is the last time we see each other in this era."

Bernard came up to Gromana, activated a portal, and instantly disappeared there together with her, leaving me alone with the disgruntled cat. His anger manifested itself in his tail swishing madly from side to side. The catorian asked in a deceptively sweet voice:

"What player with a Higher demon? Whatever for do you need a Higher one?"

Something in that voice indicated that the catorian was truly outraged and was barely restraining himself from sending me to respawn. Perhaps my initiative spoiled his game. Not wanting to end up at Bernard's mercy earlier than I had to, since I had not yet changed my anchor point, I started my explanations:

"Yesterday in Moscow an unknown player performed a ritual sacrifice. You were there hanging around with me; you should have seen it."

"You mean in Tsaritsyno Park? While you were entertaining NPCs, I was busy clearing the area of Lumpen's sidekicks!" Archibald retorted. "I had no time to stare at the bodies."

"Ok, so then I'll be brief. Four NPCs were killed, and their souls drained. Next to the seal, NPCs faint. I called a necromancer, and after performing his ritual and before respawning he told me that they were drained by a Higher demon. Demonologist Erhaville assured me that no one had called up Higher demons in our world for the last fifty years, and that he was ready to repeat his words in front of Madonna. Also, he supposed that perhaps some strong player had that demon on a leash, so to speak. A traveling player. Bernard would know who that player was. That's it."

"So Erhaville: then?" Archibald said slowly and pulled out his comm.

"I will have problems if someone finds out about your call." The demonologist's voice replied from the comm in lieu of greeting. The catorian put it on the loudspeaker again.

"I know, so I'll do it quickly. Did a Higher demon appear on Earth?"

"Yes, I checked the bodies myself. It was definitely not brought in through the seal. The astral plane is clear. You know that, or else we would have hired you already. Safety above all. So that means someone brought in a demon as a pet. I don't know who. I've been trying to get information all day through my channels, but nothing so far. It's an outsider, too – there is no one like that among our people. So we have a dark horse here."

"Thanks. If you get info, call me right away." The catorian finished the conversation and turned his attention to me. "Show me the video."

Steve had prepared the video back when we talked to Erhaville. Archibald tensed and stilled, quickly receiving the file. Grunted something incoherent about the appearance of the victims, for a few moments he was lost to the world, watching the video again and again. Something was bothering him, so he started thinking aloud.

"Suppose this really is a demon. Suppose you are right in thinking that Bernard would know the owner. But then, where are the tracks?" The catorian scratched himself behind his ear in contemplation. "Higher demons are large and clumsy beasts, they always leave behind some kind of tracks. But there is nothing here. That's number one. Number two — why is there an NPC standing right next to the seal and talking as calmly as can be? You babbled something about them fainting!"

"This is the investigator on serious crimes. He is immune." I ventured my earlier guess. The catorian only snorted:

"Immune ones are few and far between in the Game. We ended up having to drag Monstrichello in from another world. Anyway, it's not important. We'll figure that out later."

"Teacher, I am starting to worry." The catorian looked bothered by this whole story, and this scared me.

"Never mind. I hate Higher ones." The catorian nodded, watching the video once more. "No, that's not going to work. I will have to see it for myself. Activate the portal; we are going to Moscow."

All the way to Tsaritsyno Park the catorian was glum and reserved. I was left to guessing what all of that meant.

Even though it was not a workday and the park was crowded, we reached the crime site quickly and without trouble. In the crush at the gate no one paid any attention to two FSB officers who turned off into the thicket on the left. Vesnin and his bunch had already removed the bodies and the tape, and only crushed grass served as a reminder that someone had been killed here last night. There were neither NPCs nor players in the clearing, the same as it was at night. Until the completion of the investigation the Game would not allow strangers access to the crime scene.

It was funny to watch Archibald, who did not care about conventions, appearances or me, settle down on all fours and started sniffing around the ground just like a common alley cat looking for a place to piss. The catorian didn't miss, it seemed, a single stone in the clearing and in its vicinity trying to discover signs of the presence of a Higher demon. After circling the area about three times he sat on the ground and stared at me in bewilderment.

"There was no Higher demon here." Archibald stated unexpectedly. "Either as a pet, or from the seal."

But what about the video of the necromancer and his dead body?" I reminded him just in case, even though I was certain that the catorian recalled it all very well.

"You see, my lazy student, I have been hunting Higher demons for a very long time. So long that I can literally feel them. It's a true gut feeling. Now I am certain that there were none here. Someone else drained the souls." Archibald seemed puzzled despite all his extensive experience.

"Who can do such a thing other than demons?" The investigation was proving even more complex than I had initially thought.

"There are a couple of creatures..." The catorian said vaguely. "But a park on Earth is not really a place for a chance encounter with them... Did the Game assign this investigation to you?"

"No." It was my turn to snort." Personal directive from the Great One. She dumped this great joy on the Judge Supervisor in the middle of the night You did see it for yourself — I was just enjoying my last days. Madonna allocated me just ten days to find Merlin."

"Why does it not surprise me that you didn't bother to mention the most critical thing!" Archibald suddenly perked up and mumbled under his breath: "How could I forget about you, my dearie!"

The catorian extracted a curved knife made of a whole piece of obsidian crystal, and sliced his wrist. A few drops of dark thick blood fell on the ground and were absorbed with a hiss by the soil in the seal area. A symbol appeared in its place, a bloody outline resembling the letter M.

The catorian uttered an elaborate curse as he healed his wound with an elixir. However, grave concern melted away from his face like snow in the spring. I looked from the flaming letter to Archibald, waiting for some explanations.

"If you tell a soul that I performed a ritual with my own blood, I will tie you up and ship you off to Madonna in a gift box in a sexy rabbit suit. Even though no one would believe you anyway." Having warned me, the teacher extracted a flame thrower from his inventory and calmly turned the area where his blood had sunk into a small piece of flaming inferno. "Can you guess who the 'higher demon' was, Guide?"

"Madonna? Merlin?" I groped, as there were only two options after Archibald said it.

"Much as I would like to ascribe whatever atrocities to the lady we both know, it is not so this time." My teacher shook his head and pointed his finger at the flaming symbol. "This is Merlin's sign. Whenever he does something, he always leaves his mark. Don't try to find it on your own; it only reveals itself in response to the blood of a few. It's somewhat of a privilege not granted to many.

"Did you know him?" I blurted out.

"Yes. In the previous era. I can't say anything good about him though," the catorian replied dryly.

"So then Merlin did not only respawn secretly, but set up a sacrifice in the middle of Moscow." My indignation knew no limits.

"Why do you think he did it secretly? The Game announced it about six hundred years ago. But you should not confuse respawn with incarnation. That has not happened yet. Merlin has gained awareness of himself, but opted against building strength, choosing to play in the shadows. Oh well, like always. He does not wish for Restart; he is too attracted to the easy unencumbered life of a simple influential creature. It's funny that every time he lives as a jerkoff; he wastes his strength in parties, orgies and such; he likes luxury and women. As for the sacrifice... Merlin needs Energy, and he can't get it from open Sources because he is like a vacuum cleaner. He'd suck any Source dry and not even burp. So he entertains himself by taking souls. He learnt that trick in the era before the previous one, he learnt that from demons. You saw the bodies: they were prepared in advance. Merlin has an estate somewhere and he set up a human farm there. And it's somewhere in Russia."

"So then, that is not the first sacrifice?"

"We'll need to look at the data. I'm sure it's not. Madonna must know something, since she sent you here. Stupid as she is, she senses Merlin. He is her teacher after all. She can't stand him."

"Maybe the enemy of my enemy..." I started, but Archibald interrupted me:

"No, that won't work for us. Merlin is a true Light one. Do you know about Atlantis?"

"It's an island described by Plato that sank because of a natural disaster." I was glad to show off my education.

"Rather, a separate Game world from a previous era: a sister world of Earth. For some experiment or other Merlin needed a lot of Energy; so he devised nothing better than becoming the god of Atlantis and demanding that the entire population of it sacrifice themselves. Everyone. Women, children, old people. That was the end of the Atlantians, but Merlin's experiment failed anyway. There was a factor he failed to take into account. You think that stopped him? Not at all. His next sacrifices were the Aztecs, then Mayans, then someone else... All in all he sank seven worlds before the next Restart put an end to his passion for experiments. In his prime Merlin is bloodthirsty and inventive. It's a truly horrendous sight."

"But why?" I asked in surprise.

"Because he is a creature of absolute power. Madonna with all her peccadilloes is merely a child compared to him. Well, not even that — rather like a sickly sperm without much hope to ever reach an egg. Merlin is not yet bored with this world, since he confined himself to merely a respawn. We do need to find him urgently. We cannot allow him to gain strength and reincarnate.

"Where and most importantly, how do we find him?" I asked. "There are no tracks, no souls and no witnesses. Nothing is known!"

"There is one thing that is known for sure. If we need Merlin, then, as it was with Madonna, we need his diary. That is why I'm still here, my silly student! Because without you we will not be able to enter the Citadel of the Paladins, and without me we will not be able to enter into the classified section of the library. Is that not the area the access to which you were requesting from my former Head?" my teacher asked me testily, and he winked.

CHAPTER THREE

DAY TWO

AFTER MY VISIT to Tsaritsyno Park the teacher gave me his blessing to leave for home with my guards, while he worked on preparing the visit to the Citadel. In response to my generous offer to help he just waved me off carelessly and asked that I refrain from adding more trouble for him and the guards he had hired elsewhere, and just go and enjoy my Doll until he called me. Which is precisely what I did.

The rest of the day sped away as I basked in the love and care of my affectionate girlfriend. I was joyfully greeted, bathed, offered a drink; my hunger for food and sex was sated, and all of that without a trace of messing with my brain because of my sudden departure in the middle of the night. That was just great!!!

Lying in my comfortable bed, half-asleep, I was playing with a lock of Helen's hair and contemplating happiness. If at that time the Game had offered me a trade — a quiet life as an NPC with Helen instead of what I had at the time, I would have traded that very instant. It's the moment when you realize that ignorance is bliss. I did not want to know anything about restart, eras, Merlins, and all that. Thinking of what my life with Helen could be like, I drifted off to sleep. I slept soundly without dreaming, and for that reason I did not wake up with the first ring. My watch showed 2 AM. Someone was ringing the doorbell insistently.

Though I forced my feet to shuffle towards the door, my brain totally refused to wake up:

"What, your official housing provided by the Game was not to your liking?" Archibald was standing in the door of my comfortable premium class place, smirking. "You, my student, are in disfavor, and ought to be breathing mold in the company of other riffraff for the next — and the last — month of your life. And you are putting on the Ritz instead!"

Not waiting for me to invite him the catorian stepped into the apartment. In response I just thanked him sarcastically:

"Well, at least you did not teleport straight into the bedroom."

"Spare me that. It's a total perversion to watch your student copulating. So I'd rather do it the old-fashioned way." Archibald grimaced, staring at his reflection in the large mirror in the entrance hall. His previously new armor was now tinged with rust and looked as though he'd been through a battle.

"You could have called me on my comm." I looked at Archibald, puzzled.

"I could have, but it would not have had the same effect. Wake up, it's time for us to go hunting. I have set the bait already. We'll wait at your place till they take the bait, and then we'll depart."

Overwhelmed by that news I rushed to the bathroom to try and get rid of the last traces of sleep. Archibald had managed to prepare everything awfully fast. I had barely managed to relax after my night adventure which had gradually turned into a daytime skirmish, and he showed no signs of fatigue. Apparently that was the hunter's skill, honed during all those centuries.

"Yari, why don't you invite the guest in? You didn't even offer him coffee." In all of the commotion it had not occurred to me that Helen would wake up. The fact that we had guests in the middle of the night did not phase her in the least.

I remembered very well how other players treated Dolls, so I tried to make sure that Helen would stay as far from the catorian as possible, leading her back towards the bedroom.

"He does not like coffee and he is in a hurry." The girl was stretching her neck, curious to take a look at the strange guest: my Doll was of the opinion that everyone loved coffee! How could it be otherwise if Yaropolk really loved coffee?

"I reeeeally do like coffee, honey. But I don't like Yari so reeeeally much. He is very boring." The furry bastard purred right behind my back. I could not see where he had got the time to creep up so silently. Helen beamed, cast a reproachful glance at me and disappeared into the kitchen.

"She is cute." Archibald looked over my Doll's figure with an appraising glance. I felt a pang of jealousy. "It will be hard to part with her."

"I am not going to part with her." I frowned. "I like everything about her."

"Count me surprised! It is impossible for you not to like her." Archibald snorted and rolled his eyes. "She is the ideal the Game pulled out of your head. But even ideals have some drawbacks. For example, Dolls cannot have children..."

"That's about the last thing on my mind." Mocking the teacher, I also rolled my eyes. "I am about to be wiped out, what children?! Is that why you invited yourself to coffee, to give me a hard time for living with my Doll and try to straighten me out?"

"You are welcome to live with a fat-ass domineering opossum rat if that is your preference – see if I care! Before we leave, we need to talk about further plans. Here I am safe. My hunters have reported that since I appeared there are no threats around. That is good to know."

I heard the clinking of dishes from the kitchen followed by Helen's voice:

"Yaropolk, everything is ready. Ask the guest to wash his hands and bring him to the table."

"What is this world coming to?!" Archibald could not refrain from a barb. "My student is being ordered about by his own property!"

The first cup of coffee just sank into me, perking up my sleepy body. The second one I was able to enjoy, as I was able to clearly perceive the world around me. So as soon as Archibald called blushing Helen a "blossom" for the third time I sent her away from the kitchen. Her hair, ruffled by her sleep, stood around her head like the halo of a dandelion. But I still considered that my teacher flirting with her was not acceptable. It seemed that that was what Archibald had been waiting for:

"What's the deal with the Coordinator's right to issue orders, and why do you need the anti-grav?"

"Bernard considers that I am his mental slave." I started from a remote point.

"And you..." the teacher prodded me.

"And I am not. At the Lecleur estate Bernard gave me 'Lumpen's Diary', but it turned out that gift smelled fishy. If I had activated it, I would have received complete mental enslavement in addition to the hundredth level of Darkness."

"You really did not activate it?" Archibald verified, looking at me closely, and I shook my head to emphasize. "What do you need the anti-grav for, then?"

"So that Bernard would think that I activated the diary." I twisted the facts confidently. I did not feel like explaining to Archibald how I received a hundred of Darkness without the diary.

"For example." Archibald failed to notice that I was bluffing, and continued questioning me. "So then Bernard would consider that you found a way to ignore his orders... Fine, let him be distracted; that will work in our favor. What did you do with the diary?"

"I gave it to the Temple of Knowledge." I did not hold that back from him.

"I hope you requested something valuable in exchange?" The catorian raised an eyebrow.

"Of course," I reassured him, proud of myself. "The most valuable commodity in this game is information."

The teacher was quite skeptical about my statement, and to stop me from dragging my feet, he asked me to show him the video of our bargaining. Well, "asked" would be a bit of an overstatement. He ordered it, to be precise. Understanding that I would not give up the details easily, he swore by the Game that he would kill me here and now, sending me to respawn at Bernard's estate, by way of saying hello. My teacher is so funny. Never a dull moment with him.

"So, what's the result of the data processing?" the catorian smirked, after finding out about the list of players I had received. The one encouraging thing was that I managed to keep my secret—the true reason for which I had requested that list. I had long since come up with a plausible explanation for Archibald.

"The category 'Insanely Vast Amount of Knowledge' includes twelve players. These are creatures from the first era. 'Crazy Amount of Knowledge' includes three hundred and twenty players. They are from the second era. 'Vast Amount of Knowledge' includes twenty thousand. The third era. I was not even thinking of the fourth era- there are plenty of players from there. Actually, if I manage to stay alive, I will try to get in touch with someone with the 'Insanely Vast' status, to level up my artifact. He would not care – the first era is water under the bridge – while it would be useful for me to find out more about the Game."

"Ah-ha-ha!" The catorian's sincere laugh rolled through the air. "You traded Lumpen's Diary for some rotten crap from the Temple of Knowledge? Student of mine, your naiveté astonishes me! Do you really think that the creatures possessing, as you put it, an 'Insanely Vast Amount of Knowledge' would even deign to speak with you?"

"Well, you did." I looked contentedly at the catorian's suddenly long face. "There will be others."

"Ah, so you have already processed the data? Highly commendable." The catorian smirked and his joy vanished without a trace. "We'll get back to that later. Now we need to concern ourselves with survival. The first priority is finding the trace of Merlin's Diary in the Citadel."

"Are you allowed to visit the Citadel?" I asked in surprise.

"Not by portal, no. We'll have to storm the castle using our very own paws. Why the sad face, my lazy student? Have you forgotten how to use your limbs? All we need is to use the teleport to get as close as we can and then walk, just like real pilgrims. Don't be afraid: it's not the first time, and probably not even the last one, that the Great One has stripped me of class and rank, so I know what I am talking about... This seems to be part of her mandatory program at each incarnation: to make the slaves remember their places and know who is the master. Predictable and boring!"

"And yet she entrusted her conscience with you, as her only confidant." I didn't believe him.

"That's different. She was not the one who asked me..." Archibald lifted his claw and meaningfully let the sentence drop. "Let's get back to Merlin. It is not difficult to enter the Citadel. The hard part is entering the classified section of the library. I've worked it all out. We only have one chance."

"Gerhard promised to help..." I started saying but then I saw the catorian's grin.

"Since I am here, consider that he already has. Now we are waiting for our long-eared Chance to swallow the bait, and then we'll start working with him closely, while being very quiet in the reading room," the catorian said, glancing at a little device with a screen that he was holding in his hands.

"I was hoping for more concrete help," I grumbled. "If Garlion is your Chance, things aren't looking great. I have not yet told you about what happened when we met the last time."

"I am sure that the atmosphere was far from friendly, but that long-eared twit will pay for everything. Tell me now." The catorian did not lose the line of conversation even as he was looking at his screen worriedly.

I was not able to tell on the elf, because my cell phone started ringing right at that moment. Archibald gestured for me to answer. Major Vesnin was calling. I took the call, and by the way of greeting heard more bad news. It seems I have forgotten how to expect good news any more.

"We have a new sacrifice. Eight bodies. Kolomenskoye Park, main entrance. I will send someone to meet you."

The conversation with Archibald dwindled on the spot. Having heard this new information, the catorian stuck his little device into his personal inventory and immediately prepared for a portal jump. Following him I relied on my luck and my teacher. Perhaps the new crime scene would offer the catorian some clues to help him uncover the person who was Merlin. I was sure that this new case was his doing.

The portal brought us directly to the police line. The cool night air affected me like another double espresso. But apparently it did not work the same way for the local police. The sleepy guards were despondently strolling under the street lights, and yawned continuously without even bothering to cover their mouths. They paid no attention to us. This behavior could not even count as negligence: it was unlikely that anyone would show up at the crime scene. The hour was too late for decent citizens, and there was too much commotion for indecent ones.

The sergeant, whom I remembered, quickly saw us in the dim light of the street lamps, and hurried to greet us. We were taken to the crime scene itself in the official vehicle. This time our guide simply pointed out the direction, indicating where we should go, turned around and left. After walking in the darkness for about five minutes we ended up on the riverbank where major Vesnin was standing by the water, periodically pushing up the glasses that kept sliding down his nose.

"General Archibald." The catorian demonstrated an empty hand to the major, causing the latter to stand to attention. It did not matter, after all, to which service the general belonged; the important part was that he must be an outstanding and useful person. So I could readily understand major Vesnin: it would do no harm to stand to attention for someone like that, particularly since FSB was always known to have great capabilities.

"Major Vesnin, Senior Investigator, Tsaritsyno Police Department! Currently I am the lead for investigating the case of a serial killer. This crime and the one in Tsaritsyno have already been combined into a single case. All the characteristic features are present." After such a perky report I thought a little less of Vesnin. He was looking at Archibald a little too obsequiously. Steve agreed with me, and offered some suggestions to explain the major's subservient behavior. Definitely the investigator was hoping to use my advantageous acquaintance for his own purposes, whether work or personal. Time would tell.

"Where are the bodies?" Archibald asked. As was proper for high-ranking individuals he glanced at Vesnin only in passing, and got to business right away. The major pointed the beam of his flashlight toward a nearby area:

"Here, right by the water. It's a blind spot for the external surveillance cameras. My people are already analyzing the records in order to establish how the victims got here. There were no witnesses.

The bodies were discovered by a couple looking for a secluded place in order... for the purpose of... well, they were hoping to get romantic. They are currently hospitalized and being treated for shock. The staff psychologist is already there expecting to work with them.

Vesnin was reporting all that to Archibald's retreating back. He was confidently walking towards the bodies even though it was pitch dark. Vesnin was trying to offer some light to the catorian, but the latter simply ordered in an irritated tone that he take the lights away. Unlike Vesnin and myself, my teacher did not need additional sources of light. I started after him with the major. Our feet kept getting entangled in the tall shore grass, and that was not something I could deal with by using the flashlight, even though the major was kind enough to provide me with one.

"Make everyone step back as far as possible," Archibald ordered over his shoulder, bending over the seal. Vesnin immediately turned back, lighting his path and sighing sadly. The major was deploring a lost opportunity to see a real FSB general working in the field — not some pen-pusher! Yet he did not dare disobey a direct order.

I stood next to the catorian. The new seal looked similar to the previous one: the same view of the broken bodies set into an eerily beautiful pattern. Archibald let a drop of blood fall on the nearest body and again the odious letter "M" floated above the victims. Which is what we set out to demonstrate.

When Vesnin returned it was already over. The catorian pointed at the body which had his blood on it and stated in a way that brooked no argument:

"I am taking this body, and my colleague will work with the others. Any questions?"

The major just nodded submissively without questioning the reason for taking the body. Vesnin's submissiveness and lack of curiosity astonished me more and more. Had I not been certain that the investigator was an immune creature, I would have thought it was some useful skill that Archibald had. One of those that I was introduced to at the Academy, thanks to his other student, Dolgunata. May her consciousness rest in peace, buried under Madonna's.

My teacher turned towards me:

"The next sacrifice will take place tomorrow. There will be sixteen bodies. We need to figure out the location. Merlin never does anything without a reason. Get your necromancers over here — you need to work on the standard version that implies a demon and report it to your management."

The catorian disappeared among the trees, fading in the darkness of the night. Moreover, he did it so skillfully that the demonologist and necromancer I summoned through the Judge Supervisor did not even notice him. The now experienced demonologist informed me that the seal was fake and it would not have been possible to summon a demon using it. The necromancer tried to raise a body and went to respawn, first letting us know that a Higher demon had been there. Hearing that, the demonologist scratched his head, mumbled something to the effect that it must be some weird error, and departed. Remaining one on one with Vesnin I asked him about coffee, not really hoping for much luck; predictably, the answer was negative. The major reported the results of the work of his team — the guards kept away from the crime scene, the same as the previous time.

"They checked out all the homeless folks around, just in case someone saw something." The investigator's tone was once again calm and businesslike. "But everything is quiet. Both here and in Tsaritsyno. It's as if the bodies just materialized here on their own. It's a true mystery. There are no clues indicating how they appeared in the parks. There are cameras at all the entrances and around the park perimeters. The records from here have not been analyzed yet, but nothing was found in Tsaritsyno."

"Right, only you can't stick a mystery into a case." I supported the major. Vesnin's complaints, together with his servile attitude to the FSB general, led one to certain conclusions. Of course, I had only known the investigator for a short time, but admitting one's inability to do things from the start was about equivalent to acknowledging that the Ministry of Internal Affairs for which you had worked for a couple of decades was totally incompetent. Normally institutions working in closely related fields never showed much liking or respect for each other, instead exhibiting rather unhealthy competition. But Vesnin, for some reason, was resisting the system. I even became curious about what bothered the fat investigator.

"My boss called me. They are taking the case

away from me. Too many dead bodies and no progress to show."

I kept quiet, not knowing what to say to that.

"I'd love to nab that bastard, but they have cut my wings now. I've been up for almost two days, nose to the ground, and still..."

"Leave your nose alone, and leave the ground to the swine as befits their nature. In the morning you will take unpaid leave for a week, and will work with my subordinate here." Archibald's voice came from behind, addressing the major. "Now hand over the shift and go sleep. Three o'clock in the morning is not a time to be constructive and efficient. In the morning the colonel will clarify your new objectives. The city department won't be able to do crap. It's way out of their league."

Hearing the joyful "Aye, sir general!", Archibald nodded to me, indicating that I should follow him, and set out for the thicket again in broad confident strides. Vesnin just stayed still where he was. The joy in his face was so sincere that it seemed he straightened, looking taller and more slender all of a sudden. Like a hunting dog that has caught the scent of a quarry. Or a normal person inspired by an opportunity he had been waiting for, perhaps, for his whole life.

All the way to the thicket I did not ask the "general" any questions, but once we left sight and hearing range, I immediately coughed very expressively, calling on the catorian to clarify why he needed that NPC. Instead of an answer I heard:

"Tomorrow you'll call the major and order him

to not leave his house. Under any circumstances."

Not understanding my teacher's logic, I asked the main question any sensible person would:

"What for?"

This is the kind of question with which I have had a special relationship ever since I visited the time pocket for the first time. I generally considered that this question should be the cornerstone in the life of every sentient being. A timely question "what for" would solve most of the world's problems by eliminating complicated excuses, and would save scores of individuals from reckless actions. Besides, if one could force everybody to answer that question honestly and provide explanations, it would be so much easier to separate jerks from normal people.

"Let's get a dog!"

"What for?"

"It will shit on the lawn, providing me with the joy of observing someone step in it."

"Well, that's an argument."

"I am going to run for the governor's office!"

"What for?"

"I want to start my own small business with the money from kickbacks and bribes!"

"Excellent goal in life!"

"Let's get drunk tonight!"

"What for?"

"To get drunk, of course!"

"Sounds like a great reason!"

Given that all beings are used to view themselves as extremely positive creatures, such thoughts would not even occur to them. Of course, "I am not like that!" It's a pity that in reality they come up with various arguments that make them look much more dignified.

"A dog is like another member of the family. It will help me feel less lonely."

"Ever since I was a kid I have wanted to serve the people!"

"I get drunk because I want to forget about my problems: mortgage, blasted work, stupid boring wife... You know it all, what am I telling you all that for?!"

The ability to ask oneself this question and answer it honestly distinguishes a sensible person from empty-headed spin doctors.

Thinking those utopian thoughts, I heard my teacher answer with another question instead of providing an answer.

"Is your video recording activated?"

"Yes." The reason for this interest was not clear to me.

"Excellent. You may record this for yourself now, but make sure to delete it later. I will check," the catorian said without looking at me. Archibald's eyes were wandering through the darkness, searching for some clues visible to him alone. "You were right, and I was not. Vesnin really is immune. Have you recorded that? Good for you. You may watch it a couple of times, to boost your sick feeling of self-importance. I allow you. Vesnin, meanwhile, needs to be locked up at home so that he can be isolated from everyone. You get it: right – why has an immune one appeared precisely at this time?

"Merlin is looking for his diary so as to activate it and reincarnate." One does not have to be Nostradamus to predict the actions of that mysterious creature "Vesnin will be needed as the sacrifice."

"Yes. He will die in any case." Archibald finished the thought. "Either form Merlin's hand or ours, depending on who finds the diary first. It is impossible to destroy a diary that has not been activated. I've checked. As for an activated one — it is possible.

I sighed heavily. Everything seemed to be logical and justified, and fully in line with common sense; there was an honest answer to the "what for?" question, but it still weighed heavily on my soul.

"Yaropolk, you are becoming sentimental. Is this the influence your Doll has on you?" my teacher said suddenly in quite a friendly voice. "Remember — no pity or compassion for NPCs. Their lives are shorter, but they bring more problems."

"Have you figured out a way to get into the library?" I asked, deliberately changing the topic. Amazing, but Archibald's mentor voice affected me even worse than his habitual sarcasm.

"Speaking about the library: you wanted to tell me an interesting story; you will do so along the way," the catorian said, and opened the portal. While I spoke about the incident in the Citadel, we jumped through portal after portal, just like jumping horses at Royal Ascot Races. Archibald kept looking for something in his navigator screen, and sometimes mumbled under his breath in a language I did not know, However, at the appropriate points in my story

---

he made sounds indicating that he was still with me. Only after I finished did I remember Sharda's words, which he had asked me to convey to Archibald. After I did that I gathered enough courage to ask what those words meant.

"Word for word they mean that your opponent is mistaken in his conclusion. This is being pointed out to the said opponent in a very emotional manner," my teacher enlightened me.

The catorian stopped at some kind of cemetery. I had not yet explored that area, so the map did not show anything other than darkness. Steve projected the coordinates to the familiar globe, and stated with certainty that we were in South America, at La Recoleta Cemetery in Buenos Aires, to be precise, if it existed in this version of the Game world. Moscow was somewhere on the opposite side of the globe.

"What does that mean? He asked me to cuss you out?" I came to an interesting conclusion.

"Yep," Archibald agreed easily. "Our good old Sharda was quite upset. But on the whole I agree with him. On my mark you follow me and don't lag behind. Got that?"

"Sure. And what are we waiting for?"

"Ofelia del Plata... These long-eared ones are so mischievous." My teacher grinned into his whiskers.

I used the break in order to do a keyword search through the local internet for "Recoleta" and "Ofelia del Plata." While Archibald was staring at the spires of the unique necropolis I learned the melodramatic story of the unfortunate bride. But before it brought tears to my eyes, Archibald rose quickly and rushed into a passage between the crypts, making a sign for me to hide. About twenty yards away, something white showed briefly, resembling a female silhouette in a dress. The sorrowful figure gently glided along the streets of the cemetery straight towards the exit. We followed it, but were too late. As soon as "Ofelia" disappeared behind the gate we dashed after it at full speed, but we were too late. The street behind the gate was empty. Archibald approached the road and was carefully selecting a car for us. I was quite indignant at such pickiness — if we were chasing that "Ofelia" we needed to hurry! Finally, a Bentley showed up in the distance. My teacher softly jumped onto the roof and disappeared within the car. Less than a minute later the Bentley turned around, and the passenger door opened in front of me:

"What's keeping you? If we don't make it because of you..." I jumped into the seat and briefly noticed the body of the erstwhile owner of the car in the back. Another random NPC victim.

We were rushing down the road at over a hundred miles per hour. The car was quite sensitive to my teacher's sudden maneuvers, leaving strips of burnt rubber on the pavement, and making me clutch at my seatbelt. Alarms on the dashboard were beeping pitifully, emergency blinkers activated, the car nearly skidded, but the computer managed so far. Stepping on the brake, Archibald, without waiting for the car to stop, opened the door harshly and stepped out as if inertia simply had no effect on him. I turned around quickly, hoping to watch the cat doing somersaults on the pavement, but no such luck. Archibald, looking unperturbed, was standing on his own two feet and looked off into space, while the door of the luxurious Bentley obviously felt the full force of inertia and reacted in full agreement with Newtonian physics. The door jammed, and once the car came to a halt, it was sticking out like a broken wing. I rushed towards my teacher, but was greeted by another bout of displeasure:

"You are moving like a snail! Is that the expression they use there on Earth?"

Ignoring his barbs, I stood next to him silently. Well, a couple of yards away, just in case. In any case it was impossible to sway the catorian anyway, since his weighty argument would never change — "I have lived through four eras!" and there was nothing I could say to counter that. Even though Archibald never said that out loud, his entire behavior in the role of teacher practically screamed it.

"Let's go," the catorian said with satisfaction, and started forward slowly. I followed closely. After we covered a couple of blocks passing along narrow city streets, we stopped in front of a compact three-storey building.

"A small transit portal for the select few. The long-eared ones always thought they were the ones." Archibald nodded at the building. "Wait for me here."

The catorian faded in the dusk, and no matter how hard Steve tried to find him, all his attempts failed. Concealment lay at the very core of my teacher. The entrance door of this odd building opened slightly for an instant, and immediately shut again without a sound. I knew for sure that Archibald had just gone inside, but even after watching the video a few times I was still unable to see him. The teacher, who returned ten minutes later, found me doing exactly that. A limp body wearing a long loose white robe was draped across the catorian's shoulders. It turned out to be Garlion. The elf was unconscious.

"That's our pass to the library." Archibald easily dumped the body of my long-eared enemy at my feet and gestured to me, indicating it was my turn to play pack animal. I heaved the elf up, and now his lifeless form was draped across my own shoulders. I could smell a characteristic sweet odor coming from him; that indicated that this quietly snuffling creature had been subjected to some chemical soporific rather than a hefty bonk over the head. Frustrated, I cursed and slapped Garlion on the head, turning his face away from me. Archibald simply grinned and opened the next portal with a broad gesture. Without much ado I launched the elf's body straight into the portal. I was not going to treat him gently after all he did to me at the Citadel. Let him serve as a test case now. I jumped into the portal after him. The catorian was in the rear, as he wanted to make sure that there were no "friendly" necromancers hanging around.

"Make yourself comfortable." Archibald appeared right after us. I looked around with interest. The place where we landed was a plain apartment in a city. Unfortunately, it was too ordinary to suppose it had any personal significance for my teacher. Beyond the window a panorama of some alien megapolis could be seen, drastically different from Moscow.

"What, the explorer in you has woken up?" Archibald did not miss my interest in the apartment. "I will have to disappoint you right away: this is just a stopover. Just to check for uninvited followers and take a breather.

"The probability is 90 percent that no one is living in this apartment." Steve confirmed the words after analyzing the available data. *"Too much dust."*

It was true. A cursory glance at the sparse furnishings demonstrated that the comment was justified: a thick layer of dust had settled on everything around. While I had never noticed Archibald being sloppy.

"You ought to treat our library warrior with a bit more care. Or else he'll go to respawn before he has a chance to tell us everything." The elf had in fact landed badly in an armchair, falling upside down, his feet dangling in the air.. His face was smudged; apparently it had slid through the dust, slowing his fall; his right hand was twisted unnaturally. The robe rode up, demonstrating his long legs in leather pants.

"Nothing will happen to him..." I mumbled, but took his feet off the armchair and settled his body on the floor carefully. "What was that masquerade he put up at the cemetery?"

My teacher plopped down in the other armchair, having first cleaned it from the dust.

"Have you not noticed how many elves there are here?" I nodded: it would be hard not to notice. "Elves keep very close family ties; they maintain the records of their genealogy from the time of each restart. In each world they set up their communities.

Elves are the most common race on Earth, so they go to some extremes. They build crypts for themselves. Monuments. They try to preserve the memory of those who were wiped out irrevocably. They are strange creatures. I fed Garlion a suggestion that I had destroyed his family crypt: to hell with all of his ancestors! He rushed to check if it was true. These long-eared twits use robes to scare off NPCs and curious players. Given the way they are built, that kind of robe makes them look more like women, so that's how a fair number of legends originated."

Despite his calm voice and seemingly relaxed face, Archibald's posture was still tense.

"You think someone is going to follow us?"

"Let's wait a few minutes." Archibald shrugged. "A portal to the other side of the globe is expensive. If someone was in fact tracking us, they'd at least have to pay for that. And you, student, take note of that. It's useful to have a number of stopover shelters around the world. That makes tracing you much harder.

"This won't help if I have tracers on me." I could not guarantee that either Gromana or any of the necromancers Archibald had killed had not attached something like that to me.

"That's why I made sure to clean them all up a while ago," the catorian brushed away my comment."Once we get to our destination I will teach you to do that on your own. Iven was right — it's not good when your students shine like a beacon for the entire Game world to see. That makes me look awful... Fine, let's keep going. You will carry Garlion."

The next portal brought us to a warm igloo home in the middle of the white desert of the Antarctic. That was followed by an actual scalding hot desert and then, to my childish delight, by an air bubble floating somewhere in the depths of an ocean. Archibald took extreme care to ensure that no one accompanied us along our path. Within the bubble the catorian finally decided to remember that he was a teacher, after all. But before that he set a curtain of silence over us:

"In our line of work" – presumably he was talking about head hunters – "only those who are lazy place excessive trust in equipment and tracers. A player should actually work his ass off in the area where the portal is open in order to follow his prey. There are no hunters on Earth who would be able to track me down, but Lumpen or Bernard could hire the best from other worlds. No matter how good they are, however, they have their weak spots. Most frequently it would have to do with the environment they need. Some cannot tolerate cold, while for others heat or water would be fatal. In case they teleport to a hazardous location, they instinctively activate all the protection available to them. That induces a disturbance in the ambient Energy. That's when we get…"

The catorian's sword swished out of the sheath and pierced the air above his head. My teacher pulled the weapon towards him; there was an unpleasant squelching sound and a brown furry creature fell to the bottom of the dome. I did not see any eyes or mouth. Nor were there any limbs. It looked like a ball of fur, or like a decorative pillow. The creature crashed to the floor of the air bubble, and Archibald kicked away a healing potion vial that seemed to have appeared out of nowhere: the pillow wanted to restore its Energy. The catorian bent over his enemy and said with his inherent politeness:

"Darlangir, tell your owner, if he wants to pay his respects to me, I am always at his service. He knows how to reach Earth."

A tremor went along the surface of the furry ball, and Archibald finished the creature off with his dagger. The body shimmered as it went for respawn.

This concluded the pleasant "caring teacher" interlude; no one bothered to explain what had just happened. The catorian opened the next portal and extracted a time bomb from his inventory. This location was compromised and had to be destroyed.

"That's more like a den of an old hand of the Game," I drawled, looking at the new location. The portal brought us to a dark room decorated in stone; it was equipped as a state of the art mad scientist's lab. My map went crazy trying to figure out our location. Dark areas in different continents flashed one after another, without settling on any particular one.

"Don't count on much hospitality. It's not really my forte, as you know." Displeased, Archibald appeared next to me and deactivated the portal that had brought him in. "Keep close to me and do be careful with Garlion or else he won't make it to the final stop."

I did not bother to hide my disappointed sigh,

for I really wanted to explore, take a look at every nook and cranny, and actually in fact take advantage of my host's hospitality. With a sour look I dragged the elf closer to my teacher. The catorian flicked his paw, and a glimmering platform lowered itself from the ceiling; it turned out it was an elevator. Its smooth movement and absence of inertia made the trip down very comfortable. We were traveling through openings in the partitions between the floors, but once we were below a ceiling it closed again. After passing through three or four levels the platform stopped and disappeared, leaving us standing on the floor. I looked around and swallowed nervously: we were standing in a real torture chamber. Archibald walked to the nearest table like he owned the place, and indicated to me where I should unload our still unconscious elf. I was noting my teacher's confident moves as he restrained the body. It was clear that for him it was a commonplace event, not worth any moral anguish. Archibald poured some green liquid into the elf's mouth and settled on the edge of the table.

"A plague on you, catorian!" Garlion woke up loudly. Amazingly, the elf came to instantly, and as instantly became aware of the changes in reality around him. Humility was never his strong side, and so at first he wiggled silently, but it only made the straps tighter. As he was becoming exhausted, the raging elf starting calling on whatever powers to rain all sorts of troubles on my teacher's head. Many years of working in the library had made him an amazingly creative curser; he only paused now and then to take a breath. But Archibald was not impressed by the elf's efforts. Garlion suddenly fell silent — now all he was able to do was open and close his mouth without making a sound.

"There are two possible scenarios. Number one: you will give me the access key to the closed section immediately and tell me where Arthur's notes are kept. I will send you to respawn as a matter of gratitude.

"Stuff it up your..." Garlion actually managed to spit in my teacher's direction. "Gratitude? You know very well that the Game itself will wipe me out for breaching my obligations!"

"Then I have no other choice." Archibald grinned "Before you give me the key and information I will try all the torture methods known to me. Believe me, I know some things that will come as a surprise to your curious librarian's mind. I am sure that you will not have encountered those things in your books. And after that the Game will wipe you out anyway."

"The strength of Elrads is with me!" Garlion laughed hysterically, but beads of sweat on his face betrayed his doubts. "You will not be able to do anything with me!"

"I will." Archibald stated without unnecessary emotion. "I have this right."

"You Are not the Head!" Garlion's voice turned into a squeak.

"I am not, but due to certain circumstances the strength of Elrads will not hinder me." Archibald loomed menacingly over the elf, who shrank in fear. "You are mine, Garlion. And mine alone. Welcome to the legendary Avalon!"

The elf's face fell as if he had heard something horrible. The information we heard helped neither me nor Steve to figure out the specific location. I had never heard about Avalon and the strength of Elrads. While I was trying to figure out the meaning of the dialogue between the elf and the catorian, Garlion made an attempt to disappear. The effort made sweat roll down his face, his nose started bleeding, his body shimmered and began to fade, yet it did not disappear completely. Apparently that was the strength of Elrads. With a sigh and a moan the elf, unconscious, crashed back onto the table. Another instant, and his body regain solid form. Archibald poured a healing potion down Garlion's throat, waited for him to come to, and continued:

"Now that we both understand the situation as it is, again I am offering you a choice."

"I cannot." The elf looked pitiful. Tears were about to roll down the high-born one's face. "The Game scares me more."

"And that is your mistake." Archibald whipped the elf across the face with his tail and took out a hand-held saw. "Nothing personal, Garlion. "You just happen to stand between me and my goal..."

Garlion surrendered half an hour later. For me just a few minutes proved to be enough. The catorian was true to his word. Without useless sentimentality he was like a great musician who extracted ever new tones of screams and pleas for mercy using Garlion's body like a musical instrument of his own invention. I did not have the courage to turn away completely—the catorian would never have forgiven me that – so I stared at the floor and tried to feel detached from what was going on. It's easier to torture someone than to watch torture. At some point you inevitably catch the right frame of mind, and the leaden understanding that torture is necessary is replaced by pleasure. But this time I was grateful that Archibald did not force me to help him and forgot about his role of the strict teacher. He preferred to not share his experience in this field, and I decided, faintheartedly, that since restart was close I didn't really need to know how to burn the hair off of live players or how to make a snake-sucker eat their eyes out.

As I was standing by the door, unable to shut out the sounds, I felt respect for Garlion practically despite myself. Thirty minutes is a very long time, when every second is filled with unreal torment. He tried to stay strong to the last, every time choking on his own screams, vomit and blood, as he whispered the next portion of the key to the restricted section. And every time Archibald made him swear to the Game that he was telling the truth. From the first time, as he would not name a single password. I don't know what the poor guy hoped for, but the Game betrayed him, cloaking him in black fog that brought a new wave of pain and suffering. Even listening to all of that was torture in its own right.

"Enough... Stop... I have told you almost everything..." What used to be a mouth could produce only a hoarse whisper. Garlion had lost his voice a while ago. The elf gave up completely and croaked, calling the Game to witness that this time he was telling the truth. The snow-white glow confirmed his words. The deed was done. The elf's head lolled listlessly, but Archibald did not leave his victim alone. Any forgotten trifle could jeopardize the entire plan.

Another healing potion brought Garlion to, and the catorian continued his interrogation:

"How much time will we have before the protection activates?"

"Thirty seconds," the broken-hearted elf responded listlessly, and the white light confirmed that too.

"Where are Arthur's notes?"

"The thing you seek is located in section twenty-five, the eighth item from the right." The librarian's memory was perfect, and he could easily find his way around the library without catalogues and such. "Only it's not Arthur's notes. They were destroyed during the attack of the demons. Remember? You are looking for Merlin's Diary. The document I mentioned will bring you to the Diary. I swear by the Game!"

White light flashed again. I forced myself to look up. The elf's mutilated body was in the same place. It was the first time that I had seen a creature cry without tears, for it had no eyes and no tear ducts. Just a jumble of bones, meat and blood.

"You see, we just lost so much time... and you lost your pretty face." Archibald summed it all up and touched an electronic panel on the wall next to him.

"You promised to send me for respawn," Garlion whispered. The table on which he was lying started sliding down into a pool that opened underneath. I felt a cold blast and a frosty fog cloaked the body as it was being immersed.

"I promised, but I changed my mind. You are too late. It's unwise to leave behind enemies, particularly those that are holding a grudge against my students. Sweet dreams, elf."

"Curse yo..." Garlion's scream drowned in the fuming liquid. Steve analyzed what we were seeing and concluded that the elf had been stabilized and placed in liquid nitrogen so that the player would not respawn.

"Come on. I will do you a favor and show you something interesting," my teacher said curtly. He easily moved Garlion's frozen body to a cargo cart and called up the elevator we had used earlier. After putting the cart on the platform we went a couple of levels down and reached a huge frozen cave. I looked around, but did not see anything particularly interesting. The view was obscured by columns covered in frost, and some stones that did not look like much on the face of it.

"Mister Archibald's Ice Museum." The catorian roughly pushed the cart, and frozen Garlion rolled to the floor with a clunk. Not quite sure what he was talking about I took a closer look at the nearest column and saw that some features of a humanoid figure showed vaguely through the frost. A couple of scratches on the icy surface convinced me that I was not mistaken. All those columns and rocks had been frozen in the same manner as Garlion. It was quite a company he had collected there.

"Three hundred and two." Steve could count a lot quicker than I. My subconscious was shocked with

the scale of the catorian's personal cemetery. *"Three hundred and two frozen players! The catorian is a monster!"*

I fully agreed both with him and Archibald. One needed to keep one's enemies close. What could be closer than one's own home? He was a bloody genius, living on top of a crypt full of his enemies. Hopelessly frozen. That was far better than if they had respawned and prepared for another battle, having leveled up their experience and skills.

Admiring, I wandered among the bodies that doubled as monuments to themselves. Steve scanned the statues and highlighted two of them so that I would pay special attention. The first one was the statue of Don Fabio. His presence did not surprise me: the necromancer deserved a fate far worse for all his misdeeds. If I had been Archibald, I would have simply wiped him out. The other statue bewildered me. How did it happen that Dolgunata's brother ended up in the company of jerks, bastards and the catorian's enemies? Unlike the other "inhabitants", Sakhray's face and posture were calm, as if he had voluntarily agreed to be frozen.

"You should be grateful to me, Garlion. I put you next to the great ones." Archibald was working on placing the elf, lifting the echoing silence by his conversation with the new exhibit.

"You meant to say 'laid him at the feet of the giants'?" I responded, thinking of the elf's shattered limbs.

"For him, even lying at the feet of such players is an honor." My teacher snorted behind my back.

"Enjoying the view!"

"What did Sakhray do to deserve such a joy?" I nodded in the direction of the statue and looked at Archibald. Some ideas flashed through my head and I hinted openly at the most realistic one. "Bad luck in relatives?"

"You guessed it right. He is the anchor that can bring Dolgunata's mind into her body." Archibald confirmed. "Madonna is looking for him, and if he were conscious, she would have wiped him out already. Given his ability to hide himself... So this way it's less worry for everyone."

"It would be silly to ask how soon you are going to need Sakhray again, right?" I tried to find out gently what were Archibald's plans with respect to Dolgunata. It seemed that I was too hasty in discounting the druid: Archibald has a few aces up his sleeve in his play against the Great One.

The teacher did not even bother to reply to me, turned around and started towards the abandoned cart. I followed him and prudently changed the topic to something as interesting to me:

"My navigation map is still going crazy since it cannot figure out our location. Will the greatest of the teachers enlighten his dumb student about his mysterious Avalon shelter? Don't be mean, Archibald: I am not trying to get ahead of myself, and I am being obedient. Even Garlion knew more about it than I do! I went all over my artifact — Avalon is not mentioned anywhere!"

"I agree, that was an error on my part. But, as you saw, gaining access to the restricted sections was not easy, so as to delete information about my lair from there as well." Archibald grinned. "Ask me something else."

The catorian pointed his paw at the cart ordering me to pick up my carrier job, and called the elevator.

"You have so much interesting stuff here. This elevator is obviously not from our era, yet you use it without a problem, and you are not worried that the Game will destroy it. Is Avalon like the Academy? Like a territory outside of time and space?"

"You mean you won't leave me alone, right?" Archibald was starting to show irritation. The tension of the last few hours was taking its toll.

"May I at least look at the library?" I asked in dismay, realizing I would not be able to find out anything about Avalon. "Or is Archibald's collection not for dummies?"

"What a smart little boy." The catorian's nasty smile spoke volumes, so I simply shrugged and pretended to lose all interest in the castle around us. Steve would record everything in any case, and sort it out by category. Meanwhile, I was not going to humor Archibald by attempting to hide the curiosity that I was bursting with. But I was hurt.

This time our final stop was Archibald's personal office. Fire in the fireplace, soft leather furniture, antique writing desk and other things showed the teacher to be someone who preferred the comfortable British style. Sophisticated and tasteful, like everything about Archibald.

"Welcome. But don't feel at home." The teacher

said curtly, and settled down in a chair next to the fireplace. Watching the catorian grunt and carefully cuddle his feet in the soft throw, I did not immediately figure out a place for me to sit. The sofa was too far away; the chairs by the wall were not suitable for trusting conversation... so I finally selected the other armchair, with the same throw as the host's. After some contemplation I set the throw aside. After all, I had been told directly not to overstep the boundaries of hospitality.

"So, oh-my-student-who-suddenly-grew-a-brain," Archibald said after a rather lengthy pause, still looking at the fire. "I suggest that you become my vassal and change your anchor point to Avalon."

"I accept," I hastily agreed, realizing that I didn't have time to look for hidden traps, and that I may never get a second chance like that. I needed to change my anchor point as soon as I could, and there was not a ton of choice... The Citadel and Avalon. But I would choose the latter over a thousand Citadels!

"Good. Repeat after me." Archibald said the words of the vassal oath, not even bothering to stand up from the chair. Nor did he bother to move at all—as if all of it was just a trivial thing—while my palms were sweating with worry. Once lightning flashed between us, confirming the agreement, a mechanical manipulator lowered itself from the ceiling and quickly drew the emblem of my new suzerain on my shoulder. A silver hammer against a golden shield. I barely had time to look at the new tattoo when the manipulator covered the drawing, making the area the same color as my armor. I was somewhat bewildered.

"It's not a good idea to advertize your new status to anyone," Archibald clarified. Did it seem to me, or had his voice in fact acquired a barely audible hint of warmth? At least I was not hearing his former sarcasm in it. "Place your hand there, to change the anchor point."

Another mechanical arm came down from the ceiling, scanned my retina and fingerprinted me. The machine hummed for a while, then clicked, and I felt a slight prick. A drop of blood fell on the pad, and as it was absorbed a message flashed in front of my eyes, notifying me of the change in my anchor point. I was quite astonished by this automated change of the respawn point, and asked my teacher what was all that.

"It's a mechanism from the third era," Archibald clarified, pleased with the effect it had on me. "The Emperor kindly allowed me to keep three objects from each era, including the first one, for personal use."

My inner explorer immediately developed an obsession that must have been readily reflected on my face.

"No, my impatient student, don't even dream of that. Maybe at some point... for some outstanding... well, actually, just no. But I promise to give you little treats from time to time until restart. Now let's get to business! Let's discuss the critically important things."

A small metal item was thrown at me, and it

took me some effort to catch it. Once I had it in my hand I realized that it was a solid box with a mechanical timer.

"Local tracer cleaner," the catorian commented. "I don't have time to teach you now. Turn the timer one full circle. This device will automatically clean others' tracers off you once per hour. This is enough to ensure relative safety."

"Of course, yours are not among those others," I wanted to add, but I didn't bother with such empty statements. That was clear from the start. The catorian explained to me how to embed the device control into my interface and make sure that it was hidden from others, so that 'informed' creatures would not notice it and take it away. In this respect Archibald knew no equals. He looked closely at my outfit and enhancements. Then the displeased catorian ordered me to throw away all the amulets. Not to put them onto the auction but to trash them entirely. Because one could rarely see such disgusting trash as what I had received from Bernard. The only thing that pleased Archibald were my ten-level enhancement gems that I had brought from the Dungeon. However, after brief contemplation he told me to pull them off my armor as well. To my questioning expression he commented that such gems may be really cool for me, but way beneath his level for his vassal. According to Archibald his vassal should not wear such things; or maybe as decoration only. He rummaged through his own stocks; then the catorian generously dumped in my lap a pile of twenty scintillating stones. My teacher did not hold back. The properties of each of those gems were several orders of magnitude superior to the level of all my own paltry treasures combined. And all those riches were installed without the participation of any NPCs or other players. Apparently, for every activity Archibald had a special robot or mechanical device. The complete repair of my armor was a pleasant added bonus. The last time I had respawned had happened before the reincarnation of Madonna, so the damage my armor sustained at the Lecleur estate still marred my armor. The metalworkers in the Citadel had simply patched it up, restoring the protection, but its appearance really sucked. I was never a show-off, but flashing the patches was no fun either.

"Now come here – we'll do a little body art, or rather, armor art," Archibald continued, now that he was happy with the way he had equipped me. To implement his idea he pulled out a sharp stylus from his inventory and started drawing power lines right on top of my armor. Using his own Energy of Light to apply the lines, Archibald was turning my Daro set into the Legendary variety one, and I was glad to no end. Really, like a creature completely unused to receiving anything for free, I had just received, in addition to all of the above, an anti-grav, which would enable me to soar like a bird to a height of up to one kilometer, and a triple velocity accelerator. Really, I was literally ready to worship my teacher for this incomparable sensation of being all-powerful! It was like being accepted at the club of deities at Olympus!

The blue lines on the armor kept sparking and crackling from the enormous amount of energy that had been just poured into them, before they faded, leaving barely noticeable traces on the metal. Now all I needed to do was to find out from the catorian what the upgraded properties were.

"Defense and attack. Now, if some Gromana decides to have a talk with you without my permission, she will quickly change her mind." Archibald stepped back to fully appreciate the result of his work. "You will not make her drop dead, but now you will have some serious bite. Most important, you will be able to survive. And finally, dear Cinderella, you need practice in order to learn how to use all that. Or else you'll turn into a pumpkin. I think I promised you a training range..."

I don't know how I was able to refrain from the impulse to wrap the kind catorian in a hug and dance around the room. Perhaps what stopped me was the thought that he would not appreciate such an outburst and would take all the presents back. So I just stood there and smiled from ear to ear, beaming with unreal happiness. There was just one thought dashing around my head: I hoped it was not all just a hallucination after seeing what I saw in the torture chamber. But no, the catorian was snorting into his whiskers, and demonstratively brought me down to earth from my wanderings, trying to quickly explain to me how that magical device worked. Finally he got tired of staring at my puppy eyes, and sent me off to train for six months.

For six months I tested my new outfit, learning to use my new armor both for defense and attack and contemplating the eternal. The eternal was — my teacher's motives and unexpected desire for my Doll.

At first I was just feeling down and considered that I remembered Helen so frequently just because I was lonely. But the more time passed the more I realized that I was sinking into self-deception. Gradually my slight infatuation grew into attraction. This realization made me really angry with myself: restart was just around the corner. The time was just completely wrong for this corny fluff. All this was just getting in the way. What an idiot! I needed to concentrate on business!

I thought about a lot and re-evaluated even more. The main question that bothered me was — why did Archibald need to nurture his Madonna, turn her into the Keymaster, and then embed there the consciousness of her old incarnations? It seemed to me that the reason would define the entire Game by Archibald.

Returning practically at the same time when I left, I found nothing better than to ask the question that worried me directly of the author of this multistage plan. Archibald did not rush to answer, as if considering what part of the truth to tell me.

"In order to explain I need to tell you a long story. Are you ready to listen?" I simply nodded and prepared to absorb information. "Until the first restart the world was wonderful. Just imagine: the entire Milky Way was populated by sentient beings. Everybody lived in relative peace and wealth. The balance was maintained by them without any external supervision. There was one rather ordinary Player; he lived quietly, did not show any superior strength or intelligence, and he loved his Doll. The Player adored his Doll so much that he decided to grant her freedom and turn her into a player too. That's how the future Madonna appeared. After she was born, as any extremely spoiled woman, she gradually lost all the features that the Player most valued in women. All the love between them was in the past by then, and at some point Madonna decided that she deserved something better. She left the said Player, seeking a stronger teacher and mentor.

"While she was searching, her personality changes reached drastic proportions. Her fame spread about; she was portrayed as an aggressive and cruel warrior, and an ambitious one to boot. It seems to me that had she been a normal woman, the future Merlin would have never noticed her. She was searching for the strongest one, and she found him. A maniac teacher and his bloodthirsty student. She was mirroring his inclinations, sharing his predilection for atrocities and experiments. Together they hated the world and one another, but their alliance enabled them to reach unprecedented heights. Absolute power and lust for blood did what they were supposed to: galaxies vanished at their hands, but the Game bore everything. I think, an assassination attempt on the Emperor became the last drop. This couple wreaked havoc on the Game; in effect, they precipitated the first restart.

"When he learnt what was in store for them, Merlin somehow struck a deal with the Game. He would voluntarily sacrifice himself, his student and another player for the sake of the new world, and for

146

this the Game allowed Merlin and Madonna to create the list of the chosen few allowed to transition to the next era. The Game did not care how the selection was done; all that mattered to it was to maintain the power balance and make sure that the three players would have the vast Energy potential that was needed during restart. Merlin pushed the point that since he and his student were going to die anyway, he wanted to take part in the creation of the new world. Merlin and Madonna, pleased with themselves, convinced the Player I mentioned to join them. It was easy, since he felt guilty for Madonna's doings. So that was how the first participants of the restart were defined. After that Merlin and Madonna had the justification to start the purges."

"Was there a need for that? At restart the Game would turn the players who did not make the list into NPCs." I asked for clarification and received a confirming nod.

"This is true now, but the first time they were the ones doing it. Merlin and Madonna had planned all that with a single goal in mind: becoming more than simply players – becoming an integral part of the Game; naturally, they were not planning to really die during restart. Before implementing his cunning plan Merlin ran experiments for a long time. I was present at those experiments, and helped to create the mechanism for the personality matrix transfer. The idea is simple: at some point the player's consciousness is backed up and saved into a crystal matrix. Following restart the matrix from the crystal is transferred to the body and the personality is restored; however, the person will not recall the events between backup and restoration. The first problem those two ran into after restart was incomplete recovery of personality. Merlin was primarily concerned with preserving all the knowledge and skills after transition; he did not care at all about integrity of consciousness. The second problem was occupying their important roles in the new era as well. That's when the Diaries appeared. They are used to transfer, among other things, the necessary knowledge about the restart process itself. These are the rules embedded in the Game. Now the entities go through two stages of recovery: the primary initiation, when the personality matrix is embedded in the body of the subject, and incarnation, when the Player receives the activated Diary.

"Now, the answer to your question. What is left of Madonna and Merlin after all these restarts is uncontrollable and extremely dangerous. Their power increases from restart to restart, and so do the changes in their minds. They must die, or else the Game is doomed. Madonna will die first, after she transfers the right for restart. Then I will find a way to eliminate Merlin as well. This is not my first attempt to destroy them. I spent a lot of effort on Dolgunata. I made her strong, both morally and physically, taught her everything, made her the Keymaster and made the Game accept her. And only after that did I transfer Madonna's matrix from the crystal. All that impatient twit had to do was to follow my orders. But Nata considered that she was clever and independent, clutched onto that Diary and let the genie out of the bottle too soon. She was not ready yet. She was too emotional to win. Now she is losing in a mental battle with a crazy and experience opponent, but Sakhray may help to weigh the chances of winning in her favor, I am sure of that."

"Madonna definitely won't be able to get to him here," I asked worriedly as soon as Archibald stopped.

"Correct. Only two beings have access to this place. Both of them are currently here."

"Good. I have a couple more questions for you. Why is it not possible to simply not activate the matrices of Madonna and Merlin?"

"Because it is impossible to violate a direct order. Besides, Merlin learnt to transfer consciousness without the crystal and without external assistance, although with some injuries."

"Who asked you to transfer the matrix?" I asked a question to which I already knew the answer. I needed to check the extent of Archibald's "truthfulness", as there was a chance that all of the things he had said earlier were just a pretty fairy-tail for a naïve calf whose name was Yaropolk.

"The order was issued by the one you call the Nameless," the catorian answered without hesitation. "The third participant of the restart. The Player who lost his Doll. An auxiliary part of the mechanism, and the outside observer."

I nodded, accepting the final version of what was going on. It was time to move on to problems at hand.

"When are we setting out for the Citadel?"

"As soon as we buy you rock-climbing

---

equipment." Archibald grinned, looking at me as my face fell.

"What for?" I swallowed. Fear of heights had followed me throughout my life.

"So my student can accompany me to the summit of Pobeda Peak; that's where our Citadel is located. Portals don't work within a hundred kilometers of there."

"I did not expect to say that, but with you I would go to the ends of the Earth," I blurted out, glad that I would not have to go alone.

"The end of the Earth is really not far from there, so we'll also buy you a steel cup for your balls. Because it will be scary. I promise," the catorian said cheerfully, and opened the portal.

CHAPTER FOUR

DAY THREE

THE SNOWY LANDSCAPES of the Tien Shan mountains are worthy of the cameras of the greatest photographers. Regal and immovable, they breathed peacefulness. They calmed you down better than any sedatives or antidepressants. Had it not been for the hellish wind, one could stay there for a long time, contemplating the beauty around. Even more, one could spend a lifetime staring at them and forgetting about everything.

Another blast of wind threw a handful of snow on my visor, obscuring most of my view. In addition, it brought me down to earth from waxing poetic.

The Daro set, the second in the hierarchy of the Paladins' types of armor in the Game, protected my body well from the cold and the wind. I pushed the visor back and with pleasure inhaled as much air as I could. The lack of oxygen immediately made me dizzy, and the dizziness was replaced by complete euphoria. The world in front of me went dark, my legs buckled, and I barely had time to thrust my palms forward, when I crashed into the snow with my visor open. The biting cold cleared my mind for just a second, but it was enough to close the gap in my armor, under the guidance of my cursing Steve. The pressure equalized, air composition returned to normal and I felt a slight prick on the shoulder: the analyzer of my body condition that Archibald had added deemed my condition to be less than optimal, and administered a shot of elixir. I tried to jump to my feet with vigor, glancing at the portal that was still open. The catorian had apparently lingered, occupied by transporting the snowmobiles for our expedition. Naturally, I would rather keep recent events secret, since it clearly demonstrated a lack of intelligence in certain individuals. The only thing I could possibly say to redeem myself would be that I had never been in the mountains.

"The Citadel of the Paladins is over there." I heard Archibald's voice, but not from the side of the portal, as I had thought; rather, it came from behind me. I turned around, cursing under my breath. The catorian had traveled to the Tien Shan using the second portal, and our new shiny modern ATVs were already sitting right next to us. Not leaving the teacher any time to mock my inglorious attempt to conquer the mountains, I quietly took my place on the ATV and lifted off. My delight in this monster machine was so pure that I completely forgot about my recent failure. It was a comfortable, nicely purring machine flying through the air. Well, actually, it was not really flying — it was more of a hovercraft. The vehicle hovered just a couple of feet above the ground. However, this hovering flight was very comfortable. It moved softly, without jouncing on bumps and holes; the vertical lift and landing were praiseworthy on their own. That was the kind of "horse" that would be worth half a kingdom. My hands itched to try this baby on a road.

The portal brought us to the summit next to Pobeda Peak. The Citadel was a good hundred kilometers away. Half of that distance was a hellish descent, and the other half — a climb just as hellish. Archibald's meaningful silence was the answer to my question as to why we could not use a glider, a plane, a helicopter or some other flying machine. So I had to trust his experience, activate the camouflage mode to avoid unwanted attention, and follow the catorian. To my regret, we did not get to test the upgraded ATVs in the mountains at full capacity. Archibald brought it to barely a dozen miles per hour, making me adjust to his speed. Steve did a simple calculation and "gladdened" me with the news that at that rate we would make it to the Citadel sometime in the evening. I hoped that the Judge Supervisor would be satisfied with my formal letter yesterday, and would not bother me; it would be very hard for me to explain what in hell I was doing in the middle of Tien Shan rather than looking for the murderer in Moscow.

After at least half an hour of monotonous and

slow descent I heard a long moan over the howling of the wind:

"Player, help me!"

Bewildered, I looked around as we kept moving; but I dropped the speed to a minimum. All around me was virginal white; the snow sparkled so brightly and uniformly that there was virtually nothing to catch the eye. Perhaps the rarefied air was affecting my mind again, causing audible hallucinations. Once I pushed the accelerator, the same voice moaned I the exact same tone again:

"Player, help me! I beg you!"

No, that was not an illusion. I stopped and turned off the engine. Steve, never at a loss, quickly analyzed all around trying to pinpoint the source of the sound. Meanwhile the figure of the catorian became significantly smaller in the distance, as he had not noticed that I was lagging behind. I had to call him on the comm and ask him to return, ignoring all the insults he cared to heap upon me. I could not just get up and leave; the plea for help had been repeated for the third time.

Archibald flew over ten seconds later and demanded an explanation. As soon as I opened my mouth to speak, there it was again:

"Player, help me! I beg you"

"Here! Did you hear that?" I stared at the catorian demandingly. He shook his head slowly and, strange as it may seem, negatively, while staring at me all the while. This really freaked me out. If I were losing my mind, that would really mean "game over", since madmen were not tolerated in the Game.

"Where is the voice coming from?" My teacher asked for clarification and Steve pointed definitively to the left. Archibald turned and flew in the specified direction. I followed him and in about ten yards we found a frozen body. Only the remnants of his clothing enabled us to identify him. There was not much left of the unfortunate mountaineer trying to scale the local peaks. Next to the body a shimmering copy of the creature that it had once been hovered in the air, staring at the world with empty eye-holes. It was that ghost that was moaning:

"Hee-e-elp!" It whispered again and, swaying in the wind, rushed towards me.

I stepped back, worried about some unpleasant surprise, but the ghost could not fly too far from the body. The soul of the dead mountaineer was tied to the corpse. Archibald noticed my movements and asked:

"What do you see?"

My first thought was to prepare a video file, but I had to give up that thought. Steve warned me that the camera would not be able to record the presence of the ghost. There was the frozen corpse. There was Archibald. But the ghost could not be seen. After hearing my brief explanation, the catorian hemmed, but did not exhibit disbelief. Looking at the body dispassionately he just asked me:

"What are you going to do?" Well, actually, I was hoping to hear the answer to that question from my teacher. The ghost picked up his howl again, making me make my own decision.

"I am a player! What should I do to help you?"

The ghost stopped moaning and flew around the perimeter of the area available to it, as if he did not notice us. Cursing, I turned off the invisibility mode. His stare immediately focused on me and the ghost scowled.

"Player, find Kathryn. Find my Kathryn! Help me!"

All my attempts to find out who was that Kathryn and where one was supposed to look for her were ignored. The ghost kept repeating the same thing over and over again like a stuck record, interjecting the commands to "find" and "help". By the way, my ephemeral employer either could not see Archibald at all or just chose to ignore him. After making a couple of circles around the corpse just for appearance's sake the catorian firmly stated:

"You need to search the body."

I was rather skeptical about that suggestion, but pushed my ATV towards the corpse. The ghost reacted with a quick dash in my direction. I hastened to pull back:

"Can you guarantee that it's safe?"

"No." Archibald stated the obvious. It was easy for him to talk, the ghost just couldn't care less about him approaching.

"Maybe you could search the corpse yourself?" I came up with another bright thought.

"It wouldn't work, the task is linked to a specific person. Quit whining—you are better protected than Fort Knox!" the teacher cut me off. "It won't do anything to you. Come on, get to work!"

"Listen, let's forget about it." I really didn't want

to get down to the ground. "We have stuff to do, and here we are, goofing off instead."

"The Citadel is not going anywhere." The catorian was getting annoyed with my stubbornness. "Get off already and search the boy, or I'll help you down!"

Under my teacher's unwavering stare I finally did get down, and immediately sank in the snow to my knees. Using my anti-grav, I approached the corpse by air. The ghost gladly rushed towards me, touched my protective shell... and instead of the bright flash showing that a threat had been blocked, I felt the space change around me. Within seconds I found myself in a personal viewing theater. A small screen opened in front of me, demonstrating a silent retro film. At first I saw a newlywed couple. They were young, they loved each other, loved the mountains and both were into mountaineering. They decided to conquer their next mountain. They put together an expedition, hired the guides, purchased the equipment they needed. Nothing spelled trouble, yet my intuition suggested that the tragic moment was coming. As if responding to my thought, a squall suddenly assaulted the small group. Strong wind blew the climbers off their feet, but they struggled on. Someone suggested that they go back, and the young husband supported that sensible idea. The lady, however, turned out to have a quarrelsome character, and was not too strong in the brains department. Predictably, she stomped her foot and proudly continued upward — alone. The husband called to her to come back, but to no avail. Deciding that the stubborn girl would sulk a while and then come back, he stayed with the others to set up camp. However, the girl did not return — neither an hour later, nor by nightfall. Failing to see his wife or good weather, the husband rushed off in the twilight, searching for her. None of the guides or other hired hands dared to join him, to risk their lives in the dark and in foul weather. Having made up his mind that he would go back only after he found his other half, the man froze to death twelve hours later, but never found her. The show was over.

"Find Kathryn," the ghost's sad voice rustled again. "Help me!"

I wanted to tell him that this help would not do anyone any good any more. Since he was a milquetoast, he had perished himself and failed to protect his wife. Whatever it was that she had wanted. Maybe her PMS demanded some "sulking" and "emancipation"? Had he slammed his fist on the table everyone would have been fine! The wife should have freedom in selecting what to eat for dinner, or choosing the names of future children. After all, she is the one giving birth. But all safety issues should be definitely the men's domain! But instead of offering this belated advice I simply nodded to the poor guy, accepting yet another pointless quest.

"What happened with you? Did you see something?" the teacher called to me. He was unusually happy. I raised an eyebrow quizzically. "Make your face look a little simpler. Don't be a party pooper with your sad mug."

"You will offset it with your happy one. Let's do

it this way: you share first; maybe that will light me up like fireworks. What the hell, Archibald? Why is it that I can see and hear the ghost, and you cannot? And with all that your mug is just about bursting with pleasure!"

"Less pathos, my dejected student! The teacher is supposed to know more than his student, right? There is a simple explanation. You are the Guide, and you have encountered difficulties in finding the restart participants. Before the Game presents them to you on a platter, it will generate certain hints, clues, messages, encounters. Whatever it takes to force your limited mind to act properly. Actually, that is a hint already. Everyone can see the body, but you are the only one who can talk to the ghost. Got that?"

This information did not fill me with as much delight as it did Archibald. Whatever the hint meant was not known, while I already had a huge pain in the ass in the form of one corpse on my hands and the need to search for another. Without responding to Archibald's words, I searched the body, but did not find anything worthwhile. The ghost quieted down and just circled above me, sobbing from time to time. It was time for another brainstorming session with my teacher.

"The only way she could possibly go would be up." I finished my story and looked at the mountain sadly. What was the point of going down just to have to go up again? I pulled out a rope from my stash and started tying the frozen body of the hapless mountain climber to the ATV. That surprised the catorian.

"In my past life I was an experienced gamer," I

said shortly, continuing to do it. I needed to verify that the ghost was attached to the body and not to the location of his death. Otherwise my idea would not work. I dragged the body a few yards, and gratefully waved at the ghost flying after me. He was rather stunned, and started looking around and calling his love with new enthusiasm.

"What does this have to do with your previous life and this corpse? Is gaming somehow related to necrophilia?" Archibald asked, not passing an opportunity to mock me.

"Only if the corpse was yours. Finding Kathryn is just the beginning of the quest. Once we find her, she will ask us to drag her love to her, since she won't believe our words. Then we would have to go back. Or else they will demand that we help them complete their journey and drag them to the top. Or something else. What, have you never run into stuff like that?"

"Not at my level. I must have forgotten the way it works at the lowest ones." The catorian brushed me off, taking my self-esteem down a couple of notches with just one phrase. However, taking into account my statement he sensibly decided to use the ghost as the navigator. We made a large circle around the location with the hapless guy in tow and I determined where his reaction was the most frantic. By experiment we figured out the trajectory of the ascent and started back up guided by the "force of eternal love". That was really the only way to define it.

It took us an hour and a half to reach the summit. Mostly the top was flat, with good visibility. On the left there was a huge snow-covered boulder resembling a hunched person looking into the abyss. That's where the ghost rushed as soon as the boulder became visible. It was getting so impatient that the body was dragging along after it as the apparition concentrated on its goal. Archibald reached the boulder first and brushed away the snow. Once I stopped next to my teacher I saw a body curled in the fetal position on the leeward side. The woman deserved some credit for her stubbornness or determination: ultimately, she did make it to the top. Unlike her spouse, Kathryn's body was perfectly preserved; but her soul was restless as well. The girl's ghost was standing next to her body, greeting her love with silent tears.

"Player!" The mountaineer called me loudly once again, still a few yards away from his wife. "Help us again! Put my body next to Kathryn's! Let us complete our mission!"

I jumped down to the ground, unceremoniously dragged the body over and set it down next to the dead woman. The quest, just as I supposed, had multiple components that did not show in the list.

"You found her!"

"You found him!"

"You brought him!"

"You brought me!"

"You brought us together!"

The ghosts were quickly marking as complete the tasks that had been identified and the ones that had not, which looked rather silly. The script must have not been compiled properly. Whoever had written the code for this part deserved only a kick in the ass! My mood was not improved by the fact that once all the thanks were over I did not gain any experience, nor the promised suggestion as to where to find Merlin. All that happened was that I wasted two hours of my precious time! Frustrated, I turned to the ATV when Kathryn called after me:

"Wait! Release us, player! We have fulfilled our destiny."

"Are you sure? Maybe you are supposed to tell me something, or hand something to me? And I am supposed to release you as a form of gratitude?" But the happy couple of ghosts just stared at me in surprise.

"No! You should release us first." The mountaineer shook his head, embracing his wife.

Feeling like an idiot, I could think of nothing better than borrowing the trite phrase from the movies and the Bible-thumpers.

"I release you. Rest in peace."

I heard the cat snorting with derision. The ghosts, instead of being finally completely and quite sincerely dead, told me what this process involved.

"Burn the bodies. That is the only way for us to leave."

Annoyed that getting information from them was like pulling teeth, I bled a bit of gasoline from the ATV and poured it over the frozen bodies. Now just a small thing remained... that I did not have. I had neither matches nor a lighter on me.

"What would you do without me?!" Another verbal jab from above, followed by a lighter that fell right next to me. The Game overcame logic and the laws of physics once again: the bodies burned like a torch. The flames flared ten feet into the air, devouring the bodies of the hapless newlyweds. After it was all finished, I expected that the ghosts would float up to the sky or just disappear. Shining surrounded them, and as they were finally disappearing, Kathryn shouted:

"Complete what you have! Good luck in your search, Player!" At the last word the wind blew them away like smoke. At least someone got what they wanted!

"I am all ears." Archibald reminded me of his presence. "What was the hint?"

Without much enthusiasm I repeated Kathryn's last sentence word for word. It did not help me much. But my teacher came to my aid:

"How many active cases do you have to your name now?"

"Two cases for the Judge, received a week ago; they should clear soon." I did not even have to look at the case list. I remembered it quite clearly. I had received those cases against NPCs, basically, by accident: I shook my head while driving — some hotshots cut me off and the Game immediately suggested that I punish them. I felt magnanimous and decided to ignore the offer.

"No. Keep going."

"There is one quest: the Explorer's quest. To find a treasure based on a map drawn by a child."

"That's it!" Archibald was actually fidgeting with impatience. "That's the search for which they wished you luck! Once you complete the task with the map it will bring you a step closer to Merlin."

"Are you sure?" I asked warily. "This was a beginner's quest issued to a young Explorer in the Sanctuary's library. What does Merlin have to do with that?"

"You don't have any other choices anyway," Archibald concluded, and jumped onto his ATV. "Off we go. There is still a long way to the Citadel!"

The next ten hours could be described as "boring and riding". Completely so. I became fed up with the landscapes a couple of hours into the trip. At the end I was just about sick of the monotony. Several times I nearly fell off the ATV, lulled by the sameness of the surroundings and the smoothness of the ride. Archibald did not want to talk via the comm to brighten the long hours of the journey. Thinking of different things I recalled today's sacrifice and felt guilty that I could not do anything to counteract Merlin. I needed to find him faster!

By the time we approached the shimmering fog curtain I was in an extremely depressed mood.

"Let's get down." Archibald dismounted his ATV, landing silently on his feet. Even though they were covered with steel armor. He did not even trample the snow. I decided that repeating this feat would be not quite within my reach, so I simply lowered my ATV and took a position immediately behind the catorian, who was preoccupied with yet another device he extracted from his inventory.

"We'll leave our machines here," my teacher warned me. "We can drop the blocking field for a little while. On my command — run as fast as you can.

Don't overtake me, don't lag behind and, most importantly, don't think until I tell you to! Your main task is to keep close to me."

Despite the warning and my readiness, I nearly missed the moment when Archibald rushed forward. And there was no command, the blasted mangy cat! A hurricane force head wind started blowing from the fog wall. I fell on my knees to improve my stability and diminish the surface area. Moving forward was extremely hard. In my case "running as fast as I could" amounted to "crawling like a turtle". Archibald was not too far ahead either. Bending almost double, he demonstrated amazing steadiness. The wind strengthened, dragging me back. With a shout I crashed my fist into the stone underfoot, making a dent onto which I could hold. That made fighting the wind easier. Making a similar dent with my other hand, I pulled myself up and fixed myself firmly in place with the toe of my steel boot. My muscles were ringing with tension and demanded a respite, even if it were just a short one. A blow, then another. Pull, steady... The wind stopped as suddenly as it had started, but I hit the stone again due to inertia before I could stop myself...

"Enough – we made it through." I heard Archibald's voice above me. I crashed onto the stone, exhausted. My hands trembling, I tried to extract an elixir. But I failed: the vial rolled out of my trembling hand as soon as I pulled it out of my inventory. I was shaking all over from straining too hard; my nose started bleeding.

"A sorry sight," my teacher concluded, and

rolled me over onto my back with his foot. "Dolgunata would not even have felt this wind. You will need brutal training if you want to survive."

Archibald did not wait long enough for me to answer. He lifted the fallen vial and poured the healing potion down my throat. Warmth spread through my body, followed by an intense cramp. As if every muscle tried to remind me of its presence with burning pain. But this was followed by total bliss. Pain and fatigue vanished without a trace. Archibald hemmed and said:

"So why in hell did you rush into the hole after me?"

"What?" The point of why he was giving me this flak escaped me. "You ordered me to yourself..."

"What does it matter what I ordered? Where is your critical assessment of the situation? Where is your analysis of information that is available to you and your ability to draw conclusions from it? Why are you staring at me like that? What was that fog curtain? Right, it was the protection of the Citadel from undesirable visitors. Are you one of those? No, and you won't be at least for the next hour or two. Therefore, you could cross the curtain quite easily in any place other than where I tore it. And then you would have been waiting for me here without all that strain!"

"You could have told me!" I was earnestly offended. "What if the image of one's aura went to Gerhard as soon as you cross it! How would I know?"

"You could have asked, knucklehead! Or do you think that Paladins only move around by jumping through portals? This is the standard 'friend or foe' system here. In any case, I hope you remember this for the future. Even though watching you with your ass in the air like a crab was funny!" my teacher chuckled. But within I was seething at his unfair scolding.

I had no desire to get into a pointless quarrel, so I proceeded to "assess the situation" and "draw conclusions from it". The fog curtain had restored itself behind us and I found nothing worthwhile there. Actually, there was nothing ahead, either. We found ourselves in a stone cul-de-sac whose walls were unnaturally smooth. Perfectly polished, without a crack or any other defects, they rose on three sides around us high into the air. Steve estimated the height at about fifty yards. There would be two ways to overcome that obstacle: either to scale them or to dig under them. However, since we had no equipment for either method, we would need to find a third option. My teacher's behavior did not offer any insights either: sitting by the right wall he was calmly doing something with his navigator, as if he could not care less about our surroundings. I was too proud to ask what we were waiting for, so I decided that Steve and I would explore the walls more thoroughly. Let's proceed from the assumption that the Paladins actually use this entrance from time to time. It's not like someone lowers a rope for them, right? Steve studied the bottom of the wall and happily highlighted a section which, on the face of it, was just as nondescript as the others. I went straight for it. As soon as I approached the wall the section that Steve identified shimmered and disappeared, revealing a passage.

"You already solved it? What a good boy! Found the entrance all on his own! Apparently, it's very useful to give you a piece of my mind," the catorian said, immediately appearing next to me. Without wasting any time he pushed me aside and dove into the darkness. I was stricken by yet another instance of his insolence.

"Are you playing dumb again?" My teacher's face peeked from the passage. "Come on, the most interesting things are ahead of us!"

Night vision did not help much in the dark labyrinths of the Citadel, and during the first few minutes I basically felt my way. Archibald ran off ahead, forgetting about me; I took advantage of that in order to move at a speed that I found comfortable. After making a turn I ran into the catorian, who had been waiting for me. He immediately lit up a small blue light, dimly illuminating the corridor. I just snorted to myself at this attempt at courtesy.

"A brief introduction." Archibald showed a 3D map of the Citadel with all its nooks, wings and pockets. I appraised the tool enviously. The teacher gestured, zooming into the map. One of the hallways showed a green dot. Steve, like myself, was practically drooling at this new thing I wanted badly, and failed to immediately realize that the green dot was marking our location. I would run to the auction for a thing like that! I just needed to remember and find out what it was called. Pleased that I was able to listen to him again, the catorian continued:

"We are here. The library is there. This is our route." A red dotted line appeared on the map. Steve and I gasped in admiration. "Now to the most interesting part. For most of the way you'd have to carry me along. I cannot stay conscious within the Citadel."

"Why did you come here altogether then? I would have entered by myself, easily, as it turned out," I grumbled with annoyance.

"You would have entered. You would have even made it to the library. But you would not be able to leave without me. Any more questions?" Archibald barked angrily; obviously he had not expected such discontent on my part.

"How should I carry you?" I sighed heavily, resigning to the inevitable.

"Whole and undamaged. Here. You will pour this into me once we reach the location. Go strictly along the indicated route. The artifact will help you. And generally, fewer questions, more actions."

Archibald passed me a vial full of yellow liquid, then took out a different one, gulped it down and crashed onto the floor.

For some time I looked at his unconscious body indifferently, without hurrying to do anything. A host of questions was rushing through my mind, and the fact that there were no answers only exacerbated my mood, which was far from bubbly anyway. Really, I was so fed up with Archibald. He never explained anything; he ordered me to fulfill idiotic tasks, and his overall behavior was abominable. To him this was wrong, and that was not right! From his exceedingly long life, his brains must have dried out — old age dementia in full bloom. Had it not been for Madonna's ultimatum indicating that without looking for Merlin I would be history, I would never have agreed to work with Archibald.

I listlessly kicked the unresponsive body a couple of times, but did not come up with anything better than to grab the teacher by the feet and drag him in the direction of my goal, not caring much about his comfort. If I were to run into some Paladins now, it would not be worth it to even bother about explanations. Who would even listen to me if I had the "Great Exile" with me, in plain view? But fortunately, I did not encounter anyone. Steve was being useful by highlighting our route, but strictly speaking that was not necessary: so far there was no way to turn. The hallway not only had no guards, it had no other doors or halls. There was altogether nothing there other than the bare walls of the narrow corridor, lit by our little blue light. At the first sign of fatigue I stopped to rest and opened the map once again. Steve scratched his beard in contemplation and shrugged, unsure where we were, where everybody was and when we would reach some kind of a familiar place. Then we pressed on, but literally after the next turn I heard muffled voices from behind the wall. I put my ear to the wall and started listening:

"What are you going to do?" the first voice asked.

"There's not much space for maneuvering," the second one replied. "It's either us or them. I'll visit the Head tomorrow, and propose a plan of attack. The

Pilmans need to be fully destroyed. They only have two anchor points; if we join forces with the hunters and priests, those bastards wouldn't have a chance."

"It's not so easy to get to see the Head." I could hear doubt in the first guy's voice.

"I know, but Demitre promised to help. He needs a skirmish now like no one else. Iven — he did have a name. Demitre is just another nobody so far."

"Well, that's a sensible thought. If Demitre helps us, then..."

The voices retreated and gradually faded. I explored the wall thoroughly and found two spyholes. It was interesting that they were perfectly suitable for my average human eyes. Looking into them I saw the large empty hall on the other side of the wall. What had my currently unconscious teacher said? Paladins use this passage? Sure, sure. They stroll every evening through the secret labyrinths of the Citadel, enjoying some peeping as an idle pastime! I would bet that only very few knew about the existence of these passages. It's not surprising that no one had seen Gerhard for so long; the Head must have been peacefully wandering these hallways all on his own. Keeping tabs on all things hidden and present. Most likely these hallways were also capable of penetrating the Dome of Silence. By the way, speaking about the Head, it would be really awkward to run into him now. Something suggested to me that the Head would not be happy to see me at this time. These new circumstances made me reconsider my mode of transporting Archibald. His armor rattled too loudly against the stone floor; I did not need that extra noise.

With this heavy burden on my shoulders and in my soul I soldiered on. Steve, in addition to lighting the route, started looking for more spyholes. Even though I was doing fine with this myself, now that I had figured out the pattern of their location. Each hall could be seen from three or four different angles. Whoever designed the layout of the Citadel was obviously a maniac for hidden observation. We passed one hall after another, but there was nothing interesting going on. The halls were either empty, or the Paladins in them were engaged in some routine work. No conspiracies intrigues or investigations. At least that allowed my soul to have some rest. Half an hour later I made it to the destination and was happy to lower the catorian onto the floor. The library was waiting for us behind the wall.

My first thought was to just leave the catorian there and get into the library by myself. However, studying the walls did not yield any result: there were no mechanisms capable of opening a hidden door; nor was there an actual door itself. Steve spread his arms, assuring me that he had not noticed anything unusual. The wall was just solid.

"Wake up, sleeping beauty." There was nothing for me to do other than pour the reviving potion into my teacher's mouth. He'd have to get up and work now. I did not sign up to do everything for him.

"What took you so long?" Archibald, as always, was unhappy with me. Looking at his dirty armor with annoyance, he said through his teeth: "While I am busy, make up a worthwhile explanation for what happened. And it had better be a battle with trolls in which you had to use me as a weapon rather than your petty desire to humiliate your helpless teacher by dragging him on the stones. Get that? Now move aside!"

A huge hammer appeared in the catorian's hands. After setting up the Curtain of Silence, the teacher swung it and whopped the wall mightily. I jumped to the side, shaking off the stone crumbs. I had not moved far enough, and ended up in a cloud of dust and crumbled stone. Archibald paid no attention to my displeasure: he dealt blow after blow with abandon, as if he was working for the gnomes part time. The wall cracked fairly fast, and soon a huge stone fell into the common hall, forming a passage. Archibald administered a few more blows, widening it, after which he rushed into it head first. I followed him.

"Stick the stone into your inventory," my teacher ordered me, while he dashed to the nearest statue and lifted it above the floor together with its stand. The statue was placed right where I had just cleared the stone — not only to enlighten the masses with beautiful artwork, but also to cover the hole from strangers' eyes. Archibald looked his work over critically, extracted a portable vacuum cleaner from his inventory, and cleaned up all the dust and plaster. Of course, the unusual location of the statue could pique the interest of some observant Paladin, but all of that would happen later, when we were no longer there.

The library was closed, since it had lost its chief supervisor. Archibald quickly dialed a code on the electronic alarm pad at the door, opened it a little and hastily disappeared within, gesturing to me. I followed him, also trying not to open the door too much. As soon as I entered, Archibald shut the door; I heard the lock click. We needed no spectators or curious rubber-neckers in there.

"You have two minutes." Archibald said. "Don't waste them."

I felt taken aback, not sure what would be the most efficient way to spend the minutes allocated to me, but then my glance caught the nearest shelf with the books. Everything became clear as the brightest Game day. This was the Paladins' library! Even the unrestricted section would have rare manuscripts that would be extremely useful for an Explorer. I would easily level up my artifact to unprecedented levels! It seemed my hands acted on their own, knowing precisely what to do: one was activating the infinity training range that Archibald had given me; the other held on to the shelf tighter than if it had been my beloved. Taking the books in batches would take too long; I had to risk it and try to grab the entire shelf. The space blinked, and there I was, outside of time and with about three hundred books that I had craved. Greedily, I pulled out the first one and started the scanning process. I had two minutes. Two minutes to go through the bookshelves, one by one. Steve counted several dozen of them there and was not going to skip a single one!

"You have 'Context Search' of course." Archibald greeted me back in the library with the statement rather than the question. I nodded, confirming his guess.

"Excellent. You need to bring it up to level 50. Together with 'Neuronal Network'. Everything else can wait till later."

"Why?" I came up to the next shelf and looking at the catorian questioningly. A second passed, and another, but I waited, not disappearing into timelessness, demanding my answer. Archibald clarified with annoyance:

"Because at level 50 of 'Context Search' you will be able to materialize the books you have read. And manuscripts. And other sources of information. The restart is coming. You are guaranteed to become one of the representatives for this era. You need to increase your value for the future! Your artifact would have the entire open library of the Paladins! Don't waste time! We have one hundred seconds left!

My teacher's comment was fair, and I stepped into timelessness once again. I could bet that I was going to hear a lot of new, useful and interesting things from Archibald, but it would come at a price. And the catorian did not sell anything cheaply. I needed to think of that while I was still there.

I looked at the next book, beckoning to me with new knowledge and highly desirable experience points, and set it back on the shelf. Before leveling up, I needed to sort all of this out.

"As an Explorer and the Guide I need information on what is going to happen to the information from the current era at restart. Will it be relevant? Will it be possible to use it without breaking the rules of the Game?" I shouted into space.

Hoping once again that the Temple of Knowledge would not be too hard on my humble self, I prepared to insist that the reason to let me into the Temple was well justified. My hopes come true, however, without the need to argue: a moment later I was staring at the old guy inviting me towards a small desk, waving his wrinkled hand. I nodded to the keeper and started on the materials. With each new fact my mood sank further, leaving me more and more disappointed. I was correct about the price. By generously allowing me to copy the books from the current era, the catorian was putting me into a very nasty corner. Conflating some facts and the information I had just learned, I used my right for an additional question to clarify:

"Was Garlion an Explorer in the previous era?"

A small nod of confirmation from the old man was my answer. Perhaps Archibald was a truly outstanding teacher and a wise being, but his methods could not be called humane. He would dump you into a bog full of shit and watch, adding more shit with little stars. If you manage to climb out, you would earn some honor and respect, and the stars would go on your shoulders. If not, you were only fit to die anyway like a bug in the code, unworthy to be called a "player". Or at least something like that. Even though it was hard to argue: this place was not for weaklings.

Why did players not like to recall the past? Archibald was not too eager to share that he was a creature from the first era, even though he could have made an exception for a student like me. There could be nothing better for an express level-up for an Explorer: a unique source of information, practically a fount of untold wisdom. But he kept quiet about it... This had never occurred to me before because I ascribed it to the teacher's character, but now it all became clear.

As for Explorer players — they were very few. And so the Game favored them, enabling them to accumulate and replicate information. Yet there was still one caveat. Every time a player for the first time replicated information from a previous era in the informational space from the current era, he lost part of his personality core. Not immediately, but at respawn, when the Game "printed" the new body and inserted the backup copy of the consciousness in it. This process was irrevocable. You could not remember something from your previous life unless you cleared some memory for it. Now I understood Archibald's sarcasm regarding conversations with creatures from the previous eras. No one in their right mind would agree to lose a part of himself. I had been long bothered by this question: where did Garlion get the money to buy minion status for his son, and then player status as well? Had all elves been so rich, the Earth would have long turned into their playground. But I did not see a huge prevalence of elves' youngsters here. At the same time the elves carefully guarded both their own lives and those of their young. The conclusion was rather obvious. He had sold his soul to the devil. Or, rather, transferred the library of the Paladins from the previous era into this one, and paid with his own mind and personality. That's why the elf had phenomenal eidetic memory: each book was a part of himself. It was a horrible trade: the son's well-being in exchange for madness. So that was the fate my dear teacher envisaged for me! Fleabag bastard!

My first desire was, after returning from the Temple of Knowledge, to leave the training range and stuff a couple of books down the throat of the old puppeteer. But, after a few Templar's Blows, I cooled off and finished scanning the entire shelf. Forewarned is forearmed. In the current era it was vital for me to develop, otherwise stagnation would be the death of me. Nothing could force me to replicate the information if I did not want to do it. Archibald was right — I had to be careful. And trust nobody, least of all him.

This time when I returned Archibald was waiting for me.

"Stop now!" He barred the way to the next shelf and stared at my face closely, looking for non-verbal signs in my expression and gestures. Anger and indignation still prevented me from reacting even-headedly, and of course the catorian noticed that. He was never stupid.

"You went to the Temple of Knowledge," the teacher asked me again in his affirmative style. Son of a bitch, he had not read that in my face! He must have scanned my internal Game interface with the visit counter which was supposed to have been hidden from others! How did the catorian get such admin rights? That was some armor upgrade I got from my teacher! "Did you learn something new?"

Both his tone and the question itself were virtually dripping with sarcasm.

"I received some clarifications regarding the meaning of 'Context Search'." I tried to imitate precisely my teacher's tone and pauses in his speech and again reached for the next shelf. Archibald prevented me again.

"Will you share your new discoveries?" The catorian was not willing to release me from his paws, getting only more excited by our argument. His behavior betrayed that he had guessed the true purpose of my visit to the Temple of Knowledge, and now wished for me to acknowledge that aloud. I had nothing to lose except time:

"Oh, just a minor thing. For example, the way your new exhibit managed to get hired as a librarian. You were thinking of steering me down a similar career path? Thank you, I am not interested!"

"I had no doubt about that. But now you have realized how useless it was to have the entire list of the players from previous eras. No one would ever betray any information to you. The Game does not forgive attempts to bring back the past, and everyone prefers to die in sound mind." Archibald raised an eyebrow eloquently, and moved aside. "Process this shelf. The other shelves in unrestricted section have no value."

Archibald finished intimidating me as suddenly as he started and moved further into the library. There was a door into the next section. Still aggravated from talking to the catorian, I went off with the last shelf. Returning a moment later I joined

Archibald. He was stuck at the door.

"I am glad to see that you are developing vestiges of critical thinking. I take it as a credit to my good work. Don't touch anything in the next section, or else we'd end up with some visitors."

"Why? Is Gerhard van Brast not supposed to know that you are in the Citadel?" I asked the question that bothered me. While Steve busily scanned the books and I was routinely turning the sheets, I had some time to think of my teacher's behavior. The only reasonable explanation that I could come up with was that Archibald had rendered himself unconscious so that someone could not feel his presence in the Citadel and prevent the meeting. · And that not so very mysterious someone could only be the Head. Gerhard and the catorian were very close; he had the wherewithal to accomplish that. Would that affect me as well? Would I end up stripped of my class also?

"He already knows that I am here." Archibald did not bother denying the obvious, instead, enthusiastically trying to open the lock. Unlike the entrance to the library the passage to the next section was locked with a common padlock with magically protected hinges and hasp. "Your question is posed incorrectly. I don't want him to know that I am in the library."

"Fine," I continued, "why do you not want him to know that you are in the library?"

"Now is not the time! Ask your questions later! And if you as much as touch anything here, there will be nobody asking them altogether!" Archibald cut me off sharply. "All the books are alarmed and there is no way to deactivate it here."

The lock screeched and turned. The door slid to the side, letting us into the next hall. There were a lot more books, but their inaccessibility drove me to despair. Archibald hurried to the next door, keeping an eye on me. I did not care about his distrust, and since that was all I could do I slowly walked along the rows of books, demonstratively keeping my hands behind my back, and videotaped the backs with the names. Steve promised to analyze them and come up with a hypothesis as to what kinds of books were located there and why they had been removed from the public access section. The goal of this campaign was a non-descript steel door in the corner. It was completely smooth — no handles or holes. Once I approached, Archibald pushed a small dent in the wall, the size of a human finger pad, and called up a projection of a numeric keypad.

"Enter the password." My teacher ordered.

"Why me?"

"Because you are the Paladin here." The catorian's whiskers twitched disgruntledly and he rolled his eyes, appealing to the creators of the Game to help him teach the stupid student or, in the very worst case, to help him to get rid of me. But I was not so easily deceived. I knew that the reason was not at all in me being of the Paladin class. It was much simpler: the one who enters the password on the keypad would be accused of burglary. Gerhard would be immediately notified of that.

Seeing that I was in no hurry to follow my

teacher's command, Archibald whipped his tail against his legs and said quickly, clarifying his order:

"If I were to enter the password, the Head would appear here in a couple of seconds. We won't have enough time to find what we need. While if you do it, Gerhard will want to catch red-handed not the petty gopher, but the mastermind behind this whole daring operation. He won't come here: on your own you would never be able to get out of the library you broke into, and he can't see me here. So he will be looking in a different place. We will have precisely thirty seconds to find what we came for.

Satisfied with the explanation, I touched the keyboard decisively. My name immediately appeared in the projection. The protection of the restricted sector identified me and now expected the password in order to determine my right to access. After I dialed the code, the panel lit up with cheerful blue light, confirming that access was authorized.

"The security of this section is tied to the librarian." Archibald explained while the automatic door was opening. "To his normal mental state, that is. So dragging the frozen Garlion here would not do the trick. The password is used when the librarian is dead... or almost dead, like today. Everyone who enters will have precisely thirty seconds to press a special button on a device from Gerhard's personal inventory; otherwise the library will block all the ways in and out. At least that's what it was supposed to do when I designed this protection."

"You did?" I looked at my teacher in surprise. "And you did not leave a loophole for yourself?"

"You overestimate me and underestimate the Head. That's two mistakes! The Citadel is Gerhard's home."

The door opened, revealing the sacrosanct core of the library to us. Ancient books were sitting on small desks under glass domes. Some of them looked so decrepit, it seemed a simple breath would reduce them to dust.

"Here they are, the most valuable treasures of the Paladins." Archibald whispered as he crossed the threshold before me. "As far as I am concerned, they are worth thousands of minds of those like Garlion... Don't pick up."

The order came a fraction of a second before my comm rang. It was Gerhard. The Head was already informed that I had entered the classified section, but, just as Archibald had predicted, decided to "bring me back into the fold" by the phone call, and catch the main perpetrator on the spot. It was hard to just ignore the call. As if I were ten years old again, had run off from my classes, and my mom got the call from the school. So she was now calling me to yell at me, and if I didn't pick up I'd catch hell later. But it wouldn't be now.

The comm rang for ten seconds. During that time Archibald and I split, each doing his own thing. Archibald dashed about like a whirlwind between the desks, trying to find what we needed, and in between smashing the protective domes. I tried my best to keep up, grabbing one rarity after another out of shattered glass and stuffing it into my inventory. Steve counted down the time remaining to lockdown.

"Here!" Twenty seconds later Archibald was standing by a desk with a rather small piece of paper on it. The catorian was in no hurry to break the lid — he was waiting for me. I sped up, grabbing the last pieces together with the glass shards.

"Scan." The teacher ordered as soon as I was near. The countdown was nearing zero. Steve was fast as a lightning. Not only did he scan the document, but he also noted the location of the explosive charge in the dome. That was why Archibald had not broken it.

"Ready!" I reported. Archibald shattered the dome at the nearest desk. We just had a couple more seconds to grab some extra documents.

That was the last manuscript I touched, but there was no time to throw it into my inventory. My voice and body stopped obeying me. I froze in place, staring at the broken dome and clutching the book in my hand. Archibald was standing still somewhere in the periphery of my vision. We did not make it. What let us down was simple greed, that prevented us from leaving four seconds before the deadline. Time ran out quickly, the zeroes blinked one last time and faded, followed by the rattle of the lowering barred partitions. The invisible vise released me, and in the door of the restricted section I saw the Head of the Paladins of Earth. Gerhard van Brast.

It was very lucky for us — the Head did not make it either. The portal brought him to the open section, but he did not have enough time to enter the main storage area before it was locked. The bars blocked all the entrances and now one of them was

---

separating us from Gerhard. The stare of the Nameless, locked on the catorian, promised nothing good. I turned to Archibald. Unlike me, he continued to stand still, unable to move. It was obvious that he was trying to resist Gerhard, but not succeeding very well. A small box fell out of his hands and rolled towards me. I don't know what moved me — was it intuition, or the certainty that the catorian expected this from me, but I instantly dashed for the box and, still on all fours, hugged his leg as I pressed the button on the device. The whole thing must have taken no more than a second. No one expected such speed of me, least of all myself. There was a brief explosion of pain, followed by blissful darkness. I was wrong: the box was not a teleport.

"Now, my student, there is no turning back. Archibald noted after respawn. The catorian was carefully selecting new armor from his armory. He respawned naked as jaybird. His armory had just about everything. It even held a few Imperial sets. Archibald carelessly shoved them aside and extracted another Daro set. "Gerhard will not forgive us this entry. Oh! Here he is! Avalon on the line!"

"You have a week to find Merlin." I heard the Head's dry voice. I had never heard him speak like this. I never even knew that one's voice can change in such a way because of a fit of anger. "If you fail to produce a result, I'll kill both of you. And you owe me for the library separately. The timer is on."

"No, there is no turning back for both of us," I smiled bitterly, and called up the projection of the page with text. "The question is only whether this was worth it."

That was not a rhetorical question at all. The photograph that we had obtained, once you got rid of the extraneous words that were on the page for the sake of volume and distraction, had only one meaningful phrase left.

"Only one who takes the entire path himself will find the Diary"

And the hated letter "M" instead of the signature. Only with different monograms.

I saw confusion and disbelief in Archibald's eyes. Of course, on the face of it there appeared to be more information on the page. Without wasting time to argue, I projected the initial appearance of the document; then Steve removed all the extraneous bits for visual clarity. Archibald was silently digesting what he saw, accepting the bitter truth. There was nothing he could tell me.

It seemed with each new clue that we obtained we became entangled in this search deeper and deeper, and inevitably ended up with a shorter deadline.

We were obviously in for a fun week.

CHAPTER FIVE

DAY FOUR

CONDITIONED REFLEXES are definitely useful, unless you are the dog. That occurred to me once I woke up at five in the morning, roused by the trill of my cell phone. My conditioned reflex to throw that damned phone the hell away was not yet quite formed, but after another couple of such awakenings my subconscious threatened to overcome my awareness. Before that had a chance to happen I petted Helen soothingly and climbed out of bed.

The number of the caller was not identified, but at this point I really didn't give a rat's ass who was going to inform me of the crime that had been committed.

"General Ryabov on the line!" I heard a loud voice from the speaker and had to quickly escape to the kitchen so as not to wake up my sleeping Doll.

"Another crime has taken place. Sixteen victims. We are waiting for you at Izmailovo Park. Details at site. Over!"

Another bigwig with general's stars. It did not matter that we represented different organizations. They got a mighty kick in the ass for twenty eight bodies and no clues, so they were broadcasting their ability to use their command voice to everyone around, right left and center.

"Good morning to you too, sir general. Don't you worry about calling early. I got plenty of winks yesterday, thanks for asking," I mumbled under my breath.

"What kind of snotty nonsense am I hearing, my crybaby student?" My teacher appearing in the middle of my kitchen reinforced my belief that good and morning don't go together. It would have been so much better if yesterday he had cleared out for his Avalon, rather than spending the night at my place. "You are complaining. Aloud. In the kitchen. To yourself. You should have at least taken the trouble to get dressed..."

"I did not invite you here," I snapped back, moving back towards the bedroom to retrieve my armor. Safety is important of course, but wearing armor while having sex is truly a perversion.

"Why Izmailovo?" I heard Archibald's contemplative voice in my bedroom. Indignant at such insolent barging into our private space, I hurried to dress as quickly as I could. I was no prude, but preferred to clean up after sex without spectators or applause. And anyway, the bedroom is the private territory of the hosts.

"You expected it to happen elsewhere? I asked, still nonplussed, pushing Archibald out into the hallway.

"Next to Paveletsky Railroad Terminal," the catorian clarified, after thinking it over again. "So what did I miss? And how much longer are you going to dawdle?"

His complaint was excessive, as I was already standing there in full battle armor, ready for new great deeds. The catorian appraised my sarcastic expression and opened a portal to Izmailovo Park. I felt a pang of envy again. Wasn't it nice to be able to wave a hand and open a portal to wherever you want, without any scrolls? But it would take me a lot of time and effort to reach those heights, if I could reach them at all. Of those whom I met personally only a few had that ability: Gerhard, Madonna, Archibald... Even Gromana, or, say, Bernard used scrolls.

Now that was interesting. Archibald was in the same league as Madonna and the Nameless. Showered with gifts from the Emperor, enjoying unique preferential treatment and his own private Avalon; Archibald who could open a portal to anywhere with one flick of a pinky, and whom the Nameless always trusted to transfer the matrix of his former Doll. So who are you, Archibald? And what connects you and Gerhard? After our escape we did not discuss the events that had occurred in the library, but that did not meant I had stopped thinking about them.

So then. "You owe me for the library

separately." For what? For me transferring to the next era the Library of the Paladins over which they hovered so much? Nonsense, that was in Gerhard 's own interest. It was quite likely that we had entered the Library with his silent blessing. Otherwise Demitre would long since have dragged me into the Citadel himself. So there was something else. What got Gerhard so mad? I reviewed the entire scene in my mind once again. I was blocked. The bars fell. I freed myself and saw Gerhard outside of the room. The Head was enraged but he concentrated fully on the catorian. My teacher was still being controlled like a low-level noob. That's it! That looked like a punishment! The Head stared like Bernard had when he was really unhappy with me! And Gerhard was furious. That had been an act of open defiance on the part of Archibald, and a demonstration of power on the part of Gerhard! The catorian won that time, but the Head would still make him pay for that later.

The cool morning air cleared my head right away. I was following Archibald towards the entrance to Izmailovo Park and glaring at his back.

"Now what?" Archibald sighed heavily and turned. "You are huffing as if you have developed another thought in your head. Fire away: I'm in a good mood today."

"Call the Game to witness that you don't have a mental, physical or other type of dependence on the being known in the current era as Gerhard van Brast." I voiced my suspicions. If he were Gerhard's vassal, I needed to know. The difference between working as a team with someone else's marionette or an independent puppeteer was tremendous. "Then we'll keep going."

"And what if I don't?" Archibald asked sarcastically, but from the twitching of the tip of his tail I suspected that he found the question unpleasant.

"Then don't count on my unconditional support. Now we are pretending that we are cooperating, for the sake of destroying Madonna. Otherwise I will play strictly for myself to survive at any cost," I parried, and tensed. I did not like the teacher's reaction. He didn't like mine either.

"What would prevent me from breaking your neck now, and continuing to do the same in Avalon until I wipe you out completely?" the teacher hissed angrily, right into my face.

"Maybe lack of time and a good candidate for a Guide? You put so much at stake. It's unlikely that the master would forgive his underling such disobedience," I responded, not dropping my gaze.

"Maybe," Archibald responded with forced gaiety, but I did not understand to what it pertained. His eyes, however, stayed cold and relentless. "Gerhard was my teacher and suzerain. Now I am neither his vassal, nor his mental slave. Don't worry: my relationship with Gerhard will not stand in the way of what I have planned. The Game will confirm my words. Is your curiosity satisfied now?"

White light flashed around Archibald, and I had to agree. The catorian, as always, used very careful wording. What the teacher had planned could be dramatically different from what he had told me. I would not get a confession here.

Now was not the time to continue the delicate topic, and I scolded myself for my lack of restraint. Had I given it more careful thought, I would have been able to predict the catorian's answer and pose the question in such a way that he would not have a chance to avoid a direct answer. Having reached agreement we continued on our way, each with his own thoughts. This was a conversation we would have to continue later.

"Your budding brain is starting to bother me. I am starting to lean in favor of partial lobotomy," Archibald grumbled as he was letting me enter the park before him. Had I just received a compliment?

The line of hunched policemen around the crime scene was a familiar sight. And in general the whole thing was shaping up like groundhog day all over again: early morning, another park, cold policemen, and again a pile of bodies in horribly beautiful poses. Except for the main core actors: the extras and supporting actors were different in every scene. This time another sergeant greeted us instead of Lartsov. A short guy, turning blue from the morning cold, timidly blinked his sleepy eyes and saluted the caravan of government cars with beacon lights with a shaking hand. That's how the Game presented the arrival of the FSB representatives.

"Hail to you. C-c-come with me," he said, his teeth rattling from the cold, and pointed at the police car nearby. Archibald and I had barely made a few steps when the blue-faced sergeant jumped in and shut the door behind him. The line policemen were silent. They looked at the sergeant sitting in the car with a mixture of envy and indignation. They envied him for sitting in a warm place, and protested that he had not offered this opportunity to his superiors before getting in himself. This kind of slip was unlikely to ruin his career, but could easily ruin his reputation with the boss. I felt pity for the kid. His brain must have been so frozen that he had practically publicly disrespected an FSB general.

"Report," Archibald ordered, getting into the car. The sergeant, already dizzy with the warmth, warming his hands in front of the air grille, did not catch on at once that the order was addressed to him. Once he realized whom he had just about ignored, he turned red and blurted out all his information, stuttering from fear.

The overview was clear and familiar. Again, no one had seen anything, again there was a strange pattern made of the specially prepared bodies; again the NPCs felt quite unwell at the crime scene. The only new fact was that when experts reviewed the crime scene photographs with the bodies, it did not affect them in that way.

The sergeant led us to the cordon tape and returned to the car. The morning sun had barely risen above the horizon, and together with the bright floodlights lit a significant area in the park and the figures that were wandering there. There were two. Vesnin, who should not have been there at all, and a general — apparently the one who had called the day before. The rest of the support group were as usual outside the forbidden area.

I lifted the tape for Archibald, as a lower-ranking official was supposed to, and I walked behind my "boss" as befit my rank. The policemen turned at the sound of steps, and Archibald and I got a chance to look at the new guy. Unlike Vesnin, who was not affected by the Game magic, the older policeman fully felt the effects of the seal. His face was tinged with blue, his nostrils and pupils grew wide, his breathing was labored and fast. But his poor condition did not at all affect his bearing. He was standing as straight as if he were at a parade, and his stare was penetrating as if he could read your entire dossier on your face. People like that persevere by sheer willpower and a firm conviction that the general cannot be weaker than his subordinates.

Civilian clothes did not hinder the general from determining who was the boss between the two of us. He greeted Archibald with a nod as an equal. So we started discussing the issues in accordance with our rank. Archibald with the general and I with Vesnin.

"What are you doing here? You were removed from the case. We agreed that you would stay home and wait for my call," I told the major by the way of greeting, once the higher-ups strolled off to talk privately.

"Livanov called me a couple of hours ago and asked me to come here. Well, 'asked' may be an exaggeration," Vesnin chuckled, pleased, as he adjusted his glasses that slid down his nose again. "People like that simply order you to report right away. So I was just restored to working on the case. I will be working with him!"

Wow! The Game did not like that we interfered and attempted to isolate the immune one. So it generated a script on its own and returned him to the midst of the action. That was an interesting turn of events!

"And this Livanov, who is he?" I asked the major, and nodded towards the peacefully talking superiors.

"Come on, colonel, it's a shame not to know such people! Livanov is the legend of the ministry of Internal Affairs!" The major was not simply indignant at my ignorance, but seemed genuinely insulted. "He is an incredible detective, hundreds of solved cases, not a single cold case for the thirty years that he'd been working. It's odd that you don't know him; he works with your folks a lot. They bring him in for the most sensational cases. Take the terrorist case in Moscow a couple of years ago. He was the one to find all the terrorists then, and to prevent a series of terrorist attacks."

"Oh, wow, so that's him!" I tried to correct the situation. Actually, my respect for the old guy, who looked as though he had stepped off a recruitment poster, was genuine.

After this introduction I looked at the epic NPC differently. Strong face, indomitable character, backbone of steel and computer-like mind. If Vesnin was right, a lot of interesting quests and scenarios might be related to the general. He was too colorful a figure for the Game to allocate so many resources to him without reason.

"You got any good news for me?" I asked, as a

matter of protocol mostly, nodding at the bodies, and received a negative answer. For NPCs, players' affairs were beyond understanding, and they preferred to write it all off to some higher powers or mysterious influences.

What remained was the necessary ritual of smoke and mirrors: calling up the necromancer and the demonologist to confirm the absence of the souls and the presence of a Higher Demon. So I started on that, dumbfounded by the message visible only to players that the world was going to disappear in six days. This time Archibald did not bother to run experiments with his own blood to verify that Merlin had been there. Everything was already clear except for one thing: where to find the damned murderer. We needed just one clue, one small but significant hint!

"I have an idea, but you'd tell me that I am barking mad." Vesnin's contemplative voice brought me down to earth again. He spoke as if continuing an earlier conversation, so at first I did not understand what he meant. Steve alerted me in time that I had blurted out my last sentence aloud, attracting the major's attention. "But it's not to be put in the report. That's definitely not anything you can put in a case."

"Fire away. At this point any nonsense is better than nothing. And 'nothing' is what we have been getting for quite some time."

Vesnin looked around to make sure there was no one listening, and wiped his glasses.

"This is not an ordinary criminal." He seemed to have trouble finding words.

Despite all his precautions, Archibald appeared

next to us instantly, showing his interest in the conversation. The major looked down, not expecting a new listener, but I reassured and supported him:

"Major, quit your blushing! No one doubts your knowledge and experience. Surely you understand that any lead, even the strangest one, might work out after a joint brainstorming."

"He is a two-face...I mean, I wanted to say, this man, he is not like a man, really... He has two faces, I mean, two appearances..." The major was totally embarrassed.

"A psychiatrically unstable person with several independent personalities?" Archibald made a suggestion.

"Yes." Vesnin sighed with relief. He was glad that the "FSB big gun" did not consider him crazy.

"Why do you think so?" Archibald pressed on, but the major's face already was showing regret from having said too much. The fat man shuffled his feet awkwardly in place and shrugged his shoulders, unwilling to cooperate any further. My teacher asked him a few more questions, but Vesnin really clammed up, and all Archibald heard back from him was that it was based on his intuition.

"Serge, I'll take Vesnin for today, OK?" The catorian turned to Livanov, who had just crossed the taped border. "I need to work on a clue with him."

"Serge" by then was ready to entrust the sly catorian with anything, including Vesnin as well as the most sacrosanct secrets of the state. Without any further questions we left in the general's car, since jumping through portals with an immune NPC would be too risky for his mental state. We would need Vesnin in the future.

In the car Archibald ordered the driver to move towards the center of the city. The major became agitated, and once again tried to convince the catorian that he knew nothing specific, and that his intuition was to blame for everything. But Archibald was not listening to him; deep in his own thoughts he was looking elsewhere on the road.

As soon as we reached the Garden Ring Road, the teacher issued a new direction for the driver: to find a decent watering hole. Three pairs of eyes stared at the catorian, bewildered. The driver, obviously speaking from experience, objected that by six in the morning all decent watering holes would already be shut. Besides, neither Vesnin nor myself were sufficiently upset with lack of the results as to drown our sorrows so early in the day. The catorian was not convinced by our half-hearted objections, but he kindly agreed to any place nearby that served alcohol.

Fifteen minutes later we were entering a practically empty strip club. There were no customers, nor were there any girls working. Security was checking the place, preparing to close, and tired waitresses were cleaning up the last tables and finishing their shift. Considering that he needed no table to implement his plan, Archibald moved towards the counter. A tall young NPC greeted us with a drowsy stare and informed us that the place was shutting down, so he could not serve us. To be more convincing he called over the security guys in case we didn't cooperate. The catorian did not stand on ceremony; he leaned toward the bartender and said something quietly. The guy's eyes glazed, he waved off security and three shots of vodka appeared in front of us.

"Drink!" The teacher ordered, and took his shot in his paws. I followed his example, beginning to understand what Archibald was after.

"I don't drink." The fatso tried to resist, but the teacher forcibly shoved the shot into his hands. That was followed by a question about his strong feelings for Archibald personally and the FSB in general.

"Respect for our work is the basis of success. Right, major?" Archibald lifted his shot higher and pronounced his toast. "To the success of our investigation!"

There was nothing Vesnin could do other than acknowledge his profound and sincere respect for that organization and start drinking.

Everyone who ever lived in Russia would know the difference between "drinking" and "having a drink". "Having a drink" would be something that we would do frequently but a little at a time. To relax, to lift one's mood in case of really bad stress, or from joy. While "drinking" was something that did not require a reason; people drank from despondence or moral weakness, but definitely a lot. A whole huge lot, till they started seeing mermaids dancing on the ceiling. What Archibald and I set out to do was to get the major to drink. The catorian's thinking was that since the Game magic did not affect the major and we were unable to interrogate him by force we needed to engage the magic of alcohol. Because a drunk guy is chattier than any woman.

Archibald was the first to gulp his shot down, without any food to chase it, grunt contentedly and playfully scold Vesnin and myself for our tardiness. Just like Vesnin, I was warming the glass in my hands, gathering my resolve. Ever since adolescence when I was an NPC, I just did not like strong alcohol. I was more of a beer aficionado, but now was not the time to be picky. The burning liquid flowed down my throat, leaving a fiery trail and spreading warmth through my body. It took me only about half a minute to start feeling tipsy: from lack of habit and on an empty stomach one shot felt like three. A warning came up on my internal interface. Steve became wobbly and he informed me, slurring his words, that soon we'd all feel "reeell bad". I heard a hum and a click: the Daro set was demonstrating its unique capabilities. A slight prick at the base of my neck restored my clarity of mind and brought Steve back to normal. The embedded medical analyzer diagnosed my state as alcohol intoxication and counteracted it. The warmth still stayed with me, I even felt slightly euphoric, I just was not drunk any more.

Vesnin's face kind of fell at once, and, cursing mightily, he gulped down his shot. Lurching away, he got off his chair, trying to shove the shot glass in his pocket, and said he needed to use the restroom. But Archibald did not want to let him out of his sight. Archibald set the major back forcibly in his chair, put a new shot in front of him and poured the shots himself. The drinking procedure was repeated. Then again. The major did not resist any more and simply poured one glass after another down his throat as soon as Archibald filled the glass. Once we reached the third bottle, elves' potion was poured into Vesnin's glass so that the major would not black out too early. Once Vesnin was sufficiently relaxed from alcohol to forget our previous conversation, Archibald started speaking for the first time since we began this thing:

"Why do you think that the killer has two faces?"

"Think?" Vesnin, who was deep in his cups, measured us with a proud stare. His idiotic glasses slid down his nose again, and seriously interfered with his "eagle" image. Drunkenly, he placed them back up, and after a pause said he condescendingly: "I don't think so! I know for sure!"

At that time the curtain from the private dance section opened on the right and a gorgeous semi-naked goddess strolled right by us. She winked at Vesnin, whose jaw dropped, and then disappeared behind the "Employees Only" door. The major looked at me sadly and said plaintively:

"Maybe we should get out of here."

Instead of an answer there was again the sound of vodka being poured. Apparently, the major had not yet reached the state the catorian needed, since he was still able to ask for mercy.

"How did you find the first crime scene?" After Archibald's unsuccessful attempt to get Vesnin to talk, I started on the task. The major's attitude towards me was generally more favorable.

"Ah, what is there to find when you know where it's gonnna happen?" Vesnin waved my question off. Now quite drunk, his control was poor and he gestured too much. "Only: hush! Not a word to your boss!"

"Really, major! We are, like, buds! For you, I'd..." I was frantically trying to recall the behavior patterns of the drunken bros in my 'burb. But probably I was still too sober to do that and not feel like an idiot.

Vesnin's grunts made us realize our main mistake. In front of Archibald this fatso would keep mum. The teacher figured that out as well, and disappeared in an instant.

"Come on, there's no boss here. He's gone. He's done in. He couldn't keep up drinking with us at this rate." I was trying to allay Vesnin' s vigilance.

He frowned, trying to understand when the boss had managed to leave, and why the major had failed to notice that.

"Oh. He's gone, alright. And I didn't notice!" Vesnin's mood noticeably improved, and he leaned closer to me. "You understand, colonel, no generals should get a whiff of a thing like that. Especially your guys. They'd just scoop one up right away! And I still want to live, and preferably live well.

"That's an excellent wish. Can you see the future?" I asked, no less secretively, also leaning towards Vesnin. He turned once more to look at Archibald's chair to make sure it was empty, and shook his head no:

"Not the future, but I see some things. Normally it all turns out true. I've never had a vision turn out a blank. Don't look at me like that! Better think how I managed to stay in the police force with a body like this! Livanov himself called me up! Eh? There! I'm trustworthy. I only got a couple o' them cold ones. An' that's when I was young an' dumb!"

"So how come you're still a major, and even that in some stinky district office?" I replied skeptically, pushing on all fronts.

"Because there are corrupt jerks everywhere! They think since you can buy and sell them, that means I have a nest of stool-pigeons in the area, too. They tell me: 'You, Vesnin, are good, but in your own place. Once we move out somewhere, all the stats will go to the dogs until you settle into the new place.' They keep promising to promote me to lieutenant colonel... Bastards! Now they can stuff that up their ass! Livanov and I, we'll show them..."

Nothing new. Glory and admiration, "life that is long and comfortable, and death that is quick and painless". Now it was clear why Vesnin was so eager to get on my good side, as well as Archibald's and Livanov's. The major was grasping at every opportunity to advance his career. If it hadn't worked out in his own institution, perhaps in ours he would be well appreciated by someone who could be of use to him.

"And so it will be. What kind of visions do you have?" After clarifying the moot points I returned to the main topic.

"I have dreams. Various ones. Mostly the crimes and those who committed them. And in the morning I remember every detail. The images come bright and clear. I see where the perps threw out their weapons, what kind of evidence they left... In Tsaritsyno I just saw the bodies. I woke up and hauled my ass there right away. And I had a vision about that coffee, too. I rarely ask my mom to make coffee, and here in the dream I saw that I needed it. Cause an important guy would come, who would like it. So I waited for you. I knew that you'd come. So that's how the dreams work, colonel."

"I got that. So when did you see the double-faced one? What did he look like? Can you recall his face?" My surprise knew no bounds, but I tried to conceal it the best I could. As if it were not enough to have an immune NPC on our hands; he turned out to be a clairvoyant!

"It was today, just before Livanov called. I didn't see his face — more like two different patches of fog. One white, one dark. They slid over each other like... damn, I can't even describe it. But I know for sure that he is the double-faced one. It's like he has two different core aspects. The dreams never lie, particularly ones like that."

"Like what?" Again I steered Vesnin towards the topic I needed.

"You locked me up at home. It was driving me up the wall. I had to ask for help.

"What help?" I perked up, but Vesnin suddenly balked.

"That's something one never talks about. Never!"

"What secrets can be between us?" I feigned a dramatic show of being offended. "What if I were in the same situation and needed help? You'd begrudge me that?"

"No, but there wouldn't be help for you. I asked my mother, you see. She knows some stuff about occult lore, even though I shouldn't say that, given our line of work. Her neighbors call her a witch behind her back, but that's really crazy. In the past people like that were called soothsayers, 'those who speak the truth'. People would come to her with their troubles, and she'd help some, and some she'd turn away, if they were planning something evil. So then she helped me too, 'cause it's no good when guys get killed."

I gave up being surprised by whatever stuff was associated with this immune one. Vesnin's mother was a witch? Whatever. So she was, then. Archibald briefly appeared behind Vesnin's back, gesturing me to continue the topic about the witch. He found that interesting, and so did I. We had looked at the major's origins. His mother definitely was not a player.

"Why do you think that your mother won't help me? Am I the wrong kind for that?"

"Something like that. One of your guys was too thin-skinned. She helps common people gladly, but not those in power. They're all rotten, she says. They are just trying to cover that up by pretending they care about the people and the state. So for that they rounded her up. They kept her in jail for three years, that's even before I was born. So, no offense, but she won't help y'all."

Archibald gestured so eloquently, suggesting that I arrange to visit the major, that it made me smirk. The teacher obviously sensed something.

"Let her tell me that herself! I can't pass up such a chance, major! Let's go see her, let her think about it. Now is not the time for petty grudges. People are being killed!" I piled all my weighty arguments on him.

"I have already asked." The major sighed. "She said no. She said it was over her head. It's useless, let's not drag my mother into this."

"That's enough, guys!" Archibald came up and slapped Vesnin cheerfully on the shoulder. "That's plenty of drinking for today: it's time to get to work! Now we shall go to our respective homes, get ourselves into decent shape and return to the trenches!. Major: you have any coffee at home?"

"Sure..." Vesnin was a little overwhelmed by this forward proposition.

"Well, excellent then! Where shall we take you? I need you chipper and sober today, and you are sitting here drinking!"

"But you..."

"What about me? I poured vodka down your throat? Don't you try to pass the blame! Get home, get yourself in shape, or else I'll report to Livanov what kind of dashing guys he has on his team. How they guzzle vodka by the bottle starting at sunrise!"

Vesnin surrendered under the barrage of unfair accusations, and told us his home address. Getting up from the chair, the major realized that he was unable to stand straight on his own. The elves' potion wore out, and the effects of the alcohol overpowered him again, making the major lose control of his mind and body. I hurried to help my drinking buddy, letting him lean on my shoulder like a wounded warrior, and left the bar. Hopefully, the search for Merlin was moving off square one.

By the time we left the smoky club it was after seven o'clock in the morning. It was a work day, and the city streets were busy with rush hour — people hurried to get to work. I really loathed the idea of negotiating the traffic crush, and so I quietly tried to lull the fat guy, hoping he'd soon fall fast asleep, and then it would be possible to transport him home via a portal. Vodka, fatigue and fresh air soon overcame the major, and he started snoring like a chainsaw. We were halfway there. Now it was Archibald's turn.

Vesnin's apartment was on the outskirts of town on the south-east side, in a bedroom community. A typical high-rise building in a typical bleak courtyard. As soon as we exited the elevator the door of the apartment we needed opened wide. A woman was standing at the threshold — not too young, but attractive; her appearance was like a Cossack from the Don region. Her cheeks were flushed red, her closed dress showcased her shapely body; her black hair was braided in a thick crown around her head. Only her stare was at odds with this lovely and enthralling picture. Her jet black eyes stared heavily and unswervingly. I shook my head to dispel the glamour. The woman did not go anywhere, but the aura of attractiveness vanished. The appearance of the woman suggested that she might have been Vesnin's older sister, but definitely not his mother.

"Come in. Put him there," the owner said, as

she stepped back into the apartment. "Let him sleep it off till the evening."

The attributes of the woman that appeared before us indicated that she was in fact Vesnin's mother, an ordinary NPC with a strange name: "Mama Marfa. Not Margaret, for example, or something equally elaborate. Just "Mama Marfa". Quite an odd name for the appearance she had selected. It was more appropriate for a much older woman. Unless that was a high quality illusion, Marfa really was a very professional witch. None other would be able to control time and its effects on a body.

"You prefer coffee, or something stronger?" Mama Marfa turned to Archibald, ignoring my humble presence. Without fussing about it I obediently unloaded Vesnin onto the bed and went to the kitchen, where Archibald had already settled as if he were at home. He gestured to me immediately to indicate that he was the one to speak with the old gal.

"I have heard you prepare the most wonderful coffee." Archibald's voice was smooth as honey. "I am quite an aficionado. If you were to show us your great kindness..."

"Oh, you are too sweet," she blushed coquettishly, and beamed a broad smile The subtle aura of attractiveness appeared again. But this time I got just a glancing blow; the spell was aimed precisely. The witch decided to show off her skills, and the catorian for some reason decided to support her in this farce.

For the next half an hour I observed the verbal dancing of two experienced mature beings. Archibald and Mama Marfa talked about everything and nothing, as if testing who would lose their cool first; then serious talk would begin. They bantered about weather, politics, real estate prices, food, tickets to the Bolshoi Theatre; they discussed the problem of illegal immigrants, and even a current pop diva and her new image for a popular fashion magazine. The old woman was the first to rush it.

"Enough of that. It's impossible to drag this out forever. What brought a high warlock into my home? I follow the law strictly and don't break the rules.

"If you had not, then you would not have been expecting guests," Archibald parried at once. "You know very well, Marfa, why I am here. Judging from your preparations you have been waiting since last night. But you miscalculated: you thought they would send someone not so high up. And for a witch like you it would be a matter of seconds to distract their attention and send their minds wandering. But it didn't work, now you have to answer according to the law.

"It didn't work then?" Mama Marfa hung her head despondently, and kind of shrank. The illusion disappeared in seconds. First her face covered with deep wrinkles, then her body kind of dried, her skin sagged. A large hump on her back made her look like Baba Yaga from the fairy tales, and practically doubled her over.

"Just tell my son that I died of a heart attack." The tired old woman was slurring her words with her half-toothless mouth. She was obviously confusing Archibald with someone else.

"You tell him yourself once you are about to die." Archibald waved her off, showing no reaction to the changes in her appearance. "We'll have a talk now and I'll decide what to do with you. Do you understand?"

"You are not from the Inquisition." Mama Marfa bunched up her bushy eyebrows as she studied the teacher closely. "They don't waste time talking, and the outcome is always the same."

"The Holy See manages splendidly without us." The catorian did not bother to argue. "Calm down, they don't have any questions for you, even after what happened yesterday. But I do."

Archibald extracted a round clay tile from his inventory and placed it on the table in front of Mama Marfa. That just about did in the poor witch: she became deathly pale under her age spots. She clutched her bony hands in a gesture of supplication, her mouth opened and closed without a sound. It looked like some kind of seizure.

"By the right of the founder I order you to answer the truth," Archibald said. Mama Marfa confirmed hoarsely:

"Go ahead and ask, First One! I acknowledge your right in everything."

"What did you do yesterday?"

"I killed an unborn child. The mother took that grave sin fully upon herself, so I am clean in the eyes of the law. She will repent that in Purgatory on her own. The mother was quite a young girl, and became with child from a guy who raped her. She asked me to remove the child before anyone could find out. That is all. In all the other matters I work according to the law."

"Did you burn the embryo properly? Did you not take any blood from it? Not a bit of heart? Not a lock of hair?"

Archibald was listing the details confidently, as if he had many times taken part in such rituals. He looked quite infuriated. Mama Marfa looked down and confessed reluctantly:

"I did... I took all of that, the blood and the heart. Even the nails. That's why I was expecting the Inquisition." "You will destroy everything you took. And you will tell me how you already used what you used. Now tell me about your son. Tell me everything."

Mama Marfa sobbed, and tears rolled down her cheeks. She would have been glad to omit some things, but no one gave her that opportunity. The catorian had bound the witch very tightly, so that she was unable to argue or disobey him.

"He was weak and sickly. When he was born, he didn't cry. I knew right away that he was not going to live–that was the punishment for my grave sins. I didn't expect to become pregnant when I was close to sixty. Until then, I had no children, God sent me none. I decided I didn't care, I'd never be a pure soul in heaven, and I couldn't afford to lose him.

"How many lives did you take?" Archibald wanted clarification.

"Fifteen hundred. I went to war for that. There's always a war here or there, so that's how I found donors. I didn't do anything untoward in Moscow. I held the ritual to ensure life and health for my son. And I have no regrets for what I did!"

"Why does he have those dreams?" The catorian was relentless.

"I make a potion for him, to help him in his work. My grandmother devised the recipe for this potion — it opens the third eye. Without that he wouldn't be able to keep his job in the police. And this way he can see assaults and murders before they even happen. He can see everything — who murdered whom, with what weapon, and how they disposed of the weapons, or where the stolen goods were hidden. This kind of help is pleasing to God!"

"Who is the two-faced one?"

"You'd know better than I, First One." The old woman lifted her gaze from her clutched hands and stared at Archibald in surprise, not having expected such a question.

"Who performs sacrifices in Moscow?" The teacher tried a different approach.

"I am telling you: that's out of my league. I would not have enough strength to see that. I can only sense when he does his evil. Everything alive can feel that pain, the animals howl, the trees fear to rustle! Even the first time my head was ringing like a bell, and the last time I was thinking of committing a grave sin just to stop hearing their pain! He just tormented the poor sufferers, damn him! A simple murderer would never do anything like that."

"By the right of the First One I release you from the obligation and free your will from my bondage. Go make me some coffee." Archibald abruptly finished the conversation, and once the old woman got busy, activated the dome of silence.

"What would you say?" he suddenly addressed me. "There are several thousand dead bodies to her name. Decide, Judge: pardon or execute.

No matter how unexpected that question was, I had already made my choice without excessive moral qualms. Internally I justified to myself whatever Mama Marfa had done back when she was still being interrogated. I could not initiate a case against her and sentence her to death, since I would have done the same thing. I would kill any number of people to preserve the life of my child. The witch was not evil — she just had her own definition of morals, which did not go against mine. Even if she were to die soon, at least it would not happen because I sentenced her.

"That's what I thought. Prudence is better than fake justice. She is an NPC, and whatever one NPC does to another does not concern players. There are no quests associated with her. Once she is caught, the inquisitors will have to sort this out themselves. If she is caught, of course."

I nodded in agreement and asked the teacher:

"The First among witches? When did you manage to do that?"

"Right after restart. The plan to replace Madonna was already active. I thought she would come back as a witch. Founded an order among NPCs, so that it would be easier to control them. But the priests interfered at an inopportune time. They didn't like the order becoming stronger. That was at a time when there were more witches among NPCs and players in this world than fleas on an alley cat. I had thought the Holy Inquisition had gotten rid of all of them at the time, but no, it seems they are hard to eradicate. Two thousand years underground. Good for them wenches! I'll need to let the witch players know about them. Maybe something good will come out of that."

Once things started heating up, you abandoned your witches and made Madonna a druid," I smirked. Archibald shrugged indifferently. "By the way, why did you choose a druid among other classes? You didn't want Gerhard to influence her?"

"Right. In addition to that druids always march to their own drummer, they are obsessed with being one with nature. They are taught concentration, self-control and the ability to be detached and meditate from the moment they appear in the Game. So that was a couple more points in their favor when I considered the struggle of minds. So the priests' interference turned out well, after all. A witch's chance for survival would have been slimmer. So, let's get back to this old one. There seems to be no reason to punish her. She knows nothing new about Merlin. Her coffee is shitty. I don't understand how you could drink this crap and praise it. Do you want me to tell you what she dumps into it?"

"Better not." Archibald's words made me remember the taste of that coffee. Now it seemed to me that slightly bitter aftertaste that I had thought piquant resembled, in fact, not the most pleasant substances. I felt slightly nauseous. If I had the choice of not knowing what lent the coffee that bitterness I would rather stay ignorant.

"So there is just one thing," Archibald took out his comm and pushed a few buttons. "Hi darling, it's disgusting as ever to hear you! Who's working with NPCs for you? I have one nice specimen here on Earth that I wanted to give to you to reform her."

"What is your decision, First One?" Archibald finished his conversation and removed the Dome of Silence. Mama Marfa dared to bother him then. She had not tried to escape, nor to poison us. At least my Daro set did not find any strange or unknown ingredients in the coffee that she had prepared. The old woman was humbly waiting for her fate to be sealed by the head of her order.

"Your power is dangerous," the catorian responded. "It is not great, but it is well beyond rituals on cats. You know that yourself and you must understand why I cannot let you stay here...." The old woman lowered her head despondently, but the catorian did not stretch the pause for too long, and finished his thought: "You will now spend some time among the sisters. They will take care of you and teach you a lot of things appropriate for your level of power. Do not worry about your son; you will be allowed to visit him from time to time. Tomorrow you will go to Zurich. You will be met there. Any questions?"

Mama Marfa stalled, trying to figure out what to think about the sentence voiced by the catorian. Of course, she would be more pleased to stay till her final decline next to her son. She would tell fortunes for the local girls using dead cats, about when they hope to get married, or cure the clap for men and women who screwed around. But on the other hand there was not the slightest reason to be unhappy with the decision of the First One. Effectively that was not a punishment but a dramatic change in her life. Very few get such a chance in their later years. Mama Marfa nodded, and thanked the Head of the Order sincerely for the honor bestowed on her.

"Excellent. After you finish your training..."

Mama Marfa did not find out what was going to happen afterwards because the door to the apartment slammed and we heard a woman's voice:

"Mama! Would you babysit Dima today? I have been called to work!"

A young woman's head appeared in the hallway that led to the kitchen. She was followed by a kid of eight or nine. His mother gently pushed him towards us.

"Sorry, you have visitors? I apologize that I didn't call first."

"They are my son's colleagues." The old woman found a clever explanation, and the visitor's look sparkled with interest. The woman looked about ten years younger than Vesnin, but addressed the old woman quite reverently. Apparently she was the major's wife. The guy was no dummy — even though he was quite a fatso, he somehow got himself a very pretty wife... Or else his mother chose very carefully. That would be quite like her! So that meant we were seeing Vesnin Junior ... Wow!

"We are already leaving." I was barely aware of Archibald's voice. "Yaropolk! We are leaving!"

I radically disagreed with Archibald. The last thing we needed was to leave, but I was unable to explain that as I was staring at the system message:

You have discovered the author of the Explorer's drawing

"Do stay," Vesnin's wife protested. "No need to run. Dima will stay out of your way. Mama, will you look after him?"

"Sure I will, dear. But I will be leaving tomorrow. Your hubby got me a voucher to travel to a resort through his work. So after that you'll have to be on your own." The old woman quickly came up with an explanation for her impending departure.

"Oh, that's so good! Don't worry; I will take him in the evening. Oh, is he here then?"

"He's sleeping after a night shift; don't bother him." There was a hint of steel in the old woman's voice and for a moment the eyes of her daughter in law glazed over. Mama Marfa did not hesitate to cast her spells right under the nose of the First One, trying to get the woman to leave as soon as possible.

"Gue-e-ests!" The kid drawled suddenly and lifted his head. My back turned cold, as if I were watching a horror movie. The boy stared unblinkingly at the floor and kept pulling at his sleeve incessantly. There was something wrong with him. Ever since he came in he had never looked at us. Absence of common curiosity in a child was definitely not normal.

The entry door banged as the woman finally

left; that scared Dima. His whole body jerked, and he hugged himself, still looking down. We heard a ragged sigh.

"Come on bunny, I will give you the chess set. Set them out, and I will come in a few minutes," Mama Marfa started to fuss, but I grabbed her by the arm, not allowing her to take my "luck" away from right under my nose.

"Archibald, it's him!" I nodded at the boy. "He's the one that drew the map!"

"The Explorer's quest?" The teacher understood me at once, and asked Mama Marfa, who was afraid for her grandson, to stay where she was. She was obviously worried, but settled on a stool obediently.

"Do you believe in random coincidences?"

"Do I look like an idiot?" I heard a trace of indignation in Archibald's voice.

"It seems that we are in luck. Dima, did you draw that?"

I extracted the sheet of paper that I had received back in Zurich, and put it in front of the boy so that he would stare at it instead of the floor. The kid reacted to this invasion of his personal space by rocking intensely from side to side and humming loudly. 'Damn, it seems he is sick!' — it finally dawned on me.

"What is in this drawing?" Not willing to give up I raised my voice a little, but then Mama Marfa came to his aid:

"Don't. He understands you; he just can't answer. He's autistic."

"Gue-e-ests," the boy said slowly again, still

rocking. "Pe-e-ople..."

"Give me this thing." Mama Marfa carefully took the sheet carefully. "Yes, that's Dima's scribbles. A couple of years ago he would produce them every day, It's as though he was obsessed, he'd just draw them non-stop. Where did you get it?"

"Doesn't matter. Are there other drawings?"

"No. I burnt them all. I am no dummy, really. Don't get mad, I just want a quiet life for my grandson. But apparently it's impossible to cheat fate, since I missed this one. Have pity on the kid — don't take his childhood away from him. Even though he is special, he is loved. I'll tell you myself whatever you need. Those drawings that I burnt, they were not like this. This one is kind of, like, incomplete."

Mama Marfa turned the sheet this way and that, but to no avail. She only remembered that she had decided to burn them because all Dima's maps had dead people on them. I was getting desperate when Archibald interfered:

"Has he been like that since birth?"

"Yes, it's my fault," Mama Marfa said repentantly. "I interfered too much with his father; now the baby is paying for it. I wanted to cheat fate, so that I would not be the last of my line, but I only postponed the inevitable.

"Cut down on the fatalism," the teacher grimaced. "In the end everyone will die. How is he with animals?

"He likes them." Mama Marfa thought for a while. "We used to have a cat a while ago. Dima would often play with it. More's the pity it didn't live long.

Dima saw a program on TV about space, and I was doing some laundry... and he stuck the poor beast into the washer. He was trying to train it to be a cosmonaut, that is... we ended up having to throw the washer away just like that, with the cat and all..."

"Fine. Get out of here. I need to talk to your grandson one to one. Don't worry, I won't harm him. I will try to help."

"Sure, sure." Mama Marfa caught on and disappeared out of the kitchen, I rose to my feet as well, but Archibald stopped me:

"Where do you think you're going? I'll make an exception for you, fine. Sit and watch. Just keep quiet."

I gladly plopped back onto the stool and prepared to watch. Archibald activated the protective dome in the room, so that Mama Marfa would not be able to come back or peep. Then he went down on all fours.

"Purr, meow!" said the catorian and smoothly glided over towards the boy. The kid stopped rocking, and some interest reflected in his face. It was fleeting, but still enough for Archibald to hang on to the trace of emotions. The catorian started purring loudly, rubbed affectionately on the boy's legs and tickled his pale cheek. Dima smiled absently and squatted, spreading his legs awkwardly. His skinny hand stretched towards my teacher's ears.

"Purr." Archibald would not let the boy touch his ears and quickly rolled over on his back. The boy readily moved his hand to the cat's belly, covered with steel armor. With a contented smile he petted the cold metal, thinking that his hands were touching long thick fur.

"You gre-ew." Dima said suddenly. "Space good."

"Space good," the catorian reassured him. "Silent there, and no people.

"Good. I want no people. So many everyone. I like silence."

"To have silence you have to work. You want?"

"I want. You make silence for me?" For the first time the kid lifted his eyes from the floor and concentrated on Archibald.

"Yes. You will have silence. No one will bother you until you want it yourself.

"Good. Your silence is not death? I won't die?" the boy asked suddenly.

"No." Archibald stopped pretending he was a cat and squatted next to the boy. "Death is nothing. There is nothing there, not even silence."

The boy nodded seriously, indicating that he understood and was pleased with what he heard. At that moment his eyes were normal and conscious.

"I cannot die. Mom and dad will be sad. I don't want to upset them."

An amazing statement from an eight-year-old. It was not that he "didn't want" to die, it was that he "could not" die, and he was worried about his parents' feelings. An amazing kid. There is so much in the world that we cannot understand and therefore label as inferior. Even though it is quite possible that it is the opposite. We are all freaks here. This kid was the way nature had intended. He was self-sufficient. We simply got in his way with our expectations and demands. Wonderful!

"I will give you your own world full of peace and silence. You will be able to stay there as long as you want, and come back to your parents sometimes so that they will not be upset. But for this you will have to do some work."

"Own world. I want. You kind. What I have to do?"

"Do you remember this drawing?" Archibald took the sheet and presented it to Dima.

"No. Not a drawing. Map." Dima fell silent, waiting for the next question.

"Fine. A map; but it is incomplete. Finish this, and you will have the present.

"Pencil." The boy knelt, put the drawing on the floor and stretched out his hand demandingly. This time Archibald's vast inventory failed him: the catorian had no writing implements. Steve scanned the area and highlighted a shelf. In a holder I found a short lead pencil there.

Dima started rocking again, repeating words and phrases anxiously, and sometimes shouting loudly:

"Stole! They stole the map! Look, space! Everything is wrong. Too simple. Everything became simple. Bad map. Won't give me a present, because it's empty. I need to correct! Correct!"

His hand holding the pencil fluttered back and forth, leaving thick lines. He was trying his best to do it well and earn his gift. After a couple of minutes his child's scribbles had turned into quite a decent map.

With the new details its meaning changed. The treasure was a chest on which Dima carefully wrote an "M". I had no doubt that it was Merlin's Diary. He marked another important detail: the initial starting point for the search. It resembled a starting field in board games:

"This is the starting point. You need to find the entrance, or else it won't work."

Four human bodies in a strange but familiar position served as the entrance landmark. Dima worked on that part especially thoroughly, drawing details with great precision. I didn't even need Steve's help as he created the projection of the site of the first sacrifice. I remembered where I had seen all of that already. To make it crystal clear Dima drew a tree and a crown next to it. That undoubtedly indicated the Tsaritsyno Park.

"This is all." The kid extended the finished drawing to Archibald. "Map is complete. You can search. I want silence. Your promise."

"You are great. I will give you silence." The catorian was not going back on his words, and picked up his comm again. "It's me again. Quit your screaming; my ears are not your property! Yes, she is flying into Zurich tomorrow. Yes, you will need to send someone there. No, I cannot send her from here via a portal. What do you mean, why I am calling again? No, no more witches. I remember that you aren't working anymore. Do you need a prophet?"

Judging by the grin that spread on my teacher's face, his interlocutor had stopped swearing.

"From Earth. A boy, eight years old. Two years

at least, and then — who knows. Yes, he really is a prophet. He is autistic. Enough! One more question and I will call the priests! There! That's better. Here are the coordinates — I will be expecting you immediately. I don't care if you are busy! You have one minute! Over!"

Archibald turned off his comm and looked for someone on whom to vent his irritation. He could not yell at the boy, Mama Marfa was not around, so I was the only one habitually fitting the role of punching bag. As soon as the teacher opened his mouth to launch into an irritated tirade, Dima rose from the floor and stood between us:

"Don't be friends with him. Bad!"

"Who is bad?" Archibald calmed down at once, and his attention switched to the boy.

"Him." Dima pointed at me. "Bad! Now good but will become bad. They will look for him. To punish. Don't be near. Could punish you too. Take you from space."

I was taken aback by such prospects. I wondered if prophets make mistakes? Or did the catorian? I would be happy with either option. Otherwise my number of days in the Game would tend towards zero, with everyone going after me. In other words, I would not be able to leave my respawn point. I would end up stuck in Avalon till the end of time. Or until Archibald finished me off or turned me into another exhibit in his personal ice figure museum.

"Treasure will make him bad!" Dima insistently tried to persuade the catorian to have nothing to do with me. "He will find it. With this map. But not at once. First he will open the entrance. And let out evil. Everyone will look for him. Is this my silence?"

The boy instantly forgot about me as soon as he saw the blue glimmer of the teleport opening. Archibald, just in case, pulled his sword out and stood at the ready. A second passed, then another and a third, but no one was in a hurry to step out.

"You are losing your grip, long-tailed one!" A pleasant female voice came from the door, and its mysterious owner glided into the light. Her face and head were covered with a male kaffiyeh.

"Look to the right," Archibald said sarcastically, quickly sheathing the sword, as he did not need it.

The lady took his advice and tsked: a silver arrow was vibrating less than half an inch from her head, as if impatient to pierce her skull and splatter her brains. The arrow vanished in the air as fast as it had appeared. That last trick was intended for the guest: by a slight vibration of the air Steve determined that the dangerous object was in the same location. Archibald obviously did not trust our guest.

"I agree, we all make mistakes; sometimes even grown monkeys fall out of trees." The witch — and the lady who appeared belonged to that class — did not look embarrassed. Nodding at the boy she inquired: "Is he your gift to me?"

"Poor one." The boy moved close to Archibald and took his hand, staring at the floor again. "Why did you chase her out of space? She is offended. You hit her."

There were simultaneous exclamations from

both sides "I did not hit her!" and "I left on my own!" Now that was an interesting turn of events!

"He's a funny... kid. Capable. Sees through to the crux of things." The guest frowned, displeased with the boy's comment. Dima had obviously touched on a topic that was not much to her liking.

"He just sees reality in his own way," Archibald remarked, annoyed by the recent accusations.

"Quit your hair-splitting. If you are trying to justify yourself, I will admit that no, you did not physically hit me!" The witch brushed him aside and ran out to the adjacent room, to evaluate Mama Marfa.

"I'll take Marfa as well," the lady stated with satisfaction, and then asked: "What do you want in exchange?"

"You know my rates." Archibald shrugged. "But since there were two in the case, there will be two on my side as well. Cleanse my student too. He hung out around Gromana recently."

"Eww! You should watch your menagerie more tightly, and the company they keep, Archie!" The witch grimaced at the mention of Gromana. "The cleansing procedure will take a while. I am not going to hang out on Earth so long."

"Avalon?"

"Sure, that's fine with me. I hope you didn't touch my room there?"

"So far I have lifted seven seals," Archibald confessed easily. "I am working on the next one, but they keep distracting me all the time."

"No problem — I will update everything. You

will have something to play with for the next thirty thousand years..." The witch pulled out her comm. "All clear. Come and take both; start working on access to Altair right away. Special control for the boy."

Finally, some guests emerged from the portal. Two scrawny creatures, wrapped in black robes from head to toe, took Dima and Mama Marfa, who was in a trance, into the portal. The portal vanished and the witch deigned to look at me, just about for the first time.

"Guide. Explorer. Judge. Paladin. Why do you need him?" The witch looked at the catorian in surprise. "Nata fit really well with your teaching concept, but this... I don't even know what to say..."

I was in shock — the witch just gutted my mind without any problems or restraints, treading over the most private corners of my personality. The feeling of someone's sticky hand rummaging through your head was truly nauseating. I was disoriented for a couple of seconds, unable to gather my thoughts that were scattered throughout my brain as if by hurricane Andrew. And it stung all the more that even after such a deep scan she found nothing to interest her.

"Dear Clarissa, in general you are a very smart witch, but on occasion you can be as stupid as a lump on a log," Archibald drawled with pleasure. He was obviously flattered that the witch failed to see what he saw. By the way, this question bothered me quite a bit — what was it? Steve started a keyword search for "Clarissa, witch" in the database of players that we had received from the Temple of Knowledge, and just one heartbeat later he turned into a bloodhound on a hot trail. Witch Clarissa was a creature from the first era; apparently she lived on a private planet in the vicinity of the Altair Game world.

"What's going on with him?" Clarissa frowned, seeing astonishment in my face."

"He just found out when you were born." The teacher properly interpreted my behavior. "After all, I don't call you an old hag for nothing."

"So he is worth the time you are spending on him? I want to know the reason. What do you want for that?" The witch did not bother to play a blushing innocent, and immediately started bargaining. But for some reason with Archibald rather than me.

"Let's first deal with the curses, and then with the rest. I hope you haven't forgotten how to open a portal to Avalon?"

"It was my home for thirty thousand years, 'darling'." The witch stressed the last word, loading it with sarcasm. "One can never forget that. And quit calling me 'darling'. It made me immediately want to check to make sure I didn't have fleas."

"That was rude, 'darling'. You drank so much of my blood over those thirty thousand years that at this point we might as well be considered blood relatives." Those two were in tune and enjoying this process.

"So can I hope for an inheritance?" I could see the witch's broad smile even through her shawl.

"Hope — yes, get one — no," was the catorian's reply.

The witch waved her hand, opening the

passage to Archibald's home, and I was thinking about what I had just heard. Only a strong woman would be able to tolerate the catorian close to her for thirty thousand years. A very strong one, OR one in love. In view of these new facts, I was looking at the witch's back with something like sympathy. The catorian added his power to the already created portal, giving permission to visit Avalon.

"Wait here — I'll be quick." Clarissa instructed us as if she owned the place, as she took the elevators to dash off to her room. We remained standing in silence; it would have been silly to expect from Archibald any comments or clarifications regarding his personal life.

"There are three curses on you. Two from Gromana and one from Soluna," Clarissa concluded, having looked at Archibald through a red crystal. "There are thirteen on your student. All from Gromana."

"What are they intended for?" Archibald grimaced after hearing the unpleasant conclusion. Only witches were capable of working with curses, but the catorian was unhappy with himself: he had been unable to get rid of this nasty thing on his own.

"Your student has the standard set, for undermining his luck. Basically, he would be unable to eat a sandwich without choking. Yours are more elaborate. I see the overall idea, but it will take me some time to unravel the whole bundle. Are you ready?"

While Clarissa worked, smoking Archibald and me with yellow acrid smoke, I realized that I knew what Dima had been talking about. I knew why I would become bad and everyone would hunt me. And this knowledge was not making me one bit happier.

CHAPTER SIX

DAY FIVE

FTER THE CLEANSING I woke up the next morning in bed, wrapped in a throw up to my ears. Next to the bed on the chair I saw a cup of coffee and a light breakfast, which I finished off immediately. No surprise there: the last time I had eaten was at home in Moscow almost twenty-four hours ago. Even if this care did not come from Archibald personally, it was still nice to realize that someone had thought about me. At least a couple of robots from his numerous metal army. My teacher wanted Avalon to become a hospitable refuge for me. A smile appeared on my lips, stretching muscles that were falling into disuse from lack of joy in my days. When you don't expect anything good from other beings, even a modicum of care is perceived as something extraordinary and touches your soul. Then, recalling my mother, I realized that customary care was frequently devalued and treated as a matter of course.

I sighed, thinking the breakfast could have been more plentiful, and asked Steve why he had been hovering in front of my eyes ever since I had awakened.

"What do you want?"

"While the noble one was sleeping and taking his breakfast, his humble serf bent his backs to advance his owner's well-being," So, I am starting to talk back to myself? What is this world coming to... I have a subconscious that is easily offended?

"I was wrong. I will try to correct my ways, oh my provider," I played along with Steve. "Did you find anything interesting?"

"I have made a video for you. It's quite curious. The visuals are not that great, but the sound makes up for it."

Steve set the video to play without bothering to verify whether I wanted to see it right that minute. As he warned, the picture was only so-so: it showed the ceiling of the office where Clarissa was working on removing the curses. I didn't need to watch it, just to listen:

"Don't get underfoot! I nearly sent him for respawn now!" I could hear the witch breathing loudly right next to me.

"No problem. If you do, he'll respawn here in an hour and you'll continue." I heard my teacher's voice nearby."

"Oh really? You tied him to Avalon?!" The witch's voice rose. After a pause, in a voice that was calm again, she added: "Who is he, Archibald? And why did you call me?"

"Did I not call you in order to give you the witch and the prophet?" Archibald answered with a question.

"Drop it, you could have brought the witch to the Sanctuary on your own, and taken the prophet for yourself. For an NPC like this they might have even returned your class to you."

"They might have," the catorian agreed. "But then I would not have a excuse to see you. Maybe I was missing you."

"That's a good joke." Clarissa laughed heartily in response. "Don't, Archibald. Don't make it worse than it is."

"Sorry," the catorian responded, and I nearly choked, hearing this simple word from his lips. It sounded sincere and without sarcasm. "I had a serious reason for which I wanted to see you. I didn't want to speak of it via the comm. Restart is coming. Paladins will be the leads in the coming era."

"That's it? I had started to think it was something important." Clarissa snorted in disbelief. "You have any problems arranging for my transition? Normally you don't warn me. I simply receive a notification that I am on the list."

"Not this time, Clarissa," the teacher responded. "Talk to Gerhard yourself. I am sure you will find a way to buy a spot for yourself."

"You have problems with Gerhard?" Concern slipped into the witch's voice.

"I would rather not speak about it now." Archibald stopped her.

"Because of him? He's totally out — don't tell me you have forgotten how to read auras."

"I can see very well what condition he is in. But I also know what he is and what he is capable of."

"Then share this information with me. You drag him along everywhere; you have tied him to Avalon; you didn't kill him when the kid revealed our relationship, and he knows that I am from the first era. Maybe he even knows who you are?" The witch insisted.

"That honor I only granted to you, sweetie. Value that and keep mum." Despite his facetious tone there was menace in the teacher's voice. "Knowing too much will bring wrinkles even to the face of an experienced witch. You don't need that. Let's have some fun instead, like in the good old days."

"Go to hell. It would be better to not survive the restart than to be with you again..."

The recording stopped. Apparently, Archibald intentionally provoked Clarissa. So what could he have possibly done that she still could not forgive him? The little prophet caught it right on: the witch was still feeling hurt. And still loved him. This was obvious even without Dima's abilities. I wondered if I were to ask Archibald: would he ignore me or send me for respawn? Maybe I should try my luck with Clarissa and offer her a trade. She wanted to know who I was; I wanted to know what had happened between her and Archibald.

"You are thinking about the wrong thing," Steve interfered. *"You were told point blank and clearly that Archibald is not who he pretends to be. You have no idea with whom you have tangled."*

My subconscious was correct: I had in fact been moving down the wrong path. I needed to get Archibald into a corner and find out who he was and what tied him to Gerhard. But I would have to work out the script really well and take into account the nuances... A ring of my comm cut short the gallop of my thoughts. I looked at the screen and cursed: it was the Judge Supervisor. Yesterday I had not sent him the daily report, so he was going to scream now. I was right.

"Where is the report?" I heard a threatening shout instead of a greeting.

Actually, it was easy being a prophet if one were to use his brain and the deductive method. So, it was six in the morning, and the Supervisor was not only up and running, but also extremely mad, the way only really sleep-deprived people were. The telepathic abilities I suddenly discovered in myself suggested that the reason the Supervisor did not get enough sleep was another sacrifice. Merlin had had some fun again and the number of items they had found would be thirty-two victims this time. Damn, I was counting people as items. Great.

"Where was it this time?" My dealings with Archibald had taught me that it was not worth bending over for each displeased prick with a modicum of power and I should rather set my own tone for the conversation. If there was no report, it was that way on purpose.

"Are you crazy? I am asking you where is the report?!" The Supervisor was one of those people who considered that absence of the result was due to insufficient volume rather than the unwillingness of their interlocutor to answer. I did not want to talk to a player who was obviously not himself, so I simply hung up and after that would not take incoming calls. After the third call he gave up. It was a pity that cell phones did not work in Avalon; I could use a call to Vesnin. I would have to jump with Archibald — first home, and then to the crime scene.

My teacher did not pick up when I called his comm. I was hoping that he was in fact in Avalon, rather than doing his murky deeds hell knew where. I jumped out of bed cheerfully in order to find Archibald as soon as I could.

My room had four identical doors. Steve stated that he had no idea where they led, because we were brought into the room by a local elevator; however, I had never been told how to call one. I shrugged, and like any common mortal, opened the door that first came to hand and called out into the dark corridor. An echo answered me. Not used to lengthy contemplation, I started down the hallway. After ten yards or so I came up to another fork in the road. This time I had to choose one of five doors. The situation was becoming amusing. The left door took me to another room where Archibald, obviously playing a mad architect, had installed six doors. I chose the third one from the right.

"This completes the proof." I was greeted by my teacher's sarcastic voice. "Great, Clarissa, you did an excellent job."

The catorian and a hologram of Clarissa were sitting at a huge virtual desk with figures remotely resembling chess pieces. The witch had already left Avalon, but agreed to keep Archibald company until the completion of their experiment.

"So you doubted my work?" the woman grumbled, looking at the pieces on her board with some displeasure.

"No. But you doubted my student." The catorian waited for the witch to make her move and immediately took her piece off the field. "You lose. You remember the terms?"

"I do, but I would like to point out that I lost the bet and lost just one piece. The game is not over yet." I was completely lost in this exchange, without any idea what they were talking about.

"This is not for long, dear," Archibald purred. "You may start working on fulfilling your obligations on the bet you lost. Get some training before you lose the entire game."

Clarissa deigned to pay attention to my presence:

"A Judge has the ability to purge himself from all the burdensome influences, both physical and mental. Including curses. So-called "Purification": it is available directly before sentencing. In order to use that option it is enough to call on the Game requesting it to purge you from any influences in order to decree a just and objective sentence. It's shameful, young man, not to know the basics of your specialty!"

I felt embarrassed for being scolded like a kid, even if it was for good reason.

"Play and learn," Archibald seconded the witch as if he had nothing to do with me. "You disappointed me. I had thought that my student had grown older and wiser, and you don't know about such an elementary thing as mental freedom before decreeing a sentence. Or else you don't want to know and you actually enjoy being spied upon at all times. Sort of like twisted exhibitionism."

"What do you do: like teacher, like student," I replied, hurt. "I play to the extent you have taught me. I blunder along and suffer, being hurt at every turn instead of strolling through life like a king."

Clarissa smiled at my attempt to push Archibald:

"Boys, I am going to wish you have a good time, but without my further presence."

"Wait: you must complete the game." Archibald protested. "You wanted so badly to find out who he was.

"Archie, the bet is done. I lost and I paid my debt. And as for the game in general... I don't recall promising to finish it within a predetermined timeframe. See, dear, I am not giving up my interest. It's just right now it's not a priority for me. We'll finish the game some time later... after the restart." The hologram vanished, leaving Archibald empty-handed.

"The Supervisor called. There was another crime. Thirty-two bodies." I thought this was an opportune moment to let Archibald know about the incident.

"Good," Archibald nodded, even though I did not quite understand what was so good about it.

"May I find out what was the bet about?" I could not but ask this question while my teacher removed the desk by a wave of his arm.

"Nothing much," Archibald grumbled. "Just checking Clarissa's work and your luck. I bet that if she removed everything you would still reach us safe and sound.

"What do you mean by safe and sound?" I was taken aback by this turn of events.

"I mean that you were stupid enough to drink the coffee and eat the food without bothering to check them for poisons and lucky enough to get the sequence of eating right and not kick the bucket."

All I was able to do in response was to curse mightily and with feeling, recalling Sintsov's vast vocabulary.

"So be happy that your luck is with you. Otherwise your death would have been painful. Clarissa worked well. And the fact that you picked the right doors is a hopeful sign as well." Gromana had dropped my luck to zero, hoping to make my life hell. The witch did not consider, or simply did not know that I already had level two Luck, which counteracted her curses, partially or completely. So that means Archibald had decided to check my luck, using this highly elaborate way that was so much in line with his twisted imagination. It really had been with me, enabling me to avoid a painful death and respawn.

"Wrong doors would have been painful and deadly as well?" I asked, now without enthusiasm.

"Right. One mistake — one painful respawn." The teacher explained like it did not matter, and opened a portal to Earth.

Archibald at that point did not know the precise location of the crime, and neither did I. So we disembarked next to my apartment. Two semi-transparent shadows flew up to Archibald and reported that there had been no attempts to break into the apartment over the last 24 hours. Bernard had fastidiously followed the agreements making Lumpen leave Archibald and me alone.

The catorian ordered them to keep up their guard duties, and the shadows disappeared. I felt guilty. I should have been the one to care about my Doll, not my teacher. I seemed to be getting completely confused, noticing sometimes positive and sometimes negative features in the catorian's character. That was complex: as with me, this being was either good nor bad.

"What's up?" Archibald asked once my cell phone found the network, which was just about bursting with incoming voicemails. There were twelve from an unknown number, twenty-two from Vesnin, and also one text message from him:

"Gorky Park. I have video!"

We didn't bother to go into the apartment, and hurried right away to one of Moscow's landmark parks. The Game immediately generated a projection of our arrival in all its glory with blinkers, sirens and police escort. Vesnin welcomed us himself. He nodded as we greeted him, took out a tablet and offered it to Archibald. Apparently the video had gone viral on all the mass media channels. The recording was shown on the front page of the leading news portal.

The video had been taken from the air using a new device popular among NPCs: a drone. The camera made daring and dangerous turns among the trees, sometimes running into things. This suggested that the pilot was a novice rather than an experienced user. As it soared one more time, for a fraction of a second it captured the clearing with a multitude of bodies. Then the video went black. The staff of the news channel singled out the frame, which made it possible to see in detail the thirty two bodies and a creature in a dark robe. His eyes were glowing red from a huge deep hood, but it was completely impossible to tell the player's class. At the time when the picture was taken the player pointed his arm at the camera. Perhaps that was why it had been damaged and stopped recording. But in any case, there were no extraneous objects in the field of view before it stopped working. Then the broadcast was expanded by the opinions of the local experts and some such. Archibald stopped the video and handed the tablet back to Vesnin.

"Have you found out who took the video?" Archibald asked.

"No. The video was sent to the publishing house from an anonymous account. It was registered two minutes prior to the sending of the video via torrents and anonymizers and removed immediately afterwards. The guys are still attempting to trace it.

They tried to check it out through the drone registration database. These machines are subject to registration. Nothing there either. Our experts are saying that the operator was learning how to operate both the camera and the drone as he was filming. It's possible that some local piss-ant show-off was learning and accidentally flew it into the crime scene. The video was uploading directly to the server, that's why it stayed available. There was no debris found from the drone."

Vesnin suggested we continue the conversation as we walked towards the crime scene:

"I think it's a real video, not a staged one. All details from the location and the dead bodies match. It seems that could be your maniac. The general sent the video to the facial guys' department for processing. Perhaps we might get his features."

I experienced sincere sympathy towards the IT specialists who had been ordered to improve the quality of the image in the way that brooked no argument. We approached the seal and Vesnin left: one of the police meat wagon drivers felt sick and his colleagues needed some help to remove a guy built like a bear from the forbidden zone. Vesnin, since he was built pretty much the same as the unfortunate driver, was acting as the towing vessel, saving the hapless worker.

"Are you going to show off your brilliant intellect or do you need help?"

"It's a trap," I stated categorically. "Merlin decided to have some fun. He wants to confuse us by showing us a vampire."

"And here's an excellent explanation for the immune one's visions. A two-faced creature with red eyes. You have to agree: a vampire would be a perfect match. Two transformations, two faces."

"Vampires have a lot more transformations." I showed off the knowledge I had acquired, receiving a nod of approval from the teacher. "The main point is that NPCs cannot record the activities of players. The Game will not allow that. Therefore, the operator was a player. Merlin, as far as I understand, is too careful and foresightful to get into a random recording. So that means that he is not only the main producer of this video, but also the director. But why was that done?"

"So that the Supervisor would have a plausible excuse to kick you in the ass for failing a simple task," Archibald stated gravely without a hint of sarcasm.

"Well, this morning he really was screaming fit to burst the speaker," I confirmed.

"That's exactly what I am talking about as well. Madonna is not his boss any more; he is under the protection of the Emperor. I could bet that video is much longer than what we have seen. We have gotten too close to Merlin. Check your task list. I'm sure you're in for a surprise."

Steve showed me the list, and it confirmed my teacher's words. The quest of finding the maniac had been removed a few minutes before I woke up in Avalon, that's why I hadn't seen the system message. The Supervisor's call had been nothing more than a desire to personally show an upstart his place. The petty revenge of a mighty elf on Madonna's "protégé".

"You cannot yet see the cases initiated against you, but the first Judge you run into will sentence you to respawn. A double or triple one."

Archibald knew how to make you feel "positive". While Vesnin helped with loading the bodies onto the transport, I was thinking about my life. I was glad there was no need to call up the demonologist and the necromancer. I was tired of those pointless rituals. I wanted to see the full version of the video, but calling the Supervisor with a question like that would be beyond stupid. Only to needle the elven bastard, in case he had already calmed down. In effect, all that was left was to live through those five days, show up in front of Madonna or Gerhard and humbly wait for the decision from the great ones. Damn, I didn't want to die. The thought that I had better be honest with myself floated to the surface of my mind right in time. I had made the decision a while ago that I was prepared to face the fate foretold to me by Dima. If the alternative to death was to become a serial killer... why was I any worse than Merlin?"

"So what's your conclusion?" Archibald was reading my mood like an open book, but I had no time to answer. A huffing Vesnin literally ran right up to us:

"Quick! Flee!" He wheezed, huffing from a shortness of breath. This sprint of a hundred yards had not been easy at all for the fat guy. "Livanov called: the upper management have called in an order to arrest you. Your own people have betrayed you and in addition blamed all they could on you. They took me off the case again. Cops from headquarters are on their way here. Go! I will cover you."

Archibald nodded, and hastened to leave the crime scene. I was following on his heels. After we were behind some trees, the catorian activated a portal to Avalon. I had barely caught my breath when a bright flash flooded the arrival hall with light. The helmet compensated for the brightness. That enabled me to see the frozen player. An uninvited guest jumped into the portal after us and was caught in Avalon's protection system. It was Darlangir, a furry brown creature that looked like a pillow; the same one that had had the misfortune of chasing Archibald before.

"Life does not teach morons anything," Archibald sighed looking at his hapless pursuer. "Why did you have to press your luck, Darlangir? There was a reason I spared you the last time. But no: you keep pushing as if you were immortal. Determination is a good quality, Darlangir, but not when we are talking about attempts to get to me! Now, where will I find such a cute enemy again?"

I realized why Archibald had put up a set of checkpoints before we dragged Garlion into his castle. In order to let head hunters have a chance to stay in the Game. Had he jumped to Avalon directly, the local security system would have easily caught all those who came without invitation. While this way almost all the followers were lost somewhere along the way. To their own benefit, too. Now I understood the history of the appearance of the ice sculptures of mysterious Avalon. The catorian stopped at nothing to conceal the location of his castle, and the most insistent visitors received the right to stay there forever. Darlangir's fate was sealed once he risked jumping in after us.

I was right. The already familiar robotic arm came down from above, picked up immobilized Darlangir and doused him with liquid nitrogen right there in the air. After that the local elevator sent the furry pillow into the deep bowels of the castle. The Game had lost yet another head hunter.

"We stopped with you having some sort of an epiphany," Archibald returned to me. He looked crestfallen.

"You knew what needed to be done to advance, but you didn't tell me." Archibald didn't bother denying the accusations, so I continued: "'Only the one who follows the entire path.' That's number one. The kid prophet foretold that I would become bad. That's number two. You were not going to tell me. You waited till I figured it all out on my own. In order to find Merlin and his Diary I have to make the same sacrifices. Follow Merlin's entire path. Right?"

"And this is coming from the Judge who executed a prostitute for just offering her services." Archibald sighed, trying to needle me. All I could do in response was shrug confirming that this indeed was a fact of my life. But now the circumstances were different.

"You got the gist of it. I realized that back on the mountain, but did not want to force you. All in its own time." The frivolity of tone had disappeared, revealing to me a serious and concentrated teacher. "I warned you from the outset — I do not have the ability to drink souls, so it would be impossible to pretend there was a Higher Demon. The Game community will figure out who was behind murdering the NPCs. You should get ready to be hunted in earnest. The Game will do everything to destroy you. Do you realize the scale of the consequences?"

"I do now. But I see no alternative. I just cannot sit quietly and happily through the remaining five days and just die at the hands of Gerhard or Madonna." I stated out loud what I had been thinking about for the last half a day. "The most important thing is to select the victims correctly. Maybe the Game will not consider the sacrifices to be murders."

"Yes, your specialty can help us gain some time," Archibald said in support of my line of thinking.

"We need to find NPC criminals. So that the Game would not have any doubt at all of their guilt, then there will not be any idle questions for us. The method of execution is determined by the Judge. Can you help with the first four?"

"I have a couple in mind," my teacher said mysteriously. "I was saving them for myself, but for the sake of the initiation of my favorite student as the greatest villain of this era I am willing to contribute them. Here: hold the files... and hold on to your self-restraint. Or else my collection won't live long enough to make it to the sacrifice, and all because of your love of humanity."

This last warning was justified. Ten seconds after learning about the depravities of the first candidate my hands itched to stuff his tongue and teeth into his own throat. He was a cannibal who exclusively ate little children, no older than six. The file contained the list of his victims and a description of recipes that he had developed individually for each child.

I shuddered. During the time that I had spent in the Game I had seen a lot, but the things that NPCs inflicted on their own kind was just beyond my comprehension. The main question was why the Game would allow such atrocities? Why did some beings torture other beings simply to satisfy their depraved instincts? Murder for the sake of murder: what could be more atrocious? My desire to find the only remaining Creator grew to an unprecedented level. To find him, look him in the eye and ask about the main concept of the Game. And only then drive the spikes of my artifact into his eyes and repeat this procedure until his last respawn. Because someone who decided that things like that have a right to exist does not have a right to live!

"There are only three here," I finished perusing the files Archibald handed to me. The teacher responded by suggesting that I look for another candidate myself.

"I will need a portal to Tsaritsyno Park. To look around and find the fourth sacrifice," I was thinking — where would I find a proper candidate at high noon?

"Go without me; I will catch up with you in ten minutes," my teacher warned me as he opened the way. "By then the problem must be solved."

My teacher was right: this was not the time to be sentimental any more. The portal dumped me directly at the clearing where the first crime had taken place. Not the most popular strolling spot for park visitors even during the weekend, let alone the middle of working hours. All those tree-huggers were currently shackled to their hated jobs attempting to earn some money. So there was no one I could possibly catch in the clearing. Walking along the path created by the police, I ended up on the main avenue of the park. It was time to do some hunting.

"You: punk, what are you doing here?" I didn't understand immediately that this was addressed to me. Once I turned around to look for the potential aggressor my hand was grabbed by a small old lady. Her childlike height did not at all hinder the valiant warrior in a flowery shawl from attacking a full-grown dude. Looking at the old hand clinging to me I was not sure why she latched onto my case or what to do with her.

"Get away from me, lady! I could hit you by accident!"

"You could, and it would be no accident, but you would say it was! Police! Police! Help! Help! Dearie, do help an old woman to catch a drug addict!" The old lady, still clinging to my hand, asked for help of a teenage girl of about 15 who happened to be running by. The girl, casting one scared glance at us, ran faster. "Good for you! Run away, dearie! No need to be around druggies!"

"Ma'am, I am not a drug addict. Let me go," I said listlessly, realizing what the problem was.

"Please."

"That's what you all say! Look-see, how you suddenly turned polite! The police will be here any minute now. And why do you, with all that reverence of yours, jump through the bushes in broad daylight? Doing your drugs, er, or you raped someone? Or even killed them?!" The victim of news broadcasts and TV crime shows was getting her second wind.

"Really, I did not do anything untoward." In order to get the old hag to calm down I did not make any attempts to extricate my hand or run away. Quieting, she looked me over questioningly."

"Not even taking a crap in the shrubbery?" she clarified, already understanding that she had made a mistake, yet hoping.

"Unfortunately," I said with a smile, but immediately corrected myself. "Fortunately, I mean. I am an entomologist. I was looking for local insects for a lecture at my college."

The legend appeared in my head as I recalled the way this old biddy latched on to me like a tick.

"Well, entomologist or not, no one is allowed to crap in the park!" The old hag stated definitively and launched into "good advice" mode: "You should let your conscience be your guide! You must attend church! Yeah, our church even accepts entomologists! You need to repent, and confess and live quietly, even though you are... er... whatever it was you called yourself? Well, then no one will think badly of you. Or else, what is it, you clambered out of the bushes and your eyes are red like you've been drinking. Did you get drunk or what?"

The time till Archibald's arrival was inexorably getting shorter. I tried to chase away the thought that the boring old hag would become the fourth participant in the sacrifice... because if you sentence people for being boring and imposing, there won't be any pensioners left in the entire land.

"Do you have children?" I asked for some reason. "And grandchildren?"

"Three kids and seven grandkids, I do," the old gal immediately switched modes as soon as I asked her about family. One question, and my status of "alcoholic atheist" was replaced with that of a "normal person". The old biddy started telling me how her daughter married well, and her grandchildren had just started school, how they studied, what the teachers were like these days, how her sons had gone into business and now help people because their own childhood was so hard... She had found what she thought was an attentive listener and was bending my ears with all her might. She was so happy that I just could not bring myself to stop her. At some point I realized that the stream of words had stopped. The old hag was frozen in midsentence and glum Archibald came out from behind her. The catorian decided to take matters into his own paws, and so he put the potential victim into stasis.

"Why the hell are you stuck here? Did you pick her? Good. Drag her to the site: we don't have much time." The teacher grabbed the old woman, preparing to transport her to the clearing. I blocked his way.

"I have not. Let her go." I said with a leaden voice. May the whole world go to hell, but I could not use that old biddy for the sacrifice. My mother's upbringing came up at the worst possible moment.

"We are losing time." The catorian took a step to the side, trying to go around me. I blocked his path again.

"Let her go," I repeated. "She will not be the fourth victim."

"So you are going to take her place and become a sacrifice instead? Did I hear you correctly? You chose this old specimen who threw her own children out into the cold, made her husband an alcoholic and is making her neighbors life hell? Who will, besides, croak all on her lonesome in two and a half Earth years? Really?" The catorian said, surprised, but stopped nonetheless.

"No! I did say that I have not chosen yet! First — this old hag is not going to be the fourth sacrifice. Second — nothing will happen if the choice takes me another ten or fifteen minutes. And don't try to convince me otherwise. You were ready to wait for me to decide on my own to go down this damn path; this means I still have time. I don't want to stay in the Game generating exponentially more cruelty."

"What will you do, little goody-two-shoes, if I force you?" The catorian's voice was fit to chop ice, it vibrated so heavily in the air around us. The teacher became almost a foot taller, and darker, as if his fury that had been accumulating for centuries now found an outlet; he loomed over me as if trying to crush me like a flea with his mere breath, but to no avail. I held my ground, firmly convinced that I was right. My activated artifact took its usual place on my arm; the protection was set to maximum; in my other fist I held several stacks with the Templar's Blow, preparing to defend the old hag with all the means available to me. I'd rather kill her here and now, if the teacher ignored my demands, than to allow the irrevocable to happen. I would try in any case, since there was not much I had to really oppose Archibald.

"I can see that you did level up on your stalwartness and determination. Good, you will need these qualities during restart," Archibald said and suddenly all the tension drained out of the situation. The teacher returned to his normal height, the darkness faded, and the old woman was placed on the nearest bench. Her calm breathing indicated that she was sleeping peacefully. I looked at her beatific smile. I hoped that she was seeing a sweet undisturbed dream without drug addicts, killers or rapists. This world really needed more kindness.

"Consider that you passed the test," my teacher told me briskly and went striding to the clearing. I looked after the catorian, confused, but hurried after him right away, trying to match his broad strides. Was this a test? Something like what Gerhard had done to test me before he allowed me to use Leguria? Or was Archibald trying to pretend things were better than they are and show that he is in control of everything?

A few minutes later I realized that the first guess was correct: there were four bodies in the clearing.

"The fourth one was not quite so outstanding as the first three." The teacher handed me the file for the new victim. "Just a common murderer. There are tons of those in this world."

Indeed, compared to the first three he was just your garden variety serial killer. Killed twelve women. Motive for murders: revenge for his wife's adultery. She was the first victim.

"In response to your question — no, we cannot wait. Tonight Merlin will sacrifice sixty four people. He is almost at the final stretch. One or two days, and he will complete the search and incarnate. We have to press on. My guys are now combing the city looking for the right victims to sacrifice for all the seals. We cannot guarantee that we will make the right number. But we must give it all we have!"

"If you thought it all through and took care of everything, what was that circus with the old hag for?" I could not keep down my question. Archibald actually deigned to turn his mug towards me and cast a sour look over me.

"I must be sure that you don't go bonkers. Yes, you did decide to perform the sacrifices, but you retained your overall moral principles with respect to the players, and, what I find interesting, with respect to common NPCs. You are the Guide. Which is a being that is guaranteed to transition to the next era and has no right to be flawed. We've had enough of those during restarts. Deficient players result in imperfect restarts. Every time it was the same thing: one's own interests overshadowed any values whatsoever! The old hag was not accidental; she was the embodiment of everything that tied you to your former life and was important for you. Any more questions?"

I had no more questions. The directness and rationale of the answer won me over. Even though, frankly speaking, the motives presented for the test for me were unexpected. I did not find this distrust insulting in the least, since I acknowledged Archibald's right to doubt. My teacher, just like anyone else, doubted. Not me, but his choice.

Now was the time to implement what we had devised. I needed to get into the right frame of mind, to feel the righteous wrath and determination. I opened the files again and carefully reviewed the crime scene photos. It made me want to personally strangle these creatures strewn on the ground now, to wipe them out completely from the memory of the Game. But the Judge in me quickly took control. Case initiation. Sentencing. The right to execute it was, of course, mine.

"You should not be doing this." An unexpected visitor approached me as I was preparing for the ritual. I was setting the bodies of those sentenced into the shape of the first seal, breaking their arms and legs without pity. Whoever that new arrival was, let Archibald handle him. I was hoping that we had already reached the level of mutual understanding at which we did not need words. I cast a glance at my teacher and immediately dropped what I was doing to activate protection and take my battle stance. The catorian was not there. Well, actually, his physical body was still in the clearing, but his mind was somewhere far out of the surrounding reality. His glazed eyes, raised hackles and the nervous twitching of his limbs indicated some grave struggle in which

Archibald was involved in the depths of his mind.

Suddenly a semi-transparent projection of a player appeared before me. It was a human creature dressed in a simple robe without any indication of class. He was floating in the air, sitting relaxedly in the lotus position. Sort of like a monk with a gorgeous mane of white hair and eyes that looked like molten gold. The longer I stared at this enlightened visage, the more it made you want to lose yourself in his wisdom and acknowledge his power unequivocally. To my dismay, he had the right of the stronger, since this was none other than the First Counselor to the Emperor. The second strongest creature in the Game.

"Killing these beings through the seal will result in a number imbalance of NPC souls." The Counselor clarified his thought, staring at me as if I were an insect. His upper lip twitched in a funny way, showing his teeth, which had been sharpened into fangs.. Archibald was still comatose in whatever psychedelic vision had been produced by this intruder.

"Do not concern yourself with the fate of the creature that calls itself Archibald," the Counselor said, as if reading my mind. "You should be only concerned about your own. This is the philosophy of your teacher, is it not?"

Another strike against my teacher. I will deal with this later, once I kindly and carefully see out this pesky guest.

"My sentence was confirmed by the Emperor," I started defending my position carefully. The Counselor nodded, confirming that:

"No one is challenging your right, Judge. We are here only to warn you about the consequences of your rash decision."

"Are you talking about the seal?" I nodded towards the four already twisted bodies. The Counselor nodded. "So what will be the consequences?"

"A case will be initiated against you, for respawn until complete wipeout." Well, that wasn't exactly news to me.

"Why do you not initiate a case against Merlin?" Irony was showing openly in my voice. "Or is it that quod licet Jovi non licet bovi?"

"That creature has our permission." The Counselor pretended that he did not notice the sarcasm in my voice.

"Then issue me one," I countered with a logical proposal.

Archibald whimpered, and I jerked reflexively.

"Listen, what is that flexing of the muscles? Both Archibald and I know very well who you are. Do you have problems with your self-esteem, or some grudge against my teacher?"

"It's just a precaution, nothing more. Archibald should not hear our conversation, nor influence the choice. Which you will make independently. Now. This is our word. The level of your importance for the Game is too low to issue you permission to form the seals. You have been warned. We must stay impartial. In the Game everyone has a right to act the way they consider necessary up to a certain point."

"How do I find Merlin then?" I asked, not seeing

a way out of this.

"This does not concern us. You are the Guide. It is your task to bring everyone together. If you are unable to fulfill your purpose within a hundred years, the Guide status will be transferred to another being. Your soul will be disposed of."

The Counselor spoke in a calm emotionless voice. As if the value of a life equaled zero if the creature did not fulfill the assigned role.

The Game had demonstrated one more time that it included the chosen ones as well as those who didn't make the cut. This exchange with the First Counselor to the Emperor confirmed that I had made the right decision. I would go down that road no matter what. For the sake of eradicating from the Game those like this immortal higher jerk. I was ready to kill living beings even for the sake of an illusion of a properly structured world!

"The choice has been made." The Counselor demonstrated excellent skill at reading minds and remaining unperturbed. I wished I could have this level of self-possession for the next day or two. "We accept your choice. We confirm that it was made without the influence of third parties. You do not need to be concerned about preemptive action on the part of the Game due to the choice you have made. That is not part of the rules. I ought to wish you luck in your Game, but given the circumstances I consider that unnecessary!"

The Counselor disappeared without any additional special effects. At the same moment Archibald crashed to the ground. I rushed to him instinctively, taking out a healing potion as I ran. The catorian's body was convulsing so badly that I was unable to open his mouth right away. I had to transform my artifact, to use the claws on it for that. Finally, I was able to give him the potion, but it did not seem to help at all. He was still unconscious and thrashing in my arms. Confused, I did not know what else to do other than pour a couple more potions into his mouth. After the third vial the catorian stilled, sighed deeply and went limp. I placed a stone under Archibald's head and instructed Steve to prepare a video of the events. Archibald would want to see it all for himself. I sat on the ground next to him, waiting for the teacher to come to. Starting without him was too risky.

"Amazing." The catorian came round within a couple of minutes, but needed a bit longer to restore his strength. He used it to watch the video. "The student rushes to defend his teacher. Contrary to the philosophy that I am following. That was stupid. You should have rather tried to bargain with the Counselor."

"The way you say 'thank you' sounds odd. Do you remember anything? All your fur stood on end. Why did he do that to you?" I was curious about what was behind the Counselor's excuses.

"I do, but I am not telling you. I need you in a sane state," the teacher shrugged and grinned: "During the first era I hunted Counselors for fun. Three lost their wings. I even made it dangerously close to the Emperor, but... it was not to be. Well, on the other hand, the Emperor graciously agreed to give me Avalon for my exclusive use. Not bad, right? The Counselors were renewed, the holes in their defenses eliminated, some things were upgraded... and, unfortunately, they were made immune to players' attacks. They should have instead put some benevolence into those vindictive pests! Now at every encounter each Counselor considers it his duty to torture the poor catorian. It's not deadly — they are not allowed to interfere with the Game process. But it is always a torture, painful to the extent that it makes you want to respawn. Those bastards never repeat themselves, but that just adds extra fun to our encounters. If you had been in my place, you would have lost your mind within the first few seconds."

Wow! I had guessed that Archibald's game was full of adventure. But guessing was one thing, and knowing interesting details was quite a different matter. Thinking about what I just heard I caught one phrase:

"You said that the Counselors are not allowed to interfere with the Game process. Then why did he barge into our game with his warning?"

"This was not interference, merely some simple advice. Merlin has been long considered an inalienable part of the Game and as such is protected by it. No matter what he does, the Game perceives it as its own actions. We are now creating a potential threat for Merlin, and, therefore, to the Game in general. The old guy guessed that we want to find his Diary and him. He doesn't want us to come close until he wants it himself. The Counselor was sent to warn us."

"There will be open season on us," I noted.

"You knew that before," Archibald looked me over. "Want to backpedal?"

"No, of course not. Are you rested?" I rose to my feet. "How is the seal activated? I have put the bodies in the right pattern, but I don't know what to do next."

"Next, my diligent student, is the most interesting part. We do not have the ability to drink souls, so here. This is a Mayan ceremonial blade. Just slit their throats, the knife will do the rest. It's your quest, so go for it."

The bone handle settled in my hand as if the horrific knife with its curved blade had been made especially for me. Dark engravings of skulls on the blade flashed menacingly, anticipating blood. This knife knew very well what it was intended for, and did not need any control from me. I felt nauseous. Good thing the breakfast had not been light and had happened a long time ago, or else I would have been barfing under the nearest bush by now. It made me want to throw the knife somewhere very far and wash my hands, like, ten times.

But my transient weakness was suppressed with a firm determination to finish off the criminals and get rid of this knife. At least temporarily. I bent over the first victim. One pass, and for him it was over. The bloodthirsty knife did not let a single drop of precious liquid fall to the ground. After a mere thirty seconds there were four bloodless corpses in front of me. Grey and frozen in a beautiful post-mortem composition.

"The choice is made!" I heard the Counselor's voice in my ears, completing a slew of system messages. The Game informed me that the world-wide hunting was open. Quarry: one item; anyone could become a hunter, that was a public offer. I didn't read the details of the text describing the offers for killing me for the sake of preserving some semblance of equanimity, and concentrated on the line that was actually important for what we were trying to accomplish:

The Explorer's map has been updated

Immediately the piece of parchment was in my hands; two heads bent over it searching for the new detail. The dotted red line traced its path from the first seal that Dima had designated the "Entrance", and stopped at the new seal in Kolomenskoye Park. So far everything was going in accordance with the known plan.

"Congratulations, student of mine, you have grown in the eyes of the Game community. I had not expected to say that, but it is quite an honor to have had you as a student! An entire ten basic granises for each respawn is really great. Given that you are at level 79 right now, your murderer is a potential rich man."

Archibald laughed merrily, seeing my face fall. That furry ass was pleased with himself and his successful joke; meanwhile all I could think about was how much my murderer was going to make from me.

"We were unable to cheat the Game and gain some time. I told my fighters to bring in the next candidates by portals, individually. If they are discovered, just make the seal out of random NPCs. Delay equals death for you. Remember that." Archibald opened the portal to the riverbank where the next sacrifice was performed in Kolomenskoye Park. "I will provide protection. If there are not enough victims, find more on your own. Hurry, it's going to get hot soon. Basic granises for killing someone like you is easy money."

To my misfortune only six candidates were lying on the bank. The fighters from Archibald's army disappeared; presumably they were guarding the perimeter.

"Could you perhaps open a portal to a prison?" I suggested, but Archibald refused.

"Prisons are the domain of the inquisitors. All those confined there serve as material for genetic experiments. It's closed territory — stronger than the Citadel. It's not as though they are invulnerable, but it would be a lot of trouble."

Together we walked to the central gate of the park. It was a lot more crowded than Tsaritsyno Park. I glanced over the crowd and grimaced. Now I was supposed to pick those for death row. Whether they had any plans for this life or not did not matter. The important thing was that they satisfied my requirements. It would be great to find out what the great requirements were, before crossing a couple of living beings out of this world.

"I would hurry if I were you." Archibald disappeared and reappeared several yards to the right, singing his sword sharply. The air shimmered and revealed a player neatly cut in half. Oh yeah, a member of Perfectionists Anonymous! The halves blinked a couple of times and disappeared, indicating the player had been sent to respawn.

"Very soon the entire hunters' elite will be here. From Earth, to begin with." Archibald clarified. "I will be able to protect myself, but you will end up going to Avalon for sure."

"Those two." I pointed at two young men insolently drinking beer sitting right on the grass. An older man pointed out to them it was wrong, provoking a good deal of aggression from the young misfits. One of them was eager to physically assault the concerned passerby. This was quite a common scene all in all, but I didn't have any other criteria to select the NPCs.

"Done." Archibald threw two darts making the future victims freeze in place.

I would not say that this was easy for me. Just a few minutes ago I was desperately defending an innocent old hen, and now I was seeking vices in people for which I could kill them. Nonetheless, I could not just pick the first two random NPCs. The Judge in me protested. I would have to initiate a case against myself.

"This will scare the rubberneckers," Archibald stepped onto the bank out of his portal and placed a small device on the ground that generated visual waves. I nodded indifferently, and started setting the bodies into the seal. I was not going to open the files and review the cases in detail, preferring to rely on the diligence of the players responsible for collecting the candidates. I would find out if I was correct or not as soon as the Emperor responded to the death sentence I decreed. Every times the bones crunched it made me startle, but I forced myself to refrain from pity. None of the victims uttered a sound; they had been prepared for the procedure perfectly, frozen in stasis. I was grateful to Archibald. Alone, without his preparedness and experience, I would have broken down already on the first seal.

I received a strong blow on the back just at the moment when I finished shaping the last body. My protection and the inertial blocker held, preventing me from falling on the practically finished seal. I braced myself for the second blow, but it never came. Either the attacker had hoped for an easy victory, expecting to send me to respawn with one blow, or he suddenly faced other problems. However, I rolled over to the side, quickly turned around, and activated my artifact. A stack of scrolls slid into my other hand in case my invisible opponent returned. There was no one. Archibald stood still nearby, scanning the area. At the same time he kept in touch with his team over the voice loop. From the erratic bits of conversation I understood that they had had a breakthrough at the perimeter. The number of intruders that had made it into the clearing was unknown. Simultaneous flashes to the right and left indicated that there were at least two opponents. I fell to the ground, and two fireballs whistled above me. There was a loud clap and crash: the trees standing behind me crumbled into dust.

Things were getting tough. We needed to finish working on the seal. The fireballs showed that these opponents were way beyond me. My teacher had outfitted me with great protection, but I did not really have much by way of attack capabilities. The scrolls would stun my attackers, but they were unable to pierce through advanced defenses.

"Close the seal!" Archibald voiced my own thoughts and disappeared into the air.

I rolled over towards the seal, initiating the cases as I went and sentencing everyone to death, pulled out the knife and slit the throat of the nearest victim. A shimmering dome appeared over me, and the aimed and ricocheting volleys of lightnings dissipated, crashing into it above my head. A couple of fireballs buried themselves in the ground right at the perimeter of the protective dome. Archibald was taking care of his student even as he was busy hunting. My knife worked at the speed of a meat chopper, and yet I nearly stopped at the eighth victim. The guy, one of those whom I had picked, opened his eyes and realized what was going on, horrified. He could not talk: for the seal pattern I had to dislocate his jaw, but he did feel the pain. From the emotional stress, or from pain shock, his body was shaking wildly. He could not control himself, and this threatened to break the seal. Delay could cost me seven useless deaths, so I slashed his throat while looking him straight in the eye. I had always thought that it would be difficult to watch life leaving a person's eyes; for any normal person it would be an unbearable sight. I had thought that I was normal. The feeling of enormous disgust with myself made me puke bile right over this guy's body.

There was a waterfall of system messages again. The Game had increased the reward for wiping me out, raising the price for each death to twenty basic granises. In addition, the quest was now expanded to the players of the entire sector ruled by Bernard. The map updated as well, showing the dotted line to the next point: Izmailovo Park.

A ruffled Archibald appeared next to me. He grabbed me with one paw and opened a portal to Avalon with the other. We tumbled out of it into the teacher's private rooms. The catorian's appearance concerned me. Even his strength and experience had not been able to prevent critical damage to his armor. My teacher took off the destroyed set and went to fetch himself another. It was a while before he responded to my surprised look:

"Being stripped of class has its drawbacks. Zork and Devir are very well aware of my weak spots. Truly, I was close to respawn. This is sad. After the next sacrifice there will be a quarantine set in Moscow. We need to prepare well."

I had thought that we were already prepared well. Archibald's normal nonchalance had disappeared. He was now looking like an old tired cat who was being forced to mouse by the circumstances of life. Just recently Archibald could have laid his paws on the entire arsenal of the best abilities available to Paladins, but now, without his class alliance, the going was tough for him. There's not much you can do in battle with your bare hands, no matter how agile, experienced and wise you are. You still don't have any advantages.

"We need to act quickly." Archibald continued his thought and put a blaster on the table. "The players don't know yet what we are up to. They don't understand why we created the seals and are summoning a demon. But this will not last. You will not be able to create the seals if there is an ambush at each location in the city. We cannot allow that. Here. Using this thing is not difficult; you should be able to figure it out. We are setting out in three minutes."

My teacher disappeared until the time he had specified, leaving me to familiarize myself with the new weapon. The adaptive settings system activated as soon as I picked up the weapon. One of the walls in the hall rode up, transforming the room into a training range. Multistrike-8810 easily blasted into atoms the mannequins used as moving targets. Controls were easy indeed: the gun's dimensions automatically adjusted to the person holding it, it fully integrated with the armor, there was a laser aiming system right on the internal display. This wonderful device shot high-temperature plasma enhanced with additional battle spells. So first Archibald had given me the shell, and now he handed me the teeth.

"It is dangerous to involve my fighters beyond this point. Every kind of loyalty has its price, and the reward for your body exceeds all reasonable and unreasonable payment schedules. So still your love of humanity in advance," Archibald warned me before opening a new portal. "We'll just grab any NPCs that come to hand. Forget that you are a Judge, or else you'll just croak. Devir will figure out our location in eight to nine minutes. By the time he shows up in the park we must already be at the next point. We need to do this before the quarantine. After that portal transportation will be entirely shut down in Moscow. Both in and out. We won't be able to jump to Avalon, nor will we be able to respawn, or else we won't be able to get back to Moscow at all. And then everything will have been in vain. I don't remember this much agitation for a long time. The Game activated additional resources. Now it's playing with the big boys."

I nodded, confirming that I understood it all to the last word; for the first time I started praying. No, not to some hypothetical god, but to the developers of the Game, pleading with them to not force me to kill kids and their mommies. If we couldn't find any other candidates, Archibald would force me to kill just about anyone. Because when it's your own life at stake, people on Earth turn into Game NPCs, and it didn't matter that at one point I had been one of them.

I don't know what helped, my prayers or sheer luck, but once Archibald activated a scanner to search for NPCs, it gave us a satisfied purr. A few hundred meters away from us there was a running track and, by a fortunate coincidence, there was a regional contest underway. The sportsmen, conveniently bunched at the starting point, were just beginning a new lap. Archibald did not bother with stun darts, just released the drones from his inventory with the command for individual hunt. At first there were indignant exclamations and calls to get the foreign objects off the trail; those were replaced with sounds of struggle and the frightened cries of girls. The drones completed their task perfectly and dragged to us, along the shortest path through the thicket, sixteen wriggling bodies struggling to break free.

Archibald threw a dart, stopping the cries of the nearest runner, and his stiff body fell to the ground. My teacher tried to work fast, but we were unable to prevent the hysterics totally. Once we reached the third victim, the others realized the extent of the danger and launched into a cacophony of stress reactions. Guys threatened us or offered ransom, girls pleaded that we let them go, talked about their children. It seemed to me that it would never end. My hands shook and I wanted to howl together with them, but my body kept doing the work, adding one sacrifice after another to the seal. Finally, silence settled over Izmailovo Park. All sixteen guys and girls were dead.

"We are too late," Archibald grumbled. My field of view was obscured by a stack of information messages on the introduction of the quarantine in Moscow, on the change of the status of the quest to kill me to "global" and the increase of the reward for each respawn to one hundred basic granises. I received a new unique designation achievement of "Mr. Jerkeverse".

"There he is!" I heard a familiar voice. The Supervisor of Judges had been the first to figure out what we were doing and showed up personally to stop the horrendous criminal. Plus the basic granises would serve as excellent consolation for his wounded pride. The Supervisor brought company — a couple of Judges somewhat lower in rank. They immediately surrounded the Supervisor and themselves with a protective field and prepared to attack. Perhaps they specialized in the execution of sentences."

"I sen..." Multistrike-8810 demonstrated excellent results not only with mannequins, but with real enemies as well. As soon as the Supervisor opened his mouth, I pulled Archibald's present and shot a dozen great balls of fire into the Judge. The first eight were blocked by the protective field, but the rest reached the target. The plasma left just the bottom part of the disrespected Supervisor standing; fortunately it was unable to deem me guilty nor to sentence me to death. The subordinates followed their boss on the road to respawn. I looked admiringly at my super-weapon and blew away the light smoke curling from the heated barrel.

"Happiness is a warm gun, right?" my teacher concluded with an approving slap on my shoulder. We were both pleased with the outcome of this meeting with the Supervisor.

"Let's get out before any other players show up here," Archibald said curtly, pulling a skateboard out of his inventory. The teacher jumped onto it, soared into the air and made a couple of circles around the clearing, deftly maneuvering around the trees. Having confirmed his level of skill he approached me and grabbed me onto the board without even slowing down. I was barely able to hold on, clinging to

Archibald. I didn't know what speed this device was capable of developing, but according to Steve we would be in the park in no more than an hour. Actually, Archibald had his own plans. Instead of dashing at full speed to the next point, he hovered in the treetops at the outskirts of Izmailovo Park. For my every attempt to find out what was going on, I received an insulting whack with his tail on my head. My position was literally too precarious to insist, so I waited silently for the outcome. Finally the teacher gained speed and we flew onto the sidewalk at full speed. The landing was not soft, but this was no time to discuss driving style for flying skateboards. The teacher pulled out a sewage manhole cover sharply, kicked my body straight down into the well, and then followed me. Sinking knee-deep into the sludge, I tried not to look down; it was enough to smell the odor to understand where we had ended up. Archibald was fiddling with setting the manhole cover back in place, while dusting the edges of the hole itself with some kind of powder. To the pitch black darkness of the Moscow sewage system was now added the humidity and the stench.

My teacher lit a little light, casting a greenish glow on the insides of the sewage main.

"Now for the most interesting part," Archibald grinned, as he was feeling one of the walls. "What do you know about perfection, my naïve student?"

"That it has no limit," I blurted out the first answer that came to mind. I hated those charades! If I were to see my teacher under acid some day, I would never be able to guess, since his random thoughts and weird behavior were just normal shit for him.

"That's a wrong thought. If perfection had no limit, then perfection would not exist at all. That's the right thought." I just grunted meaningfully in response. After all that emotional turmoil I was crashing, and so I was glad that Archibald did not need me to actively take part in that conversation. He went into the "teacher" mode. "The Game, my dim-witted student, is a huge machine, governed by trillions of players and NPCs all over our Galaxy. Whatever its mechanism is, it is limited with respect to resources. Which is fortunate for us."

Part of the wall gave, moved toward Archibald and to the side, opening a secret vertical shaft with a spiral ladder leading down.

"What is the good side for us in that finality?" I was trying to grasp the main idea of Archibald's soliloquy as I was following him down the stairs since we were descending without any hurry.

"Don't rush! I am working on your education, by the way! First you don't listen, then you accuse me of bad mentoring in front of every Tom, Dick and Harry. As I mentioned, the Game is limited; for this reason it has four main environments in which players reside; each of those is divided into three more layers. Each layer is enclosed within itself, and practically never intersects with the others. That brings us to the idea that the underground hasn't heard either about the quarantine, or the seals."

"Are you trying to say that the task to wipe us out was sent only to the residents of the Game who live on the surface? Even though the status was set to 'global'?"

"Not 'us', just you. You have to bear personal responsibility for what you have done. I do dare hope that the developers have not yet discovered this hole in the global quest."

"It seems more like cheating," I frowned. We had gone rather far down; the air was becoming rarefied and humid. "So then it's possible to wreak havoc in one layer and in another be an honest and respectable player?"

"Why not, if the Game gives you wings, gills, and lungs?" the teacher hemmed. "Or if you are sufficiently rich and powerful to develop your armor accordingly. It is impossible to get where we are going in standard or even advanced armor. Which, as you understand, limits the number of such cheaters dramatically. The owners of Daro or Imperial armor we can cross off right away: their religion would not allow them to think about such ideas.

"So Devir will definitely follow us. For him religion serves more as a shield than a visor." I reminded the catorian about our opponent.

"Devir?" Archibald actually stopped to think. "No, he won't be able to figure it out on his own. You can't cure stupid. He has plenty of strength and a grip of iron, but as for the head.... it's pretty thick. In order to win a battle you need to preempt your enemy's moves, you need to think like him. If there is a problem with that, no amount of experience can help. Rushing in, chopping everyone up, killing them — that's his strong point."

"From what you are saying it seems as though

Devir would be an excellent weapon." I summed that up. "Maybe he doesn't need to think. Maybe he has found someone who does that for him."

"Let's hope it's not Gerhard. Enough of you being a smart-ass! Generally, you ought to be a little more dumb! Look, even Clarissa thinks you are a mediocrity, and she is an experienced witch — she knows what she is talking about. So then, before you spoil my mood any further, I want to say the most important thing: Delrada kon Zagardash! Archibald and his student are seeking refuge!"

The latter was obviously not addressed to me, but to the two giant earthworms that were guarding the bottom of the spiral ladder. Their dimensions were more reminiscent of pythons — about three or four meters. The main peculiarity, though, were additional limbs in the form of three-finger tentacles. Those growths acted for the worms just like hands. One of the guards took out his comm, but I was not able to hear the conversation. A Dome of Silence appeared around the worm's head. The guards of this passage were players!

"Zagardash agrees to admit Archibald and his student," the worm said in the Common Game language after finishing his conversation. Then he pointed a tentacle at me. "The weapon should stay here. There is no place for that in our world."

"Give me Multistrike," Archibald ordered, taking away my only means of defending my position in an argument with my enemies: "The right to carry this device was granted to me by the Emperor. Would you like to challenge it?"

"No, oh Ancient One. The passage to the Underground World is open to you," the worm said, acknowledging the truth of Archibald's words. The worms hid their coils in the depth of the room and opened a round door in the ground wall. Beyond it we saw a railroad with a wagon that took us through the long corridors to the mysterious Zagardash.

"Are your fighters still at my apartment?" I asked as we were traveling, because I was worried about Helen. He shook his head negatively. Damn: I did think that morning about my Doll's safety. Some player could use her to get to me. That was not to be allowed. The wagon was moving slowly, giving me time to resolve my problem. Archibald refused right away, saying that one ought to deal with his own property, he was not going to allocate people for that, and it was a silly thing to begin with. I didn't want to get into an argument regarding Dolls and went through all the numbers in my comm, until I found what I thought was the optimal solution.

"Greetings, Brother Yaropolk!" Alard answered with joy in his voice. He was the only player to whom I could come, regardless of the tasks out there to kill me. "I had no doubt that this was a mistake. How is it possible to issue a task to kill a worthy Brother? If this is the case, the Game must have lost its mind, and I am within my right to not accept such tasks. There is no honor in killing a noble Paladin! Take care of yourself, brother, and don't tell me where you are — infidels could be everywhere!"

"Thank you, Alard, I never doubted you, my brother!" It was a great pleasure to hear the words of support from the orc, even though I did not deserve it. I didn't want him to find out the truth and be disappointed in me. "I came to you for help."

"What do I need to do?" Alard responded with understanding.

"While I am being hunted, my Doll could be in danger, as I am unable to protect her. I was going to ask you to take care of her while I am away."

"Helping a friend is the holy duty of Paladins! There is no honor in leaving your brother in his time of trouble! Don't worry! Mizardine and I will look after her! Good luck to you, brother! I am glad to know you are alive!"

"This attachment will bring nothing but trouble." Archibald just could not keep quiet; he had to voice his opinion, even though I had not asked him. Particularly because I had not asked him. I didn't bother to explain myself, choosing instead to concentrate on the vista of the underground city that had opened up to view. As in our layer, there were both NPCs and players, but their appearance was unusual. Worms, snakes, bats, slugs, centipedes, even moles — all those were merely approximations that my imagination provided with respect to the local inhabitants. They were all sentient and capable of speech. On the whole, if you disregarded their looks, it was quite an average town with a common bustling life.

Archibald was correct: no passersby became excited, recognizing a horrible criminal in me, when we approached. Either they didn't care or they had enough of their own business to mind.

The wagon swerved several times, turning along the main street, and stopped at a large building. Judging from its decoration, Zagardash occupied quite a distinguished place in this world. That was only to be expected, since Archibald dealt with him. Several quick worms saw us into the reception hall where our host was already expecting us. It was a huge two-meter-long slug.

"My good old friend!" The slug's body vibrated, making the air produce sounds. Our host did not have a mouth. "I am glad to see you still have your tail. What has brought you to our abode?"

"You are not even considering the possibility that I decided to drop in to see an old friend of mine?" Archibald bowed low to the slug. "I am glad to see that your slugness has not changed."

"Ho, ho: only dawdling twits go around with idle visits, my restless friend!" Zagardash vibrated his belly, offering us a seat. "Should I congratulate you?"

"On what? Did I miss something important?" Archibald twitched his ear irritably and looked around.

"Don't be so modest! To train a student who is worthy of his teacher is something to be proud of. My ears in the middle world reported to me that he has made an attempt on your law and order. Even here we have heard the echo of that. Is my understanding correct that I have the honor to see the culprit in person? Or is it an honor?"

"Don't make hasty conclusions, Zagardash." My teacher rose to his feet.

"Archibald, like any ruler I want to avoid chaos.

Our subjects are worried that because of the actions of your protégé the borders between the layers will be erased, and then chaos will become inevitable!"

"So then: you are refusing us shelter?" Archibald clarified. The nice thing was there was no small talk. The parties just proceeded to business right away. Even though it was no fun that the business concerned both my life and our entire undertaking.

"I didn't say that. Why do you accuse me of things that have not happened?" the slug responded. "On the contrary, I told you that I was glad to see you. But as any ruler would, I expressed my concern about the current situation."

"What do you want for the possibility of visiting with you?" I could hear tension in Archibald's voice Apparently, he had expected a different reception from Zagardash.

"A mere trifle. Tomorrow is the opening day for the Nardine Games. I strongly recommend that you participate as my fighters. Very strongly recommend." The slug's body puffed up.

"Yari, we are leaving." Archibald turned around in order to leave the inhospitable house, but actually stayed in place.

"Archibald! You want to offend me? If you go out, offended at dear Zagardash, our subjects will think that I am a bad host. They will stop respecting and obeying me. Why obey such a disrespected slug? Ho, ho," the slug said self-righteously, rubbing his tentacles.

I turned around to see why the catorian had

never made a single step towards the door. The door had flung open and I saw the one whose presence Archibald had heard a moment before he appeared.

"Archibald, out of respect to you I will let you go to Avalon, but only if you give Yari to me. Now." The ideal weapon, the stupid mage Devir was standing in the doors, gloating about his luck. His small army of high-level players was crowded behind him, leaving the initiative to their leader.

"Devir, I am not glad to see you. Not at all." Archibald was mocking as usual. "If you had been in Yari's place, I would not have hesitated for a second. And you know why? Because you are a stupid meathead."

Devir rushed forward together with the other mages, but a wall appeared in front of them, halting their approach.

"I dare hope that was the acceptance of my offer to stay for a while as honored guests?" The slug gleefully threw some oil on the fire. "I have heard that Avalon is really delightful, but not as a prison. Isn't that right?"

"That's right, Zagardash. Your hospitality knows no bounds," Archibald made up his mind and turned back towards the slug. There was no need to worry about a blow to the back from Devir now. But just in case, I checked my hotkey panel and realized that the Templar's Blow was unavailable.

I would have liked to think that my abilities had been blocked by Zagardash's house, and not by the underground world itself. Otherwise events would take a decidedly unpleasant turn. Trying to equal

Archibald in turns of the ability to withstand our enemies by sheer force would simply mean death for me.

Steve analyzed the hall around us, putting yet another nail in our coffin. There had been nothing indicating a friendly meeting from the very beginning. Steve counted several dozen strange niches and bumps on the walls; there was high probability that they were used to discharge unfamiliar weapons. This news did not make me happy. I was not sure that my protection would have been able to withstand that assault.

"We will be your fighters in the Games, my cunning friend." The catorian confirmed his proposal with finality. "Moreover, we will win them for you. This is what you want, isn't it?"

"What do I hear in your voice, Archibald? You disapprove of your old friend? Ho, ho, come on. You know what kills those like ourselves, those who have survived many eras... It's boredom. Right, my friend? There is nothing more pernicious than that bitch; because of it we lose our taste for the Game." This slug did not even need a mouth to make it clear how glad he was. "Look at the bright side of this! Old Zagardash will do you a favor and dispel your boredom. What stirs your blood more than a threat to your freedom? You win, and you will be free. I will take care of your unlucky student and his companions. You lose, and I will personally check that they drive ice arrows through your heads. That's regarding the question you did not ask about your reward."

"It's not up to you to take my life or freedom," Archibald's voice was quiet and menacing. "They are mine in any case, and I don't trade in them. My conditions. If you want a victory, you will have it. But do provide passage through your domain to the location I specify and furnish thirty-two NPCs for the sacrifice. You are welcome to do with Devir and his entourage as you wish, but they must not pose a problem any more. And the icing on the cake for you, my artful friend: In case we lose — which is impossible in principle, but still, according to the rules I have to say it — Yaropolk and I will become your slaves until the nearest restart. If you want, you can give us to Devir, if not, we will keep alleviating your boredom. We are pretty crazy guys. Deal?"

"The rules of the Game prohibit the use of external objects. Just abilities!" I heard Devir shout. Archibald ignored him, waiting for the slug to answer. The latter was lost in contemplation, thinking of that proposal. It was attractive, and I completely did not understand why he was lingering. I totally refused to think of my teacher's motives, hoping that he had a plan or a miracle stashed in his inventory.

"Deal." Zagardash emerged from his reverie and the Game registered the contract. "Until the Games you shall not be harmed. This is all."

"Madonna will be against this," Devir warned the slug.

"That is exactly why she will not know of any of this," the slug responded. A huge glass jar covered Devir and the rest of the mages. "I don't like surprises. Everything should be the way I want it. Till tomorrow, my warriors. By the way, Devir, you and your fighters will be participating as well. I have spoken!"

Archibald closed his eyes and bent his head down, as if preparing for something. I was smart enough to follow his move. For an instant fierce cold gripped my body; it was followed by darkness. Our day had been short, but busy. In my case I ought to be glad that I would definitely live long enough to see the next morning. Who cares if it would be in the form of a piece of ice? A new day will bring new solutions.

CHAPTER SEVEN

DAY SIX

I WOKE UP in a terrible state. Neither the armor nor the several potions I downed helped immediately against the tremor as my limbs were thawing out. But the worst was my eyes. I couldn't see anything, My eyes were burning as if they had been pierced or burnt; only after a while did I start seeing the world again, in black and red. It was quite a while before I not only felt the cold of the steel bars of my small prison, but also appreciated the panorama beyond them.

A large number of bird cages were hanging high up in the air, swinging from careless movements; inside them were all the lucky guys like myself. The cages were small; it was impossible to stand in them at full height. Neither could the inhabitants of this

---

"bird market" stretch themselves out on the floor. The group was varied: there were both players and NPCs of all sorts of appearances, sizes and levels. Some were still unconscious, some, in futile fury, were trying to chew through the bars of their cages with their huge fangs. Altogether Steve counted fifty-two cages in which fifty of my opponents were confined. I was in one cage, and my teacher in another. Steve quickly found Archibald among the participants. My teacher was unconscious, and I was worried because he still had not come to. I was counting on his help..

About a dozen cages away I saw a familiar face. Devir was fully ready to do battle, actively instructing his fighters, who were in their cages nearby; they nodded and made suggestions to develop their tactical plan for the battle. One could but envy their excellent teamwork.

Some more time passed; I spent it looking around to check out where we were. A sand arena was shining below like white gold. Apparently the contest was to be held right here. Its entire perimeter was surrounded by an impenetrable dome that concealed the spectators from us. I took out my comm and tried to get through first to Archibald, then to Alard. No luck. The scrolls didn't work either. My initial idea had been correct: the dome completely blocked us out from the outside world.

Finally, all the participants except Archibald had regained consciousness. Feeling trapped and without a plan, I called the Temple of Knowledge:

"I need information about the rules of Nardine Games!" Damned Archibald had signed up to this weird enterprise both for himself and for me, without giving any indication at all as to what would be the right thing to do.

"The inquiry is considered insignificant, but due to elevated reputation the visit to the Temple has been permitted. You have two informal visits remaining. Additional questions are not available during informal visits."

Once in the Temple, I breathed. Prior to this no one had told me that I could visit the Temple without a "proper" reason. But this surprise was pleasant and came at a good time. The scroll I needed was set on the table as usual.

The overall picture was pretty bleak, even though I would not call it unexpected. The adage "Bread and Circuses" worked for any society, and the bloodier the circus, the more satisfaction it brought to the spectators. So these were sort of gladiatorial battles the Nardine way. The good news was that it was possible to form teams of two-three participants straight at the arena. You could turn an enemy into an ally and at the end no one could force you to fight with your allies. All the winning team members were declared winners together, The purpose of the game was simple: to kill them all, figuratively speaking. In fact, only NPCs could actually die; the life count of the players, while they were in the arena, could not go below one. As for the bad news, using any outside devices was strictly prohibited. Only one's own artifacts and developed abilities. Under those conditions NPCs were sort of "warm-up cannon fodder" armed only with the potential fury written into their software. Therefore all of them were huge mean monsters capable of breaching medium-level defense and inflicting quite a few holes on the slow players. Well, of course, only hardcore. By the way, the reward for the winners kind of sucked, too. Had they come up with something more attractive, maybe they would have gotten more volunteers for this bloodbath. As it was, it was "just" freedom, which was granted to anyone by the Game at the first spawn, and which now had to be won back. The battle continued until the winner was declared. After that the players who lost were kept on ice until the next Nardine Games, which were held at least once a month. This way, in complete isolation, one could lead a pitiful existence until the end of time. The slug was not joking by saying to Devir that it would be a long time before he could report to Madonna.

I finished reading and scratched my head, confused. It was completely unclear what the catorian counted on, promising us victory. He had been stripped of his abilities, and was unable to use his toys from previous eras. I agreed, it was better to sleep through everything, dumping all his problems on Yari with his double luck, rather than be shamed in the eyes of his students. Only, what was I supposed to do? The Templar's blow would only make my opponents laugh, and all that was left to me was to hope that they'd die laughing from staring at my futile efforts.

"Have you finished reading, Dark one?" The old guy asked, emphasizing the "Dark". I nodded, preparing to return, but the keeper of the Temple of

Knowledge was not in a hurry to send me back.

"You are facing a hard battle, Dark one." He stressed the word "Dark" once again. "Sometimes we protect those who don't need it, because Darkness itself takes care of those who want to conceal themselves within it. Remember that."

The portal sucked me into its whirlwind, returning me to the cage. Steve and I looked at each other, confused. I wanted to believe that the Game, in the form of the Keeper, was offering me support and some clue because it was trying to protect the Guide. All I could think of was Leguria — my dark ability, at which the Keeper could be hinting. But if I were to use it, Archibald would be affected just like the others. I could not predict what Leguria would do to the catorian, and without him I would definitely not be able to finish off Merlin.

"Your teacher never came to," Steve pointed out.

"I'm not blind," I snapped at Steve, thinking that I didn't know what the last statement from the old guy related to.

"I agree, you aren't blind, you're just dumb," my subconscious parried. *"Leguria reacts to emotions and/or movement, just as it worked with zombies and other raised offal at the Lecleur estate. The old guy was talking about Archibald. It's because of him you hesitate to use Leguria. But look: Archibald is unconscious, he doesn't project any emotions and is not moving. So for your dark ability it is the same as if he did not exist!"*

Steve had just enough time to finish that thought when a bell sounded under the dome and some voice said pompously:

"Rejoice, residents of the Underground world! May the sand of the battle arena of Nardine fly in the air, to be settled only by the strongest! Let the battle begin!"

Preparing for the unknown, I grabbed the bars of the cage just in time. The bottom disappeared, leaving me hanging by my arms, but I was able to brace myself and jump down on the sand, rather than crash down like a lump, which is what happened to most of the participants. I activated my defense purely reflexively, so I blocked the blow that I immediately received from the mages. The monster nearest to me jerked his head, and my inertia neutralizer grunted glumly as the blow sent me flying several yards. The blow exceeded all my defenses, sucking the Energy from my crystal like a siphon. There was a silver lining to it though: a huge chunk of ice dropped to where I had just been, catching the monster on the head. His roar shook the whole arena, and the creature switched to the new target, forgetting about me. The Game algorithms helped the beast figure out who was the overconfident idiot who had dared attack it.

Before I caught a blow from someone else, I found Archibald with my eyes. Devir and his team had made it to the catorian before me, and had thought of nothing better than to waste energy and time on my helpless teacher. They were absorbed in trying to beat him up, apparently considering him their main threat. The teacher was just lying on his back, the same way he had been in the cage, his paws spread every which way. Lightning bolts, icicles and fireballs kept pelting his body. A couple of seconds were enough for me to see that for Archibald the game in this arena was over. Only the mages' fury was preventing the organizers from dragging my teacher's body to the side. Another lightning bolt hit the catorian, his body shook, and I saw the gleam of a vial with a familiar potion in his paw.

"Look!" Steve zoomed in on this. It was the same potion I had had to pour into the catorian's mouth in the Citadel, to make him regain consciousness. The old guy and Steve were right! That was Archibald's plan. No consciousness meant no emotions. No emotions meant no food for the one who would bring us freedom.

"I am Leguria!"

My human consciousness lingered for a couple of seconds. I remembered that I had fifty opponents who were going to turn into the vessels full of fear and other tasty emotions to quench my thirst. A breath, then another, and Yaropolk faded even from the memory of the dark creature. Only Leguria remained, now in control of the entire arena and everyone within it. The tentacles stroked the nearest vessel tenderly, trembling with anticipated pleasure. From affectionate my embrace immediately became passionate, unable to hold back the all-encompassing thirst. Leguria sank into the brains of its victims again and again, and clung, like a traveler exhausted by the long road to water, to the areas responsible for pain, suffering and agony, drowning them in their own horror. The arena filled with screams that sounded like music in my head and made me work faster. Sometimes my sensitive tentacles were burnt by an unexpected defense, and then I, with shouts of disappointment and grief, searched for a gap in their protection. I was so indignant at this flirting! My food wished to play with me instead of granting me my pleasure right away. The walls crumbled easily, proving the pretence of this resistance, and I drank deeper from the brains of the vessels, extracting the most horrible phobias and fears. I made sure that all the space available was under my control and wholly gave myself to pleasure, hoping that this food would quench my eternal thirst at least for a short while.

The awakening was always the same. I woke up, suffering from thirst, drank up the small fragile vessels until there were no more (and it happened very fast), and fell asleep again, just as hungry and unsatisfied. But today everything was different. Well, more than half of the vessels ran out as quickly, but the remaining ones continued to bring me joy for an interminably long time. They screamed, suffered, but would not run out, dripping ambrosia into my bottomless belly. Several times other vessels came from behind the wall and were immediately entangled in the network of my tentacles. Only one of those joined the ones that I liked so much. Twenty two vessels intended for my pleasure, what could be better? With gusto and gratitude I went deeper and deeper into their brains, lovingly moving from one area to another.

I did not know how long this feast lasted. But at some point I felt that I did not feel thirsty any more.

I felt the wonderful feeling of contentment that I had never felt previously; it was replaced by sleepiness. Petting gently the vessels in farewell as if they were my beloved children, I closed my eyes blissfully, sinking into untroubled dreams.

I felt my human body as I was lying on the warm sand. Large grains of it that had somehow gotten through the visor were stuck to my cheeks. I felt very reluctant to open my eyes. On the contrary, as soon as my memory came back I shut them as hard as I could, postponing the inevitable, and trying to make peace with it. Once it made no sense to stay down any longer, I rose to my feet and assessed the scope of my doings. Thirty-one NPCs were lying lifeless on the sand. They were dead. Twenty-two players were candidates for a psychiatric ward. They were rolling on the sand, flailing their limbs chaotically, fighting off invisible opponents; they drooled, stared into space and made horrendous sounds.

One of Devir's mages twitched and grabbed my foot, but it was just a mindless twitch. He let me go and attacked an NPC corpse. Looking at what I had wrought, I would not allow Leguria's feelings to penetrate into my own. I was not the one who enjoyed pain, I was not the sadistic murderer. That was the only way. There is not enough pity for everyone. I forced myself to concentrate on my current problems, the most pressing of which was time. Leguria had been around for seven hours. Merlin could have already made the last sacrifice and laid his hands on the Diary. I could have simply taken too long.

Archibald was still lying in the same place where I had last seen him, half buried under the bodies of the mages and Devir. Throwing the insane mages aside, I bent down to the catorian, trying to pry the potion from him. He was clutching it so tightly that I ended up having to transform the artifact, uncurl his fingers, or whatever it is that cats have, and release the vial. As I was doing all that the silence was complete. No one was in any hurry to declare me the winner or take away the losers. The protective dome still separated the oh-so-scary me from the spectators, who, I supposed, had been satisfied by the sight. I grinned, imagining the faces of those scumbags. I ended up having to pry the teacher's jaws open with the artifact claw as well, but I managed quickly and gave him not only the yellow liquid, but also a couple of healing potions. The catorian had been first frozen, then thawed, then beaten by lightnings, fireballs and what not, and finally left lying around for seven hours. It would have been naïve to have expected Archibald to have his normal reflexes after such a brutal punishment. He could not do without them, and I could not do without him. Whoever he was.

"You couldn't be a little more gentle, dummy?" Archibald grumbled, rising to his feet. He was moving awkwardly like a jointed doll. Despite the view he was staring at, his displeasure was caused by the scratch that I had accidentally given him when I was trying to take the damned potion from him. Having stared at the little wound for a while he licked and healed it by blowing at his hand slightly. Without waiting for a response, Archibald immediately added me to the group, thus closing the Nardine Games. Two winners, fifty losers. Not a bad trade for freedom.

"What took you so..."

The teacher just began to scold me when he froze like a stone once again, and only his fur standing on end indicated that he was conscious but not accessible. I had seen this sight not very long ago, and so, without even bothering to look around for the source of this attack, I demanded:

"Counselor, let him go!" There was no response, and I looked at the guest we were seeing far too frequently as of late.

The Counselor of the Emperor was floating in the air nearby, fully engrossed in assessing the condition of the players. Lifting one of those unfortunates close up to himself so as to easily look him in the eye, the Counselor sighed heavily and airily waved his hand at the player. The latter dissolved in the air like a sugar cube in hot tea. Once he disappeared, I received a message:

You have killed a player with his last death. Token "Killer" received

The Counselor started on the next player, ignoring my presence and request. I got angry. What the hell? The rules of the Game should be the same for everyone, even for the second strongest creature.

"For interference with the game process, for unjustified blocking of the being named Archibald, and taking away from him the opportunity to develop I deem the Counselor of the Emperor guilty and request that the Emperor himself decree a penalty commensurate with the trespass. By the right granted to me by my specialty, if the Emperor confirms the verdict, I remove all constraints from the afore-mentioned being and plead with the Emperor to protect that being in the future from unfair discrimination of any sort on the part of the said Counselor. My decision is final and may you all go up in flames!"

The Counselor stopped what he was doing and looked at me. Not a muscle twitched on his face, and his golden eyes stared me with a dead stare; only his head tilted to the right shoulder indicated there were some feelings there. Perhaps curiosity. A second passed, then another, then a third. The Emperor was in no hurry to help me put this bastard in his place, and even the Game refused to initiate the case against itself. The Game was infallible, and there I was, way out of my league...

"You have no right of justice over me, Dark Paladin," his upper lip rose, showing his sharp teeth and making the Counselor look disdainful.

"This is against the rules of the Game," I continued to insist. "Now I am acting not as a Paladin, but as a Judge. My duty is to serve justice. You, Counselor, are breaking the rules set forth by the Game and the Emperor. If you disrespect them, how can they be upheld by those under your command? I could readily believe that the catorian made a transgression against you personally, but if that happened, I am sure the rules allowed such an action at the time. The rules were changed later, but as we know, laws are not backdated. Particularly since your vendetta against the catorian has been accomplished many times since. On what basis do you block the player every time you appear? Please justify this action to me as a Judge, and I will admit that I have been wrong. Show me the rule for that in the codes for this era, and I would be the first to agree that Archibald needs to be punished in the harshest way. Or are you saying that you are the law?

There was a pause, as if the Counselor was thinking whether I was worthy of an answer. So we just kept staring at each other, neither of us willing to back down.

"The Emperor is willing to grant you an honor and accept all the "Killer" tokens that have been issued to you today." The Counselor changed the topic.

So that's why the Emperor was in no hurry to resolve our argument: he was discussing with the Counselor the elimination of the players who had lost their minds! If the Emperor is willing to confer an honor on me I must not sell out too cheaply. Oh, how I needed the catorian right now! I had no clue what those tokens did, and how much one could ask for them.

"I am flattered by the honor extended to me, but I cannot discuss the details of the deal, as I am waiting for a response from my Emperor." I tried to make my message as mild all possible and still indicate that without the teacher there would not be any bargaining. Let's see how much they needed the tokens.

"You might have to wait for a long time, Dark

Paladin. Now they were checking to see if I was bluffing.

"Well, if the answer is no, so be it. The tokens will not weight my inventory down," I responded forwardly.

Verdict is deemed justified.

The Counselor showed no reaction to the message, and I gladly got back to the catorian, who had come to. He nodded at me, unable to say anything, and gulped down a bunch of healing potions all at once. My teacher was unsteady on his feet, and in order to keep his balance and save his dignity, had to lean on his sword. While I was helping Archibald get back in shape, the Counselor, as if nothing happened, resumed disposing of the players who had hopelessly lost their minds.

You have killed a player with his last death. Token "Killer" received

The Counselor relentlessly eliminated twenty one players, sending me a "Killer" token every time. Seven hours of Leguria had done them in: the players lost their minds from pain, and this required interference on the part of the Game itself. There was no place for crazies in this world. At number twenty-two the Counselor stopped: a mumbling Devir was hanging in the air in front of him.

"As the teacher, I would like to reclaim my student." Archibald interfered with the work. Those are the rules, aren't they, Counselor?"

"You are within your rights, Archibald. Do you confirm your illogical request to leave alive your enemy, who used to be your student, and are you assuming responsibility for him and his actions as his teacher? We would like to remind you that this player does not consider you his teacher. You are not in his hierarchy of significant people, even though you are on his list of especially dangerous enemies."

"That means he is smarter than I thought. So much the better for Devir. He is, of course, a black sheep, but still of my flock. And I will decide when he croaks." Archibald did not hesitate for a second.

"So be it. Dark Paladin, are you ready to give your tokens to the Emperor?" The Counselor turned to me as soon as it was clear that the disposal process was over.

"By all means, Counselor: as soon as you remove the hunt mark from Yaropolk and enable us to finish the remaining sacrifices." Archibald was right there, and I was glad to no end. My teacher was glad of an opportunity to get a bit of his own back at the expense of the Counselor.

"We cannot allow that."

"Then Yaropolk will have a large pool of 'Killer' tokens, and we will be bargaining next with the heads of classes," Archibald snorted. "I am sure the Marunians will be very glad to send twenty-one players to Earth and ensure decent protection to my student together with the set of NPCs to sacrifice."

"The Emperor cannot allow that." The Counselor's voice betrayed his displeasure.

"But you don't have much choice." The catorian was pleased both with himself and the situation, and was not hiding it. Knowing that we would win this, he was already standing on his paws firmly without support. "Either you stop harassing my student, or you get a crowd of Marunians on Earth. There is no other option."

"We are ready to approve the exchange of the tokens for the removal of the mark." The pause was long, but in the end the Counselor gave way.

"And allow him to perform several more sacrifices without invoking additional marks," Archibald added.

"And we will allow him to perform the necessary number of sacrifices to resolve the Explorer's map puzzle," the Counselor repeated obediently.

Archibald rubbed his paws with pleasure and clapped me on the shoulder:

"Fine, now you can agree to transfer the tokens, my lucky student."

"The token gives one an opportunity to turn an NPC into a player?" I clarified before approving anything. Twenty one new players. Archibald was right. For a gift like that any class would happily protect me against any assaults by the Game.

"Yari, in principle, if you wish, we could discuss other proposals, but as your teacher, I strongly recommend that we accept this one," Archibald concluded.

"I agree to transfer the tokens on the conditions that have been specified," I stated, anticipating getting rid of the mark.

"Accepted. The task of eliminating Yaropolk has been cancelled. Yaropolk has been granted the right to perform the sacrifices. I am taking the 'Killer' tokens."

A host of system messages flashed before my eyes, informing me that all the tokens had been transferred, and I was not subject to hunting any more. I could breathe now. After that the Counselor returned to Devir. One pass of his hand, and the mage disappeared, only to reappear immediately and fall on the ground. He was unconscious, but breathed calmly. The Counselor disappeared, not bothering to say goodbyes. Archibald poured a healing potion into Devir's mouth and looked up.

"Zagardash! We have completed our part of the deal!"

In response the protective dome was strengthened. Energy was being pumped into it. Archibald grunted and returned to the mage. It took another couple of vials with the healing liquid to bring Devir out of his faint. Finding himself in a strange place and in odd company, the mage was rendered speechless.

"Welcome back, my prodigal son." Archibald spread his paws, enjoying the mage's confusion. "Tell your kind teacher what was the last thing recorded in your memory, and you will receive a bonus kick in the butt in the form of information on how the hell you ended up here, and as my student again!"

"Why Nardine Arena?" Devir showed an excellent awareness of our location.

"As always, my meat-headed student, you have provided the wrong question instead of an answer," Archibald sighed heavily. "You are saddening me again. Just as you always do."

"Student?" Devir frowned even more, and for a few moments his eyes glazed. The mage was reviewing his interface. With each second Devir's eyebrows climbed higher and higher, until he shouted:

"Three weeks?!" What, have I been killed to the final death?"

"Ah, that's already better," Archibald nodded. "But still quite bad. Come on, Devir, don't disappoint me so completely."

"What do I owe you?" Devir's shoulders drooped despondently.

"Here we go!" Archibald drawled with pleasure, raising his finger pedantically. "On the third attempt. I have not figured that out yet, but I will let you know as soon as I need something."

"Now that the main question is out of the way, maybe you can tell me what the hell happened here? The last thing I remember is the Lecleur estate. What am I doing at Nardine Games and why in hell am I your student again?"

"Yaropolk?" Archibald did not feel like dealing with Devir, and he pushed the unpleasant task onto me. I didn't feel like dealing with him either, so I stuck to short answers:

"You respawned last in the Lecleur estate, that was your last image. That's number one. You died in the arena because you were caught in Leguria. That's number two. The alternative to being Archibald's student was for you to die completely. That's number three. And you ended up in the arena because you chose the wrong allies. I think this covers all the questions you had."

"Good! Clear, precise and concise." Archibald praised me and turned to Devir. "So then, my new old student. I can see you have not fully realized the depth of the hole in which you are going to find yourself. Open your properties."

Judging from muffled cursing, Devir did not like what he saw one bit.

"You are at level one. Any death would be final for you. You are a new player, so you shall go to the Academy again with the next set of recruits. The old Devir was weighed, measured and found wanting. So your memory is, basically, a nice bonus from the Game for your earlier outstanding achievements. Any questions?"

"No questions... teacher," Devir pushed out painfully. Archibald extended a group invite to Devir as well, making him part of our team.

"Great. Now I am positively getting annoyed! Zagardash, could you hurry the organizers with issuing the reward, or else my Judge will initiate a case against them. He is very quick to punish and quite bloodthirsty! According to the rules we won, and yet we are still here! You have a minute, and I am now counting!"

I tried to keep a poker face, in line with the reputation of the awe-inspiring Judge, while wondering how did I get to this: that others are scaring players with me. Had it not been for restart, I would probably live on in the local folklore and they would be scaring disobedient kids with me: "Do it now, or else Mr. Jerkeverse will come and his Leguria will get you!" With some variations this threat could also be used against disobedient wives... I must have been really tired if such nonsense coursed through my head.

In any case, Archibald's threat worked. The organizers, scared by Leguria, decided not to run any unnecessary risks.

"Hail to the winner of the Nardine Games, honorable Zagardash! May the days of his Game be forever! Glory to the hero!"

The dome blinked and disappeared. The Nardine Arena was a typical amphitheater with countless tiers for standing spectators. The top levels faded somewhere in the dark, creating the illusion of infinity. For those especially, there were large screens all around the arena's perimeter, showing all the action close up. But there was some trouble with the viewers. The bleachers closest to the arena were empty, perhaps half way up the first tier; the first rows were covered in something green and so stinky that the filters in my armor activated automatically. Had Leguria's aura penetrated the protection then? I calculated the range — thirty yards immediate effect zone, the range of discomfort and mindless submission to Leguria was about a hundred. Right: about one third of the bleachers would have been within range. I didn't think any kind of tragedy had occurred there. Maybe a couple of players had gone to respawn, but mostly they were just scared to the point of producing this stinky green goop.

Several worms, bristling in their protection spheres, jumped to the arena and formed a live corridor, while trying to maintain their distance from us. Part of the lower tier disappeared, and the "honorable" Zagardash, the winner of the Nardine Games, slowly floated up to us on a hover platform.

"My old friend!" the slug started vibrating as if nothing happened, addressing Archibald. "You brought ambiguous feelings to my house. Both the joy of victory, and sadness at the way that victory was won!"

The naïve slug, fearing Leguria, decided to cover himself up from me with Archibald; he stopped in the place where the catorian was between us. I took a couple steps to the side, coming out from behind my teacher's back, and the slug immediately moved on his platform to restore his original position.

Are you hinting that we have won dishonestly?" Archibald asked in surprise, and now moved himself to check Zagardash's willpower.

"Ho, ho, was that what I said?" The platform glided, following the catorian's move. "I said that victory should bring honor and respect, and instead fear overcast my house with its shameful shadow. Who will answer for that? Poor Zagardash suffered losses, our subjects do not respect us, our partners are afraid to deal with us. That is bad, very bad. How do I fulfill my part of the bargain if the original agreement was quite different?"

"Oh, really?" I did not need to see Archibald to know how furious he was. "Did it just seem so to me, my cunning friend, or you are hinting that by winning these games for you we caused damage to your house, and so you refuse to honor your part of the agreement? Think well before you respond,

Zagardash, since my student is a Judge. Repeat once again that you do not acknowledge that we have fulfilled our obligations, and that you refuse to provide to us the thirty two bodies! Let's see what Yaropolk says."

Archibald again used me for intimidation, but I was in fact ready to initiate a case. Zagardash would in the end receive what he had asked for: alleviation of his boredom for about three hundred years going forward! I could not understand how Archibald could deal with him altogether. It was quite obvious what kind of a rat this slug was!

"Ho, ho, my friend!" Zagardash immediately backpedaled. "You know me. Who in our town could say that Zagardash does not keep his word? No one, no one, my dear. My house is famous for honesty and decency. I would not have even thought to violate the contract. I only lamented my problem, my trouble, to you, as to an old friend. And I asked for advice — what to do about the contract. Because I had two fighters. And there are three players here. And there were supposed to be two winners. Such was the contract. And I promised that if you win, I would take Devir. What is poor Zagardash to do?"

The slug was trying to wiggle his way out of this like crazy. Now that everyone publicly denounced him, he regretted tangling with us in the first place, but there was no changing the past. We were not going to take pity on this schemer. He was playing his part perfectly well: he was doing it all for the public, accusing us of unfairness to try and justify himself in the eyes of his subjects; on the other hand he was trying not to aggravate his dangerous "friends". I was really tired of his shenanigans, so I said:

"For the breach of the contract I decree..."

Zagardash snorted amusingly and rushed to Archibald for protection:

"Don't!" He played the part of a victim perfectly.

"I did warn you. You have seen yourself what Yaropolk can do. He might sentence you to complete wipeout and there would be not but a memory of the honorable Zagardash. I will miss you, my cunning and evasive friend."

"Thirty-two NPCs will be waiting for you by my residence." It was obvious that the slug was having a hard time vibrating to produce the sounds.

"The NPCs must be humans," I hasten to specify, given the world in which we were currently.

Zagardash made a hoarse sound of displeasure and sent his hovercraft towards the exit, forgetting all about Devir. We followed, but the worms escorting Zagardash stepped into our path. In response the catorian pulled the blaster out of his inventory and handed it to me:

"The Emperor granted me the right to own it. It's yours now. The Game will confirm the transfer."

White shining light appeared around Archibald and his weapon slowly, as if reluctantly. Several system messages flashed in front of my eyes, informing me that I had received an achievement, but I did not see anything particularly important. My attributes stayed the same except I was the owner of the impressive weapon called "Multistrike-8810". This meant that no one could take the blaster away from me, even if they knew I had it in my inventory.

The worms stepped away from us, clearing a space; I didn't even have to threaten them. As far as they were concerned, I was a maniac who had killed twenty-two players at one fell swoop, and there was nothing holding me back from expanding that list. Particularly since Zagardash was already pretty far off and couldn't see the cowardice of his servants.

"The master requested that we accompany you." The leader of the worm troop was the least lucky of them all. The order needed to be followed, and at the same time he needed to save face in front of his subordinates. He saw us to the carriage and shut the door tightly behind us. The carriage started slowly towards Zagardash's house. The worms kept a close eye on us, looking more like a convoy than an honorary escort.

"Yari, are you getting all this honor after Leguria?" Devir piped up; to him all of this looked like absurdist theater. The catorian and I chose to ignore him. Archibald was concerned about something, so he was deep in thought, and I was simply annoyed by Devir's presence.

Fortunately we made it to the back door of Zagardash's residence without any more adventure, but accompanied by the loud and annoying squeaking of the wheels. We were on edge already without that. A glum crowd of thirty-two people was waiting for us near the gates. The worms guarding them were shocking the people with electricity, making them crowd closer together, even though there was no need for that. The NPCs were quiet and docile, and tolerated the guards' assaults without objection.

"The master has left due to urgent business, but he has fulfilled his obligations under the contract," our companion stated as he opened the doors of our carriage. "He requested that you make sure you have the right number of NPCs and depart from the Underground World together with them immediately. Zagardash does not grant refuge to Dark ones."

The worm practically whispered the last sentence, fearing my anger. So then, I had been correct and the underground layer on Earth was a Light world. Using Leguria had terrified the inhabitants and made them want to get rid of the horrible Dark one ASAP. To them it looked as if the Counselor had showed up personally to quiet my Leguria and stop the players' suffering. Good thing there was nobody there to explain to the morons that the Counselor had showed up at our party to confirm that the players were beyond recovery and dispose of them. That procedure could not have taken place without him present. Those were the rules.

"We shall not go to Gorky Park," Archibald declared once he came out of his reveries. "They won't let us perform our sacrifice, there are too many players and NPCs. The hunt was stopped very recently, so it would be dangerous to show up there."

"Agreed." The teacher was right. The Game had accepted our terms, but that didn't mean it wouldn't try to interfere with us. "But we can't wait. Merlin has either completed the next sacrifice or is about to start it. We will not be able to beat him to it."

"So, you are going to kill them? Devir looked at the crowd of future corpses in surprise. "That means I was hunting you? What was the reward for you?!"

"One hundred basic granises for each of my respawns," I responded to Devir, not without pride.

"Did you down a Counselor or did you try to assassinate the Emperor?" Devir whistled in astonishment. Instead of answering I just shrugged vaguely. Let him suffer, trying to guess. Meanwhile I had our own problems to deal with, and so I opened the map. The sacrifice had to take place in a location with specific coordinates. A wild thought shot through my mind. The map was drawn in two dimensions; therefore there were only two coordinates. There was no vertical, so theoretically it was possible to perform the sacrifice underground. I lifted my head, staring at the ceiling of the giant cave that housed the underground world.

"Dear sir!" Archibald spoke to the worm. "It depends on you how soon we will fulfill your master's request and depart your world. Tell me quickly, what is the place with those coordinates?"

"Oh, that — that's at the city dump." Asking our escort was not like pulling teeth. He was hoping to get rid of us as fast as he could. "It's the liquid waste processing site. That's all I know. It really is not a place for Light beings."

"So then it will be just right for us Dark ones," Archibald responded, and turned towards me: "How much time do you need to assemble the seal?"

"Fifteen minutes and twenty seconds if the NPCs are immobilized." I had the answer prepared in advance. Steve had calculated it right after Izmailovo Park, expecting that we would be preparing the next seal in about as much of a hurry.

"You will have two minutes at best! Recalculate it!" The teacher stunned me, and without giving me any chance to rebel, switched to Devir:

"And now, my new old student, we are going to learn. Prior to the Academy you are allowed two abilities: one for defense, one for attack. Your defense ability will be Narlin Dome."

"I will be able to hold it for three minutes and twenty three seconds." To give Devir his due — he plugged into the new task at once and estimated his Energy stock and external accumulators. At level one the basic Energy hundred didn't get you very far.

"No need for more, Yari will make it." The catorian was an efficient manager. He calculated the potential for each of his underlings and set forth a plan of tasks on the basis of maximum capacity. On the brink, but quite doable. Steve updated his calculations and confirmed that it was indeed possible to fit the procedure into two minutes, with advanced preparation. In order to make it, we would have to break the bodies here and now.

"Get on with it." Archibald froze the first NPC. I didn't know how he managed that, but the others were just listlessly awaiting their fate. "Devir, come here. This is your scroll. I will become a very angry teacher if you forgot how to use that."

I detached myself from it all and did not wonder who my victims were as I absently broke their bodies in accordance with Steve's instructions. My internal Judge shut up and watched the process silently, feeling the cognitive dissonance. Part of me realized that I was a criminal and a murderer, and the other — that if I were to be dead I could not help anyone, and without me the restart would be defective again. Yes, I really believed in the higher purpose behind this whole enterprise. Maybe that's why there was not a case initiated against me after all.

"I see you have some funny ways of entertaining yourself." Devir had learnt his defense and was observing my actions. I finished working with the last victim and was barely able to straighten my back. Archibald was waiting for my go to open the portal. I was able to brace myself and nodded at him, at the same time instructing Devir:

"It will get worse now. Don't even think of dropping that dome!"

Devir was the first to jump into the portal. I waited out a couple of seconds just to make sure, grabbed the first four mutilated elements of the seal and followed the mage. The landscape on the other side was sinking in the toxic green smog, but I tried not to be distracted by the scenery. Thankfully, Archibald kept passing me the bodies to be sacrificed. Making sure the finished seal was in order, I pulled out the ritual Mayan blade and started with the killings. I had thirty five seconds left.

"But you said you destroyed him!" I heard Devir's tense voice even through my concentration. Cursing under my breath, I worried that Devir would become too agitated and collapse the dome.

"Being held in my Avalon is the same as

destroyed. Keep on task!" Archibald cut Devir short. I was maintaining my pace as I finished with the last five victims. We made it. I heard the deafening clang of the bell in my head; colored circles danced in front of my eyes. I shook my head to clear the faint feeling and read through the system messages carefully. The Game accepted the sacrifice and updated the map. The next location was right in the middle of a river. Well, in this quest we had not had to swim yet, I could agree with this. The Counselor to the Emperor kept his word: there was no new hunt called on me.

"That's it," Devir grunted, and the foul ecology of the place came to take revenge on humanity, represented by us. The green fog filled the area where the dome used to be, and started on the seal, eating the bodies like acid. Without waiting for the poisonous fog to eat through Devir with his useless noob armor, Archibald opened the portal, and unceremoniously threw Devir into it. I followed and found myself in my own living-room. Archibald didn't want to jump into Avalon with Devir in tow, but the removal of the quarantine was good news.

"Brother Yaropolk! I knew all that was a misunderstanding and you were not guilty!" Alard greeted me very warmly and heartily. Helen was working in the kitchen, not yet aware that we had arrived. I hurried to her, leaving the whole company, as I was concerned that Devir would be interested in my Doll. I took the coffee and cookies from her, and instructed her to stay in the kitchen and not show her face to the guests. After coming back I talked to the orc: I needed to thank him for his help and make sure that he was out of harm's way:

"Thank you for your help, brother. You really helped me out. Do you mind letting us have a talk here? I need to discuss something with Archibald and Devir privately."

The orc should not be in that room as we discussed our plans. I respected my red friend too much to have Archibald turn him into a statue. Remembering that the orc was completely incapable of getting hints, I explained everything to him point blank. As I supposed he would, the orc showed great understanding and left, assuring me that he would always be nearby in case I needed his help.

Archibald set up the Dome of Silence and started planning for the next stint:

"We will not be able to perform a sacrifice in the middle of the river. We would need a platform for that, otherwise there's no way we could keep the seal on the water or in the air. However, my intuition is telling me that we won't have to swim. I have looked at the subway map. There is a line that goes right through the point we need."

"That's logical. But first we need to find out if Merlin has finished his seal. I don't know what it's supposed to look like." I voiced my main worry. "on the map the picture is too small; I can't see all the sixty-four components."

"So: Merlin, then?" Devir cut into the conversation at precisely the wrong time, annoying me. I didn't understand why Archibald had had to drag him here. Why hadn't he sent him straight to the Academy?

"Vesnin has been taken off the case. He won't be able to help us. All the information is classified, the Supervisor keeps vigil over it day and night, searching for you to show up somewhere on the horizon." Archibald spoke with such certainty that I had no doubt he was well informed. "If Merlin has already done it, and according to my calculations the sacrifice was supposed to have taken place at night, there will be a surprise waiting for us near the seal. The old guy is afraid the word will get out too early, and we are nipping on his heels. Even in this era he has more enemies than a stray dog has fleas, and it's not in his best interest to reveal his secret identity before he gains his full strength. Two coordinates are not enough for me to calculate a portal to the location of the seal. I need a third. Where do I get it?"

"Look, this is the subway station closest to where we need to be," I took out my laptop and opened the map of Moscow. "Let's jump there, walk along the tunnels, and see on location. We can gather the NPCs for the sacrifice in the subway itself."

"Devir, you stay here. You are responsible with your life and limb for keeping all of Yari's property safe. And as your teacher, I recommend you keep your hands off the most valuable property. This is a direct order," Archibald said, not wanting to risk the life of the mage, who was at his last life already. The mage looked back at me, not understanding, and I kindly obliged and provided an explanation.

"Any death would be fatal to you, and any attempt on my Doll would end in you dying. Got that?" I was far from pleased with the thought that

---

Devir will be staying with Helen in our apartment, but there was nothing I could do about it. Archibald's order reassured me somewhat, and as I was stepping into a portal after him, I was surprised at the cause of my displeasure. Most of all I disliked the idea that Helen would be talking to Devir, smile at him... I felt like returning and throwing the mage out of there by the scruff of his neck, out of our home. I have never felt so proprietary. It was a pleasure and a torment at the same time. It was a pleasure to have a person so dear to me, and a torment to realize that our common future was so uncertain that the probability we would actually have one was negligibly small.

However, I would be lying if I said that every time as I killed those NPCs I didn't hope to increase that probability in the end. Yes, I was so attached to my property, to my Doll, that I was dreaming of our life together after the restart...

It was the middle of a workday, and the passenger flow of the Moscow subway was not too thick. Columns of zombified people blindly followed their routes, standing still on the escalators in order to stuff themselves into the trains or spill out into the streets. Somewhere among those NPCs, with a few beggars and musicians among them, my future sixty-four sacrifices were hurrying along.

Archibald quickly maneuvered among the people, and reaching the edge of the platform, jumped down onto the rails. No one paid any attention to him. The Game itself concealed the actions of a player from NPCs. I lingered for a bit: the rule for not approaching the edge had been drilled into me since childhood at the level of my reflexes, but as I saw Archibald beckon to me I hurried towards him. I briefly thought that I needed to be careful since there was the high voltage rail there, but I did not have time to fully think it through. There was a train coming right towards me.

"What: missing Avalon?" Archibald grabbed me out of the train's path with one hand and stuck me flat against the wall. The engine driver didn't see me, just like the other NPCs, so he didn't apply the emergency brake. Pushing with my back against the wall, I silently stared at the faces flashing by as the train was slowing down. The grey glum alienated crowds were traveling in the carriages; most were staring into their phones or tablets. Some were trying to sleep, some were off in some kind of nirvana, senselessly contemplating the glum world. I didn't see a single happy face, either in the train or in the station. That made me sad.

"Come." The train had passed. Hurrying to disgorge its load of passengers at the next station. We had about two minutes until the next train was due. Archibald got out his flying skateboard, and we rushed along the tunnel. The catorian used a bright flashlight to search for doors or branches along the way, but there was nothing like that. We let by a couple of trains and finished our search. There was nothing to show for it...

"Any ideas?" Archibald cared to ask for my opinion. Ideas, actually, I did have.

"There is no passage in this subway." I played Captain Obvious here, but the teacher understood where I was going.

"In which is there?"

"I have heard that for selected NPCs special lines were built — the so-called 'Subway-2'. I do hope very much that it was not just idle talk."

"Why have I never heard about this?" Archibald frowned.

"You never lived in Moscow. No one ever acknowledged officially that it existed. Or maybe it was because, fortunately, you never needed to use it. Supposedly it can serve as a form of backup evacuation route. According to the rumors Subway-2 starts in the Kremlin and ends out of town at some restricted access military facility. Every kid has heard about this 'secret'. Either that's what we need to find, or we'll end up having to learn to walk on the bottom of the Moscow River."

"If we have to, we'll have time to dive later. Let's work from your version We simply cannot access the Kremlin," Archibald noted. It was hard to talk with the trains rushing by, so the catorian transported us to Avalon just like that, skateboard and all. "You are at odds with the Judge Supervisor, and no one will help me since I don't belong to any class."

I took out my comm, but was not rushing to use it. First I had to plan out the conversation I was about to have. Archibald would not be able to help me, so I decided against explaining my idea to him in advance. After I was in the right frame of mind, I pushed the button.

"Speaking." The severe voice of a very busy person was coming from the speaker.

"Sir Yurmil, this is Yaropolk, appointed by

Madonna. We met recently."

"Could be," I heard the annoyed response. "I can't remember everyone I happen to meet. Where did you get my number?"

"You gave it to me yourself, along with permission to call if I encounter problems. So I am doing that."

Archibald looked at me, grinning openly, after he heard whose name I invoked. However, for the Registrar the magical name of the Great One was enough that he would not hang up on me right away, and he let me spin my line.

"What does such an important player as Madonna's appointee want from a humble registrar?" Yurmil asked, with barely veiled sarcasm in his voice. As a player, he must have been very well aware of the quest initiated against me, and even after it was revoked, it did not add many points to me in his eyes, and neither did the fact that I brought up Madonna. Since my patroness herself had allowed for me to be hunted, my usefulness to the Registrar would be dubious at best. However, since he was still talking to me he considered he had a chance to get something.

"In order to accomplish the task issued by the Great One, I need access to Subway-2. Would you help me with the map and the access?" I asked plaintively.

There was a silence in the comm suggesting that Yurmil was weighing all the "pros" and "contras".

"Ten granises." I added some weighty coins to my words.

"A hundred," Yurmil deigned to respond,

hearing about the immediate profit he could receive instead of something long-term far off. Archibald shook his head in surprise. Even the catorian was impressed by the appetite of this dude. But I had other plans:

"No, you don't understand. It's not I who will be paying ten granises. You do. To me. For providing access to Subway-2 and the map."

By hanging up Yurmil showed what he thought of that proposition. I dialed him again and received the message that my number had been blacklisted. Archibald frowned, unsure where I was going with that, but did not interfere. I dialed the next number.

"Good afternoon, Mr. Yaropolk. How is your search going?" The voice of Madonna's personal assistant was quite loud. Archibald could hear the chameleon full well without me even putting him on the speaker.

"I am close to success, but I have run into some problems, and you can help me to resolve them. I figured out where Merlin will appear very soon, but the Moscow Registrar refuses to provide me access to that place. Oh, of course, I introduced myself properly and indicated who my patron was. Mr. Yurmil, however, is demanding one hundred granises for his help. I am sorry — perhaps it's my fault to some extent — I was not able to set the right tone to that conversation. But my last few days in the Game have been very stressful. I apologize for bothering you, but I do have to seek your assistance."

"Are you sure that you need access to this place?" The chameleon did not believe me overmuch.

"Yes. If I have access, I will know who Merlin is by tomorrow. May the Game take me if I don't believe what I am saying. I do hope to be there in time, so that the Great One can save us all."

"I heard you." The chameleon gave in. He could not see the white shining that enveloped me, but the fact that I was still talking to him showed that my oath had been accepted. "I will convey your words to the Great One. You will know of her decision."

The comm went dead again. I had done all I could, now all I could do was wait for the results.

"I can congratulate myself: I was successful in teaching you. Student of mine, you are starting to bring me joy," It did not take Archibald long to figure out my intrigue. "If this works, you will receive an interesting achievement."

"Two granises on it working." I had no doubt that Madonna would spread the unfortunate registrar in a thin layer all over Red Square once she learned that Merlin was nearby somewhere. I really did get the Registrar into a pickle, but he did walk right into it. I valued my own skin more.

Archibald did not accept my bet, since he was thinking the same. Precisely three minutes later I received a system notification of receiving the new achievement that Archibald had warned me about:

Achievement received: Level 1 "Impressive Fink"

My comm started vibrating almost immediately. Yurmil was on the line.

"You just lost all fear, you bloody sorry excuse for a Paladin?"

"I am warning you that this conversation is being recorded and will be sent to the Great Madonna," I interrupted the Registrar. It took him half a minute to brace himself so as not to make his situation worse by being too hot-headed. Finally, a really annoyed voice came from the speaker:

"Access to Subway-2 is granted. The coordinates of the entry point will follow via a message. Anything else?

"What about granises?" I reminded the Registrar.

"What granises? You bas...," Yurmil's breath caught at my insolence, and he simply broke up the connection. I wanted to finish this set and sent a follow-up message: "I expect the granises by the end of the day in my bank account. Thanks for your help! I look forward to the coordinates!"

It was clear that Madonna was not going to sort out my money quarrels, but I banked on the very fact of insulting the Great One through me. Who could suppose what her reaction might be? The head of the Clerics had also thought that he could not be touched, and where was he now? I thought it was honest to insist on compensation equal to the amount of the bribe that was not to be.

"You do accumulate enemies pretty much at the speed of light," Archibald commented neutrally.

"Let's consider that the little nabob went too far and received his last warning from a Judge." I felt like I was Robin Hood, taking the money away from the rich and giving it to the poor. "By the way, just out of curiosity, what level is your achievement of this type?"

"Like I would just go and tell you! There are the coordinates," Archibald nodded at my vibrating comm. We never brought up the topic again.

Yurmil did not deceive our expectations: the portal in fact brought us to the starting station of Subway-2. A thick layer of dust and the absence of lights made it clear that it had not been used for a very long time. The current NPC rulers preferred to move by air. Archibald extracted his skateboard, and we flew forward through the tunnel, looking for the right location.

Once there were a couple of hundred meters left to the spot, Archibald cast the Dome of Silence and stopped, staring into the darkness intently. My vision, even enhanced by my abilities, left a lot to be desired, so I pulled out my Multistrike just in case and made ready to shoot at any target.

Moving forward slowly. Archibald pointed down at a few trip wires underneath. Had we not been using the skateboard, we would have definitely been caught by one. There was about fifty yards left till the end of the tunnel, when I heard monotonous mumbling. Someone was there.

We flew to the opening very quietly. We saw the wide platform of the cross connection station, just as dark and dusty as the ones before. In the center, in the dim light of a candle, a single lanky figure in a robe was standing. From afar it really looked like the creature we had seen in the video from the park clearing. This unknown person was working on putting together a seal.

Archibald pulled out his sword, played with it,

---

but then put it back into its sheath. No matter how strong an artifact was, without class allegiance it would be useless for fighting Merlin if that was indeed he. My teacher pulled out a weapon that was exactly the same as my Multistrike and nodded at the guy. I aimed for the dark figure and indicated I was ready.

Archibald started counting down, crooking his fingers. I swallowed, preparing to do battle. There was no fear, just the tension that made my palms sweaty. Here was the moment of truth! If I found out whose mask Merlin was wearing, it would resolve a good deal of my problems on its own. For this I would be even prepared to shoot at the guy's back. Archibald bent the last finger, and plasma enhanced with deadly spells shot out from both barrels at once. Three hits were enough for the Judge Supervisor, so how many would it take for Merlin?

The Dome of Silence dispelled with the first shots. The dark figure turned around, raised its hand in defense. The plasma stopped short of the target and dropped to the floor, burning a hole through it. We kept blasting away. Another volley. Three. Five. Ten. The defense of the dark being easily overcame our attack, but it was impossible for him to fight back. Finally, at some point, the enemy lifted his head and the red embers of his eyes shone from under the hood. It was so unexpected, I stopped shooting. A vampire? Merlin was a vampire? Taking advantage of my mistake, the vampire attacked Archibald, melting his Multistrike. I resumed shooting, covering the teacher, while he pulled out another blaster, and I hoped that I would be able to shoot a few more times before my Multistrike followed suit. But instead of attacking the vampire put up an energy shield, opened a portal and disappeared without attempting to complete the sacrifice. I completely failed to understand: what in hell had just happened here? Merlin could have attacked me, or could have simply held the shield and finished the seal. Instead he chose to simply run away!

"Video!" Archibald ordered. Steve put together everything he was able to record, and zoomed in as closely as possible. But there was nothing we could see except for the red eyes.

"Garbital should know who that was!" the teacher said angrily, and pointed at the seal that was already prepared. "Is it complete?"

For several minutes Steve and I compared yet another monstrous creation with what we could see on the Explorer's map. The final conclusion indicated with 60% probability that the seal was complete. Archibald kept silent, letting me make my choice on the fate of those already crippled people. They had been prepared for this since birth. The ritual knife was the only way to check if the seal was actually complete. Sixty four swipes later we saw the system confirmation that was truly the case. That had in fact been Merlin.

"That's unexpected...," I said in astonishment, looking at the updated map. There was no new seal, and the inscription with coordinates appeared under the picture of the chest. I handed the ritual blade to Archibald: "Here. I think I won't need it anymore."

"This is becoming funny." Archibald assessed

the changes, and the tip of his tail started twitching with impatience. "Let's go — we need to prepare. We set out tomorrow at sunrise. It's better not to try to get in there today; Bernard is hosting a reception.

Again and again the Game forced me against Bernard. Now one more time we would have to visit his residence, because the damned chest with the letter "M" on it was located in his library. Section twelve, case seven, shelf three, second book from the right. When I was visiting Bernard's residence I had lacked a mere couple of hours to get to that shelf. Then all these adventures could have been avoided. It was a pity it was impossible to return to the past and correct things there.

CHAPTER EIGHT

DAY SEVEN

IT WAS FIVE in the morning. It was Avalon. Archibald's hospitality disappeared together with Clarissa, so instead of a breakfast and coffee I was in for yet another discussion of our whole enterprise. The teacher started with the bad news:

"This is Bernard's residence." A 3D model of the estate appeared between us. Steve compared it with the floor plans that we had and nodded respectfully: our maps were not as detailed. "Last night I tried to enter it myself."

"By 'tried' you mean you did not succeed?" I asked. Archibald normally either did something or not, but I had never heard of him trying and yet not doing it.

"Yes, my inquisitive student. I tried — that

means that I made attempts, but was not successful, even though I tried very hard. Without excessive modesty I would say that I know all modern security systems like the back of my paw. But the protection of this estate is at a different order of magnitude."

"Is this bad?"

"It brings up questions to which there are no answers. That's what's bad. How did Bernard get protection from previous eras? He is a creature of this era, I have no doubt about that. This protection has been there for a long time — I checked; and we can rule out Lumpen's help. I don't see who else could have helped set up the protection; I checked through my channels as well. All those who would be capable of doing it, deny it."

"Could it be a gift from the Game, or from the Emperor, that came with the position of Coordinator?" I made a suggestion, but then corrected myself: "But the Game would not provide anything that comes from previous eras. Only from the current one."

"That's the whole point."

"What about Madonna? Or even Merlin himself?!" I had an epiphany. "Really, that's the deal! Bernard keeps Merlin's Diary, he let it slip that he knows where to find the old coot. Maybe he even became the Coordinator because of Merlin? Doesn't he need helpers? Why not Bernard?"

"No," Archibald shook his head confidently. "Neither he nor Madonna, and both can be ruled out for the same reason as Lumpen: the protection was installed before her incarnation. As for Merlin... I think if he had had a hand in this, Madonna would have sensed it and made mincemeat out of Bernard together with his residence."

It was in fact quite improbable that while Madonna stayed at Bernard's for such a long time she would not have determined who had designed the protection or sense his unseen presence.

Yet Archibald started thinking:

"You know, my lucky student, on the whole I agree with your line of thinking, but it is not Merlin who is involved in all that. I need to think some more about it — who of those from the previous era was in the play, but after restart lost their influence and made an alliance with the Coordinator?"

"Could it be Gromana? She became close with Bernard immediately after she came to Earth," I reminded him of something I knew. "Should we be looking in this direction perhaps? They did not even know each other before meeting here on Earth."

"That's out of the question," Archibald waved me off. "That was Soluna's doing. When she cursed Gromana and sent her to exile on Earth, she had asked Bernard for access. Before granting it, he carefully reviewed the black witch's file. Gromana had no other option than to stay with Bernard and accept the status of being his vassal. She drank a fair share of Soluna's blood, and the Coordinator was at an advantage from whatever angle you look by providing protection to the witch. There's no point in barking up that tree."

"Sorry that I can't help you any more with this. The list of players of the previous era does not indicate their levels, only names and locations," I said sadly and caught my teacher's glance, loaded with sarcasm. I did not even bother feeling offended that Archibald perceived me as whatever, but definitely not someone able to help.

"What difference does it make where Bernard got this protection and who is his ally if you cannot access the library?"

"You are not paying attention. I did say that alone I was not successful. We will have to go together."

"So are you hinting that you need my help?" Now it was my turn to be sarcastic.

"Not at all. Stop speculating, silly student! I need someone to accompany me. It doesn't matter who it is — you or some stupid player," the teacher parried. "If we can't enter Bernard's residence the ordinary way, we'll go via the Path of the Dead."

There was a lengthy pause. Archibald either expected me to ask questions, or at this point believed that I was well informed; in either case, he did not hasten to explain what this path was. Steve just spread his hands — there was no information available. I decided that since any stupid player would do for the task of accompanying Archibald, I would find everything out along the way. All that was left to do was to get up and ask when we were setting out. My teacher simply squinted his eyes quizzically and called the elevator. We moved to an unfamiliar and interesting room. The central part of it was taken by an arch that looked like a large Greek Omega. Within, it was opaque, iridescent green, and did not look at all like the portal entrances I had seen before. Its shimmering surface rippled with little waves now and then, as if someone was trying to get through from the other side.

"Only two can walk the Path of the Dead," Archibald explained, pulling out his Multistrike. I followed suit. "This is the domain of Thanatos. You will like him — he is also quite boring. Come on, there is no time to waste."

Archibald drew his Multistrike and shot a volley of fireballs straight into the arch. For a few seconds the ripples on its surface stilled. My teacher disappeared in the arch without delay. I followed him, this time without fire, as I was concerned about shooting in his direction. The green surface clung to me like sticky rubber, I had to push forward, working with my elbows. I heard the blast of a gong in my ears, and the rubber trap was behind me. Archibald was already actively shooting from his Multistrike at the ghosts and skeletons attacking him, so there was no time to really look around. I turned my head this way and that, letting Steve to register our surroundings, while I noted only the red rocky terrain of the Paths of the Dead. Now I could join the teacher and help him clear the world of the specters.

"We need to see the master," Archibald said half an hour later. The stream of ghostly attackers dwindled, even though not completely. I felt as though they would never run out. Lacking the strength or desire to answer I simply grunted. My teacher made a few steps to the right, leaving me alone against the never-ending army. I killed a couple more with the plasma, but then missed a few and was thinking that they would attack me from the back. But it turned out I was wrong. Swerving around me, the ghosts flew to the portal, striving to overcome the resistance of its green surface. I moved towards Archibald and verified that we had just wasted half an hour destroying those completely harmless ghosts. All that column was aiming for the shimmering obstacle that separated them from our world; they couldn't care less about us. Once they reached the gates, the ghosts disappeared, and new eager ones replaced them.

"Did you know about this?" I couldn't get rid of the thought that Archibald was just having fun while waiting for the mysterious "master".

"Everyone has their small weaknesses, even the Shadow," we heard a low, but unemotional voice say in the dead silence. That could be the voice of Death himself, inviting the select few to share their last steps with him, and reminding them that from now on nothing mattered. As soon as the speaker finished, sounds flooded back into the world.

"Thanatos, long time no see! It's a pleasure to see you again!" Archibald bowed his head as he put a smile on his face. But his tail betrayed his tension. The catorian did not use his customary "my friend" either. Perhaps because the local master was very particular about using the term "friend". Not clear where to look to see Thanatos, I turned my head this way and that, and then followed Archibald's gaze and looked up. Directly above us, about a dozen yards in the air, a dark-skinned young man was floating; his enormous snow-white wings fully spread out. Thanatos was dressed in a simple codpiece, but I could bet this piece was stronger than the Imperial armor set: the creature that we were seeing demonstrated quite clearly that players could reach the status of a god. So why not the god of death?

"We saw each other three thousand seven hundred and two years ago," Thanatos responded, and it became clearer to me why I could relate to him. Thanatos was straightforward and unequivocal. For the player who made himself the god of death there were only facts without any distortion. "Why did you enter my world, Shadow?"

"I need help," Archibald admitted, and as for me, I heard yet another name for the catorian. Shadow. What could that mean? "I need to enter the library of the Coordinator for sector 446."

"The price is standard." Now Thanatos' voice carried no emotion whatsoever. "Is this the advance?"

For the first time since he had appeared, Thanatos paid attention to me.

"No, this is my mirror," Archibald refused to give me as an advance. A charge of entropy surged up and settled somewhere at the cloud level. I lost all understanding of what was going on.

"I did not grant him the right to be here," Thanatos remarked. "Your mirror must leave my world."

The stream of ghosts dissipated, clearing the path for me towards the portal, and an invisible yet palpable force started dragging me towards the exit out of the world of the dead. Archibald came to my defense:

"I want to buy a single access guest pass for

him. Minimum price, without rights of functional interface."

A couple of seconds later I was released, and the flow of ghosts into our world resumed its motion.

"Follow me." Thanatos flapped his wings and disappeared in the rocks. The offer had been accepted.

"Shadow? Mirror?" I was not hurrying to set out after Archibald, requiring at least some answers.

"Hold on, my determined student. Soon you will find everything out, I swear by my tail, but not today. So let's go — we can't make Thanatos wait. He doesn't like that."

I felt like different feelings were struggling inside me. One side was screaming that I have waited for a long time and I need to press Archibald, and the second one was ordering the first one to shut up and run after Thanatos if I didn't want to leave the catorian alone in this not too hospitable world. Looking at my teacher's retreating back, I agreed with the latter and rushed to catch up with the catorian.

"The Path of the Dead was created back during the first era." An observer might have thought that Archibald was just thinking aloud rather than teaching his student. He was walking forward and mumbling under his breath when I caught up with him. "In effect, the Path is just the same place outside of normal space as my Avalon. The difference lies only in the setting and the functions that it performs."

"And the imagination of the owner," I added and clarified: "Do you pay with players or NPCs?"

"Players, preferably under level 50. Ideally

without an anchor to a respawn point. One service costs one hundred players. Now I will have to pony up two hundred at once. My stock of frozen goods is going to diminish quite a bit." My teacher continued his explanation.

"How often have you used this path?" I could not say I was surprised by Archibald's pragmatic approach. It was more like the norm for one like him. Why waste frozen bodies when it was their own fault getting that way? I was just curious to know how often he did that.

"This is the seventh time. But if I need to, I will use this path another hundred and seven times. This is the Game, my compassionate student, and there is no place for sentimentality here."

"Right. That's why Devir is lounging at my apartment rather than having been turned to dust," I quipped. "Strictly because there is no place for sentimentality here."

Archibald snorted and took several leaps to climb the nearest boulder. Rather than repeating this acrobatic feat I activated my anti-grav and glided up after him. Thanatos was standing on a small clearing, he descended from the air to the ground. Close up he looked very similar to an ordinary person except for his wings and eyes. I had never seen eyes so filled with Darkness in anyone in the Game.

I was openly staring at the local god when I heard the shooting of Multistrike. I already gotten used to the ghosts that were hovering around me and stopped paying attention to them, but one could not say that about the catorian. He was involved in shooting at the ghosts; they, in turn, were trying to get to my teacher. I really didn't like that: Archibald was the only creature capable of dragging me out of here. Thanatos didn't indicate any displeasure at the elimination of his local inhabitants, so I came to my teacher's aide. This way we kept shooting at them until the flow thinned.

"They remember you, Shadow." Thanatos indicated that he had been watching our actions. "Each one that you brought here. Soon there will be no place for you in the Paths of the Dead."

."Once there is not, then we'll talk." The teacher was showing off in front of Thanatos, concealing his tension . I stepped to one side and put away the blaster.

"The entrance will be here. I am ready. Warn your mirror," Thanatos said to Archibald, then turned his back to us as his hands started blazing. My teacher exhaled with relief as if he could not believe that the goal was so close.

"A portal will appear now, and we will only have just a few seconds to enter. It will be hard, as when we were entering the Citadel. You must constantly move forward; just one step backwards and those who will be following you will drag you back here, but this time as a present. Believe me, you are better off not knowing what you would be facing in that case. So drag yourself forward by your teeth if you have to, but crawl forward. Get that?"

It was hard not to understand such a warning. I nodded and prepared to dive into the forming portal. But something went wrong. That became clear a couple of seconds later. A new participant to all of this blocked the Path of the Dead in front of us. He looked like a most common and ordinary old man in a white robe.

"Merlin!" Archibald hissed. I didn't have a chance to take a good look at the mage when the catorian drew his Multistrike and shot a volley of fireballs towards the intruder. Even though they did not inflict any harm on the latter, because the old guy turned out to be a high quality hologram.. All the missiles shot by Archibald went right through it and exploded against a nearby rock.

"Greetings to the master of the Path of the Dead," said the hologram, indifferent to Archibald's efforts. "I have come with a proposal. Hear me out."

"Merlin," Thanatos greeted the old man as an equal. "Your payment has been accepted, I grant you the right to visit here mentally. You are using your image from the previous era."

"It does not matter what I am using. Don't open the portal."

"An agreement has been made with Shadow. The payment is received. You have no right to interfere with me, Merlin."

"I am not interfering; I am just offering a higher price," the old man disagreed. "You received two hundred souls, right? I am offering three thousand players from level 10 to 50 with free anchor points. I am sure that will be plenty to cover the return of the souls for the termination of the contract and paying the fine. In return, the residence of Bernard Kalran will be inaccessible for three days. That is all I am asking. The Coordinator is keeping an item that is valuable to me and I cannot allow it to find its way into the paws of Shadow. What do you say?"

"Restart is coming, Merlin," Thanatos shook his head. "You will respawn, and the contract will become invalid. You do not have automatic payment like Shadow does."

"You will receive your players today itself, or else the Game will send me to you to share your lonely existence. That is my word. Today nothing threatens Restart, right?"

"Right," the winged god agreed. "I must think about your proposal. Wait."

Thanatos soared high into the sky, leaving us alone with Merlin's hologram. The old guy looked at silent Archibald with a sneer and said:

"Tut-tut, aren't you being bad. Does your master know what his pet animal is up to? Did you become bored, Shadow? Decided to start a game of your own?"

"Who knows, Merlin?" Archibald was now in control of both himself and his voice. "Maybe that is my master's game and you didn't notice that you are playing it? You are nothing without your diary, just as I am without my master. Or not? You ran away so fast yesterday I didn't even have time to greet you properly.

"Shadow, don't flatter yourself." The old guy broke into hoarse but genuine laughter. "All that you have of value is the Guide. By the way, young man, your teacher owes his life to you. He drags you everywhere with him like a living shield. Well. You should at least charge him for it, Dark one! Ha-ha-ha! Serving a Light mongrel! Ha-ha-ha! Had it not been for you, the Game would have gladly wiped your teacher out from its memory, with my help. He knows, mangy furball, that I will not risk the Guide. I just don't happen to have the time to wait for another! So be careful: protect your own head, not your teacher's."

Merlin was juggling the facts and words so artfully, badmouthing the catorian, that prior to our marathon I would have believed him. But now it was obvious that the old fart just wanted to sow discord between us. We were hindering him too much — he was unable to catch up with us. I got mad at him for trying yet again to manipulate me, and a little nasty thought sneaked into my head. I could not cause Merlin any serious harm — that was beyond my level; however, I could create minor trouble and make him hurt — that was quite within the power of a Judge. The case regarding transfer of three thousand players to Thanatos initiated so easily that it surprised me. The Game did not hesitate for an instant, which boosted my determination.

I just had to wait for Thanatos to return to provide a justified verdict. He did not keep us waiting for long, gliding gracefully to the ground between Merlin and Archibald.

"Your offer is acceptable and does not contradict the rules, Merlin. I accept it. The Paths of the Dead will not touch the residence of Bernard Kalran for three days. Shadow, our contract is terminated. Four hundred souls have been returned to Avalon. Leave my domain."

The tip of the catorian's tail showed very clearly what my teacher thought about those events, but he did not argue with Thanatos. Silently he turned around and went back to the portal. I was still standing in the same place when a dark wall separated Thanatos and Merlin from us, indicating our place. The moment for what I was thinking to do was just right:

"For interfering in the Game process of three thousand players and transferring them to Thanatos thereby isolating them from the main Game world, I deem Merlin guilty, and sentence him to diarrhea for three days without the right to seek treatment. The sentence is final and I hope he explodes in his shithouse."

I had only a vague idea of what punishments were available in the Game, but since I wholly believed that my decision was fair, I hoped that the Game would find my solution possible. More so, since this punishment implied confidentiality, since the Game would not allow a premature disclosure of the old guy's identity. Everything was in the spirit of the Game, and this is precisely why Judges were disliked and players tried to kill them at every opportunity.

Verdict is confirmed

A small increase of Energy served just as a bonus to add to my satisfaction from the decision I had made. Pleased with myself, I followed the teacher, whistling a merry song, until I saw in what mood Archibald was. On the way back he was detached and strangely silent. He did not even notice, or maybe ignored, my little prank. Several times the catorian kicked stones that lay in his path, but without his customary drive. I had never seen him that depressed; he had always been sardonic and arrogant; despondency shunned him. I could see only one cause for all this: Merlin's or Thanatos' targeted spell. I could not believe that it could be due to the failed negotiations.

Sending us on our way, Thanatos had cleared the way of the ghosts, so we reached the portal quickly. Passing through it was also easier; the green veil helped you to leave the world of the dead. As soon as I stepped into the portal room, instead of the hard floor my feet slipped on something round, so that I almost fell on Archibald, who was standing in front of me. Throughout the room a huge number of small metal balls were scattered; even without Steve it was clear that these were the returned souls. They had a strange idea of souls for sure.

"The Emperor offers to buy the released souls." We didn't even have time to make it to the door when the Counselor appeared out of thin air. Avalon reacted to its guest quite moderately: its protections were ineffective against a being of that level. As the balls soared in the air and formed four regular cubes, it became clear that this offer was not to be turned down.

Archibald just nodded in response, and the Counselor disappeared together with the balls, leaving a reward for the catorian. I noted with pleasure that it was given to me as well. My level of basic granises increased by four units, one for each hundred players; unfortunately, as for granises themselves, there was no increase. Archibald, still silent, called the elevator, transported us to the hall, and settled down in an armchair, burying himself in a throw. A fireplace was burning nearby, the fire crackling and throwing bright flashes. Archibald seemed to have sunk into some sort of a trance; his eyes were blankly staring at the fire; the chair rocked steadily with the catorian in it, and I felt uneasy. That could not be that! We had done so much that there had to be a way out! There must be! Time ticked on and I felt all hot and bothered.

"Archibald!" Silence, and the measured creaking of the chair. I came closer and stood in his field of view.. No reaction. I shook his hand, but his breath didn't even change. Finally I decided that there was an hour or two available, so the catorian could repair whatever was apparently broken within him for some reason. I settled in a rocking chair next to him and started rocking; my creaks matched Archibald's. About half an hour later I heard his voice.

"You don't know who is Thanatos or what is the Path of the Dead, right?"

Well, finally! I jumped with joy, but the catorian still did not move, and kept silent. He was waiting for me to answer his question. "No. Is that important?"

"It's not important for you now. But it might become so after Restart."

"OK, I understand," I agreed; I was talking to him calmly as if he were sick. "I'm ready to listen to you."

"The Path of the Dead is the admin sector inside the Game; it provides control over all the beings. Thanatos is the lead admin, appointed to that position by the Emperor back in the first era. Every time a being dies, whether it is a player or an NPC, no matter who, his consciousness drops into the Path. There the Game determines where to send it. Either for disposal or to the printer, or somewhere else depending on the set algorithm. That is why there is an hour's delay between a player's death and respawn. The Game doesn't have limitless resources. That's from where we were just thrown out."

"So we were, and to hell with that. How did you get access to it, anyway?" I needed to get Archibald to talk, and it was not an idle question: even Merlin was in the Path as a hologram. And we had been there in the flesh.

"For special achievements. Clarissa and I had a son. Due to circumstances I had to exile him from our world. That's how the Master of the Path appeared. The portal is the gift of the Game to communicate with the one whom my son became after his exile. Or maybe it's a punishment. After all these years I still don't understand what the Emperor's point was in making the entrance to the Path of the Dead in Avalon. Normally Thanatos would only talk to players after a sacrifice. Even with Merlin. And only as a hologram."

Thanatos was the son of Archibald and Clarissa?! So, then, circumstances. Now it was clear why the witch had left him — there are very few who would be able to live with the murderer of their son, no matter how much they had used to love that person. I was not particularly interested in the catorian's family drama at the time, so I didn't dwell on the topic. I was more interested in the terms like "Shadow", "mirror" and "master", but the question was how to broach that topic.

"What does it mean that the Paths of the Dead will not touch the residence of Bernard?"

I didn't see any improvement in Archibald's state, and my patience was starting to run out. Now there was no help, and without his experience, connections and resources I would not be able to get hold of the damned diary. If there was no Diary, there would be no player Yaropolk in three days. Given the situation, even my curiosity with respect to "Shadow" was diminished.

"Besides the fact that it is now impossible to enter there through that path, it is impossible to harm anyone within the residence. Consider that everyone within its territory is in a different dimension. There is no way for them to cut themselves, fall to their death or be poisoned for three days. A local parody of immortality that will last three days. If you were to get there with your Leguria, you'd be famished and die."

"It means the status of the Sanctuary is not applicable, and Bernard's library is a really sweet piece for the Game," Steve suddenly pointed out. I frowned, not quite understanding what my subconscious meant, but then the idea floated up to the surface from the depths of my mind, and a grin spread on my face. Merlin had just signed a sentence for Bernard, even though it was not a death sentence. Since it was impossible to harm anyone within the

residence.

"Tell me, my saddened teacher, do you have a lot of granises?" I could not refrain from using Archibald's favorite tactic. The catorian stopped hypnotizing the fire and focused all of his attention on my person.

"If you are counting for an inheritance, count again! I have willed all my granises to charity after I die," my teacher snorted. And I was happy to see him come back to his usual self.

"It's too early for me to think of inheriting from you. I need to first avoid dying myself. Please give some money to a poor Paladin for an ignoble purpose."

"You make a terrible beggar. How much do you need? And for what?"

"We need mercenaries and weapons. A lot of weapons and lots of mercenaries.

"For example, and then what?" apparently, Archibald still had trouble thinking clearly. He still had not figured out what I had in mind.

"Then, my not understanding teacher, we gather the whole crowd in front of Bernard's gate, give everyone the task to destroy his extremely valuable library, and crash in, destroying everything that the eye can see. Of course, first we would take the most valuable things for us. We will not be able to harm anyone, you just said that the Game has made all the inhabitants of the residence immortal. I suspect this rule applies also to those who enter. So neither Malturion, nor Bernard, nor Madonna herself if she is still staying with the Coordinator, would be able to do anything to the attackers. Besides, we, as the clients who ordered all of this excess, would be clean in the eyes of the Game, and no one could blame us for the riots. We are just completing the task set forth by the Game to destroy ancient artifacts. It will take Bernard some time to figure out what is going on, then to ask Merlin to ask Thanatos to make everyone mortal again, and for Merlin to make the sacrifice and so on and so forth. Meanwhile we will make it to the library. We have the precise coordinates of the Diary, so what else do we need? Oh, right! Money. Mercenaries. And weapons. Lots of weapons."

It was nice to see the familiar sneer. Archibald nodded, admitting that my plan was workable, and now he was eager for action. The first thing to use was his comm:

"Ayrinessa, there's a gig for twenty granises for you and your band, plus five basic granises from the Game. You interested? I'll see you and the team at the Sanctuary on Earth in one hour — will you make it? Excellent, see you then! Engibord, there's a gig for twenty granises for you and your band..."

An hour later the central square in Zurich was a sight to behold. Due to the high concentration of professional mercenaries from our sector in the area, the Game cleared all the adjacent areas of NPCs. The rest of the players had the good sense to clear out on their own. Twenty two close-knit and very dangerous teams — including Miltay's, who was invited by me — gathered after one phone call by the catorian. Everyone was curious what the old hand had came up with and why he didn't do it on his own. The catorian was quickly making his way to the center; he had ordered me to keep close. Plowing through the crowd of mercenaries I heard surprised whispers quite often. The huge reward for my head was still fresh in their minds. At least it was good that the status of the Sanctuary protected me from belated assaults, but the fighters' looks were far from wishing me good health.

At the center Archibald set up a large tent and invited all the heads of the bands to discuss the operation. Those included all sorts — there were orcs, people, elves, strange six-legged monsters, a cynocephalian and even a flying manta ray. Miltay stared at his colleagues like they were idols suddenly come alive. Looking happily from one legendary character to another with his habitual "look here" every time and smiling happily, showing his damaged teeth. Even though he was a successful mercenary, he was still in the beginning of his career, and getting into such company was like magic. That alone could be viewed as a significant achievement regardless of the outcome of the negotiations. Archibald waited for everyone to settle at the round table, and created a 3D projection of Bernard's residence.

"Our goal," the catorian said, and had there been a mosquito in the tent, everyone would have heard it then.

"I believe I will voice a common thought," Engibord, a dark elf, cautiously began. "Archibald, this is the residence of the Coordinator; it is located in the Sanctuary, and currently the Great One is staying there! Have you decided to get rid of all the professional mercenaries in the sector in one fell swoop? Or are you not feeling well?"

"I hear panic in your words, Engibord." Archibald's voice projected confidence. "As if you were not a professional mercenary, but a newbie freshly graduated from the Academy, or a veteran whose only dream is a warm chair and some yogurt. I am of sound mind. I would like to remind you that nothing has happened to the law of the mercenaries, so what are you afraid of?"

The Law of the Mercenaries stated that all responsibility for completing a contract rested with the client, but only if the mercenary did not cross certain boundaries in his actions. For example, if the mercenary was supposed to get rid of one specific player, and he killed a bunch more to boot, he would be punished precisely for that bunch minus that one player. The client would be responsible for that one.

"The Sanctuary status," Engibord fell silent, but Ayrinessa came to his aid: a demonologist with a horrible scar that marred half her face. Her hoarse voice matched her appearance. Steve provided some information: the demonologist was a player from the third era. Archibald excepted, this lady was the oldest in the present company.

"This is my problem." Archibald was not going to show his cards all at once. "Those who venture to follow me will not be punished for the attack on the residence. But only that. If you decide to attack someone else — for that you will be held responsible."

"I am curious about the basic granises." While other heads of bands were thinking, Miltay piped up.

"For what will they be awarded?

"I was not finished." Archibald zoomed into the hologram, highlighting the library. This is our final goal. The library with artifacts from previous eras. Does everyone have the quest?"

A concerted nod confirmed that all of the mercenaries had received the quest back then. The only one who did not have it was me, and Archibald immediately corrected that. The point of the quest was to completely destroy the library; each participant of the raid would receive five basic granises for that. Destruction of individual artifacts did not count, nor did it provide any additional bonuses. While I was Bernard's vassal, I didn't have that quest. But now, given my status of an "unattached" player, I could quite easily, equally with others, try my luck and fulfill the Game's request to destroy the unnecessary artifacts.

"You can't as much as spit there before being thrown out through a portal, with a quarantine for a month," Engibord frowned, apparently remembering his previous attempts.

"There are traps, blockers, freezers... The Coordinator's Residence is better protected than Fort Knox," an orc confirmed.

"That's why I called on the best," Archibald cheered everyone up. "There won't be much to do with magic. We need brute force here. We will move slowly, burning out everything around step by step."

"Fine, but coming back to my question," Ayrinessa was extremely skeptical about the upcoming enterprise. "How are you planning to get around the Sanctuary status? We won't be able to as much as sneeze in the direction of the residence, when the punishment will find us. And our law won't work here, it would hit us directly, not the client. Clarify that, or else I am out. I will not sign up for something that doesn't make any sense."

"Today Thanatos turned his face away from Kalran's residence," Archibald stated, and Ayrinessa's widened eyes indicated she knew what he was talking about. But that obviously did not apply to the others, who looked at each other in bewilderment.

"I'm in." After her initial surprise passed, the demonologist agreed. Looking at the others, Ayrinessa shrugged. She was not going to share information about Thanatos for free, and there was no one willing to buy the knowledge there and then.

"I'm in too. Look here, if Ayrinessa signed up for that, it wouldn't be right for me to pass it up. The reward is good, and this will be a bang of a campaign."

"How about the rest?" Archibald looked at the mercenaries, since there was no immediate response.

"I'm out," Engibord said after thinking for a little while. "I don't like signing up for things I don't understand. The client doesn't wish to be frank, so I'm not risking my band. Good luck!"

The dark elf rose and left the tent. The mercenary's dealing was quick: for some paltry twenty five granises, even though five of them were basic, he was not going to get involved in this. Especially in the Sanctuary.

"Who else agrees with Engibord?" Archibald

didn't look upset. Even the tip of his tail did not twitch, betraying frustration. The catorian had expected this turn of events. One after another the heads of the mercenaries left the tent until only four players remained within: Archibald, Ayrinessa, Miltay and I.

The demonologist was the first to speak, turning towards Miltay and giving him a brief quiz:

"What do you have? How many people? Access level? Completed quests? I need to know who is going to stand next to my people."

Miltay did not lose his nerve, and answered her questions not as a student called up to the front for the first time, but as an experienced band leader. I would bet that was precisely why Ayrinessa liked him. After she was finished with the questions, the demonologist nodded to Archibald:

"He'll do. Shall we work as before?"

Archibald raised his paw, requesting silence, and holding his comm in the other paw. The Game communication gadget started vibrating, but the catorian was not surprised by the call.. The message on the display was visible to everyone: Bernard Kalran. I shamelessly moved closer to the teacher and perked up my ears.

"Don't do that," the Coordinator said by way of greeting. "We have an agreement. I am following my side of it, so why in hell are you planning to attack me? As soon as the first shot sounds the agreement will be void!"

I snorted. Some mercenary had decided to curry favor with Bernard and had sold him the information as soon as he left the tent. The termination of agreement would mean an attack on us by Lumpen and his sidekicks. And it also meant that Bernard was ready to risk his position of the Coordinator for Merlin's sake. In order to preserve his property. That was quite a turn of events!

"I honor the agreement, Bernard," Archibald parried. "An attack on your residence is not breaking it. I am driven only by my desire to follow the rules of the Game, that state that all unregistered artifacts from former eras should be destroyed. This quest, as far as I recall, was initiated over two hundred years ago, so it does not affect our agreement in any way. I could offer you a way out of this situation. Repent, turn in all your artifacts to the Temple of Knowledge, promise not to collect them any more, and the quest will close by itself. No quest — no attack."

"So we can't reach agreement?" came the response from the comm. Bernard did not wish to lose his collection so meaninglessly.

"Apparently not. Go put the kettle on and wait for your guests to arrive. On the other hand, if you don't like noisy guests you could go take a rest somewhere else."

Archibald turned off his comm with a pleased look, as if he had eaten a jug of cream in front of his master, who could do nothing about it. Following the call the catorian received a message on his comm that he read out loud:

"'Engibord.' The dark elf has been playing around too much. Ayri, I like light lirunian wine aged for 200 years. Think of what to serve with it, Surprise me, hostess with the mostest."

The demonologist cursed heartily, but accepted the levy without objection. As a student who was used to being left out of the loop I expressed my interest:

"Oh well, I am fed up with the role of an extra. Please clarify: what's the wine for?"

"For catching a rat among our glorious troops, my too curious student. I figured it out a while ago: someone is selling out on orders, forgetting the mercenaries' code. Ayrinessa didn't want to admit it, and I didn't have time to find them out. So today I had a perfect opportunity to combine business with pleasure. Ayrinessa is the coordinator of the Mercenaries' Guild for our sector, so Engibord must truly feel the depth of his transgression. And this is not a hope, Ayri, and not a recommendation. If it happens differently, I will have to step in myself. There is no place for rats among the mercenaries! Do you understand?"

Archibald was scolding the coordinator heartily, as if he had every right to do so. That's who was the true coordinator of mercenaries here, not the contrite demonologist. Even though, who knows, it's possible that Archibald had a paw in creating the Guild of Mercenaries on Earth as well. I would not be surprised.

"Now the most important thing — getting into the residence." Finally Archibald got down to business rather than playing a strict teacher. The projection was now showing an enlarged version of the entrance gate as the only means of entry. The walls of the residence were not high, but it would be impossible to take them by storm. There were portals and lots of other stuff that I didn't know about. So what was left were the gates. Huge metal gates enhanced with Game magic. "Ayri, do you still have Berta, or did you fortify your ranks?"

"Wow, good thing you did not bring up Karl too!" the demonologist responded, and a guttural slurpy rattling, which turned out to be her laughter, assaulted my ears. "I have Elsa now."

"Put Elsa in front of the gates: we are going to break them. Miltay, you provide a safe zone of twenty yards around the gates.

"Fifty," Ayrinessa corrected him.

"Even so?" Archibald was surprised, but confirmed the request. "Fine, a safe zone of fifty yards. Spread danger tape, cordon it off with trucks, do whatever, but no NPCs should interfere with Elsa. Stray players in this zone are my problem. Does Elsa need to be protected against any force majeures?"

"For about five minutes it can operate independently, even in the middle of a nuclear explosion. I worked on upgrading it myself. Keep in mind, Archie, if Elsa were killed or damaged, I would never forgive you."

That means we have five minutes for the entry." Archibald just shrugged. "Then we head for the library, burning everything in our path. Do we have the means?"

The demonologist nodded. Miltay clarified his role.

"What should we do, me and my guys?"

"Guard the rear and don't get underfoot."

Ayrinessa responded instead of Archibald. "This is not your battle. You are only coming because I liked your unconditional trust in my word. It's been a while since I encountered such... romanticism among mercenaries. We are all opportunistic pragmatists: measure thrice, sign a hundred contracts and agreements, but play it by ear. This raid will serve to educate you for the future, but today mostly just don't get in the way. Got that?"

"Sure," Miltay said bashfully, as he had not expected such a telling off. In his mind he probably was the first to rush into the library, shoulder to shoulder with the demonologist. But the mercenary overcame his internal hang-ups and showed no displeasure, earning another few points of respect from Ayrinessa. For Miltay this affair of ours was work for the long term in the hope that his team would prove useful to the demonologist, and that she would take them under her wing.

"In that case — onward!" Archibald got tired of designing grand plans and started implementing them. "Let's go: show me your Elsa."

The longer you play, or, rather, live in the Game, the less you get surprised. When you encounter on a daily basis various monsters with tails, teeth, ability to fly, crawl, etc., who are capable of freezing you, paralyzing you, gobbling up your brain or doing other nasty things, and you go to places you never knew existed before you ended up there, your ability to be surprised gradually dies off. You start viewing everything through a prism of absolute indifference. But Elsa was beyond those things. Like a child, I watched, open-mouthed, a scene that was impossible in Zurich: a dozen mercenaries were quickly and in coordination building their monster right in front of the main gate of the residence. The mysterious female name hid an electromagnetic mass accelerator capable of accelerating a missile, that seemed to be about 500mm in diameter, along two metal rails. This was the very mysterious railgun that was just starting to appear in the arsenals of NPC armies. The huge supporting rods went down into the ground, probably reaching the underground world. A slug of metal enhanced with runes appeared from the inventory of one of the lead mercenaries and dropped at his feet, crumbling quite a few pavement stones. Another mercenary wearing an exoskeleton picked it up and set it onto the guides. The first mercenary raised his hand, indicating Elsa was battle ready. It took the team just a minute and a half to build a monster that spat out metal boulders accelerated to some incredible speed. During that time Miltay and his fighters had barely finished clearing the square of idly watching NPCs, for whom those events resembled the filming of some science fiction movie. Some even took photos and videos with their phones. We didn't need to worry about it, the Game dealt with NPCs in its own way.

Ayrinessa reported to Archibald that she was ready, and he waved to indicate his "go" to begin. Along the same chain of command the order returned to the first mercenary, his hand went down, and Elsa made the whole square shudder. There was no noise, no heat. While I was watching them build the gun, some of the mercenaries had installed energy shields near the gate, blocking the damage area from us. The same shields covered Elsa's guide rails that had just spat out the missile. From the NPC crowd we heard cheering mixed with questions about the film and the actors.

The lead mercenary raised his hand again, indicating readiness for the next missile. I looked at the gate: they shone white through the infernal flames. They had withstood the first round. The second missile was fired and messages flashed before me indicating experience received. The missile ran into a portal in the gate and flew in some unknown direction, where I suppose it had more success than here. The mercenary's hand went up for the third time: Elsa demonstrated an unprecedented firing rate.

A blinding lightning hit the side of the railgun and was stopped by its protection. At the far end I saw Engibord with his fighters, preparing for a new joint assault.

"It's time," Archibald said briskly, and four things happened all at once. First, Elsa spat out yet another metal slug. Second, Ayrinessa made several movements with her hands, and shimmering hid Archibald. Third, Engibord's mercenaries attacked the gun again. The fourth and most pleasant thing: the gate to Bernard's residence evaporated with a deafening sound, opening the way.

The unpleasant thing happened immediately afterwards. Archibald fell to his knees, trying to stop the blood gushing from his nose. The shimmering around him disappeared. Ayrinessa poured several healing potions down his throat, but they didn't seem to help much. Swaying, the catorian got to his feet with the demonologist's help and looked towards Engibord and his group. On the face of it the area was empty, but Steve helped me take a closer look at the sequence of the events. It turned out that the mercenaries went down together with Archibald. But while he managed to make it, Engibord's guys were unable to get up, writhing on the ground in agony.

"Take Elsa apart. We'll have to walk from here," Archibald ordered, and sat down on the stones, exhausted. Finding me with his eyes, he grinned and cautioned: "Partial redistribution of damage. Good thing I managed to survive. Don't ever try to repeat this."

His nosebleed would not stop. Archibald wiped the blood with his paw and bent his head back. I silently agreed with the warning. Engibord's mercenaries, one after another, started shimmering and disappearing, going for respawn. Or wherever the Game sends those attempting to inflict damage on another player in the Sanctuary. Not a bad way to frame another player, by the way; you just have to know precisely where he is going to hit.

There were no more of those willing to assault Elsa, and within a minute she disappeared into the inventories of Ayrinessa's mercenaries. The catorian meanwhile felt better, rose to his feet and burnt out with a welding torch everything that even slightly resembled his blood. I always found my teacher's paranoia with respect to his blood amusing. It would be interesting to find out the reason for that, but we really didn't have time now to talk about life and stuff.

"First team go! Second team go! Third...!" Ayrinessa's hoarse voice was ideally suited for issuing commands. The mercenaries were working perfectly; they divided into small groups and moved forward towards the break. The fate of the second missile was fresh in everyone's memory, so before making a step forward, the mercenaries thoroughly showered every inch with bullets. They didn't use magic, which I found very surprising: I considered that it would have been of more use here. I asked my teacher that question.

"The portals don't activate from magic. They need a physical object," Archibald, who was standing next to me, clarified. Engibord's blow turned out to be stronger than he had supposed, so the catorian was in no rush to lead the way ahead of the mercenaries, and kept downing one potion after another. We were the last to move forward, thoroughly investigating Bernard's garden. Sometimes a slight nod from the catorian was enough for Ayrinessa to halt the whole procession and order that they get rid of the trees. I didn't know what the reason for the first two stops was, but at the third the mercenaries were too slow in burning up the specified tree and a servant of Bernard fell out of its branches. In his hands he was clutching a portal scroll, and everything was clear as crystal. Archibald's concern was not unfounded: since the stationary portal defense did not work, the defenders of the residence wanted to use ordinary portal scrolls as projectile weapons. The kamikaze caught in the act was quickly neutralized and left in place as a lesson to the others. We could only guess where this portal would have taken us and how soon one could have returned from there, should one have caught such a shot.

As for speed, our group would not have overtaken a turtle. We were moving forward very slowly, but thoroughly demolishing every suspicious object. Eventually both Archibald and myself were bored with "swallowing the dust". We pulled out our Multistrikes and started firing away at everything, not giving much thought to whether it was feasible or not. This was not much real help for the mercenaries, but we had plenty of fun shooting. I totally destroyed the gazebo in which I had first met Bernard. I could not, and did not want to, explain the vandal urge that had suddenly awoken in me. I burned everything that could possibly be burned along my path, regardless of my understanding that each object I destroyed was a work of art. Perhaps that was similar to what rioting peasants felt when they went to strip yet another landlord of his possessions. What do you do: such is the nature of humans who realize they can act with impunity.

"First and second go in, third to cover." We approached the main building and Ayrinessa rearranged her troops. The entrance doors had been ruthlessly shot out by our Multistrikes, ripping the defense to shreds; that was then followed by fire support in the form of a few dozen grenades. Only two of them actually went into the building, the rest departed in unknown directions, granting us bits of experience. Something banged loudly inside making the windows vibrate, and two teams began the storm. We received a message from them via internal comm stating that the residence was full of smoke. That complicated their advance. The players were moving by feel, unable to see each other, and following the floor plans that had been provided. All we could do was to watch their frames and wait for the signal from them.

"Oh, stinky fuckawocky," Ayrinessa cursed under her breath. One of the frames changed to "out of access area," indicating that that mercenary had gotten snagged by a portal. A couple of seconds later another one joined him. One after another the mercenaries left Earth. They started calling Ayrinessa, deploring their fate. The only way for them to return was after a quarantine, and with the permission of the Coordinator himself. All of them stated that the portals were not stationary; someone actually put them in there. No one was able to see the "bomber".

"Everyone retreat!" the demonologist commanded, but it was too late. Out of two full teams of fifteen players each only seven remained, and a couple of seconds later they shared the fate of their colleagues.

It was time to revise our tactics. Despite gusts of wind the smoke within the building did not show any signs of getting thinner, so it was unclear what had actually happened. Archibald drew his Multistrike and totally destroyed the front façade of the building, sealing the entrance with stones.

"Whatever is in there, it can set up portals

quickly and silently. We'll enter from the back. Then we'll get to the library by bringing down a side wall."

"There is a higher vampire there." It suddenly dawned on me who could be the mysterious defender. "Malturion, Bernard's personal aide and bodyguard."

"Bernard does not have any such vampire," Archibald confidently argued with me. But Ayrinessa stopped him and required an explanation from me.

"That's nonsense," I said, remembering that Nata definitely knew about this. Steve had become so good at preparing videos that it took him practically no effort at all to prepare a compilation with Malturion. I started remembering out loud. "Dolgunata definitely saw the vampire at least once, when he passed a Source of Light to me. She heard me several times when I called Malturion requesting help. You must have known this. Here."

Having transferred the video to the glum pair I was trying to comprehend the reasons for Dolgunata's silence. I didn't believe Archibald's memory was failing him. More likely, Dolgunata had not considered it worth mentioning.

"Archibald, this is an unaccounted factor. Our agreement is void and I demand compensation. If my people were affected by Chimera's breath, compensation will have to be paid out to them as well. Archibald, there is no point fighting against a Higher one with whatever we have, railguns or not. Given that Thanatos has turned away from the estate, I have nothing to slow the vampire down. Sorry." Ayrinessa outlined the situation briefly but firmly. There was nothing the catorian could say to that, and he just nodded in response. The demonologist turned on her comm and called back the remaining third team. "We are out. See everyone at the meeting point."

A portal opened, and Ayrinessa with the remaining mercenaries left the residence without unneeded goodbyes or accusations.

"Bitch," Archibald cursed under his breath, and at first I thought that he was talking about the mercenary's actions. I disagreed.

"She is taking care of her people," I said in Ayrinessa's defense.

"Who?" At first Archibald did not understand. Then, having gone through our dialogue, he clarified: "I am talking about that meatheaded druid! Why in hell was she playing her own games?"

This was followed by an unprecedented cascade of words — even Sintsov, had he been alive, would have envied it. Archibald rarely cursed at anyone verbally. Normally one look was enough to understand the catorian's true opinion on a subject. But this was a moment when curse therapy was really called for. I was prepared for the accusations to be hurled at me as well, since I was there in the heat of things and no one had released me from my function as the spanking boy, but this time it passed me by. After his verbal explosion all Archibald did was send a volley of fireballs into the building and then called Miltay, who had been wandering nearby with his team.

"There is no point for you to go any further. The residence is guarded by a higher vampire."

"That's clear. Look here, the speed and power

of a higher one, that's quite something. But we didn't just fall off the truck, and we have something. Look here," Miltay extended a small control panel to Archibald, and now waited for the verdict, squinting one eye. "Why did we come here after all? To loot? Doesn't look like it. Fighting doesn't seem to work either, they just refuse to die. So then only one thing remains — to blow everything up to smithereens. Did I get it right?

Archibald turned the control panel over in this hands, and a familiar glint appeared in his eye. He returned the panel, nodded to Miltay and pointed at the building.

"Yaropolk and I will go in. You need to hold on for three minutes, after that you may send your package. We should have enough time. If it all works, your reward will be doubled."

"Agreed! Come on guys, what are you waiting for? Didn't ya hear, summin'll come to beat us up! Put up the dome, quick! We'll show them a little rumble."

"Forward!" Archibald cheered me on, pulling out his Multistrike and diving into a break in the wall beyond which smoke roiled. I sighed deeply, as if preparing to dive, and followed my teacher. Dense smoke took me in. The visibility was so bad that I couldn't see my hands. After a couple of steps forward I ran into Archibald's back. He didn't move, and I was scared that Malturion had frozen him. But my fears were unfounded. Already in the next second the teacher rushed forward and disappeared, and the place where he had just been standing was doused with a jet of liquid nitrogen; it touched me slightly, leaving frost crystals on my armor. Then I heard a noise and the smoke started dissipating. Once visibility improved, I saw a strange device in the catorian's paws: it sucked in smoke and released clean damp air. Archibald shouted to me to work on the source of the smoke, and disappeared from my view again.

A quick glance around the hall showed me the source of the smoke. That was easy: the smoke was coming through ventilation grilles near the ceiling. Without giving it much thought I started shooting my Multistrike at the plaster-decorated ceiling, trying to collapse the ventilation ducts leading to this hall. Archibald was jumping around with his vacuum cleaner all over the place, deftly avoiding the freezing jets. I found Malturion near the far wall on a small podium. Like a captain on his bridge he was calmly controlling a couple of small drones remotely, attacking the catorian and ignoring me. Judging from his pleased face the vampire had no reason to worry. He was fully involved, not even with Archibald so much as with his toys, scowling every time he managed to flip a drone in a particularly cool way or shoot from an interesting angle.

Archibald, unlike Malturion, did not care about the flying pests, he easily avoided complex attacks, looking strictly at the vampire. Without words I understood that I would have to deal with the drones as well. A few shots turned the toys into atoms that could not even settle on the floor as dust. Without pausing between shots I sent the next three balls towards Malturion. He responded as if he had been waiting for that. He threw up his hand, getting rid of the now useless control panel, and transformed into his battle form. The balls helplessly hit the protective dome and slid to the floor, burning a hole in it. Déjà vu. I had already seen this somewhere... Holy shit!

I had not seen Malturion in battle transformation, nor had I even thought of that. The ever diffident Bernard's assistant in my mind was always just a perfect servant, who was able to show his superiority without bantering words. And, as it turned out, those were quite different things — to chat with the Coordinator's servant who despised you, or to fight a higher vampire in full battle transformation. My heart promptly sank to my boots and I realized that I had done a stupid thing. No, not because I had provoked Malturion, but because the issue had appeared so many times during the search, and here was one right under my nose all the while, but I had not once remembered him. Each vampire's battle transformation gave him unique characteristics: the shape of his eyes, head, wings.... I knew that from my books. That's how Archibald had planned to find out from Garbital, the Head of vampires, who was it that we had encountered in Subway-2. Now there was no need for that. That had just been established, and those very eyes were staring at me now. Merlin was standing in front of me.

I took a small step to the side while Malturion and Archibald were trying to stare each other down. Then I took another step. A third. Still no one cared. However, as soon as I was close to the door leading to the library, Malturion turned into a vague dark blur, and appeared right next to me. I felt his hand on my back. The vampire was not trying to hit or push me. He just attached something lightly to my back, like bullies do in school. And I knew that it would better be a sticky with the word "dunce" rather than the scroll promising to teleport me to hell in a hand basket. Everything happened so fast, I had no time to even react. Malturion activated the portal, and the air around me swirled. A second passed, but I was still standing in the same place; instead, part of a wall disappeared. Archibald could move at about the same speed as the vampire, so he managed to throw the blasted scroll off onto a wall. After that I was watching a whirlwind dance all around. Two blurred shadows, black and silver, merged into one and whirled around the hall, making various parts of the room disappear as they moved. Here and there pieces of walls, columns, furniture and curtains disappeared, showing that both parties were quite determined. I didn't meddle with them, and hurried to my goal in the next hall, hoping that Archibald would engage Malturion-Merlin for a long time. I ran headlong, shooting from both hands at once. In one hand I had my Multistrike, clearing the way of doors, furniture, walls and other material things. In the other I had a common machine gun, that cleared the way of portals. Bullets disappeared one after another, leaving only flashes behind, and enabling me to run headlong down the hallway.

The library door disappeared, and now the shelf we sought was within sight. I took a step and became stuck in something paralyzing. It was harder to move than when we were storming the Citadel, but I did not give up, pulling forward with everything but my teeth. Seconds dragged on, but I didn't move an iota. The trap held me fast. Suddenly a silver whirlwind appeared next to me, yanked my body out of the trap and hurled me directly onto the right shelf. Like in a slow motion film I saw the dark lightning materialize right by Archibald, and he was pulled into the twisting portal. I even saw the eyes of Malturion-Merlin before crashing into the shelf. The latter did not survive such treatment and toppled over. The black lightning dashed right by me and I felt rather than saw that a portal scroll had been attached to me. I had but a moment to grab the books in a bundle from the shelf and pray to the Game that all should not have been in vain. I wanted to live.

A portal flashed, and this time everything went well: I tumbled out next to Archibald, who was putting his Multistrike into his inventory. Behind the teacher I saw the smoldering spiked tail of some dark green monster, a little further lay the mercenaries who had been affected by its acid. Memory and logic clarified the picture. The dark green monster was the chimera. The mercenaries were affected by its breath, so now they were tied to this world for a month. Archibald did not alleviate their suffering because of Ayrinessa, who had left us in the middle of the raid. It would seem that she had acted honestly, but it just was not right. Therefore, Archibald acted honestly as well: that was not his team any more, and it was not his business to take care of them, just to provide compensation.

"Did you get it?" Archibald's eyes were searching over the scattered books. Without bothering to get up I started to gather them, and could barely contain a cry of joy. The small book in the dark binding was there.

"It looks like a set-up," Archibald noted skeptically, but we were distracted by a system message:

Quest "Cleanup of Ancient Knowledge" is complete. Received: five granises

Miltay had waited for three minutes and razed the residence off the face of the Earth like he promised. Three low-yield nuclear bombs are to be reckoned with even for a higher vampire. I hid the other books into my inventory, opened the dark book, and sighed raggedly. I was familiar with the language of cynocephalians in which this diary was written. It was not a setup. The Diary really had belonged to a Restart participant whose name began with an "M", and the Game itself confirmed this by a system message. But, hell, this was not Merlin's Diary! It was another Madonna's Diary!

CHAPTER NINE

DAY EIGHT

FOR THE FIRST TIME in a long while my morning was a late one. Unfortunately, there was nothing positive about it. After yesterday's fiasco — what else would one call finding Madonna's Diary instead of Merlin's? — we returned to Avalon, and Archibald rushed to the basement to defrost Garlion and shake his soul out of him. The torture took the rest of the day and all night, but the elf turned out to be a tough case. Once he had found out that his ploy had worked and we had found the wrong diary, he joyfully stretched his mutilated mouth into a smile and whispered that as the keeper of the library he had fulfilled his duty. These were his only coherent words. After that all we heard was mad laughter.

Nothing could mar Garlion's mad happiness. At dawn the Counselor showed up and put the elf out of his misery, and the catorian acquired the "killer" token. Garlion preferred to be forever gone from the memory of the Game. I could bet that the last time the elf had "broken" on purpose, in order to send us on a false trail out of a desire for revenge.

Sitting with a cup of coffee in Archibald's library, I was staring at what was already the third copy of the blasted diary that I had encountered. Two of them were in the Academy, and one here, in the main game world. This seemed logical, since the Game would envisage different scenarios of Restart initiation. Who knows where and how it had hidden several more Diaries. The strange thing was that it was Madonna's Diary specifically that was so popular.

"Malturion cannot be Merlin," Archibald noted from his chair. "That vampire has excellent reflexes and speed, honed by long practice. And Merlin, until he incarnates, is infirm and physically weak. I think that the vampire is his personal servant. So then it would mean that Merlin was just amusing himself with fake sacrifices, and watching us chase him."

"Malturion serves Bernard," I reminded him.

"We've already been though that," Archibald grimaced. "Bernard cannot be Merlin either. Perhaps that's another trick — make it all look as though Bernard is responsible for all. Malturion is serving the Coordinator; the diary is in his residence.

"Malturion is not Merlin. Bernard is not Merlin. No one is Merlin, yet he is nearby somewhere. Is your agreement with Bernard still valid?"

"No. it was terminated at Elsa's first shot."

"So then Lumpen is on our heels again? Grant my Doll access to Avalon. I don't want to leave her exposed like that."

"It won't work. Bernard has shut down Earth until noon. Total quarantine due to the attack on his residence. The Coordinator is within his rights. So you will not be able to pick up your Doll right now."

Another unpleasant bit of news for our losers' pile. The upside was that nobody could use the portals altogether, so it was unlikely that dangerous guests would visit Helen. My thoughts drifted back to the Diary, but were interrupted by a call from Miltay.

"Yari, I did catch that silly girl's tail after all!" the mercenary's upbeat voice carried through the hall. I even moved the comm away from my ear so as to retain at least some of my hearing.

"Whose tail?" I clarified gingerly.

"Whose, whose. Lady Luck's tail! Look here! Got that? Kalran signed us, like, the 3rd level mercenaries' patent! So hasta la vista! We are leaving this port, sailing close to the center! Say congrats!"

I met Archibald's eyes and saw that the catorian, like myself, would like to know the details of Bernard's noble deed with respect to the mercenaries who had bombed out his residence.

"Congrats!" I responded to Miltay's joyful gushing. "Only if you are boasting, start from the very beginning. Since I don't know what happened there after you activated your bomb. Why would the Coordinator be so generous?"

The mercenary told us all that had happened,

willingly and quite coherently. The way things were, the protection of the estate survived the nuclear explosion and prevented the shock wave from leaving the area. Moreover, the main building survived as well — only the parts at the very epicenter were destroyed. There was one positive thing though: that protection did not apply to anything within. The Energy field of the residence was a sealed ball around the whole estate, and after the explosion all that remained within that field were living beings and the main building. Everything else simply evaporated, blown apart to atoms. Everything material, including soil, objects, flora, NPC clothes, was destroyed, including Bernard's library with all the artifacts of previous eras. Miltay and his band were the only ones who had completed the quest, so the Grandeur units received by the band were beyond their wildest expectations. This new level enabled Miltay to leave our sector and move closer to the center of the galaxy, which was what he did, having asked Bernard for the patent. The Coordinator could not renege on his responsibilities, and so, fuming with fury, he still signed all the documents for the mercenary, to Miltay's boundless joy. After yesterday's events the Coordinator would stop at nothing to destroy him both as a mercenary and as a player. It would be much harder to get to him in the new sector.

"Look here: I left a farewell present for you there in the bank," Miltay finished. "I don't need it now any more, and you will find a way to use it. They don't really use them in that new sector. So then all the best, Yari! Don't hold grudges if I offended you, and once you are in our sector, drop in! I'll send you the coordinates later."

"Thank you, Miltay. Good luck to you in the new spot. And be careful there, you know, if the Coordinator really has it in for you... you understand."

"Look here, don't preach to the choir. What do you think I am — a kid still wet behind the ears? Once we get there, we'll lie low," the mercenary cut me off good-naturedly. I listened to his voice and knew that we would never see each other again. Miltay would not be playing at the third level for long. Restart was coming and no one would invite a mercenary into the new era. However, Miltay didn't need to know that. "And tell Archibald that he owes me a twenty. I'll text him the account number."

Miltay hung up and Archibald's comm beeped right away. The catorian called the bank and sent the mercenary his payment with a note that it was a good idea to pay one's debts on time.

"Right. So we did show them some rumble." I summed up yesterday's raid using Miltay's words. "If now all that's left of the estate is a huge hole, Bernard is likely to be unhappy."

"Unhappy? Ha! He is furious! With you, and particularly with me. I haven't received the report as to whether Madonna was at the estate. But it doesn't matter, As the facts are now, the Coordinator was unable to provide appropriate protection to 'The Great One'. In her situation I would have let Bernard have it. Wait... They've lifted the quarantine!" Archibald suddenly frowned. "Before it was due..."

"Would you open a portal?" I thought of Helen right away. "If Madonna didn't punish Bernard for the estate, she would for blocking the portals for sure. I don't believe those great feet care to walk on their own. I need to pick up Helen before it's too late."

"You have one minute." The teacher waved his hand, opening the portal to my home. "I gave your Doll access. Warn her not to call up her pet, or else the protection here will destroy it. Go! I need to resolve some things as well."

I jumped into the portal to my love, and was glad to see Alard there. Seeing a portal open right in the middle of the living room, the Paladin was preparing to battle an unknown enemy. Such dedication in fulfilling my request was incredibly pleasing, and I greeted my brother with a bear hug.

"Helen, get ready! We need to leave!" I shouted, still in the living-room. Helen was doing something in the kitchen, as usual. Devir by now had long left our apartment to deal with his mysterious business.

"For a while or forever?" My personal happiness generator rushed in and hugged me thoroughly.

"I am afraid that it will be forever. We are not welcome in Moscow anymore." I kissed her face, lit up with happiness and stained with flour. Alard coughed, embarrassed and went to the kitchen, stepping loudly.

"If it's forever, I'm ready." Helen took off her apron, wiped her face and rushed to the door to get her sneakers. My love did not need extra luggage to be happy. Everyday items would not be a problem, neither were clothes, and there was no need for passports for Dolls in our world. Beautiful. I waited for Helen to pull on her sneakers and headed for the kitchen to say goodbye to Alard.

"Alard, good friend, I don't know what I would do without you. Thank you! And now Helen and I ..."

I was unable to finish, nor did I make it to the living-room door. My body refused to obey me, as if it turned into a piece of wood. Helen was standing behind me, there was not a sound coming from the kitchen, and only slow and measured clicking of the heels in the hallway told me that I did not make it. We had guests.

"Weird and ridiculous are those players, who but yesterday were NPCs. The Game granted them immortality and the abilities of gods, yet they keep returning to the plebeian conditions to which they are accustomed. Really, I could never understand why we waste so much valuable resources. Those born to crawl will never fly." By the calm and contemptuous voice I recognized our visitor was Madonna a couple of seconds before she appeared in the door of the living-room.

"You are right as always, my mistress." My small apartment was under threat of exploding from an excessive concentration of high-level visitors. The Coordinator was hurrying to lick the great ass, hanging on Madonna's heels. He was obviously trying to atone for his sins.

"Of course we are right! We know that ourselves. But this Yaropolk was most likely just unlucky with respect to his teacher. What can you learn from a pet rubbing its master's feet for a bowl of milk?" Madonna walked in a semicircle around me and stopped behind my back. "Yaropolk, turn!"

Against my will I turned one hundred and eighty degrees and looked in the face of the bitchy snob. I noticed in passing how sickly pale the Coordinator was. He laughed at the joke the Great One made, but it looked strained, as if Bernard was not feeling well. I was so sick of all that brown-nosing!

"We want to know how the search is progressing." The top part of my body regained mobility, enabling me to inhale raggedly. I made an effort not to look at Helen. I could only hope that Madonna had not blocked her ability to breathe. Even though the Doll was not an NPC, without air she wouldn't live too long. Steve calculated that three minutes would not be critical for the Doll, showing me the countdown timer. I needed to solve my problems within one hundred and eighty seconds. The clock was ticking. Meanwhile the Great One kept her eyes on me, staring at me with interest as if I were a small animal.

"Yes, my mistress: I reported to your assistant that tomorrow the search would be successfully completed." I was trying to postpone the time for having to come up with "Merlin" as best I could. "There are just some minor details that need to be resolved."

Apparently, I was not successful in trying to make my external interface demonstrate reverence and adoration; neither could I distract the bitch by maneuvering my words. For that I was immediately slapped by the greatest hand across the interface that let me down.

"Silence! Did you not hear or understand? We desire an answer now! Not tomorrow!!" Madonna bent down to my face, flaming with fury, and pursing her lips into a thin line. My chest felt very tight, darkness pulled over my eyes. I couldn't breathe again, feeling pressure build up in my head until I felt the taste of blood in my mouth. I had to swallow quickly to avoid the temptation to spit it right out into the face in front of me.

"Please forgive me. I thought that since the Coordinator was here, you would have already been briefed on the details," I said, once I felt a little more like myself. I needed to throw a little oil on the fire under Bernard. "Now I see that this is not the case. Yesterday we discovered a connection between the Coordinator and Merlin — that's why there was a raid on his residence. His servant, the higher vampire Malturion, turned out to be Merlin's assistant. He performed sacrifices for him to obtain Energy. Malturion knows who Merlin is. We just needed to shake that knowledge out of him."

"What is this nonsense?!" Bernard exclaimed, but it was too late. The white light enveloped me completely, confirming that I believed what I was saying. Hedging against the possibility that Malturion had been avoiding Madonna during the time that she was staying at the residence, I added:

"If the Great One would allow me, I would provide the video that I prepared featuring this being, in order to confirm my words."

"We allow! We desire to receive proof." The ring

of steel eased off, and I gulped air greedily for the second time in the past minute. Talking to the "Great One" did not come easily. I transferred to Madonna the video that I had prepared for my teacher, and met Bernard's eyes. In those eyes I read a number of ways by which he would like to violate me. In response I simply smiled and winked, enjoying his reaction. He must have already complained to Madonna about his destroyed library. I didn't see any other reason for today's visit.

"Bernard, we are displeased with you! Why did you not report?" Madonna turned to the Coordinator, who was forced to take his eyes off me. "Do you know where Merlin is?"

"This is some kind of misunderstanding, my mistress. I surely don't! Would I have invited you to my place had that been the case? I really did have a servant named Malturion, but it has been a week since he left me, having completed his service. I was extremely surprised to see him yesterday at the ruins of my residence. I would never..."

"Where is he now?" Madonna interrupted Bernard. "We want to see him immediately!"

"He is helping to clear the debris resulting from what Yaropolk did," Bernard reluctantly admitted. "I will summon him immediately."

It took the Coordinator one call, and Malturion was in my apartment as well. By portal, too. I was getting the feeling that every player in the Game who knew me had the coordinates of my apartment. The vampire bowed to Madonna, and as she waved her hand was jerked up into the air, stuck there in the pose of a starfish, with his arms and legs spread wide.

"We wish to know who Merlin is!" Madonna voiced her demand without beating around the bush. Malturion withstood this "crucifixion" honorably, just jerked his head proudly. Madonna had not expected such stubbornness. She jerked her hand once again, and the vampire's eyes became bloodshot. But that was not part of transformation; the blood flooded the whites of his eyes as the blood vessels burst. The vampire kept silent. Madonna increased the pressure. The Great One obviously lacked my teacher's experience and technique in torture, or else she just didn't know when to stop; in any case after a few seconds Malturion's body shimmered: the vampire went for respawn.

"We demand his immediate punishment!" Madonna screamed, realizing that the vampire had escaped her torture. "Bernard, if in an hour we do not know what this vampire knows, you will die your last death!"

"My mistress, perhaps the Coordinator is conspiring with Malturion," I hastened to interject before Bernard left the apartment. "I should have reported earlier, but I was bound by the vassal's oath. Once Monsieur Kalran said that he knew where to find Merlin. May the Game be my witness."

As the white light enveloped me to confirm what I said, Madonna's face was becoming red with anger.

"Is that so?" The Great One forgot about everything, including Helen, and moved towards the Coordinator. I exhaled. Feeling the invisible shackles release my body; Helen crashed to the floor next to me, breathing noisily. I had made it! Now I had to slink out to Avalon quietly, so that this sleazebag could not get to us! I hoped that Madonna would want to sort it out with Bernard in some other place, but Kalran had his own trumps.

"May the Game be my witness! Bernard Kalran does not know Merlin's location, and is not acting in conspiracy with the higher vampire Malturion." I did not need to turn in order to see the flash of the white light of truth. Dam, I was in a pickle! I heard the voice of the Coordinator from the door, calm now. "With your permission, your Highness, I will go look for my servant."

Silence hung in the room. I turned around and saw Bernard go out of the living-room as Madonna was slowly turning towards me:

"You, a byproduct of a software bug, instead of looking for Merlin, were building intrigues around me?! But I am smart enough to know from where this wind is blowing. By yourself you are too useless to come up with that! This is all your teacher! You are dancing to his music rather than following our orders! You are too pitiful to be the Guide, but we must respect the choice the Game made! We give you time until the end of tomorrow, and if you cannot find Merlin, we will strip you of the status of Guide. We don't need losers!"

Madonna's face twisted and reddened. Her eyes wandered over me, looking for something I couldn't understand, until they wandered over to Helen, who moaned at a really bad time. I worriedly watched the

Great One start thinking another "great" thought, ready to rush to defend my beloved at any second. Luckily for us the Coordinator squeezed through the door to the living-room again, and distracted Madonna's attention.

"My mistress, I have a present for you," Bernard's face was positively beaming with happiness, and I knew that was a bad sign. "This is an instance of when mustard is good when you have a sausage in front of you..."

The Coordinator clicked his heels and stepped to the side with a bow. My heart sank. This could not be happening! I was ready to believe that I was hallucinating, or that I had been wiped out and was now in purgatory. In the door, encased in ice, was Archibald. My teacher was frozen, covering his head from an attack from above. There was no doubt that it was the real catorian: Bernard would not have put himself in that situation. I watched the unfolding drama despondently, not knowing what to do.

"I took some steps to ensure your safety, my mistress. And they were fruitful," Bernard clarified, showing himself off as a hero. "This schemer did not expect to see me here, particularly with a back-up. I think he was plotting something against you again."

"Yesss," Madonna practically hissed, without taking her eyes off Archibald. "This is a truly worthy present, Bernard Kalran! We forgive you and would like you to continue serving us. The Game values those who are loyal to us!"

Madonna once again demonstrated her virtuoso level of Game abilities. Archibald was instantly restored and brought round, and all that without a single touch. The teacher's eyelids fluttered and rose slowly. His body was still obeying Archibald reluctantly, but his eyes looked quite sharp. As he appraised the situation a painfully familiar smile sprung across his face.

"What an honor! Such high guests: the chief bitch of the Game and her loyal brown-noser! To what do I owe this visit?" Archibald behaved as if they had come to ask him for favors.

"Shut up," Madonna said menacingly, taking a step towards the teacher. He just raised a brow quizzically.

"Oh no, Great One! Even though the only thing remaining that's great about you is your opinion of yourself..." the teacher did not finish the sentence — his mouth simply disappeared. I did not know what he was trying to achieve, but Madonna was shaking with fury.

"We graciously preserved your life, you ungrateful beast! For so many Restarts we tolerated your antics, but you have gone too far and forgotten your purpose! You have neglected our gift! And now is the time for payback! You were created to serve us, but since you refused, by the right granted me by the Game I strip you of the status of player! From now on you are an NPC!"

Archibald could not speak, but he heard his sentence very clearly, fighting with Madonna's strength to the last. That's how the strong in spirit die, but do not surrender. Dark fog enveloped my teacher, and his body started convulsing as he died and instantly revived time after time, about three hundred times, until the Game brought his levels down completely. The fog turned red and the bright flame of his soul soared over Archibald and disappeared into the air. The Game had turned the catorian into an NPC.

Madonna swayed, and would have fallen, had Bernard not caught her just in time. The Great One's face was smeared with blood, her eyes darkened and her face was drawn: bringing Archibald down and turning him into an NPC had not come easily to her. For a couple of seconds she did slump into the Coordinator's arms and the released catorian fell on the floor. Used to different twists of fate in his complicated life, the teacher had not yet realized the transformation and tried to open a portal with a gesture. It didn't work. Together with his player status he had lost all his privileges, his ability to use the portals, his right to Avalon and his beloved inventory. Now, like any other NPC, he was unable to use magic. But the most cruel punishment for him was that the Game did not correct his memory. Enraged, he made some sort of battle cry and rushed at the Coordinator, who was holding the Great One in his arms. But he barely made a couple of steps before he was paralyzed, hanging in the air.

Bernard didn't need to strain to overcome an ordinary NPC. He was trying to bring Madonna out of her faint, and was pouring potions into the Great One's mouth.

The whole scene seemed incredibly prolonged to me. It was a torment to wait for the end, knowing that even an attempt to fight for my teacher would cost everyone their lives. I convinced myself that Archibald, as always, knew what he was doing. My role, meanwhile, had been written and rehearsed long before those events. There was a much heavier burden on my shoulders than blame for my inaction today. If I failed to control myself, it would all be ruined! All would have been in vain! While there was still one, however slim, chance to get rid of Madonna, Merlin and Bernard I needed to fight for it. I repeated all this to myself like a mantra.

Through the efforts of the Coordinator the Great One opened her eyes and rose to her feet.

"We will remember your help, Bernard Kalran, candidate to be our friend." Madonna spoke with difficulty, as if the Game had subjected her to maximum load for Archibald. Still wobbly on her feet and therefore supported by Bernard, she approached Archibald.

"This is not it, damn you! We do not wish for you to take up our resources! It's time everyone forgot about your existence! Monsieur Kalran, do the honors.

"With pleasure, my mistress," the Coordinator sang in response, and pulled the sword from Archibald's sheath.

Bernard chose the most dishonorable method of killing, in my view. He simply beheaded one of the legends of the Game with his own sword, not even letting him die with honor. There was blood everywhere: on the floor, on the walls, on the furniture and on my face. Helen was quietly sobbing behind my back. I was looking at my teacher's head as it rolled to my feet, and I couldn't believe it. There was a lump in my throat, and I was trying to swallow it as hard as I could. It was so ironic: I had promised myself so many times that I would get rid of this long-tailed bully, and now I was struggling not to break into tears. It was hard to realize how ridiculously Archibald's game had ended.

"Honor and glory!" Alard rushed out of the kitchen, his sword drawn. I shouted to him to stop, but as a true son of his nation, he considered it would be shameful to do nothing when a Paladin's honor was being attacked. His internal principles demanded that he interfere and punish the unworthy and avenge the weak. Even if the unworthy ones were Madonna and the Coordinator, and even if the only reward for the attempt was death.

Madonna was taken aback by the unexpected and reckless attack from a low-level player. Alard had the chance for precisely one blow; then the protection of the Great One threw the orc back onto a wall. Alard did not have inertia neutralizers, so he grunted loudly from the hefty blow against the wall, then slumped to the floor. He was unable to jump up again quickly. I shouted to the orc again that he should stop and come to his senses. But Alard, blinded by fury and indignation, was pouring a healing potion into his mouth. The orc craved revenge.

"Paladins! I hate Paladins!" Madonna spat out, and jerked Alard high, but the orc was in no hurry to surrender. It turned out that together with the potion he had pulled from his inventory a shrapnel grenade, and as soon as Madonna pulled the orc into the air, the grenade slid from his huge paw right to her feet. My reflexes from army life kicked in, so I instantly dropped to the floor, covering Helen, and hoping my protection would hold. The building shook significantly but nothing happened: Bernard had enclosed the grenade in a power envelope, which absorbed all the damage.

"You red-skinned bastard!! We strip you of player status!" Madonna's screech went to about ultrasound levels, as her face blackened once again. The Great One was horrid to behold: the consequences of wiping out Archibald were still obvious on her face, which was now distorted by deep hatred and fury. This process for the orc did not take long, and I did not lift my head, hugging Helen close and trying to muffle her sobs. Killing my friend was delegated to Bernard again. At that point I forced myself to look, wanting to support Alard at least by my eyes. I did not expect the orc to understand why I didn't do anything, but believed that he would not despise me for it. Apparently the Coordinator liked to be the personal executioner for the Great One, since he once again chose something spectacular, and tore the fearless orc in half. So died another person important to me.

Another bloody scene calmed the Great One down, and the Coordinator's reverence did wonders for her looks. Or maybe she felt comfortable in a room flooded with blood, with two bodies in it. In any case, when she came up to us she was calm and smiling, glancing at Kalran coquettishly.

"Stand up, Yaropolk. You do not need to fear us. You must be grateful to us, as we have removed you from their bad influence." I quickly rose to my feet, leaving Helen lying on the floor. I told her quietly to stay silent and not move. "You must concentrate on the search. The deadline is tomorrow. Find Merlin! Do you understand me?"

"Yes." I tried to make my voice sound firm, even though I was not succeeding too well. I was afraid for Helen, and generally after all that happened, I could not force myself to address this bitch as "mistress". But she turned out to be really observant.

"Yes what?" Her lips were still smiling, but the bitch was starting to get angry again.

"Yes, my mistress, I have understood everything," I corrected myself quickly.

"Did you understand me well, Yaropolk?" Madonna asked as she walked around me again, and put her foot on the Doll. The Doll moaned.

"I understood everything very well! I will not be distracted by anything, and by tomorrow I will find you Merlin," I almost shouted, hearing the bones crunch under the Great One's foot. "God, if you actually exist, make her stop!"

Madonna's eyes watched my face carefully. I tried to respond with a direct yet humble look. Smiling, Madonna stretched her hand towards my cheek, intending to pet it, but I jerked reflexively. My body became numb again immediately, and the bitch reached my face with her cold fingers, turning it towards her.

"Smart boy! Now I can see that you understood.

And now, watch carefully! I, as a good teacher, will provide you the necessary motivation." She lowered my head so that I could see Helen, then moved her foot to the Doll's neck and increased the pressure. Helen bit her lip and shut her eyes tightly. I could not either move or yell. There was a quiet crunch and Helen fainted. Rragr appeared next to her. Sensing deadly danger to his owner, the pet could not but try to protect her. He attacked like a small furious dog, trying to push away or bite Madonna's foot. The Great One did not make any attempts to deter the insistent pet, since she knew: he would not be able to even scratch her armor.

"What a funny animal, and even loyal. Just like her owner. But such a pest," Madonna noted in passing as she flicked the tip of her foot and sent the small Rragr flying. He crashed against a wall and did not get up, giving up his life for his adopted mom. The bitch returned her foot to the same place and the neck crunched loudly. Something broke inside me. That was the end! Why would I live when everyone was gone?! I wanted to tear Madonna into a thousand little pieces, but the field that held me captive prevented me from repeating Alard's deed! Now I was ready to do anything just to destroy this scumbag!

"No, Yaropolk! This is not the end. That would be the wrong motivation," Madonna's voice cut through the darkness that enveloped my mind. White shining flashed around Helen. "Find Merlin, and I will restore her. Completely. She is still alive, but only while my protection is there. Find Merlin! Otherwise, tomorrow after the deadline I will restore her, and I will keep killing her in a thousand different ways, bringing her back time after time... Do you understand? Good! So now you have the right motivation. Everyone should have hope!"

I heard the bang of the portal closing, and sat on the floor. I did not have the strength to do anything. I crawled towards Helen, wanting to touch the person I loved. Her head was turned unnaturally backwards. No matter how I tried, I could not feel her breathing. I turned her onto her back, adjusted the neck of my love, stroked her short hair and held her close. And only then I howled. I howled with pain, fury and my own powerlessness. I howled, because once again people whom I held dear had suffered because of me. And also from feeling my nothingness. There were no tears, just emptiness and deep despair.

The orcs from Alard's birthplace were severe, but wise: the player should not have weaknesses, or else he is weak and vulnerable. By killing their Dolls on their own, they became stronger, they transcended passion, feelings and weakness. No, that was not killing but liberation. There is no place in our scary world for beings who bring love and joy. Nothing is in store for them here besides suffering, and they do not deserve it. Nor do they deserve a life intended solely for the pleasure of another being. I loved Helen. I loved her more than I loved myself, and therefore I had to release her. Because it would be not humane to subject her to torture just for the sake of a vague hope of being with her. Those like Madonna were not trustworthy, and it would be extreme overconfidence to expect that I would in fact manage to find Merlin and that Madonna would fulfill her promise. "Sleep, my girl! May there be a paradise for you. You will be happy there, and will decide everything for yourself. I do not want someone else to hurt you." My artifact appeared in my hand as if by itself and transformed into its battle mode. I swallowed, gathering my resolve. The spikes pierced Helen's head as easily as if it had been made of paper. My beloved's body twitched and went limp. I was alone. No beloved, no teacher, no friend. From now on it was just me, duty and emptiness. Their deaths should not be in vain.

I gathered enough strength to wash my face and clean the blood off my armor. I gathered all the four bodies into the center of the room, put Rragr into Helen's arms, took out my Multistrike, and turned the bodies into a pile of ashes, destroying a couple of neighboring apartments in the process. Better that way than no grave at all. After that I went out into the street and went walking through the city. I deactivated my protection and took off my helmet, allowing warm dusty air to ruffle my clumped hair. Had someone attacked me now, those same necromancers for example, I would have been grateful to them and would not have resisted. But I was not so lucky: nobody wanted a pitiful useless Paladin, and gradually my apathy receded. Emptiness was replaced by anger. Then anger was replaced by despair and this cycle repeated a thousand times. I reproached myself for weakness, for the fact that Rragr and Alard had proved to be much better beings than I. Then my thoughts drifted towards Madonna and Bernard. There should be no place for them in the Game.

Restart would not help if this malignant tumor was going to expand and develop to a new level. Restart needed to be cancelled. I didn't know how to do that, but I was full of determination to find out.

I wandered around the city for quite some time longer, thinking about life and further plans. I had not the slightest clue where to find Merlin. I had no connections, no friends and no helpers. Archibald was the one who had all of that, and now I was dealing with the results of his lack of trust in me. Unable to think of anything better to do, I went to the bank to retrieve Miltay's present. The rivers of clerks running back and forth crossed, joined, separated, but did not stop for an instant. A low-ranking goblin with a corny and artificial smile appeared next to me immediately.

"There was a package left for me," I said by way of greeting. There was no point in introducing myself.

"Certainly, mister Yaropolk. Please follow me: your package is ready."

We merged into a dense flow, crossed the hall and separated on the opposite side. Not a single clerk could be seen slacking: even on their endless run they managed to read documents as they went and deftly maneuver between colleagues and clients. My escort, servile, opened the door and looked at me with such reverence it made me want to sock him one in the kisser. Now I hated to be looked at like that. Now I associated the reverential treatment and ingratiating looks strictly with the Great One bitch, who needed to be destroyed. Trying to breathe deeply and counting black puppies, I entered a conference room and stopped. My melancholy did not go away, but it retreated temporarily, replaced by interest and surprise. Because a common three meter long slug of metal was sitting on the table. Miltay did not waste time on trifles. Like, if you make someone a present — make it stuffed with a medium yield nuclear charge. The bank employees had put a power wrap on the bomb to avoid accidental detonation. One thing upset me: the bomb took up so much space that there was an issue of where to keep it. The clerk agreed with me and presented a bill for safekeeping and protection services. One tenth of a granis. It was a small thing, but still unpleasant.

"If it's not convenient for you to pick up the present now, we can prepare a safekeeping contract" The goblin started pushing his services, but I was already cleaning out my inventory shelves. I was not going to leave such a thing at the bank. After I left the building I activated my protection again. Enough melancholy already. Our proud Alamo will never surrender! We don't ask for mercy!

As soon as I reached the bottom of the stairs, a strange player, dressed in simple NPC clothes, but without a hint of the class armor, stepped into my way. He seemed pretty much like someone naked to me. The hood of his jacket was on his head, so I could not see his face, but his stocky build and small height indicated that he was a dwarf.

"Lift eyes," the stranger said in a thick voice.

"Looking for trouble? Get out of the way," I responded, making my helmet opaque. If someone wanted to see my face, that was a sure sign I needed to hide it.

"Package I have. I can give only if eyes show mind. So show me eyes. Don't have no plot against you. The Game me witness."

The dwarf spoke the common Game language oddly, as if he were a foreigner. While light flashed around my unexpected obstacle, setting me to thinking. Kind of too many packages for one day.

"They warned you be in doubt. Said tell you the book on the third pedestal was red. Show eyes."

My helmet became transparent again. I looked into the dark gap of the hood with interest, wondering what would come next. Steve determined that the dwarf was talking about the classified section of the Paladins' library. There were not that many players who would know the precise order in which the books were arranged there, so now I was wondering who could have sent this messenger. It must have been a farewell present from either Garlion or Archibald. I wished that it could be the catorian taking care of his student after his own death.

"Seem normal. So, good. Here: asked to give you. The shortie handed me a small sheet. I didn't see anything dangerous about it, so I asked:

"Who asked? Who sent you?"

"Says all there. My task simple — hand over and forget. All the best, Paladin Yaropolk."

As soon as the paper was in my hand, the dwarf activated a portal scroll and vanished. Nothing happened to me. In fact, I did not teleport, did not die of a horrible poison, did not contract an incurable disease, didn't even catch a curse of any sort. In my hand there was a simple sheet of paper with a brief text:

"Call Clarissa XX-XX-XX-XXX, ask for help, tell her what happened. Together jump to respawn point. Further instructions are on location. Access is granted.

Archibald

P.S. I hope you managed without wailing and regrets. Even toilet paper has its guaranteed service life."

My heart beat rapidly in my chest. He knew! Archibald knew that one way or another he would not survive the restart, and so he had prepared for it. The respawn point was definitely Avalon, the teacher was being too cautious. I grabbed the Dome of Silence scroll and activated it right there at the porch of the bank, then dialed the number from the letter.

"Speaking," I heard Clarissa's dry voice. Knowing full well that I had but a few seconds before she would hang up, I spoke rapidly:

"This is Yaropolk, Archibald's student. My teacher had been killed to the last death. I need help. My coordinates are..."

The moment I finished with the last coordinate, a portal opened next to me and Clarissa rushed out of it.

"Proof," she demanded right off the bat and I handed the letter to her. The witch read it, held it against the light of the sun, took out the lighter and heated the sheet hoping to discover a secret sign or message. There was nothing.

"Follow me." Clarissa's voice was so authoritative that even if she were to take me to be sacrificed I would not have objected. The witch activated a portal, but stalled before stepping into it. Her reflexes were warning her against the permanent deep freeze from Avalon's protection. Overcoming her momentary weakness, the witch was the first to dive into the portal. I barely made it after her before the passage closed. That was the second time that I saw Avalon's protection activate and freeze an uninvited guest. Together with us a necromancer with a strange device in his hands managed to squeeze into the portal. Someone really wanted to have the precise coordinates of the castle. But the protection worked infallibly here as well: not only did it freeze the intruder, it also blocked his device. I grabbed the transmitter and the frozen hand holding it broke off. Then I smashed the device with a blow from my artifact. The pieces were surrounded with a blue protective shimmer for a little while, which soon faded, and the necromancer was retrieved by the mechanical arm. Archibald would have been pleased: another statue was added to his collection.

The witch observed aloofly as I got rid of the transmitter, and waited for the promised instructions. Soon the elevator appeared and we reached Archibald's working office. Clarissa immediately settled in his chair as if she owned the place, and leaned back. I was still looking for a place to settle down when the top of the desk moved to the side and a small projector appeared, showing a video on the wall.

"Welcome to my humble abode," the voice said cheerfully from the screen. "Since you are watching this I must be past my expiration date. Oh well, what do you do: only Creators are forever! Now to business. This memory contains two videos. One is for Clarissa, the other for Yaropolk. I would recommend you start with number two, or else Yari risks finding this projector blown up into fine dust by my darling witch. In order to hear this message again, flick your tail. Oh, but you don't have one. Then try clacking your teeth!"

The image stopped, waiting, making the grinning catorian be still.

"Show me how he died," Clarissa asked quietly. I gave her the video of Madonna's atrocities, first having removed the deaths of Alard and Helen. The witch didn't need to know that. That was mine. That was personal. For some time we sat there silently and looked at the fire, then Clarissa stated:

"This looks more like suicide. Something is not adding up. Bernard Kalran was nothing compared to Archibald. That cat would have pulverized him, but would not have let himself be frozen!"

"You saw it all yourself," I said simply. "I don't know how Bernard caught him, and who helped. The day before we had destroyed Kalran's library, so he was mad to get back at him."

"Show me!" The witch again demanded a video. Steve, like a montage ace, prepared another cut. Clarissa studied our raid.

"Why would Archibald need Merlin?" Clarissa was talking to me condescendingly, setting the tone as if she were the boss and I her subordinate; my own pain suggested to me that it was simply a mask. It would not do for players from the first era to grieve about others, especially in front of someone. I treated her behavior with understanding.

"Frankly speaking, I don't have a clue. Looks like he had his own score to settle. The same as with Madonna. You know, for the past few weeks I went with him everywhere, and it feels as though I have not met a single person he didn't cross."

"You're right." The wall of ice cracked, and a slight smile touched Clarissa's lips. "Archibald was quite an expert at that. These days not very many knew him, but during the second era you would not have been able to find a player who didn't wish him a painful wipeout."

We fell silent, each deep in his own thoughts.

"Let's see the video number two, perhaps?" I suggested, knowing without a doubt that Clarissa would want to see the video intended for me. "Maybe at least something would become clearer, since he knew of his impending death."

There were no objections. Clarissa pushed the button with number "2", and the grinning Archibald was replaced by a tired, bedraggled cat who looked as though he had just had a bad spell.

"Greetings, my not most successful but most lucky student. Clarissa, greetings to you as well. I am sure you have not left Yari alone in his trouble; that's what I love you for. So, then, don't waste time looking for reasons and motives. Take reality as a basis that indicates that I am either dead or isolated without the right to return. Clarissa, sit normally in my chair. I hate it when you climb up there with your feet!"

Archibald fell silent for a few moments, thus

enabling me to glance at the witch's pose. She actually was sitting in the chair Indian style. About ten seconds passed and he continued from the screen:

"Fine. You're right. I can't do anything about it at this stage anyway. And yes, it's frustrating to die. I had been tricking the fates for so many eras that it almost made me believe in my own immortality. But anyway. Yari: it's time for us to make a closer acquaintance. My name is Archibald, a catorian, player stripped of class, level 362, respawn point — Avalon. I have become an independent being, while at first I was the Shadow of a player, known in this era as Gerhard van Brast. A Shadow, my student, is an additional appearance, or an avatar. Call it whatever you will, but you get the point. In order to clarify things I will say a few words about history."

Clarissa grimaced: it was obvious she didn't like hearing Archibald's confession. The catorian continued:

"Not too long ago here, in Avalon, I told you a tale about the Player, his Doll and the Doll's cruel teacher. So, then I was not quite honest. Just a little. I diminished the role of the Player and tweaked the part about his personality, because I was bound by an oath. But now it doesn't matter. You must know the truth in order to make the right choice. Or maybe I just need to get it off my chest. Who knows?

"During the first era the one you know as Gerhard, or the Nameless, had a different name. Mordor. The Dark Lord. Oppressor of the Galaxy. Horror and Terror of the Universe. Just within three thousand years from the start of the Game, Mordor became the strongest player of all time, capable of killing or resurrecting with a single glance whole worlds that would not accept his domination. He enveloped the Game like a kraken; then Mordor ran into the main problem of every all-powerful player: boredom. He had no enemies, he knew what happened at the furthest frontiers of the Game, he just about controlled the breathing of each being. Believe me, my astonished student, this is all fun and interesting for a year, two, maybe a hundred. But by the sixth millennium since the start of the Game Mordor was howling with boredom. Everything was monotonous and stable. The worlds prospered, the players worked at self-improvement, there were no intrigues, no conspiracies, nothing. That's when Mordor entered into his first deal with the Game. He convinced the Emperor to adjust the functional capabilities of the Game in such a way that it would forever limit the strength of each of the players at a certain threshold level, and add for each player an artifact that would require constant development. The Lord suffering from boredom didn't want anyone to be bored together with him. His idea was that as soon as someone reached stagnation and stopped developing, the Game eliminated him. In exchange for such a radical modification of the functional side Mordor asked for an alter ego. That would be an artificial entity without free will, but possessing freedom of thought. That was how I appeared: the Shadow of the most powerful being in the Game. I don't know for what purpose I was created. I was unable to find an answer to that question. One thing is clear: controlling me brought him infinite pleasure. Very few knew my true nature. For everyone I was simply a Paladin who had a lot of power. This led to intrigues, betrayals and scheming. Mordor played me like a computer game, making me do whatever he wanted. Then he decided to turn his Doll into a player and give her to his student, Merlin, for training. He was already bored with her, but simply killing her would have been boring. Madonna was becoming stronger, and entertained herself by killing together with Merlin, while Mordor, after some trouble with his mistresses being killed by Madonna, started using me for his affairs. Clarissa was one of our conquests. But then something unexpected happened: for the first time the Shadow separated its consciousness from that of its master. I fell in love. Once Mordor would release me, I would return time and again to my witch. Clarissa did not know anything about me, and considered my philandering to be the downside of my catty nature. A cat cannot be attached to just one being. She came to terms with that, and became my Game partner for thirty thousand years. An assassination attempt on the Emperor, killing Counselors, the second deal with the Game and the gift of Avalon, the Leruan Battle, — there was so much that happened during that time. Life was all fun and carefree until Clarissa and I had a son."

The witch's ragged sigh made me switch my attention to her. Clarissa was crying. Tears were rolling down her cheeks, and there was no trace of the former "Snow Queen". Archibald had made her relive part of their common history. Now he was talking more to her than to me.

"Mordor was adamant: the child had to die. I was unable to oppose his will, so our son was killed. I was forced to kill him. But I was still able to do something. Now I was the one to enter into a deal with the Game. Thanatos stayed alive, but he lost all emotions and turned into the Keeper of the Paths of the Dead, the admin sector. The Emperor granted me the right to visit my son, but I would not be able to go there on my own. Only a true player would have this right, and I was not among them. I could only walk the Path of the Dead accompanied by my 'mirror', that is, a player borne by the Game. It was originally intended that Clarissa would serve as the 'mirror', but Thanatos did not remember us. He was now a different being with the body of our son. Clarissa could not live with my betrayal. That was when something went awry and I started being able to leave Mordor's control, gaining independence. That was a long process. It took me four eras to be able to state with confidence: I am free. Completely and unequivocally. The Nameless does not have any power over me, physical, mental, or any other kind. What else? Oh yes, Madonna. I need to point out that our relationship didn't work out from the beginning. That moron was crazy jealous of me with Mordor, noticing that more and more often he preferred to play me, and neglected her. At this point she would not remember the reason for her loathing, but it increased from one era to the next like a snowball. After yet another crazy antic of hers I suggested we rid the

Game of this big-headed fool. The Nameless did not object. Having partially lost his memory after the first Restart, he simply shrugged, allowing me to solve this problem on my own. That's how the plan with Dolgunata was hatched, the one that you witnessed. I am afraid we have lost this era. Dolgunata turned into Madonna too early. She was not ready to fight with a strong player."

Archibald made a pause, allowing me to gather my thoughts and digest what I had just heard. In principle one ought to have expected something like that: the catorian had gotten away with far too much.

"Now that you have figured out for sure with whom you are dealing, it's time to get back to the business at hand. First: for the duration of my absence, control over Avalon is handed over to Clarissa. Darling, please try not to destroy my castle. Second: on the third level of the fourth section there is a personality solver. It is configured for automatic operation, so using it should not be difficult. Clarissa, after all that has happened you might not be able to get into the new era. Protect yourself and make a crystal. The same is true for you, Yaropolk. I am afraid without me you would not be able to find Merlin, and Madonna will kill you. Even if you lock yourself up in Avalon, the Guide will take you over. You need to back yourself up. Third: in the desk drawer there are instructions on how to defrost my exhibits. Clarissa, take Yaropolk to the basement; there you will recover Sakhray. At a certain time I taught him how to implant the memory crystals; the druid has all that's necessary for that. I have already bought him a pass to the next era. Madonna doesn't know that he is my student. This is our chance. Fourth: treat me gently and try to find me a good body. I don't want to be short, lame or crippled."

A metal arm with a dark box lowered itself from above. Clarissa snatched it with a quick move and opened the lid. A black diamond was sitting on a red velvet pillow.

"I must warn you: recording one's consciousness onto a crystal erases about ten percent of memory. This is a feature I was not able to overcome. No one knows which parts will be affected. So what reincarnates might not really be you."

Before I could make a move, the box with the crystal was thrown into a wall with such force that the crystal, even though it was protected by wood, exploded into a cloud of black shards. Clarissa's hands trembled, but the witch's face projected determination and satisfaction. The video on the screen blinked, then Archibald stated sadly:

"Clarissa, you swore by the Game that you would destroy me. You have done it. Now we are even. Send Yaropolk to the main hall while you are watching the first video. To hear this message again please press the red button."

"Come." Avalon's elevator obeyed the witch perfectly, and a few minutes later I was alone. I really did need a pause to sort through everything I had heard. The events of the day had totally drained me, and with every hour it was becoming more difficult to maintain concentration. I slapped myself several times and got back into a working mode to the extent

I could.

Archibald had told us an exciting tale, perhaps even a true one, judging from Clarissa's reaction; however, the skeptic that had developed in me with the help of the teacher would not let me take it at face value. The Game confirming Archibald's words that he was not under Gerhard's influence was still fresh in my memory, but as a Judge I also knew how to play with words beautifully and believe what I was saying. Did Archibald believe that he had gotten rid of Gerhard, or had he actually gotten rid of him? What if everything the catorian did was because the Nameless wished it? As for his motive... Archibald named it himself: freedom from Madonna! Gerhard desired to get rid of the companion that he was fed up with after so many thousands of years, but the standard methods didn't work. The Game always protected her. Then Archibald had conceived his "brilliant" plan. In my view the theory was quite plausible. Now about the tale itself: why would the catorian become so sentimental? To tell me his poor guy sob story? Nonsense! I reviewed some points of the monologue and grinned. Archibald didn't make that video for me; both of his statements were intended for Clarissa. The only difference was that in "mine" he was creating a certain mood, making her remember the past, and in the personal one he would complete the process. I would be willing to bet my last granis that the crystal with personality had been either fake or not unique and that Avalon was veritably stuffed with those crystals. The clever catorian tried to extract advantage even from his own death. Otherwise Clarissa would not give Sakhray the crystal with Archibald's personality. That was more like my teacher; not all those corny wailings about the past.

"Come." Clarissa came in and was not inclined to conversation. But her red-rimmed eyes confirmed my guess. In Clarissa's hands there was a dark box identical to the one she had broken. I was one hundred percent certain that within it there was a crystal with Archibald's personality, safe and sound. And that Clarissa would tear out the throat of anyone who made an attempt on it with her bare teeth.

The process of creating a memory crystal did not look fancy. In a small room there was a common wooden chair with a metal helmet-like contraption, like a hair dryer in the older hairdressers' shops where my mother used to go to get her hair done back in my NPC past. You put the helmet over your head; then you needed to agree to provide access to personal data, and the helmet was lifted, indicating that the process was over. Something hummed within the wall, then a window opened and a small platform extended with the crystal on it. Quick, simple, no-fuss.

We stayed in the basement for a while. It was Clarissa's first visit to Archibald's ice statue museum, and she could not deny herself a detailed tour among so many interesting characters. Compared to my previous visit the collection was significantly smaller: the payment for our presence on the Path of the Dead had been extracted automatically. That was precisely why Sakhray, with some pretty woman, was standing separately from all the others. The couple was marked "not for exchange".

"Devir's Doll? The witch was surprised. "What is she doing here?"

All I could do was shrug. My low level of skill in reading NPC attributes had prevented me from identifying the girl as Devir's Doll, so I had to believe Clarissa.

"She was frozen voluntarily," Steve remarked. *"She was not attempting to protect herself against a blow from above."*

In fact both Sakhray and the Doll were standing in relaxed poses, which made the reason for their presence even more curious. What outstanding achievements brought her here? Even if Clarissa had any thoughts on that count, she chose to keep them to herself, and activated the recovery process for Sakhray. I caught the falling druid, carried him to the main hall and started pouring healing potions into him. I recalled that process for myself: thawing out gave you extremely unpleasant sensations.

Having made sure that the druid was fine, Clarissa disappeared on her own business, ordering me to wait for her return. I had no objections: there was nothing for me to do in the main world anyway.

My ability to move around Avalon was limited. Main hall, Archibald's office and a few more rooms. I discovered a bathroom adjacent to one of them and washed thoroughly. I could not control the elevator, the doors were locked and I did not dare find out what would come out stronger: local protection or Multistrike.

Sakhray made several attempts to talk about

Dolgunata and why she was not with us, but I kept delaying that conversation. First I urgently needed to scan the books that I had recovered from Bernard's library, then the ones I had from the library of the Paladins. Miltay's present took up way too much of my virtual inventory and I had to clear out some space. Finally, Sakhray cornered me:

"Did she become Madonna? Don't fret over it, I know what we were being trained for. What do you think, I trained for nothing to implant the crystals properly till I was blue in the face? Nata went through my hands as well — I know who's settled inside her."

"As well?" That caught my attention. "There were others?"

"Sure there were." Sakhray looked extremely surprised, as if he were having to explain to me the basics of the Game. "I failed with three NPCs before I put the crystal correctly into the fourth one. Nata was number six."

"How about some more detail?" It was my turn to be surprised, since I was not familiar with the implanting method.

"There isn't much to tell. I failed with the first three crystals and the NPCs died. The next two I did right, but for one of NPCs her legs became paralyzed due to some internal conflict, and Archibald had to adjust the mechanism. With the fifth one everything went fine, and Dolgunata got her crystal without a problem."

"Were all the crystals with Madonna?" I clarified just in case, already knowing the answer.

"Yes, Archibald had lots of them. A dozen at

least, and maybe more. The Great Ones don't like risk. What if something happened to the NPC, what would you do? So they stamped out their personalities by the dozen at the end of each era. At least they were good for training."

"So what happened to the fifth NPC? Did you kill her?" I asked, just to keep the conversation going. So then, the first crystal that Archibald gave to Clarissa to destroy was a real one; he just didn't mention that he had a bunch of such crystals squirreled away.

"Why kill her? We turned her into a player that way. Archibald froze her and stuck her in his museum for some future occasion. As he said, we might need her for something."

Of course. A player, even if she had not gone through the Academy and is without levels or anchor point, would be a tasty morsel for Thanatos. Unless... a thought flashed through my mind like lightning, raising the hair on my body. Steve went through the remaining frozen figures and highlighted one, who with a high level of probability was the woman we needed. Short, homely, and also marked "not for exchange". That was definitely her. It seemed I had found a great way to get rid of Madonna. Most important was to make sure it worked, for I would not have another chance. I turned to Sakhray and started implementing my plan:

"Tell me, what is so unusual about the process of implanting crystals? Does it require anything special?"

CHAPTER TEN

DAY NINE

THE DREAM DID NOT WANT to release me. Again and again I was trying to pull myself from the kaleidoscope of yesterday's events, transformed by my twisted brain into horrifying images, until Clarissa stopped my suffering. The dawn was not even close, and the witch's glum appearance did not make our lives any more cheerful.

"The Council of Twelve has crossed me off the lists! I'm not worthy to enter the next era!" the witch announced as soon as I showed up in Archibald's office. I was unable to think too clearly, so Steve went into active mode and commented on her words. It turned out that the Council of Twelve is the highest executive and legislative authority for witches. The list was kept secret, but I was sure that Clarissa was on

---

it.

"Archibald foretold that," I reminded her. "You know that the lists will be submitted to Madonna for approval. What do you find surprising? That she would not allow Archibald's former lover to use the privilege? It would be strange if they had kept you on the lists. The witch Clarissa hung out around the catorian too long, and Madonna is vindictive."

Clarissa was silent for a while, agreeing with my statements. I understood the witch's concerns very well and shared them. She didn't want to be reborn using the crystal: ten percent of personality was after all quite a high price for a new life, and if there was a chance to avoid it, one should use it. Most likely Clarissa had tried everything to stay on the lists, and nothing had worked. Gerhard was the one preparing the lists, and an ex-lover could not offer anything of interest to him. Most likely the Nameless would try to cut off all the connections that linked him to the Shadow. Out of sight, out of mind.

"I need scrolls with portals to Avalon." I didn't feel like working as a shoulder for the "poor" witch to cry on, so I steered the conversation toward business.

"Make some for yourself." Clarissa waved me off. "Do you know how to use the elevator?"

I shook my head no. The witch wasn't happy with the responsibilities that had suddenly been dumped on her, so she updated my rights in the castle, providing extended access.

She grumbled about having to waste her time teaching me the functions and general overview of the castle, but unexpectedly she proved to be an excellent teacher and narrator. After finishing with her role of a guide, she turned back to the topic of the transition that bothered her, and provided some more detail about what was going on in the Game world. Busy with my own problems, I had sort of completely forgotten about everyone's preparations for Restart. It was not relevant to me; meanwhile a lot of interesting things had been happening. Heads of classes came to plead with the Paladins, hoping to get a coveted spot on lists of the lucky ones. Or unlucky ones: the lists were public, and each name added there triggered a whole series of quests for killing and complete wipeout. Only ten percent of the players were going to make the next era, and the struggle for each spot was vicious. The players won places for themselves by wiping each other out. No one attacked the Paladins, fearing revenge from their superiors. The rest of the players, realizing how finite their existence was, were reveling in various excesses. I listened to all of that, sighed and nodded in the right places, but felt nothing except indifference.

Finally, Clarissa finished and went to talk to Sakhray. I used the opportunity, since there was another hour left till dawn, and allowed myself to spend the time leisurely exploring Avalon. I could not deny that small thing to myself: the Explorer in me rebelled and needed to be satisfied, whispering that implementation of the plan I had devised yesterday could wait for an hour. I mastered the elevator control in a few minutes, and now scurried over all the nooks and crannies, finding and sniffing out all the interesting places, and there were plenty. Archibald's private rooms, armory and the library were, to my great dismay, closed. But I gained access to the torture rooms, the ice statue museum, to a couple of training ranges, to the office with the personality solver, as well as to the anchor room and a dozen or so bedrooms. After this brief tour I made several dozen portal scrolls so that I could return. Then I went back to the office. It was time for my plan.

"Devir, hi there, I need you to do something! Stop screaming, I know very well what time it is. Early bird gets away from Restart. I have something to ask you. I need your help. No, I can't tell you over the comm — enemies are everywhere. See, that's what you should have started with! Let's meet in the Sanctuary by the bank in ten minutes."

During the time that I had not seen Devir he advanced to level three, the maximum for players who had not yet gone through the Academy. The mage teleported himself right to the bank; he was worried about his safety and moved around the Sanctuary without lowering his protective dome. Before making a step he checked the space in front of him with a special stick, looking for traps and teleports. Having made sure there were no threats ahead, Devir looked at me questioningly.

"I need a robot with advanced artificial intelligence. Humanoid," I said right off the bat.

"In our location it is prohibited to use artificial intelligence. It requires a permit." Devir was at a loss for an answer to me, so he stated a well-known fact.

"Iven didn't need it, so you won't need one either. I need the robot by tonight. I am sure you were an outstanding smuggler. Connections are not levels — you can't just wipe them out."

"Did Archibald's death fry your brain so badly?" The mage recovered his self-confidence and he showed he was aware of the latest news.

"That's not it." I was not going to react to his barbs. "I need complete information on how to sacrifice an immune one. Requirements, constraints, sequence of actions. Everything in order to repeat this with one hundred percent guarantee of success".

"Right. I get it. Consider that we have not seen each other," Devir replied and pulled out a portal scroll. Before the mage had time to disappear I hastened to announce the price.

"All that in exchange for her. Need that?" I extended the picture to him. Devir's Doll, captured in a block of ice, looked recognizable and quite impressive. The mage needed just one glance to change his mind and resume the conversation. He braced himself and asked as nonchalantly as possible:

"And so what do you think I should do with a piece of ice?"

"Thaw her out, recover and enjoy the company. Everything functions properly. But if you don't need her, that's the end of this. Thank you for agreeing to meet with me and spend some of your time."

There was a pause. Rare passersby, who had gotten up at some ungodly hour, were hurrying by, their heels loud on the stones. The city was still sleeping. The ubiquitous noise of the cars was not at its loudest yet, so one could hear the sounds of the early morning. Devir considered it for a long time, weighing all the pros and contras; he even called somebody after activating the spell of silence around himself. I didn't interfere, preferring to people-watch absently. I had made my move, and so now the ball was in the mage's court.

"Suppose I am interested in your offer. How can I make sure that she will be okay after thawing? Archibald took her away in the last era and told me that he had killed her. How did she even survive the Restart?"

"Devir, are you serious? Archibald just told you point blank: 'I killed your Doll'? Or maybe 'she stopped functioning'? I am sure he told you whatever else, but not 'killed'. The teacher was very particular about those matters. After recovery she will be fine, and as for Restart it's quite a silly question anyway. It's your property, how could it not survive the Restart if you did? Let's get to the point. I need your help for this. I agree to return your Doll to you. If you agree, let's get going. If you don't, we part ways. Both you and I have our hands full anyway. Have you already bought your ticket to the next era?"

The mage's twitching cheek indicated that I had hit the nail on the head. He was not on the list.

"How did you find out about her? Archibald boasted to you, showing the cause of our dissent?"

"Listen to me: I don't care what bone you had to pick with Archibald! I ran into her by chance, and it was fortunate. I need your help and I am willing to offer her as payment. If the answer is 'no' I'll find someone else. All our relationships are now a thing of the past. Archibald is gone, and with him everything is gone that had to do with him! All the bans, setups and grudges!"

"That's logical. Fine, let's cooperate. What is this robot supposed to do?"

"It must be programmable; it has to be able to find several NPCs and perform certain actions with them."

"That's strange, but doable. As for the sacrifice — you need it in order to activate Merlin's diary? Like, Madonna was not enough for you?"

"Let that be my own headache," I cut him off. "I just need detailed instructions."

"Give me a couple of hours to think it over and get everything prepared. Return my Doll to me and you will get what you want. The Game is my witness!"

"No, Devir. No tickee no shirtee. I am not going to pay in advance. The Game is too unpredictable for one to afford trust. I will wait for your call until ten."

Helen's death burnt out all feelings in me. Too little time had passed for such concepts as compassion, humanity or sympathy to find a response in my soul. There was just my goal and the ways to reach it. The mage was staring at me, but kept silent without trying to convince me to change my mind. After he considered and decided everything for himself, he nodded just as silently and activated a portal without wasting any time. The first part of my plan was complete. Now it was time to use the ordinary cell phone.

"Major, good morning. I need to talk to you. Yes, I do know what time it is! It's time to get up, the sun is high and you are still not slaving away! I'll be waiting for you by the entrance. Yes, by the entrance to your building. Get down!"

Avalon was a unique place with priceless resources. I especially noted the capability to create an unlimited number of teleport scrolls to any location; the important thing was to have the coordinates. I had visited Vesnin's place once, so there was no problem preparing for that leap in advance. By the time the major came downstairs wearing an old flower-print house robe, I had been entertaining myself for about five minutes by reading the ads on the poster board. "A family of internet professionals would like to rent an apartment renovated to European standards." Some things never change, regardless of time and place.

"If someone were to see us, they would really have my ass." Vesnin was seriously alarmed. An employee of special forces who was in disfavor and hunted by his own people was not the best company for a policeman who wanted to advance in his career. Yet he came down to see me. This unconditional trust made me feel guilty. My carefully prepared plan was about to fall apart.

"Do you have anyone at home?" I was dragging my feet like a coward.

"We can't go to my place. My wife's there," Vesnin protested. "Tell me here. What do you want?"

"The last sacrifice was in Subway-2." I just needed a bit more time and I would be able to control myself.

"I know, yesterday they reported from your

office. They said they found evidence you were there. They even had some video, but it wasn't shown to me."

"We almost caught him. You were right, it was the one with two faces." It was time: I couldn't drag that out any more.

"How's that?" The major frowned.

"It's like this." I clenched my fist and hit Vesnin on the forehead with my steel glove, trying not to send him to the afterworld too early. The fat guy crashed onto the ground in a dead faint, which was useful for both of us. In order to avoid adverse effects for the immune one, I cured the wound with a potion and opened a portal to Avalon. The defense worked excellently, the major instantly turned into a piece of ice; I called the elevator and I brought him down to the others to wait for his fifteen minutes of fame. The second part of my plan had successfully been completed.

The third part of the plan was the most controversial and least prepared. Even if Devir were to say that it was fine to kill the immune being right away, I wanted to fully repeat the sacrifice ritual performed by the mages. Before the immune one it was necessary to kill several level one players. Archibald did not have any in his collection, only high level professionally trained terrifying headhunters who were trying to breach the secrets of Avalon. Yesterday I had to rack my brain quite a bit to figure out where I could come up with the missing pieces of my puzzle. Steve helped me: he reminded that players after the Academy and before reaching level ten were in the class Citadel. That was the weakest point of my plan. I needed to entice two or three players to come outside the Citadel, and do it in such a way as not to incite the rest of the Paladins against me.

After getting back to the Sanctuary the first place I visited was the auction. Three scrolls of "Widow's Kiss" cost me ten granises, but I was not concerned about the financial aspect. The seller assured me he would keep my anonymity, for most of the granises I had left after buying the scrolls. The players were extremely prejudiced against anyone who could shave off five levels with one blow, and after the deal the sellers would sell out their buyers, earning some extra money for themselves. The prospect of losing my own levels at respawn didn't bother me: if this did not work out, precisely at midnight a messenger of Madonna or Bernard would show up for me and that would be the end of my existence in the Game.

The Residence of the Paladins resembled a disturbed anthill. Players of all types and classes gathered here for the sake of the ephemeral hope of making it to the next era. The one-legged gatekeeper could not keep up with processing applications from a huge line of players requesting a meeting with Gerhard or any other Paladin responsible for including an individual on the transition lists. Here and there one could hear cries full of fury and indignation, but no one overstepped the boundaries. After I squeezed inside, I frequently felt envious glances. Everyone was by now aware of my status as the Guide, and they wouldn't mind trading places. Of course, guaranteed passage to the next era. If they had known the truth, their envy would have wilted on the spot.

I nodded to a Paladin I knew from the private areas of the residence and went to the second floor, where I used a stationary teleport. I knew the coordinates of the Citadel but did not feel like risking everything for the sake of saving a couple of minutes. Who knew what Gerhard might have done with the defenses after our invasion? What if additional teleports would send me to catch the chimera's breath? No, I really could not afford to end up there now, so I'd stick exclusively to the standard transportation methods. Once I was inside I headed for the training range where Sharda had taught us how to use our artifacts. If I were to catch newbies anywhere, it would be there.

"Brother Yaropolk! It's good to see you in the Citadel! How come?" Sharda was there as if on cue. But the one thing I had not expected was his happy smile. Knowing of his friendship with Archibald I had thought I would see a sad face. But no: the gnome was smiling, showing all his... hm... how many teeth did gnomes have anyway? In any case, the gnome was smiling from ear to ear, demonstrating his sincere joy at seeing me. That bothered me, since previously Shard had not been given to that.

"I'm just... visiting." I tried to appear as unconcerned as possible. "Wanted to find some of our young guys. I mean, graduates from the latest Academy term."

"What do you need them for?" The smile

vanished from Sharda's mug.

"I wanted to go through their Dungeon with them, but at level ten. Good for them, nice for me. Basic granises don't hurt anyone."

"What a commendable urge!" Sharda nodded his head and managed to put his short hand on my shoulder so that I nearly buckled under this "caress". "You are an honorable Paladin, brother Yaropolk! Come, I'll introduce you to some young brothers."

I did not know for whom we performed all this, but Sharda preferred to agree with me out loud while leading me to the artifact hall with a firm hand, without any chance for me to resist. Grinning at each other we quickly arrived at our destination, but no one was there.

"Tell me now," the gnome demanded, releasing my shoulder. I didn't need to be a Mensa club member to figure out that he was talking about Archibald's death. I didn't see any reason to hide the specifics of the teacher's death, and offered the video that had been prepared for Clarissa. The only difference was that I included Alard in it. Sharda needed to know that he had perished as well.

"Brother Alard was an honorable Paladin," Sharda said in a crestfallen voice; he had not expected that one more Paladin had left this world together with Archibald. "It is a pity I was not the one who taught him. It would have been a great honor for me. Why did you not take any action?"

"I didn't see much point in dying a spectacular but stupid death," I said harshly. "As for me, it is better to retreat, prepare and avenge."

"And have you prepared? The gnome asked sarcastically.

"I am preparing. Can't you see? That's why I came here: I just need one day."

"But do you have it, brother Yaropolk? Why do you think I rushed to greet you as soon as the Citadel's defenses announced your arrival? The head's order was to escort you to him as soon as you appear. I doubt very much that he was going to shower you with favors."

I stiffened my lips, preparing for battle. For an honorable suicide, to be precise: I didn't stand a chance against Sharda. Sharda appreciated my attempt at a menacing look and softened somewhat.

"If I had wanted to kill you, I would have done it already. Why do you need the newbies? Just skip those tales about the Dungeon."

"That's why." I pulled out Madonna's Diary and showed it to Sharda. The gnome had been Archibald's ally. Even though the latter was not with us any longer, and Sharda had done everything to stay away from the old plans, yet he was in no hurry to escort me to Gerhard. In any case, not right away. Therefore, there was something for the gnome in this whole affair, and therefore it was worth the risk.

"Oh," Sharda was taken aback; he obviously had not expected things to take such a turn. "But the Diary is not the one of Merlin. Madonna has already incarnated, so what do newbies have to do with this?"

"This was an unsuccessful incarnation, and I am sure that we need to try again. Without them..."

"Let's consider I have not heard anything,

brother Yaropolk," Sharda cut me off.

"What difference does it make to you?! They will all die soon anyway!" In anger I shouted at the short gnome, who was taken aback. I did not understand why he kept playing his pointless role. There was no reaction.

My artifact took its usual spot on my hand and the spikes extended in battle mode. I had no other choice than to return to Avalon, since there was nothing more I could do in the Citadel. Should the gnome try to hold me back I would stick myself with the artifact and escape to Avalon. Sharda just grinned in response to my actions and came a couple steps closer.

"Are you sure this will work out?" The gnome's question was so unexpected that I delayed killing myself, and nodded in response. Sharda continued pensively:

"I will think how I can help. I won't give you mine though, anyway. I pity them. How are you going to shave the levels off the sacrifices?"

"Widow's Kiss. I have the scrolls." Hope flared up like an ember within me.

"That won't work, you will definitely not find anyone with so few levels, You will need 'Black Death', but I'll take care of that. Have you decided who is going to activate the scrolls?"

"That will be me, myself. Somehow there were no more volunteers."

" 'Me, myself,' See, a proud one... there will be volunteers. We cannot allow Archibald's death to be in vain! Right? Good, good. Fight to the end, brother

Yaropolk. And now it's time for you to leave the Citadel. Here's the number; text me the coordinates to deliver the package. Come on, move it before Gerhard starts wondering why you have not yet been brought to him."

I nodded gratefully, and now calmly activated a portal to Avalon. Before leaving I did, however, ask the question:

"Why?"

"I told you. Because Archibald's death cannot be meaningless." The gnome did not hold back. "He asked me to help you. You don't need to know the rest. Get going."

It's a very true saying: waiting and catching up are among the worst things to do. The two hours till Devir's call seemed like an eternity to me. So much sweeter was the news I heard from the mage.

"I have information on the sacrifice. The robot is on its way — it will be here in a couple of hours. The Game is my witness. I want to receive my Doll."

"Where should I teleport her?" I was certain that Devir had prepared a place in advance.

"I'll send you the coordinates momentarily. Will I need the thawing equipment or do you have your own?"

"Do bring it. You will have to thaw her yourself. I don't want to risk it, it might trigger the castle's defenses Wait for me — I'll be there in a couple of minutes."

Archibald's instructions were rather detailed, but it was possible that Devir's Doll did not have access to the castle. In that case the system would have frozen her again, or done something worse. I reached the statue hall and walked around the Doll, figuring out what would be the best way to carry her. I did not want to put a sentient being into my inventory, even if it were frozen. There was already one there, providing me with Energy.

"Greetings, my restless student. Decided to play a thief?" I heard Archibald's voice the moment I lifted the Doll from the platform. Caught red-handed. I, however, did not put the Doll back, but prepared to jump to Devir. But Archibald's voice stopped me:

"That's right: once you have decided to do it, just do it and don't stop. So, then: I asked Sharda and Clarissa to help you. Apparently Clarissa granted you access, since you are here. That's good. Don't even think of recovering the Doll here — she does not have access rights to be in the castle. Let Devir sort out his own property. Remember, Yari, you can only trust the mage while you have him by the short hairs. Don't forget whose vassal he is. Structure your conversation and bear in mind that every word will be conveyed to Bernard. Really, I would not have gone to Devir altogether, but there is no choice. Neither Clarissa nor Sharda have the connections that he has. Don't even think of returning to the Citadel. Gerhard will not be happy with that, and that will be the end of the Game for you. Now for the most important part: in the far corner of the hall there is an inconspicuous door with a code lock. The code is the date of your initiation in the Game. Remember the first time we met? Behind the door there are memory crystals — mine and Clarissa's. I have set everything up in such a way that the copy of her crystal is kept in my safe. Sakhray is certainly a good fellow, but Madonna is too vindictive. This is the back-up version. Don't activate the crystals for the first ten years after Restart. We should become forgotten. Good luck to you, student! You must find a way to survive Restart, or I will be disappointed in you."

The voice fell silent, and I praised myself. Archibald had miscalculated, thinking that first of all I would be dealing with Devir's Doll. My teacher's warning was for the most part not relevant any more, since I had found out about both Sharda and Gerhard on my own. The only worthwhile things were the memory crystals. This simplified implementation of my own plan quite a bit.

Having collected the gift, I activated the portal from the museum and jumped to Devir. The mage carefully looked over his precious Doll and hastened to make sure that everything was fine with her. Only after that did he agree to pass me the information. The familiar cave with the altar where the mages had killed my partners from the Academy made my heart skip a beat. The memories I had of that location were far from the best. To hide my worry I remarked:

"If you survive the Restart, you will be a unique player."

"What are you talking about? Yari, I am in cooldown mode after the brainstorm to resolve all your requests." Devir stopped attaching leads and wires to the piece of ice he had received and stared at me in bewilderment.

"You are in permanent brain cooldown mode,

Devir, not just after brainstorming. Suppose you survive Restart, together with your Doll. Then you go through the Academy one more time. And then you will receive another Doll! And then you will have a harem. How will you cope with that?"

"Oh, that... Worry about your own affairs," Devir grumbled in response, but his expression told me that he was thinking not how to survive the Restart, but how nice it would be to have two Dolls at once. I didn't bother reminding him of the main condition for that. Let him have some fun for the last time.

The ice melted, and the unconscious woman fell into Devir's arms. Green blinking lights indicated that the mage's property was stable and in good shape. I sighed with relief. All that time I had worried about freezing a "non- player". What if Vesnin's mind went directly to the Path of the Dead, to amuse Thanatos? Devir meanwhile poured several healing potions into the Doll's mouth and carefully placed her on a floating platform; it turned out to be a medical robot. An energy field built around the woman; through it one could vaguely see the activity of various devices restoring muscle tone and mobility. Devir came up to me and handed me a small notebook and a sheet of paper:

"Here are the complete instructions from Levard. He did not trust electronic means of storing information. This is the only material form. The sheet has the courier's number. He'll get in touch with you in a couple of hours and deliver the package. Don't call him unless it's an emergency. That's it. We're even."

"Not quite. Bernard must not know what happened today."

"Whatever you say. That's not my concern any more. The old Devir died, and the vassal relationship died with him. I am a free player, Yari, and today I have received what I have been dreaming about for the past two and a half thousand years. I don't care about you; I need to ensure my transition to the new era. So, relax — no one will find anything out."

Devir spoke convincingly, but it didn't convince me. Precisely because the mage so wanted to buy the transition right for himself, he would have sold me whole. Activating the "Widow's Kiss" scroll took a long time, all those endless confirmations were quite annoying, so the mage's dialogue was welcome. It enabled me to prepare for the instant when Devir, pleased, went back to his Doll, and I dealt the blow. Multistrike flew out of my inventory and the last warning appeared before me. That was followed by the ability activation. I had to shoot him in the back. I pushed the virtual trigger and heard the cry of surprise before a ball of fire stopped the mage's existence in the Game. A player before the Academy only had three levels to his name. "Widow's Kiss" could remove up to five. Multistrike did the main job. Everything had been planned and was executed neatly. My internal Judge initiated a case against me, but I chased him into the back of my mind: later. Everything would have to be later. Tomorrow, if there is a tomorrow. Whether the mage had been telling the truth or not didn't matter any more. The deed was done and this was no place to be sentimental A system message appeared, notifying me that I had received a Killer token, and then the Game took its due: activation of the scroll demanded my respawn as well. So I was off to Avalon.

Levard included in his instructions for sacrifice not only a description, but also some graphics indicating the right way to hold the dagger, where to strike, in what way to place the sacrifice. I was correct: for the final sacrifice it was necessary to prime the ritual stone with two other victims. Only then would the stone be ready to absorb the blood of the immune player. The latter was somewhat of a problem, since Vesnin was not a player. Sakhray came to my aid and gave me his memory crystal. Just to protect myself I decided to turn the major into a player. By the time the courier called me everything was ready. The frozen items were brought to the location from Avalon, coordinates were sent to Sharda and the recovery platform was configured. Jumping to the location where I had killed Devir immediately after I respawned, I was wondering what to do with his Doll, who had stayed lying on the platform, but the Game took care of that: since the player had left this world, his property disappeared together with him.

The process of transferring the package turned out to be funny and sort of spy-like. The courier, an orange scaly reptilian, kept looking around in an empty small lane in the Sanctuary, and pointed his scanner this way and that, concerned that someone might be following him. The container with my robot was covered with an impenetrable Energy field. Once the courier calmed down, he explained this field prevented the contents from being scanned during teleportation. The reptilian handed me the access key to the protection, said good-bye and faded into the surroundings. It made no sense to teleport to Avalon: I was worried that the protection would simply destroy my contraband item. All I could do then was to transport the robot to the location of the intended sacrifice. I removed the protection and started figuring out the owner's manual, which was a hefty tome I set right there on the ground. That was what occupied me when Sharda appeared.

"These devices are prohibited on Earth." Oh well, teachers would always stay teachers first and foremost. Having made his statement regarding my new property, the gnome stepped aside from the teleport, letting the others pass. Two gnome Paladins whom I did not know appeared from the portal: they were carrying the victims for the sacrifice on stretchers. I grinned: today there would be three mages fewer. The newbies, tied hand and foot, would soon follow Devir. After I finished programming the robot, I could now work on the main thing. Now, regardless of how it all played out, I had a chance to survive. The robot was not officially my property, so it should not disappear after I died. There was nothing magical about it, and Restart would not affect it. It was a simple but reliable mechanism, set in a human body. The Game should not have any questions about my secret. Sharda did not miss the fact that I handed the robot three memory crystals, but he didn't interfere, understanding whose crystal I gave for safekeeping to that smart machine. I pushed the power button, and the robot's eyes came to its mechanical life.

"Task is clear and will be completed." The robot bowed his head, addressing me as a higher being. I activated a portal and told the machine to get out of my sight. In the Sanctuary the robot should be able to get lost in the crowd and not raise any suspicions. I gave it enough money to last for the first few hundred years; after that it would be time for it to complete its mission.

"We are ready," said one of the Paladins, looming over the mages. They realized that they were not in the cave for the fun of it, but there was more confusion than fear in their eyes. That did not last long, however.

"Brother Yaropolk?" Sharda had waited till the robot left our company. "Shall we?"

"We shall," I confirmed, taking out the ritual knife. The first Paladin took out the scroll and started with activating it. Unlike "Widow's Kiss", "Black Death" required a long time. The Game tried to talk sense into the Paladin who had decided to use a prohibited item; it even issued a quest for destruction and blocking his actions. It's just that no one was going to block him. It dawned on the mages what kind of threat they were facing. They started struggling, trying to weaken the ties and escape. But it was too late for fright. The scroll was activated and the first Paladin disappeared for respawn. The Game eliminated the violator. With one hand I placed the mage on the ritual stone and, without taking my eyes away, waved the blade, spraying blood on the altar. The Mayan knife did not drink the blood: it gave it all to the last drop to the more worthy object.

A minute later the ritual was repeated. The scroll activated, the second Paladin disappeared, and the altar was awash with the blood of one more player. The preparation was complete.

"Today two brothers will suffer the punishment for using the forbidden scrolls," Sharda said. "Brother Yaropolk, make sure that their sacrifice will not be in vain."

The gnome did not wait for the end of the ritual, and teleported himself to the Citadel. One could understand Sharda: Archibald's request turned out to be quite a test for him. He had to act at odds with his principles and ask two brothers in class to accept the punishment of the Game. What it would be one could only guess, and I had no doubts that the brothers would regret their agreement a thousand times. But on the other hand, the Paladins received three vacant spots. It was quite possible that they had done it for the sake of their children, granting them the opportunity to become players. Who knows?, but altruism definitely had nothing to do with it.

After I was alone, I sighed heavily, sending oxygen through my body, and started on the final part. That completely depended on my concentration and focus: as soon as Madonna's Diary was activated, I would have no more than three seconds before the high guests showed up. And it would not matter who they were — Madonna, Merlin, the Counselors of the Emperor — because they would come to kill me.

Devir's recovery platform was now mine by the winner's right, and I used it shamelessly as the winner: I started recovery of the woman with an implanted Madonna's memory crystal. After I brought her to a medically acceptable condition, I injected her with a sedative so that she would not regain consciousness. One thing I really wanted to avoid was female hysterics and tears. After that it was Vesnin's turn. My hands were working as if on their own, repeating the same procedures. The difference with the other "revivals" was that the sedative from the recovery platform did not work on Vesnin. It was magical and therefore did not affect the immune major. I didn't get that right away, only after the major tried to rush to get up, but he didn't have the strength yet after thawing. I had to improvise and tie Vesnin to the platform using strips from the clothing I borrowed from the new Madonna.

"Colonel, what the hell? What jokes are you playing?" a couple of minutes before the recovery procedure was completed Vesnin had completely come round. Finding himself in an unenviable position, the major did not panic, but rather was analyzing the situation. Years of work in law enforcement were showing. I could not interrupt the process: at the altar I needed a fully recovered immune being in order to give its blood to the thirsty stone.

"This is no joke, major! Calm down, I know it looks scary, but I am just providing medical treatment," I said calmly so that Vesnin would allow me to complete the recovery process.

"For what are you treating me? And why did you tie me down?" The major was not panicking, but he was in no hurry to trust me either.

"Don't you remember? You were hit. If I untied you, it would cause uncontrolled jerking. You would fall or injure yourself. Hang on for a couple minutes, don't twitch and I will release you. Word of a scout!"

"I remember! What damn 'scout', when you were the one that bonked me on the head?!" Vesnin shouted indignantly, and tried to fight free. The straps creaked, but held. "Let me go! Now!"

"Calm down, I tell you! Yes, I did!" I agreed "But better me than the sniper!"

"What sniper?" The major was taken aback, and even stopped struggling.

"What, you don't know anything?" I made a surprised face. "Your mother was lured by some dealers from abroad, and she easily left Russia. Despite all her principles. Even though she never worked for us, those are not the kind of people you can just let go. So the decision was made to eliminate your entire family. I remembered how you saved us at the park, so I am paying back the debt of honor. My people have already helped your wife escape. So don't worry about her. I hit you too strongly, I agree. That's why I had to tie you down."

I lied shamelessly, trying to keep Vesnin in a calm state. The major went for it, and settled down until the system notified me that he was fully recovered.

"Where are my glasses? I can't see anything without them," Vesnin complained once I finally untied him and helped him get to his feet. As he was squinting trying to see something in the murk of the cave, the major could only see the white body of the sleeping Madonna.

"They broke. It's okay, we'll order you new ones today. Here, sit down. Can you get to that white stone? I just have to finish up here. Careful, the floor is slippery."

My confidence and calm dispelled the major's apprehensions somewhat, and Vesnin trundled submissively towards the altar. I took the unconscious woman in my arms and caught up with him.

"Who is that?" The fat man frowned as he saw a new face up close. The major's suspicions raised their head again, particularly as blood sloshed under his feet. There was a huge puddle of blood around the snow-white stone. According to Levard's notes it was not supposed to be wiped up. Vesnin did not say anything, but his hand instinctively reached to where the cop would have had his holster.

"A rescued victim. I grabbed her practically from under the knife of the guy who was performing the sacrifices. She is alive, just unconscious. Wait, let me set her down and I will explain everything."

"Do me a favor, really," Vesnin grumbled. I set the Madonna-to-be next to the altar and took out the Diary:

"The whole hullabaloo is because of this book. There was a whole crowd of people killed in order to gather the right people here. Her. Me. You."

"You?" The major had not serve in law

---

enforcement for nothing: he immediately analyzed the situation and came to the correct conclusions: "So it was you that killed all those…"

"Yes and no," I admitted. "I didn't start it, but I definitely have to finish it. So, sorry bro, but today you will die."

"You bastard!" The major lost his cool. He rushed at me, trying to bowl me over with his (not insignificant) weight, but ran into my protection and slumped as he got zapped with a weak current. I managed to grab him as he fell, and dragged him back onto the altar. Then I started the procedure of activating the Diary, following Steve's instructions. The book cover turned red, the altar started trembling in anticipation of the immune one's blood. Vesnin's lids fluttered; he was starting to come round and trying to say something, but I stopped him with one blow. The major's body was convulsing, and it took me quite a significant effort to keep him in place with one free hand. With my other hand I was holding the book. Vesnin's body was becoming desiccated, turning into a mummy in front of me; the Diary was absorbing the life energy of the major and turning bright red. Finally, the message, for the sake of which I had started all that, flashed in front of me:

Sacrifice is accepted. Madonna's Diary is activated

Preparation of Game Restart has been initiated.

Attention! Diary version conflict detected. Game interference is required!

Here they were, my three seconds. Madonna-to-be was waiting for her time right at my feet. I was holding the Diary next to her, and now just dumped it onto her chest, protecting her from the incoming guests with my own body.

"Paladin, stop!" I heard the voice of the Counselor, and my body turned to stone. Too late! I had thought it all through, and the Counselor, who thought himself infallible, had no chance to protect the woman from contact with the Diary. No one had expected such prowess from the not-quite-Paladin. My stiff body fell on top of the woman when a new message flashed before me:

Player Madonna is incarnated

"What the ... Yaropolk?! Where am I? What did you do, you half-wit?!" The woman opened her eyes and pushed my body off hers. Jumping up hastily, she was looking around, not understanding, and trying to figure out what had happened. But even those movements were enough to recognize the same old Madonna in the new body. I was starting to become upset, thinking that my plan had not worked, but the third system message dispelled my doubts:

Unexpected Error
System Administrator Input Required

The second version of Madonna was taking the version conflict badly. Cupping her head in her hands, she fell down on her knees, moaning loudly from pain. I still could not move, but I could see that it was getting worse for her. The woman fell on the bloody floor and writhed around, screaming with the headache now. Her cries echoed in my ears, but nothing could mar my joy: by all appearances, it seemed my plan would work.

It was quite a simple one. I counted that after incarnation of the new Madonna there would be a situation when the same being would exist in two bodies at once. Madonna still had just one soul. Therefore, in case of the conflict, until everyone figured out what was the matter, each Madonna would see and feel the same things as the other. In that I was correct: after incarnation she recognized me at once. No matter how great a human brain was, it did not have the ability to be in two places at once. No one had previously divided a single soul in two either. I very much hoped that this time would be enough for the bitch to simply go crazy, which equaled being destroyed completely. Because there was no place in the Game for madmen, even if they were Great Ones. No Madonna — no Restart, no dead Yaropolk. Everyone would be happy.

Everything changed in one split second. I didn't even feel it happen. I was lying on the floor of the cave completely immobilized and enjoying Madonna's suffering, when suddenly there was silence and a white light that hurt my eyes. I found myself standing in a blindingly white room similar to the control room of a supercomputer. Everywhere there were touchpad panels and displays with indicators, charts and data.

Besides myself and data input and output devices there were two more Counselors, floating in the air in their normal lotus positions, a common-looking guy of about twenty, and both incarnations of Madonna. The women, like the Counselors, were also floating in the air, but in supine positions, and only their steady synchronized breathing indicated that they were still alive. Noting this fact with sadness, I turned to the guy. The moment he turned his glance towards me, my protection system howled mightily, and disintegrated. I had been too hasty to consider the guy's appearance to be ordinary. It was impossible to look into his fiery eyes; it seemed they were burning out your very soul. That's why sometimes he was called the Fire Emperor.

"This was a rash step, Guide," the strongest being in this world said, and each of his words seared my brain like a brand. Blood trickled from my ears, dark circles danced in front of my eyes, but I hung on. Once you have gone the whole way death is not what bothers you; you think about how to up the ante for your life.

"I did what I had to. This Madonna has to be destroyed."

"You assumed somebody else's functions. Your job is to find all the participants of the Restart, not to decide who is worthy of existing in the Game and who is not," said one of the Counselors instead of the Emperor. Presumably they had decided to spare me for now. "By incarnating another version of Madonna, you did not destroy her, you just launched the process of a premature Restart. The rashness of that action is that now you, as the Guide, have to name the other participants in the Restart. Are you ready to do that? Otherwise it will be deemed that you have failed your function and you will be wiped out together with all your memory crystals. That is the price of the error, Yaropolk. You have five minutes and the timer is counting."

Everything sank inside me: the Game was preserving the life of the bitch who had killed my loved one! The plan that had seemed perfect, had failed. It became hard to breathe, my head seemed full of lead as I realized my failure; yet I still had the last five minutes. Pushing all my feelings deep down I tried not to show my weakness to this computer code and said:

"Gerhard van Brast. The Nameless. The first participant in the Restart."

"Accepted." The Emperor spoke again and my legs started turning to jello; I remained standing by sheer willpower. I was tired of falling; if I had to die at least it would be with my head held high. One of the Counselors disappeared, to reappear a couple of moments later together with Gerhard. The latter smiled happily:

"What a smart boy you are! Yaropolk, I hadn't expected that! What a very pleasant surprise — you did manage to launch Restart after all!"

I did not react to the words of the Nameless, standing like a frozen statue. Gerhard furrowed his brows, shook his head and started inspecting Madonna. Then he pointed out Dolgunata to the Emperor:

"What happened to the Keymaster? Why is she unconscious?"

"There was a conflict of versions of the Great One," one of the Counselors piped up, but Gerhard simply waved him off.

"I was not asking you, a software by-product. Since when has the Emperor lost his own voice?"

Gerhard lifted an eyebrow quizzically, looking at the Emperor demandingly from a position of strength.

"The appearance of the second Madonna required my interference. The Guide has not yet named your companion. As soon as this happens we'll return them to consciousness," the Emperor responded, and the world around me faded. My mind could not stand a long statement from the Emperor, and decided to take a break. I came to because Gerhard was pouring a healing potion into my mouth.

"Oh, you were just so overcome," the Nameless smiled at me. "I had thought you were standing so still because you were frozen. But no, you were alive, Don't you worry, not many players are capable of talking to the Emperor. Now we'll make you all better, and you will say that Dolgunata was not Madonna, but the Keymaster. Understand?"

I looked suspiciously at Gerhard, who appeared so down-to-earth. His face bore a familiar fatherly smile and I accepted his extended hand in order to get on my feet. I had been out for barely a minute, so my time was not up yet. Gerhard made sure that I was standing firmly on my feet and continued.

"Don't be stubborn. If Madonna stays in

Dolgunata's body, we will have a problem with the Keymaster. Someone needs to open the door, or else there will be no Restart." Gerhard nodded into the far corner of the room. There really was a door.

"If Madonna stays in the body of this... tomato, then Dolgunata will become herself again. Your choice, Guide. You have three minutes left."

"She will be Madonna," I pointed at the body of the nameless woman, as I decided to keep alive at least someone I knew. Dolgunata was of course not much fun either, but at least I sort of knew her, so let her live. And Madonna would have to make do with this body until Restart.

"Accepted!" The Emperor waved his hand, and a silvery fog enveloped the women's bodies. A moment later Madonna in a new body jumped to her feet and screeched at a near ultrasound pitch:

"What's going on?! Why am I in this body?! Gerhard! Answer me, now!"

"Shut up," Gerhard cut her off with a grimace of displeasure. Madonna gulped some air to express her indignation, but was unable to utter a single sound. She turned red, fighting to produce just a squeak, but nothing came out. Gerhard's magic was stronger than the magic of the Great One.

"What's going on with Dolgunata?" I was worried, seeing that the druid never regained consciousness.

"It's time, Guide! Two of the Restart participants have been named. The third one still remains," the Counselor, fairly enough, reminded me that if I didn't name the third participant now, it would be pointless for me to worry about anyone's fate.

"Come on, Yaropolk, surprise me," Gerhard cheered me on, and I nearly jumped. That was the grin and the tone with which Archibald used to say that, knowing that I wouldn't let him down.

"*I have a vague suspicion about Archibald,*" Steve began, but I cut my subconscious off. Now was not the time.

What did I know about Merlin? According to Vesnin's precognitive dreams, it was some double-faced being; lately it must have been suffering from diarrhea. A higher vampire, Malturion, worked for Merlin; the Coordinator of our sector was somehow connected with him. Merlin did not like Dark players and... and that was just about all I knew about him. Truckloads of information to name him precisely within a minute. So what am I to do now? Name Bernard or Malturion for the lack of better options?

"*I would choose Bernard,*" Steve suddenly butted in. "*I analyzed it here. It' not like he is a truly unsuitable figure.*"

"We looked at him as a candidate together with Archibald from all standpoints. It's not him!"

"*Don't say 'no' too hastily. Look: We definitely know that Bernard Kalran stated that he knows where to find Merlin. That is the first fact. And now remember the first time we met him! He had told you that it was an 'echo', but how is that different from the 'double-face' that Vesnin talked about? That's the second fact. Madonna's Diary was in Bernard's library. That's the third fact.. Malturion worked for Bernard. The fourth*"

---

fact. Then, during the visit to our apartment Bernard was pale. That could be a symptom of diarrhea. That's the fifth fact. Clarissa said that Bernard would not be able to overpower Archibald, but Merlin could! And like for the Dark Ones is as fickle as dislike. That's not an argument!"

"But the Game confirmed that Bernard did not know where Merlin was," I insisted. "That ruins your whole theory."

"True," Steve did not argue. *"And now comes the twist in the tale. Imagine that Kalran is not Kalran, but Merlin himself. And always has been. And Kalran is the actual 'echo; the one that appeared during our first meeting with the Coordinator? It's like after Madonna was in Dolgunata's body: the druid's personality was pushed into the back of the subconscious. Get that?"*

"Your time is up, Guide," said the Counselor. "Either you provide a name, or we decide that you have failed your task."

"Bernard Kalran." There was nothing else I could do than grasp at the straw offered to me by Steve. "Merlin is in his body."

"Accepted," said the Emperor, and sent a Counselor to fetch Bernard. Madonna, getting used to her imposed muteness, showed me with a gesture what she thought of my mental abilities. But in the next second her eyes became very round. So did mine.

Player Merlin is incarnated
Game Restart is initiated

There were a few seconds of tedious waiting, and then there was one more player in the room. Now his personality was clear without a doubt: First advanced the aura suppressing the will; it was followed by Merlin himself. Merlin looked around and snorted:

"Oh, good to see you, dear! This façade suits you better. I always considered that female. appearance should reflect internal character. Gerhard, why did you hang the Silence on her? Take it off; let's have some fun at the end."

"Whatever you say." Gerhard clicked his fingers, and Madonna made some sort of quacking sound. The "Great One" cleared her throat and declared:

"It can't be you! I checked!"

"You owe me a bottle of Shelran," Gerhard said to Merlin, ignoring Madonna. "Yaropolk made it."

"That's arguable," Merlin disagreed. "I had to give my favorite servant to that twit. Malturion is sad and wants compensation."

"Merlin, are you mad? Your pets are asking for compensation now?! Shadow was better in that way. Do you agree?"

"Right, but what do I offer the Emperor for the Shadow? Myself?"

"We can always discuss that." The Emperor reminded of his presence, making me crash to the floor again. I decided I would be more comfortable there, crawled over to Dolgunata and patted her cheek. The druid was still unconscious.

"Enough!" Madonna was mad and insulted at being completely ignored, and slapped everyone with a most powerful spell. Or rather, wanted to slap, but in the presence of the Emperor all the players were in separate spatial planes. Madonna was unable to hurt anybody.

"Whatever you say, dear. I could never deny you," Gerhard opened his palm sharply and Madonna was thrown back to the wall. So, then! Gerhard was able to interact with other players and the Emperor!

"How dare you raise your hand at me, you horny beast!" The blow only angered Madonna, and she tried to respond in kind. The room filled with smoke, fire and lightning, but all of it was not in our dimension.

"Never mind: you will pay for this in the next era!" Realizing that using her forceful methods did not yield any result, Madonna stooped to trivial threats. Merlin turned to Gerhard:

"Dear, aren't you tired? I bet a second bottle that Yari will not explain to our flighty girl the whole extent of her misconception. Oh, hell, again..."

There was an unpleasant squelching sound, and Merlin's face turned white.

"Happy relief," I said angrily. "As for Madonna, there is nothing to explain. She will not remember any of what's happening now."

"Right, but why?" Gerhard joined our conversation, while Madonna hung on to every word.

"What, you are too much of a scaredy-cat to admit this yourself to your former love?" It was tiring to look at the strongest players of all the eras from below, so I rose.

"No, it's not scary. It's tiring." Gerhard grinned. "Besides, it would be interesting to hear your version.

There must be some result from me working with you for so long."

"You know, I don't have any suspicions about Archibald any more. I am completely certain."

"If the Great Mordor so desires, I obey," I said, bowing my head theatrically. Turning towards Madonna, I began with the same theatrical pathos: "O Great One. You will not be able to harm those two gentlemen or avenge yourself for the very simple reason that in the new era there will be a different Madonna. She will be pure and untouched and without the implanted memory crystal. While your soul will die, here and now.

"Correct, but that's not everything," Merlin recovered from his bout of pain. "Gerhard and I would like to hear the complete version!"

"So you have decided to get rid of me?!" Madonna only heard what she wanted to hear, and fire flooded the room once again. Gerhard shook his head and again cast the Silence spell on her. Not only that: Madonna was once more pushed against the wall, and now steel handcuffs grew out of it and restrained the woman.

"Yaropolk, please humor us old guys before this crucial endeavor."

"Shadow was never free. Archibald had thought that he had freed himself from your influence, but in fact you simply allowed him to think that way, observing his actions from a distance and nudging him in the right direction. Because it's so interesting to be in two places at once. You were bored with Madonna already, back in the first era, but somehow you could never get rid of her. I have no idea which one of you devised the method, but now I am certain: Merlin and Gerhard have always acted together. It was Gerhard that implanted Merlin's personality into the Coordinator, but here, it seems to me, the Game balked. Bernard Kalran was not an ordinary nobody. He was, after all, a hereditary aristocrat. For that reason Merlin came out two-faced. As to why Madonna didn't notice him... It's hard to say; perhaps at that point she didn't notice anyone or anything other than herself. After you set everything in such a way that there would be two Madonnas in the Game no matter what, you made a bet. Because it's too boring to observe the bustle of the bugs, right? It's much more interesting to push them in the right direction with a little stick. For Gerhard this stick was Archibald, for Merlin... it was himself. That's why we are all here now. All the bugs ran into the right box, and the lid has shut. As for Madonna, it's very simple. She is a Doll, even though she did become a player. I don't think that Dolls are allowed to destroy their owners. By killing Archibald Madonna actually killed Gerhard without having any idea about it. But the question is, why was that only done now? Madonna took a dislike towards the cat back in the third era. I expect Archibald had been killed previously, only he does not remember it at all. The basis of your entire plan to get rid of Madonna rested specifically on creating a second one. Because the first initiated Madonna had already been destroyed, and all the copies of memory crystals crumbled into dust together with her. The new Madonna, even though she would have the memory of the previous era, did not have the means to transfer her personality. Now we add the punishment of the Doll to that and the result is a pure, untouched Madonna in the next era, who remembers nothing. She will not in any way be connected with Gerhard, or whatever you choose to call yourself in the next era, Nameless. Well, that's about it. Oh, no, there is one more thing. You called up Lumpen on purpose so that he could transition to the next era. You need the pretence of rivalry, otherwise you'd be limited to fighting with yourselves. No, I think, that's it. Oh, and one more thing. Merlin gave me Lumpen's Diary, wanting to make me his mental slave. And only now have I realized why it was done: the memory crystal. Going to his teacher begging was not a very pleasant thought, so Merlin wanted to resolve that issue on his own. But it didn't work. Other pests got in, Gromana came, for example, and spoiled the whole plan. So the new era would have not only the pure and innocent Madonna; other participants of the Restart would not remember their past. Like hell you will make me transfer your crystals!"

"That's rough and without detail, but I have to admit that the overall train of thought is on the right track." Merlin shook his head slowly. "Agree, I owe you two bottles of Shelran; even though the last fact kind of killed the overall impression."

"Yaropolk, I don't need to convince you, do I?" Archibald's grin bloomed on Gerhard's face. "As your only and direct suzerain I order you to shut up, take the crystals and find decent bodies in the next era for me and my student. Bring me back immediately, and then incarnate Merlin. Questions? No questions? Excellent. Here."

A table materialized next to me. There were two dark diaries on it; memory crystals were embedded in their covers. I wanted to refuse, but I was unable to do so: my tongue would not cooperate. Moreover, against my will I extended my hands and put the Diaries into my inventory. Gerhard was Archibald, my direct suzerain. His orders had to be followed without objection. There it was, the real force of vassality.

"So then. I have left you my library. You already took Merlin's library. We'll sort out the rest as the need arises. That's it, Yaropolk, you may go. I don't need you here anymore."

"So you did decide to do it after all?" Merlin asked.

"Right. I am tired of this perennial chaos, it's time to reboot the Game properly. If I have to die once to do it, oh well, so be it. Turning to the Emperor, Gerhard said: "I am requesting that the druid Sakhray be brought here. The Keymaster was unable to return, assistance is required."

One of the Counselors vanished and reappeared together with Sakhray. The druid, pale with fear, saw the Emperor and went down on his knees before him. The Emperor just pointed with a glance at Dolgunata, ordering Sakhray to help his sister. The druid rushed to her, held the girl's head to his chest and started stroking her, whispering something tenderly in her ear. Dolgunata jerked and opened her eyes. At first her stare was vacant and random, but with every word and touch from Sakhray Nata woke up more and her eyes were becoming more aware.

"Enough," Gerhard ordered impatiently and Sakhray was thrown away from Dolgunata. The druid was lifted onto her feet and shaken like a rag doll. The girl's head fell helplessly on her chest. It seemed there was no life in her, but as soon as Gerhard softly lowered the body to the floor, Dolgunata lifted her head — slowly, but unassisted. I watched the changes in my formerly restless rival with bitterness rather than triumph. Broken and despondent, the druid was not at all like herself. The lively and insolent light had faded from her eyes completely. Now there was a crippled being in front of us, by the mercy of the Game not gone mad yet. Our fates were somewhat similar, even though she was whacked harder because of her own stupidity.

"Open the door," Gerhard ordered, and Nata was dragged to the door. As she approached, a touch panel appeared; the druid placed her hand on it, and then her hand dropped listlessly again. She was totally indifferent to what was going on around her, she was just doing what she was ordered, participating in the events to a minimal extent, but for the Game that was enough. The panel flashed green, confirming access, and the door silently slid aside. Gerhard again threw Dolgunata to the side with one flick of his hand, like a thing no longer needed. The Keymaster had performed its functions, and its subsequent fate was of no interest to anyone.

"Everything is ready for the ritual. The list of

players for the next era has been generated automatically," said the Counselor.

"Is witch Clarissa on it?" Gerhard clarified, and after a positive nod demanded: "Delete. No players that were personally connected to me from previous eras. That would be too much."

"Completed." The Counselor did not challenge Gerhard's right to choose players for the next era. The Game didn't care who made the list or did not. Except for those three the Game considered everyone equal.

"Sakhray, give me the memory crystals. All of them, including Archibald's and Clarissa's," Gerhard was not going to stop with the current results once he decided on a total clean-up. The druid sat his sister on the floor carefully, and on stiff legs went to Gerhard to put a handful of crystals into his open palm. Gerhard grunted with satisfaction and clenched his fist hard, crushing the crystals into dust. Shaking the remaining bits onto the floor he wiped his palm and released Sakhray. As far as the Nameless was concerned, he thought his past was destroyed. Merlin was the first one to enter the secret room. I could not see anything inside, it was dark there. Merlin came back soon and stopped in the door, holding a burning candle.

"What's keeping you? Let's be done with it already! You're the one who's going to have all the fun now, and I will have to deal with the delivery!"

"I have more suspicions about Archibald again." Steve made a theatrical pause, waiting for Gerhard to demand that I destroy the robot, but nothing happened. What if neither he nor Merlin knew about

my trick today, and the crystals that Archibald had prepared for me?

"We are taking off. The beginning of the Game will have to take place without our participation. May the new world be better," said the Counselor.

Without any special visual effects the Emperor and his Counselors disappeared.

"I hope you are going to be sensible. Ladies first." Gerhard bowed to Madonna jokingly. All the shackles fell off her, but the woman was hardly happy.

"Go to hell! You horny animal! I don't want to!" Madonna resisted with all her might, but in vain. Gerhard did not even have to strain to tear the clothes off her and shove her through the door forcibly. Merlin was waiting for her there; he took her by hand and led her further into the room. In the flickering light of the candle I saw a podium with a bed on it in the middle of the room. The place for the inception of the world was already prepared. Gerhard was in no hurry to join his former love.

"If you bring life forth in violence, how can you expect anything good of it?" I said almost aloud, astonished by what I saw.

"Right: teach me now, milksop," Gerhard turned towards me. "You will go to Avalon now. This is an order. It's unsafe to stay here during Restart. You have a portal?"

I nodded against my will, and grinning Gerhard with the gait of a conqueror went into the room and shut the door. The mystery of the inception of the world must stay a mystery.

Sakhray embraced Dolgunata and activated a portal scroll, taking them somewhere far away from the place. The druid was concerned exclusively with his sister, who needed recovery and treatment. Everything else was of no importance for him. In my thoughts I wished him luck.

My hands acted on their own. They extracted a portal scroll from the inventory, and against my will I was thrown to Avalon, just as Gerhard had ordered. There I regained control over my body and I rushed to the anchor hall. I needed a new scroll right away!

After I was initiated as a player I learnt that all my previous life had not been real. I got used to that and started building a new, game life, but they managed to mess that up as well. Everyone I had cared about in one way or another was now dead. Even Dolgunata, my strong and interesting opponent, was now crushed by the powers that be as soon as the immediate need for her was past. I would enter the new era as a new character, with a few dozen granises, downloaded libraries and a quest from my suzerain. A convenient character for data transfer. There was no doubt that as a result I would lose my current personality and turn into Garlion. The Librarian. Was that the fate I had wanted when I created the second Madonna? No! And I needed to fight for that, again!

I was unable to destroy the crystals. The direct order prevented me from doing that. My logical thinking suggested that during the reboot my Game abilities would not be available. Including respawn. I could try to use that. Steve named three numbers, and as soon as the anchoring mechanism produced the scroll, I activated it, returning to the control room.

Access is confirmed.

Access level: Guide

I had obey the order to go to Avalon, but there had not been any order to remain there. The statement that it was unsafe to stay in this room could not be treated as an order. Gerhard was in so much hurry that he made a mistake that would cost him dearly. I heard Gerhard's cry of pain coming from behind the door. A moment later Merlin and Madonna joined in. The players were giving themselves up, creating the new world represented by the new Emperor. A button on one of the panels started blinking, waiting to be pressed. I pressed it out of curiosity and one of the walls turned into a huge screen. By pushing the next blinking button I started a video. Three white figures of white fog without any signs of sex or species appeared on the screen.

"The Creators of the Game welcome you, Explorer." I heard a pleasant female voice. One of the figures took a step forward, indicating that it was she speaking to me. "And now as a sign of gratitude we want to make your time of waiting more pleasant by telling you about our Game. We are those very Creators who developed the Game and made it a reality. We hope that our creation is coping with its task and fulfilling its destiny, and so do you."

I listened skeptically and watched the patriotic video, studying the screen and trying to figure out a way to break it so that the speakers would shut up forever. Periodically one of the three Creators would step forward "making my time more pleasant" with yet another pep story.

If one were to believe them, humanity had developed too rapidly. After just several thousand years since becoming aware that they were unique, humans were actively traveling in space, destroying all the races and civilizations they encountered. People were the real locusts of the universe, they took over one world after another. This continued until all the worlds were occupied exclusively by humans. Then there was a period of quiescence, peace and prosperity. As always, sooner or later stagnation became boring. Since they were immortal and dominant in the universe, people wanted something extreme, unusual and previously unseen. That's how the first marginals appeared who were attempting to improve their bodies. Here and there it became popular to have wings, or glowing eyes, or additional limbs. Year after year, century after century, people mutilated themselves, until one fine day it became obvious that there were not many "pure" humans left. All over the place there were elves, gnomes, vampires, werewolves. Separate communities started appearing that conflicted with each other and considered "pure" humans to be second-rate beings. They were herded into reservations and demonstrated to children as if they were exotic animals in a zoo. That was when the Game appeared. The Creators were three outstanding scientists who did not want to put up with that situation. The Game mechanism was deployed on the planet that was the birthplace of humanity, Earth, which had by then become one of the less popular places in our Galaxy. For magic the Game used Elo waves, which made it possible to actively interact with objects from material and non-material worlds. 3D printers appeared for printing future players; the brains of all the inhabitants of the Galaxy were secretly scanned. After that the first version of the Game was released; it took from living sentient beings their most valuable possession: their souls. The goal of the Game was simple: to restore the previous level of importance to humans and bring them out of reservations. It's a method that left a lot to be desired. All "non-humans" became NPCs with a limited life duration; after death they were respawned as humans. The Creators did not take into account that the new generation of people would be unable to adapt to the living conditions of their predecessors. "The "printing machines" were working non-stop respawning people who immediately died again. It was decided that the first version of the Game was unsuccessful. The second version appeared, The Creators showed understanding of the fact that people were not able to live everywhere, and introduced a number of constraints on distribution and behavior. The race of humans came back again, established hegemony in all the areas and for a few hundred thousand years everything was fine. Until people became bored again. History repeats itself, and so again marginal elements appeared who wanted to change their bodies. Another few hundred thousand years passed, and humans ended up in the same position in which they had been before the Game was released: in reservations. The Creators didn't like that; so that's how the third version of the Game appeared, the one that allowed for a possibility of Restart during which all settings were reset to default. A Restart scenario was developed; it existed to this day, eliminating most of the players, which meant wiping out the anger and hatred of some beings against others. After that it went along the same well-beaten path. Another Madonna, the Nameless and Merlin would play at their intrigues, plunging the universe into the abyss of hatred and fear. From Restart to Restart the situation would repeat itself and nothing would change.

Except: there was one "but"! I rummaged through my inventory, throwing its contents out right on the floor.

"Guide, you can touch the sacred by pressing the button: cleanse the Game from stench and filth!"

The image of just one foggy Creator remained on the screen. The other two dissolved, disappearing from the circle of creation. They were tired of being immortal. Another button flashed in front of me, waiting for my action. They had thought I would believe that something actually depended on me? I grinned: this illusion of choice was simply ludicrous! I was completely certain: whether I pressed this button or not, the system would activate automatically anyway. And that was the way it happened. Failing to extract any action from me, the button on the panel pushed itself, and the Creator on the screen said:

"Restart process has been activated. All game abilities will be unavailable for the duration of one hour."

My Daro set that had used to feel weightless, now was crushing me under its weight; it felt like a granite slab. The helmet lost its transparent visor and turned into a huge metal pot that was making my neck hurt. Something was squeaking and jerking spastically, scratching my chest. My pet had gotten out of the cage that had lost power and decided to get back at its owner. I jerked several times, crushing the pet with my weight. I heard a squeak and a crunch, and it was over. The evil beast was crushed by the weight of the armor. Even though I must say that effort had cost me: my nose started bleeding from the strain, but the armor, of course, did not inject me with the healing concoction. What I missed the most was Steve. During the time I had been in the Game I had become so accustomed to his constant presence that now I felt like an orphan. I could always count on his moral support and advice. Quite upset, I was having a hard time remembering the attachment system on the gloves to get my hands out of their metal prison. While I was tearing them off I got mad at my schizophrenia, which had dumped me at the worst possible moment without as much as saying farewell. I scraped my hands and they bled, but I managed to get the gloves off. As soon as my hands were free, I immediately regretted it: it was hot in the Game control room.

Gradually the armor started heating, threatening to bake me inside like a quiche. I urgently needed to see what was happening around me, so the helmet was thrown aside following the gloves. It was a lot easier to get rid of it now that my hands were free.

The heat blinded me and I stood still, getting used to the high temperature. A couple of minutes was enough to adjust so that I could open my eyes and inhale carefully without fear of burning my insides. Sweat started rolling down my body right away, as if I were in a sauna.

There was no point in wasting time getting rid of the armor when what I needed was right at my feet. Miltay's gift. I could not bend, so together with the armor I just leaned to the side and fell over. I was able to get to the bomb, catching Multistrike along the way, by rolling on the floor. A test shot demonstrated that it worked quite well without the magic. A fireball it produced blew into fine splinters the door behind which the Restart participants had disappeared. The room was flooded with light just like the command post, but it was empty. They actually did die for the sake of Restart. So much the better.

I aimed Multistrike at the Diaries with crystals, but was unable to pull the trigger: everything within me resisted, preventing me from destroying the personalities of Gerhard and Merlin. The order worked even without the Game. Fine: not everything was lost though. I sang about the Alamo that had never surrendered under my breath to cheer myself up. I rose a bit and placed my hand on the bomb's control panel, starting the activation procedure. Miltay was an astute guy: he had configured his toy in battle mode. I just needed to press the button several times. The control panel blinked and started the countdown. Five minutes till a fiery nuclear inferno unfolds around me. I fell to the floor, exhausted, and at my leisure aimed my Multistrike at a wall. I needed to make a hole. I was sure that all the hardware was nearby somewhere; that's why it was so incredibly hot. The bomb would do its job, but I was still alive. I wanted to help it along as much as I could. I could not just wait those five minutes till my death.

I had realized a while ago that the Game needed to be not rebooted, but destroyed. The video address from the Creators only confirmed my thoughts on this count. No matter how many Restarts or Game versions there were, human anger, greed and indifference would always have upper hand, carrying this plague from era to era together with the lucky few. Again dissent, treachery and wars would begin. Again the strong would devour the weak, considering that to be the norm, and those whom they did not devour would say that such is the world, and without victims there would be no future. No. I didn't want that. If humanity was destined to die of its own weakness, so be it, but let it happen some other time. Now the heads of the former NPCs were concerned about a different problem: why did some beings suddenly stop and assume such strange appearances? I was certain: if I were to set off the bomb there and then, all the players would turn into vegetables. If there was no system for consciousness control, there was no consciousness. Everything was fair... At the same time I needed to die also. I could not abandon the crystals, nor could I destroy them. If I were to survive, Gerhard's order would force me to find suitable beings and implant memory crystals in them; then the same circle would repeat itself. That must not be allowed: therefore I was destined to die. I would at least die fighting, weapon in hand — so I would earn my passage to Valhalla.

Multistrike shot a hole in the wall and a whirlwind of fire rushed into the room, demolishing everything around. My game was over, and so was the Game itself. May people sort out their own lives and not expect some interference from on high. Whether that be the Game or the Gods. There was a brief flash of pain, and darkness embraced me. Helen, I am coming to you!

EPILOGUE

SHARDA WALKED SLOWLY along the stilled world. The silence of the city was broken by rare car honks, as if the drivers had dropped their heads on the horns, or the crazy barking of the dogs who did not understand why their masters had just turned into statues. Here and there periodically whole worlds exploded, since there was nothing to control them. Sharda only briefly glanced at the information panel that popped up before him, as he kept moving towards his goal. One world, more or less — that was just negligible production losses. What he was about to do was much more interesting. Yaropolk was wrong: as the Game shut down, it turned not only players into vegetables, but all the NPCs as well. The Game controlled all the sentient beings in the Universe

The robot that possessed artificial intelligence, brought to Earth as contraband, was turning its head from side to side, trying to adjust to the circumstances, but unable to figure out what it was supposed to do. Stand still like everyone else? Continue its actions? Its artificial intelligence was not controlled by the Game, so it continued to function.

Sharda smiled, remembering the Paladin. He had been able to bring up a worthy player, no matter how much Gerhard would have liked to have taken credit for it.

He was not the one who had stopped Zangar from killing Yari in the Academy; he was not the one who had convinced Dolgunata to go against her teacher; he had not been, after all, his inner voice represented by Steve. The incarnation of the Guide had been able to completely fulfill its responsibilities; it had turned into itself from the previous era, and finally, launched the first Restart in all of history.

The third version of the Game had impervious protection against any interference. In order to fully reboot it and reset the settings to default values the Restart participants must not only sacrifice themselves and their beings, but also destroy the current data storage. Otherwise it would not be a full reset, but a simple reboot that preserved all the accumulated behavior algorithms.

Had Yaropolk activated the nuclear warhead and left the command post, nothing would have come of it. Self-sacrifice had always been the mandatory condition.

Yaropolk had made the right choice and deserved a reward.

"Give me the crystals now." Sharda approached

the robot and stretched out his hand demandingly.

Not a single creation had ever resisted its Creator, so Sharda received what he requested.

"Wait," Sharda ordered, and sat down on the ground.

The robot obediently turned into a statue again, satisfied that now his algorithms had found the right behavior pattern. There is the master and he is to be obeyed. Pure joy for someone whose whole focus of existence was obedience.

The current owner was working on modernization. Sharda inserted Archibald's crystal into the consciousness adjuster; he was removing all the information on the catorian's personality.

It would not do for the new Game to remember the past. Just knowledge would be more than enough.

Sharda did the same to the crystals of Clarissa and Yaropolk.

At some point the Chancellor or the Academy called Yaropolk Merlin. On the whole the old guy was right; his only error lay in a small, but important detail.

Yari really was Merlin. But not for this Restart: for the next one. Archibald was destined to be his teacher again and take the place of his master, the Nameless; meanwhile Clarissa would make an excellent Madonna able to bring the new world forth with love.

There are always three involved in a Restart, two of whom love each other. That's how it had always been, including the situation with the Creators themselves.

Sharda, who, in the infinity of the past, had had the name "Merlin", finished working with the crystals and returned them to the robot. The automatic system of the Game would restore the clean data storage within twenty-four hours. The Game must go on.

— THE END —

Want to be the first to know about our latest LitRPG,
sci fi and fantasy titles from your favorite authors?

Subscribe to our **NEW RELEASES** newsletter:
http://eepurl.com/b7niIL

Thank you for reading *Restart!*
If you like what you've read, check out other sci-fi, fantasy and
LitRPG novels published by Magic Dome Books:

Reality Benders LitRPG series by Michael Atamanov:
Countdown
External Threat
Game Changer
Web of Worlds
A Jump into the Unknown
Aces High

**The Dark Herbalist LitRPG series
by Michael Atamanov:**
Video Game Plotline Tester
Stay on the Wing
A Trap for the Potentate
Finding a Body

Perimeter Defense LitRPG series by Michael Atamanov:
Sector Eight
Beyond Death
New Contract
A Game with No Rules

**League of Losers LitRPG Series
by Michael Atamanov:**
A Cat and his Human

**The Way of the Shaman LitRPG series
by Vasily Mahanenko:**
Survival Quest
The Kartoss Gambit
The Secret of the Dark Forest
The Phantom Castle
The Karmadont Chess Set
Shaman's Revenge
Clans War

The Alchemist LitRPG series by Vasily Mahanenko:
City of the Dead
Forest of Desire
Tears of Alron

Dark Paladin LitRPG series by Vasily Mahanenko:
The Beginning
The Quest
Restart

Galactogon LitRPG series by Vasily Mahanenko:
Start the Game!
In Search of the Uldans
A Check for a Billion

Invasion LitRPG Series by Vasily Mahanenko:
A Second Chance
An Equation with one Unknown

World of the Changed LitRPG Series by Vasily Mahanenko:
No Mistakes
Pearl of the South

**The Bard from Barliona LitRPG series
by Eugenia Dmitrieva and Vasily Mahanenko:**
The Renegades
A Song of Shadow

Level Up LitRPG series by Dan Sugralinov:
Re-Start
Hero
The Final Trial
Level Up: The Knockout (with Max Lagno)
Level Up. The Knockout: Update (with Max Lagno)

Disgardium LitRPG series by Dan Sugralinov:
Class-A Threat
Apostle of the Sleeping Gods
The Destroying Plague
Resistance
Holy War

World 99 LitRPG Series by Dan Sugralinov:
Blood of Fate

Adam Online LitRPG Leries by Max Lagno:
Absolute Zero
City of Freedom

El Diablo by G.Zotov
(a supernatural thriller)

Mirror World LitRPG series by Alexey Osadchuk:
Project Daily Grind
The Citadel
The Way of the Outcast
The Twilight Obelisk

Underdog LitRPG series by Alexey Osadchuk:
Dungeons of the Crooked Mountains
The Wastes
The Dark Continent
The Otherworld

An NPC's Path LitRPG series by Pavel Kornev:
The Dead Rogue
Kingdom of the Dead
Deadman's Retinue

The Sublime Electricity series by Pavel Kornev:
The Illustrious
The Heartless
The Fallen
The Dormant

Citadel World series by Kir Lukovkin:
The URANUS Code
The Secret of Atlantis

You're in Game!
(LitRPG Stories from Bestselling Authors)

You're in Game-2!
(More LitRPG stories set in your favorite worlds)

The Fairy Code by Kaitlyn Weiss:
Captive of the Shadows
Chosen of the Shadows

More books and series are coming out soon!

In order to have new books of the series translated faster, we need your help and support! Please consider leaving a review or spread the word by recommending *Restart* to your friends and posting the link on social media. The more people buy the book, the sooner we'll be able to make new translations available.

Thank you!

Till next time!